Burdens of the Dead

Mercedes Lackey
Eric Flint
Dave Freer

BAEN

BURDENS OF THE DEAD

This is a work of fiction. All the characters and events portrayed in this book are fictional, and any resemblance to real people or incidents is purely coincidental.

Copyright © 2013 by Mercedes Lackey, Eric Flint & Dave Freer

A Baen Books Original

Baen Publishing Enterprises
P.O. Box 1403
Riverdale, NY 10471
www.baen.com

ISBN: 978-1-4767-3668-6

Cover art by Larry Dixon

First paperback printing, October 2014

Library of Congress Control Number: 2013001870

Distributed by Simon & Schuster
1230 Avenue of the Americas
New York, NY 10020

Pages by Joy Freeman (www.pagesbyjoy.com)
Printed in the United States of America

To the memory of K.D. Wentworth,
friend and co-author
January 27, 1951–April 18, 2012

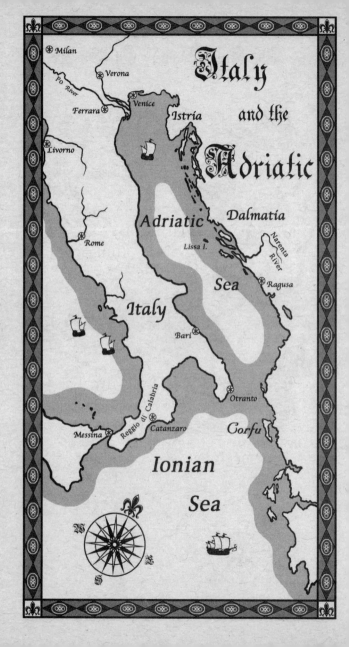

Burdens of the Dead

Prologue

Under the harvest moon, at the crossroads between east and west, a woman stood weeping. Year upon long, weary year, she came, waiting for her answer. Others had *their* answers, but never she; her child never returned, neither in person nor in word. She looked constantly to the north, to the place where the Earth-Shaker had opened the gate and drowned her land and her people; but not to the south, where he had killed one of her children and held hostage the other. The Earth-Shaker was deaf, or gone, faded into the half-dream of the forgotten. Her child remained his captive. Others were gone too, her brothers and sisters of old, gone, forgotten, faded into shadow. Only she did not fade; only she remembered. There might be nothing left to her but the waiting, yet still, she would remain until the appointed hour wherein she might, *might* have word. She would wait until that hour had faded too, she would be there until the hours when the worlds touched were over once more, steadfast as stone, sorrowful as grief itself. The dogs at her side waited, patient and faithful. Every now and again one leaned against her and she put a hand down to caress the silky red ears. She drew strength from them and they gave it to her, willingly. She had no other worshippers now.

She stood at the great crossroad, looking at the gate that had failed, until moonset. And then, as the red fingers of bloody dawn slid across Anatolia, she turned to choose her way. As always, looking at the crossroad, she took the third way. That, then, and always, was her choice.

The dogs followed Heḳate down.

She was their goddess. They were all she had.

PART I
September, 1540 A.D.

Chapter 1

Near Corfu, in the Ionian Sea

Benito and Maria stood together, leaning on the stern-rail of the Venetian galley, looking back at Corfu. The island was beautiful, with Mount Pantocrator rising out of the sea toward the wintery sky, and tiny white-painted hamlets stark against the green of her lower slopes. Maria held onto Benito, just as the magical island they were leaving clung to her, and she to it. Their lives were too entangled and confused, rather like her own. She was a Venetian canaler. They were not known for their subtlety or layered complexity of conflicting relationships, or to have conditionalities to their love or hatred. Yet here she was in a tangle of them. She loved so many: Benito. Alessia. The Mother Goddess's island Corfu. Even her winter-time lover, Aidoneus, Lord of the Dead. She loved each of them with a different part of her, and each with a "but" appended.

And all of them wanted all of her. She felt pulled and stretched in four directions, and where would that end except in her being pulled to pieces?

❀ ❀ ❀

Benito Valdosta, former canal-brat, thief, trouble-in-human-form, son of the most notorious mercenary condottiere in all of Italy, grandson of the Old Fox, the duke of Ferrara, and of late, hero of Corfu and now its acting governor-general, looked at his wife gazing back at the island they were leaving and felt both small and saddened. It was tough for a man to compete with a god and a goddess for his wife's attention. But if that was what it took, he'd have to do it. He didn't take kindly to sharing her with either the cult of the Mother Goddess or with the Lord of the Dead. But those were the terms by which he still had her at all. He'd take those terms and having her, any day, over the alternative. Benito might not like compromise—but he was used to it.

And now, to complicate things further, the Venetian Republic needed him again. The republic whose justice had sentenced him to death—and whose people had carried him on their shoulders. He'd have turned the summons down in a heartbeat, except it had come from Doge Dorma, to whom he owed... nearly everything. And they needed him, those people of Venice, the people who had carried him on their shoulders, the solid, tough, plainspoken canalers and sailors. Maria's people, even if she now claimed to be an islander and a Corfiote, needed him. They needed him because he had a real grasp of the evil they faced. He'd briefly seen the face of it when he had killed Caesare.

"Why are you looking at me like that, Benito?" asked Maria.

There was just a touch of an edge to her voice. She too was under strain; how could she not be?

He'd come…oh, worlds away from the selfish little canal-dwelling half-thief he'd been, someone who would not have seen it, or would have resented it, or have railed against what was taking her from him. *Part* of him still wanted to rant, swear, demand that *all this end now,* but—it couldn't and it wouldn't. Benito had learned to look for the greatest good, even when the greatest good required his own, personal, sacrifice. Well, there was no point in having a plate-throwing argument at this stage; trying to explain all that to Maria at this point might well send her into a tirade of *and what do you know about sacrifice* and *don't you care about me anymore.* "Trying to store up every detail of you in my mind, every chance I get," he said. "I'm going to miss you horribly every time you go back there. If I can't be with you, at least I want a picture in my mind that's better than any artist can make. They could never do.you justice, anyway." He'd never asked too much about her relationship as the bride of Aidoneus. That was ground, his instincts said, that he needed to keep off, if he was going to keep his relationship with the woman he loved.

Venice's *Case Vecchie* had a long history of keeping strict borders between these things. With its men away for the better part of their youth, and marriage being limited to one of the offspring from each noble family, to keep the family fortunes intact, they had to. It was said that Venice survived on the patience of her women. Maybe it survived on everyone turning a blind eye at the right time.

No, compromise wasn't in the least appealing to Benito, but that was the way it would have to be.

Was he becoming a politician? Maybe. There were times when he preferred the honest thief he'd been.

She smiled, though, and the temper was staved off. He'd made a wise choice. "You're all smooth tongue, Benito. I'm not some tavern wench that you have to sweet talk."

"Not all of me is smooth tongue. Or at least that's what I'd have said to one of those tavern wenches." He ducked.

"You're impossible!" He'd drawn a small snort of laughter from her. A victory. Laughter eased the strain from her face and from the muscles of her neck and shoulders. "And we can't go to our cabin right now. What would they all think?"

Benito laughed back. "They'd think I was keeping up my reputation and they'd be very jealous."

"You're impossible," she said again, "But, just for that reputation . . . if you just wait a little bit, see." She looked back toward Corfu. "I want to fix it in my mind, too." She twisted her fingers into his. "You promise we will come back?"

"I thought your Mother Goddess went a bit farther than just the shores of the island?" he asked, wishing he'd bitten his tongue as soon as he said it.

"She does. Although that is her strong place. But it's not just that. Kérkira"—she used the local name; she spoke Greek now nearly as fluently and as fast as the locals—"is the place where I became . . . me. More than just Caesare's girl, or Umberto's wife."

"You've always been that to me," said Benito softly.

Her eyes were slightly luminous and soft now. He'd said the right thing again. "Yes. But not to everyone else, or even to me. I am now. And I will always love this place for it. For the joy and the pain. I...Once I knew you were *Case Vecchie Longi*, it was hard for me to believe that, too."

He caressed an arm. "I was always just Benito. The poor kid off the canals you kept out of trouble."

"Kept *you* out of trouble?" That brought back a slight smile to her face. "I don't think that can be done."

He shrugged. "Kept me from destroying myself then. But look at the island and enjoy it, and make a picture of it in your mind to hold. I can't hate it—in fact, I owe a debt to it. It gave me something, or rather a pair of someones that I needed, too." He did not add "for eight months of the year" which just proved that he too could learn some tact. "And yes, we will come back, right on time, provided your Goddess will deal with storms or pirates or other things I can't control. I'll see that you get there. You gave your word." He hoped that would be enough, to show her that *her* word meant as much to him as *his* word.

She looked in silence, drinking it in with her eyes, but she kept her fingers entwined in his. She still had the strong hands of the woman who'd poled her boat in all weathers along the canals of Venice, but she'd spoken the truth. There was far more depth to her now.

"You know, you're right," she said after a long silence.

"I need to go and write this down at once," he said, grinning and not moving. "What about?"

"The Mother...I talked to Belmondo."

She must have felt him tense. "I know. He was a terrible governor."

"He was just weak." Benito would not speak as kindly of the man's wife, but he did acknowledge that the high priestess had also been weak, when the island, and her cult, needed strength. They had that now. They had Maria.

"Yes. But he is very knowledgable. He has many books," she said with all the respect of the recently literate. "He says statuettes of the Mother have been found in many places. In Spain. In Outremer. Old, old symbols, from before the Greek gods that he knows so much about. But he also said that we could not be sure that they were all the same, or if they were just the same idea. Fertility . . . fertility, has always been very important to every people."

"So is the result of it. And I hear the sound of ours, awake and wanting us," said Benito, vaguely aware that he'd just heard something important but not quite sure what it was. The pursuit of that thought however was lost in the task of parenting a young child. They could have had servants, a wet-nurse to see to 'Lessi's needs. But that did not sit well with Maria, and truth to tell, it didn't sit well with him, either. It was her child, and she had strong ideas about what being a mother meant. She wanted to hold and care for her, and so did Benito. She was a piece of his heart. They both were. And he would give both of them everything it was in him to give, at whatever cost.

Chapter 2

Trebizond

The night held nothing but terror and blood.

Lying dead-still next to a broken piece of wall in the eastern quarter of Trebizond, Mario Calchetti counted his time in heartbeats. He prayed. The knife-slash on his left forearm bled weakly. This ruin offered scant hiding places. They'd find him. And what chance did he have? They were plainly expert killers.

He wondered if they were Baitini; they'd had that sort of skill, that quickness, that lethality. But what would the religious fanatics want with a seaman like him? They didn't kill ordinary people. Lords and viziers were their usual targets.

But whoever they were, they'd killed Tomaso as easily as a man might butcher a hog, and too quickly for either of them to call for help. Mario had only escaped because it had been quite narrow on the stair, and Tomaso's falling body had impeded the killer. Mario had jumped the stair-rail and run; then, dived into this ruin. They had run past . . . but now one of them had come back.

11

Mario caught the gleam of a knife blade in the moonlight as the man moved, catlike, searching. Maybe, Mario thought, it would have been better to drown like the rest of the crew. But he and Tomaso had survived that; clung to wreckage, and been washed up and walked to safety along the coast. Trebizond had seemed, at last, a place of refuge. The gate guard had let them in, and they'd been climbing the stairs, arguing about just who they needed to go to see to report the ship lost—and then these two killers had accosted them. Never gave them a chance to tell anyone in authority what had happened.

In a ruined building in Trebizond on the coast of the Black Sea, where the caravans from the east met the trade-convoys of the west, someone said: "I'm Baitini. You can't escape me. Come out and I will make your death a quick and merciful one." The assassin spoke conversationally, as if he was merely inviting his quarry for a drink.

Mario pressed his bulk harder against the remaining bit of masonry, trying to will the deep shadow still darker. He was a big, solid man, an oarsman, and there wasn't much shadow. His attempt to hide more effectively betrayed him. A piece of the fallen brickwork shifted under him and something cracked. The killer, standing like a questing hound, turned upward toward his hiding place, a flash of teeth in the moonlight. He came stalking forward, knife ready.

Mario was terrified. He was a big man, and strong, but still just a sailor. Tavern brawls were what he was accustomed to, not this sort of cold-blooded murder.

He didn't even try for his own knife. He just grabbed a lump of masonry, intending to fling it and run, praying this would buy him a few more moments of life. It was a couple of bricks, still roughly mortared together. Mario had big hands, and huge shoulders from rowing. He flung the broken bricks with hysterical strength. Too late, the knife man managed only to raise an arm to ward it off and tried to move aside. But it was a nearly impossible missile to stop, and he actually moved into its path. It knocked him down.

Mario grabbed a second, even larger piece of angular mortar, and flung it two-handed at his attacker. He didn't miss this time, either. Staggering forward with a broken column base, he brought it down on the fallen killer's head, with all the strength he could muster. And then he ran.

He didn't look back to see if the assassin got up, or not. Or whether there was anyone else. The Hypatian cloister was ahead, the chapel door was open, and, as he could run no more, he blundered in. He joined those kneeling, and bowed his head very low, and automatically murmured a prayer. There were too many people for the attackers to come here, surely? He prayed again; very devoutly and very nervously, because he knew that this was only a temporary sanctuary.

He was so nervous about it that he hung back for too long. Before he quite realized it, most of the celebrants had left in groups, hastily heading for their homes, for Trebizond was an anxious place these days. And now here he was alone.

The Baitini had no respect for sanctuary, or the religion of others. All who were not of their sect were worthless unbelievers in their eyes. Mario, his eyes wild, looked at the small Hypatian sibling who had approached him. "My son, is there something you need?" the little man asked.

"Brother...I can't leave. They...they tried to kill me." He wasn't sure why he stammered this. There was no way a few unworldly siblings could protect him.

For an answer the Hypatian swung the door closed and slid the heavy bar across. Such a thing would have been odd in other places, but religious feuds were common here. There were those who resented the traders, and anyway, if there was nothing else for them to fight about, there was always religion.

"Who are they and why are they trying to kill you?" asked the Hypatian sibling calmly, turning back towards him.

"I don't know. They say they're Baitini assassins. And I've never done anything to anyone. But they killed Tomaso, God rest his soul, and they're trying to kill me. The one cut me." He held out his arm.

The Hypatian examined the cut. "I think I need to treat that."

"It's little more than a scratch, Brother, and yet it burns still. Hurts like...well it's very painful."

"It's a scratch that confirms your story, my friend. Look at the edges of the cut. That blade was dipped in adder-venom. Look at the weal, and the way it has eaten at your flesh. They do that, the Baitini. That way, even if the blade misses something vital, the shock usually kills."

Mario blinked at his arm. "He'd stabbed Tomaso with the knife already...but why us? We're just sailors." He began to shake.

The little Hypatian led him back towards the sacristy. "That sect needs no reason that we ordinary mortals can understand. Come. The wound must be cleaned and treated. It's unlikely that there was enough poison to kill you, or you'd be dead already. What ship did you come off? Have you got companions that I can get to escort you back to her?"

Mario laughed bitterly. "They're food for the fishes, Brother. We were attacked and they sank our ship. Tomaso and I were the only ones who got away. Those who attacked us were harpooning men in the water like porgies in a fish-trap. We'd come to bear the news and then this happened."

They stopped in a little stone-walled room next to the chapel, a room that smelled of herbs and other things Mario couldn't identify. There were lots of bottles and jars, a good, bright lantern, a basin and a pitcher. Mario remembered that the Hypatians were healers too. It looked as if this room was in use often. The Hypatian washed the cut with some spirits of wine. It burned like cleansing fire. "And who did you tell this news to, brother?"

Mario felt all at sea. "Well, I told the gate-guards, but no one else yet. Tomaso and I were trying to work out who to tell. We're just sailors. I thought Milor' Callaro..."

"It should be told to the Venetian podesta. He will send word of it to the sultan." The sibling paused delicately. "Who was it that attacked your vessel?"

Mario shrugged. "We saw no insignia. No flag. Pirates, I suppose."

The sibling looked at him. "But did you not sail in convoy?"

Mario nodded. "But three ships were no match for fifteen, Brother." He looked nervously around. "Are there other doors? I am scared they will come for me here."

"I doubt it," said the Hypatian sibling calmly. "The only other entrance leads by a passageway to our cloister. I think I will take you there, so you can tell this to our abbot."

Mario nodded eagerly. "I want to be with many people around me, please. Not that that will stop them. But . . . I am not a good man, Brother. I, I am scared to die unshriven, like Tomaso. I am scared to die. I prayed while I hid. Will you hear my confession?"

The sibling looked up at the ceiling; then, looked around. "Indeed. But inside the cloister, I think. There is someone on the roof. Follow me."

The Hypatian abbot was a wizened old man with bright eyes and a scar across one cheek. He listened carefully. For a saintly looking old man he had a shrewd grasp of naval matters. He also had objection to people on his roof without his permission. He sent two of the siblings up to have a look.

"But . . . they're dangerous," protested Mario fearfully.

The abbot nodded. "Yes, roofs are dangerous. Those pan-tiles can be especially treacherous. And difficult to replace."

"No, I mean the Baitini. They—"

"Shouldn't wander about on roofs," said the abbot, with what might almost have been a wink. "It's the kind of thing best left to roofers or thieves. The Hypatians draw all kinds to their ranks, friend. We will warn them. It is the right thing to do."

"But they're good people . . . the siblings, I mean," said Mario, thinking an unarmed sibling would merely be killed, but not wishing to say so.

"And if those who walk about on the roof are good

people, they will heed the warning and be told of the safe way off." The abbot stood up.

"Come," he said, leading the sailor to a spiral stair that went up into the steeple. This entire building was of stone, more like a fortress than a cloister, but this was not a place where the Hypatians were common. Nor Christians, really. There were narrow slit windows looking out from the parapet below the bells, and Mario could see the moonlit roof below and the people on it. Three of them were attempting to climb up onto a cistern. Well, two men had lifted the third up.

Mario watched as a little attic door under the roof-tree opened, and two siblings came out.

"Our abbot has sent us to tell you that the roof is dangerous and to guide you to a safe way off it, if you choose to follow the instructions we will give you," said one of the two siblings, a woman.

The three Baitini turned from their climbing.

"Kill them," said the one to his companions.

"The roof is dangerous, you really should go back," said the sibling, as the Baitini stalked toward them. "Your lives and souls are at peril if you do not go back now."

"Be still, woman," said one, raising a knife to throw, stepping forward as he did so. Then, with a scream, he slipped and fell, sliding down the steep roof; the knife in his hand skittered off the tiles, before he lost it, fighting for a hold. There was nothing there to stop him sliding, though, and he flew clear over the edge. It was a long way down to the cobbled street below.

His companion, after a look of horror, advanced more slowly.

The sibling spoke again. "I tell you again, it is not safe. If you do not retrace your steps precisely, all I can do is pray for you."

"I need no woman's prayers," said the assassin disdainfully. "Your infidel god will not protect you."

The woman-sibling was not at all disturbed by his threats. "We believe that God has many forms and that tolerance is all-important. Thus far, you have not harmed anyone here. Therefore, I will pray that you go back carefully, now." She bowed her head over clasped hands.

The killer didn't listen. Suddenly he too lost his footing. He clawed at the roof, dropping his knife, and somehow managed to cling despairingly to the very edge.

"Abdul, help!" he panted desperately. His surviving companion looked up from where he had levered the lid off the cistern. Hastily, he poured something into it, before turning to go to his companion's aid.

"Poison. I suspected as much," said the old abbot. "It won't do any harm in that cistern. Unless he falls into it, of course."

Which was exactly what happened, a moment later.

"What happened?" Mario asked, dazed by how suddenly the situation had reversed itself.

"There are weak and strong slats. We'll have to go and fish him out. I do not think we can get to the man hanging on the edge in time," said the abbot, sadly. "We did warn them."

Mario looked at the abbot, his eyes big. Had he been the witness to a miracle?

The abbot smiled at him. "The original abbot—this cloister was built in early days when times were even more uncertain—had been a knight, before he got the call, and he felt the roof was our weak point. The tiles pivot. Those men came onto the roof via the chapel, which was built later." A moment later, the man still clinging to the roof lost his grip, and fell to the cobbles.

"How will you get the last one out of the cistern?" asked Mario, despite his horror . . . and relief.

"A long pole. We'll leave him to climb out by himself." The abbot chuckled dryly. "It seems a dire price to have paid for poisoning a cistern which is kept for fire-fighting. The drinking ones are kept safe within the roof, and are much harder to get to."

"I hope he doesn't get out of there too fast and still angry," said Mario worriedly.

"It's a fair climb," said the abbot, with no sign of worry.

But in the end they had to send one of the siblings down to the harbor to borrow a long gaff, of the kind used for large sturgeon.

The Baitini shouldn't have swallowed some of the water he'd fallen into.

The abbot just sighed and said that God moved according to His plan.

The Baitini would have agreed. They believed they were guided by God, but that he had words and gifts for them and them alone. They were also quite mad enough to have believed that God had chosen to give them martyrdom, though dying unheralded because of a trick roof seemed a poor sort of martyrdom to Mario.

The bodies were given a respectful burial, although the Baitini probably wouldn't have agreed that it was respectful, or that they should be buried on the grounds of the house of another faith. But the sailor Mario saw it as a message, and applied to the abbot for a novitiate on the spot. Even the wise and kind Siblings of Saint Hypatia of Alexandria could use a pair of strong hands and a faithful heart.

And word was passed via a devout merchant to some of those who could get word to the podesta.

Chapter 3

Vilna

In Vilna, the capital of Lithuania, the Black Brain, Chernobog, continued with his plots. Many of these took the geographical power of the Grand Duchy of Lithuania far past the Bosphorus. There was some focus of his attention on Constantinople. Chernobog was aware of the watcher there, the dark one, three faced, of the moon and the sea and the earth. Such powers, lost gods and goddesses, had their own imprint on the nonmaterial world. But the watcher had never made any attempt to resist Chernobog in any way. He paid her as little attention as she gave to the walls and towers of Constantinople. They were no barrier to her, and she was no barrier to him.

After all, what did she have left? An old bone harpoon and a pair of dogs. He wondered what still sustained her, why she had not gone the way of so many other old powers? But she never did anything. Just watched and wept.

The world was full of old gods, old goddesses and old powers. Most of them were so faded, so drained, that he could overpower them easily. Still, in the spiritual realm it was hard to measure the depth of their power, so he did not challenge and devour her. Someone or something still sustained her. Why waste his strength? He had better, more immediate uses for it.

Once, the huge man sprawled on the throne had been Prince Jagiellon of the Grand Duchy of Lithuania. In his quest for power, the prince had delved too deep and gone too far. The man who had done so had been a brutal murderer, who had taken sadistic pleasure in his victims' slow deaths. What Jagiellon had become took no pleasure from such things, although he still dealt in them, as and when they were necessary. Chernobog had no real grasp of mortal emotions or of things like sexual urges. He understood they existed, but concepts like love were to him as the color purple is to a man blind from birth.

The Black Brain was a far greater monster than Jagiellon had ever been or could ever have been. But the demon possessed none of the prince's vicious desires, nor did he take any "enjoyment" from what had been Jagiellon's pleasures. Chernobog did understand that such pleasures drove the humans he worked with even more effectively than fear, but that was as far as his understanding went.

Still, Jagiellon had had a powerful mind and a strong will. The Black Brain had eaten into that, to some degree, but it was also a part of *him* now. It was the first time that the great demon of the northern forests, the fear-creature of the Slavs, had allowed a human to be this much part of him. That had advantages, but it had brought other things too.

Dreams. Or what might be called dreams.

Demons did not sleep. Maybe they were fragments of memories surfacing. Only Chernobog did not think he forgot, either. He worked with multiple deep and complex plots and plans, as he had done for millennia. He knew, of course, at least in theory, what dreams were. He provided illusions like them for some deluded humans. Well, maybe they were fragments of what the prince had been, surfacing like bits of scale knocked off the bottom of a black pool, rising to the surface only to sink back down into the depths again.

He planned, as always, to extend his physical dominion, as well as his dominion in other planes. It was what he was and always had been; among his kind one either grew, or died. But sometimes in the midst of it all of his planning, all of his knowledge, there were these—interruptions; odd, disturbing visions of a beautiful woman in tears.

Tears were not something that had ever worried him before.

He sought information from the brain he had subsumed.

Jagiellon could not recall the face. But Chernobog was aware that the vision made his human part uncomfortable, as if that gaze and those tears were something he did not wish to look upon. Chernobog too felt as if he had met her, somewhere. Perhaps in other planes. Things took on other appearances there even if their essences remained the same.

Since the death of his last shaman, and the treachery and flight of Count Mindaug to the shelter of Elizabeth Bartholdy, the Jagiellon part of him had been awaiting a new shaman. Meanwhile, he'd been forced to do some of the more risky tasks of magic himself. He had other servants, of course, but he feared letting them know too much or become too strong.

Human mages were a danger to the body of Jagiellon, and could enlist and marshal threats against Chernobog—as he had discovered when he pressed westward too hastily. But the West still drew him, called to him. There was something there he had to have.... But he didn't quite know what it was. He would conquer it in time and find out.

In the meanwhile he had deployed servants—lesser ones—to search and to spy. When it suited him, when he was sure there were no traps, he would take their bodies and see and touch and hear through them. Sometimes they lived afterwards.

From one of those he had sent out he had heard something which caused him to adjust his plans. He would not go too close to either Venice or Corfu. The ancient winged lion defended Venice, and Corfu had its goddess—she was awake and revitalized and the place drank magic. But he spied on the traffic between them. And thus he learned of the passage of Benito Valdosta, his wife Maria, and their baby daughter, north-bound for Venice. If rumor was to be believed, Benito would be heading south again soon, with a fleet to punish Constantinople.

Chernobog understood revenge. He also understood levers, even if he did not understand love.

"Bring me the blond slave," he ordered.

The servant left at a run and, along with two others, returned a little later, faithfully obeying his master's order, carrying Caesare Aldanto. He was blond still. He was also dead, long dead, and the passage of time had not improved him. The hair was possibly the only part that had not gone the way of all flesh. Briefly, Chernobog considered reanimating the slave; it was never a very successful process, though, and he discarded the idea. The spirit of the treacherous Montagnard sell-sword had long gone; there was no retrieving that part of him, either. Chernobog-Jagiellon hissed in irritation. The servants quailed.

But he merely said, "Dispose of it. And find me someone from northern Italy. There are mercenaries from all over in my armies."

Poulo Bourgo had been at the sack of several cities, and on the wrong side in a few of them. He'd known fear and terror from both sides. If he'd known that the huge slab of a man with the masked face interviewing him was none other than Grand Duke Jagiellon himself, he would have would have been deathly afraid. But since he assumed that his interrogator was just another underwashed Lithuanian noble, he was quite relaxed about it. He was a foot soldier, why would anything higher in the hierarchy than some minor functionary acting as a glorified clerk even acknowledge that he was alive?

It was a strange room, opulent, yet filthy in some way he couldn't articulate. As if a film of something vile coated everything. The luxurious trappings, the draperies and cushions, the ornate furnishings, had an air of neglect, giving the impression that the owner cared nothing for them. Poulo couldn't understand that. How could you have such wealth and not care about it?

"Milan originally, milord," he said, when asked where he hailed from.

"Did you ever go to Venice?"

"I was a bodyguard there for a while, for the Casa Dandelo. I was lucky to get out of there with my life, milord." A suspicion entered Poulo's not very fast moving mind. "I can't go back there, milord," he added nervously. "They'll recognize me."

That was the moment he realized how afraid he should have been. When that face looked up at him, and he saw the eyes gleaming dull and dead though the holes in the mask. "When I have done with you, no one will recognize you. You will not know yourself in a mirror."

Poulo might have tried to run, but he could not move. Somehow, the huge man facing him had stabbed him with a long, peculiar-looking knife. How had he moved so fast?

Poulo stared down at the blade piercing his chest, his mouth agape. From its position, the blade had to have penetrated his heart. Yet although he was paralyzed, he still lived.

The masked man lifted a small flask from a side table next to his stool. Bourgo had noticed the flask but had thought nothing of it. Liquor of some sort, he'd assumed, albeit of an unpleasant greenish-brown color.

Whatever was in that flask, however, it certainly wasn't liquor. The masked man poured the substance onto the blade and it formed into a glutinous blob, like jelly. Then the blob began hunching its way up the blade toward Poulo. He could only stare in horror as the jelly oozed its way toward the stab wound in his chest.

When the blob was an inch or two from his chest, the masked man suddenly twisted the knife-blade. The heart wound was twisted open and Bourgo's blood gushed out. Much of it, however, was absorbed by the jelly, whose color shifted toward red.

Then, suddenly, with a horrid sucking sound, the blob lunged through the wound into Poulo. Within three seconds, it had vanished completely.

The masked man jerked out the blade. Poulo collapsed to the floor. Finally, he could scream. And scream he did, for a very, very long time.

The Black Brain gazed upon him, satisfied. The preparation of the new slave had just begun, of course. Screaming and pain would continue for some time.

But there would be very little blood spilled as the parasite spread throughout its new host. The creature was a demon itself, of sorts. It would heal the wounds and consume and change the blood. In time it would kill the host, but that was no concern of Jagiellon's. It could also be forced to obey, if he needed it to. But that would be too visible, and was no part of his plan. Instead Jagiellon conditioned the new slave to obey, until obedience was invisible. Pain and magic would be brought to bear. There would be keloid scarring caused by the parasite's healing of its host; that didn't matter either. The scarring, internal and external, was necessary. It didn't matter if the slave was personable; he wasn't going to be required to seduce anyone.

When the power that had been brought to work on him had finished, the Milanese thief and bravo truly would not have recognized himself in a mirror—if his new master had made him look into one. His memories and physical ability were still accessible to his new controller—who would not pull his strings like a puppet, but rather had set deep compulsions, far harder to detect magically.

Poulo Bourgo began the long journey west, to Venice. He knew people there still, even if they would no longer know him. They could be compelled to assist him.

The Black Brain plied the paths of elsewhere, avoiding the woman, her old bone harpoon and her dogs. He went farther south to where he had taken control of those who sought holy inspiration and visions to guide them. The Baitini were unskilled in plying the worlds beyond and unskilled in magic, which they considered evil and unclean—much to the benefit of the demon who had become their unknown master, by wielding such magics.

The Baitini prayed for guidance, and for help with the Mongol yoke, whose broad tolerance they found perverted. There was only One True Way for the Baitini; their way. They would force all into their narrow path, and kill those whom they could not force.

The Baitini had not ruled by an open show of power, but by the Hidden Hand before the coming of the Mongol and the destruction of Baghdad. They'd tried those same tactics on Hulagu when the Mongols first came—and he'd almost destroyed their stronghold at Alamut in response.

Many of those who survived had fled to Damascus— also called Dishmaq, by some Mongols and Arabs—and now the two centers struggled quietly for dominance. The Old Man of the Mountain at Alamut was still formally their leader, but there were those in Damascus who tacitly challenged his position.

The Supreme Master of the Hidden Hand was one such. He now lived in the incense-reeking halls of their secret place in Damascus, far from the stark isolation of the mountains. He pulled the threads of death and fear across the lands of the Ilkhan and their vassal states, carefully avoiding open conflict with the Mongol. Instead, his Baitini undermined the Mongols by working for them, making themselves indispensable and penetrating government and serving as their functionaries—all the while seeking divine power and guidance.

The Black Brain was not the God they sought. But it was willing to take them and subvert them to its design. They were a sharp if small tool, right in the heart of the Ilkhan. They wanted visions of paradise? Nothing could be easier for Chernobog. Their paradise would be exactly as they imagined it to be.

The old man who was the Supreme Master of the Hidden Hand staggered out of the scented garden. His eyes were wild and his white robe soiled and disordered.

He could barely stand, but his words were clear enough. "At last! Our time is at hand. Paradise is ours, and so is power."

The Supreme Master of Poisons looked doubtfully at him. He knew what they smoked in the hidden, scented garden, to reach upward. He'd seen how new hands believed fervently that they had seen paradise already. He knew what they'd experienced. He organized it, down to the houris. The current Supreme

Master was an old man, and anything he said should probably be subject to suspicion. They went like that sometimes, believing too much, believing even in their own deceptions.

The Supreme Master of Poisons decided he had better send word to the Old Man of the Mountain. The Master of the Chalabis, the final arbiter in matters of religion, and thus politics and the power of the Hidden Hand, had long ago returned to holy Alamut. The poison-master wondered who would be elevated next.

The Supreme Master of the Hidden Hand grabbed his arm with a scrawny but fanatically strong hand. "Come!" he ordered.

The Supreme Master of Poisons took his own life that night. After what he had seen and experienced in the scented garden he was too consumed with shame—and lust—to go on. But not before he quietly sent a message to Alamut.

Others came to the garden at the insistence of the Supreme Master of the Hidden Hand; others proved stronger in resolution and obedience to him, to the message. New masters went out, full of religious zeal, and new orders. They remained in the same business, but with a renewed holy vigor, and rather a different direction.

Chapter 4

Constantinople

The city before Hekate's gate began to stir behind its walls. It was still a very great city, a place of assassins, sailors, whores, princes, spies, merchants, thieves, saints and cutthroats, but as the population had steadily declined under the misrule of Emperor Alexius, some of them had been obliged to take on more than one of these professions.

Antimo Bartelozzi was a spy. He masqueraded as a merchant in the Venetian quarter of the Golden Horn, and was good at it, as he was good at almost anything he turned his hand to. He'd on occasion had to resort to being a thief; and, in the service of his master, the duke of Ferrara, had killed a few people.

Fortunately, the Old Fox, Duke Enrico Dell'este, did not order death lightly or without reason. The ruler of Ferrara was an odd master, winning the love of his people by working iron himself, with his own hands. He administered fairness in a time when that was rare from nobles. But mostly the people loved him for his bravura, and for winning against the odds. For keeping them safe.

That was not why Antimo Bartelozzi loved him. Antimo had once been sent to kill the duke, and had not done so. The Old Fox had given him a reason to live, which was more important than merely sparing his life had been.

Antimo would not ever have considered himself a saint, not even here in this most venal of cities. He was reasonably generous, though, so he tossed a scrap of his breakfast pastry to a hungry-looking stray dog in the alleyway, an odd looking creature with red ears.

Antimo went quietly on down the filth-strewn street, measuring, watching, making mental notes. He didn't see the dog watching him, and then turning to follow its mistress. Antimo was looking for ways into and out of Constantinople. The dog knew some, but they were not used by ordinary mortals.

Antimo studied Constantinople with infinite care. He had been busy doing so for more than a month now. The emperor Alexius, profligate and debauched, had turned the city into a rotten fruit—ready to fall at a touch, but held in place by thorny branches. The emperor himself was not capable of directing the defenses of the city. He lacked troops, for one thing. He was scared to keep too many in the city, just as he was too scared to keep a good general there. He lacked the money for the sort of mercenary army he actually needed, and lacked the money for the sort of mercenary general, too, whom he might have been able to trust politically. Or distrust less, at least. A lot of money flowed into Byzantium, but it flowed away from Alexius just as quickly if not faster. The emperor was immobilized by his fears, pulled in so many directions, that in the end, he generally did nothing.

Alexius was fragile—but Constantinople was not. She had ancient walls and towers, and her people. Even abused by Alexius, they were a formidable force, and not one that would easily bend a knee to an invader. They loved and were proud of their city, from the Hagia Sophia to her mighty walls.

The walls and the citizenry could potentially hold off a large attacking force. Antimo explored the chinks in those walls . . . and in the citizenry. The traders' enclave was one such chink. The court of Alexius, another, although that would be dangerous and expensive to use; Alexius expected treachery there, and was always looking for it. A third, possibly cheaper chink, were the mercenary captains. Alexius used his own people and his own ships to defend Byzantium and to tax her. But since the days of the Varangian Guard, mercenaries had played a major role in the defense of Constantinople. There just were not enough of them now to form a proper force.

Mercenaries were relatively trustworthy, so long as they were paid. The emperor of Byzantium was wary about having his own generals here, so the mercenaries were his compromise for the safety of his city. The best of Constantinople's generals were in Asia Minor on the borders of the Ilkhan's satellite states of Cilcilia and the sultanate of Rum, or on the northern borders, where the tribes raided down from the lands of the Lord of the Mountains, Iskander Beg.

That worked fine for Antimo Bartelozzi, too.

Venice

In the Campo Ghetto, Itzaak ben Joseph, Kabbalistic mage and goldsmith, bent to his work. He took pride in his workmanship—and if a Jew dared to love a place, he loved this city. He felt as safe in this place as it was ever possible for a Jew to feel safe. He dared to think about the future, a future that held something other than packing up and fleeing to another place. Life in Venice under Doge Dorma was at least better and safer than it had been for the people of the Ghetto under Doge Foscari. It was still a place of Jews, Strega, even the occasional Mussulman trader. And of course, frauds and rogues, but a Jew could walk the streets without being molested.

There was plenty of quackery and trade in gray goods, philtres and charms and meaningless cantrips scrawled on strips of parchment. Still, there was real magic here, and not all of it good. Since the death of Marina, the mages had failed to unite or to accept any new leadership. The Strega families would continue with their old beliefs, but, no longer threatened by a common enemy, and without any particularly inspiring leaders, they grew more fractious.

Some drifted into areas that Itzaak would prefer not to think about. He was no great mage himself, his skills being limited to a bit of divination and his metalwork. He knew everyone, though, which was a kind of magic in itself. All news eventually came to his shop.

The latest was a bit worrying. A traveler had come into the shop, a co-religionist who had arrived from Constantinople. Besides the fact that the man wanted to convert quite a lot of jewelry into cash—of interest, naturally—he brought something of more interest. Itzaak's small magical skills related to his profession. He could read precious metals, gold especially, and a little in some gemstones. They told him from whence they had come, and what they were made of. Often the two pieces of information were part of the same thing. Raw gold had different amounts of other metals mixed in with it. And of course processed gold was frequently adulterated.

This was gold from far off. Gold from the lands beyond the Volga River. And...it was new. It had still been in the rock when Corfu had been under siege.

Gold was not a metal that, unmixed and relatively new, came into his hands very often. He smiled politely and proceeded with an assay, using the aqua regia, and carefully weighing the metal. The assay was totally unnecessary except as camouflage. It was accompanied by some equally careful fishing for information.

That was not very hard. Once he established that Itzaak shared his religion and history of persecution, Suliman ben Ezra was quite ready to tell him. "I don't know where the emperor Alexius is getting it from, my friend. But it does come from the palace. Even though the attack on Corfu failed, he is still spending gold like water. It's all he knows how to do. I think he expects Venetian vengeance, so he has been spending a little on mercenaries. This is where my gold came from. I was a seller of fine goods and perfumes. Mercenary captains run to expensive mistresses."

"It's information Venice should know," said Itzaak.

His customer shrugged. "They must have their own spies. They'll find out without me meddling. But it was time for wise people to leave there, my friend. The emperor was offering Jews as scapegoats and a blood-sop, to those who were angry about the losses. We're being blamed, somehow. Again. He doesn't quite want to destroy the Venetian quarter on the Golden Horn yet . . . but Greek pride stirs and is hurt. My family has lived there for two hundred years"—he made a face—"and yet I am still a foreigner and a Jew to them."

"Venice is more tolerant than most places."

"At the moment. But it will come here, too."

"That is the story of our people," said Itzaak, philosophically. "And yet . . . there are good people here. Marco Valdosta . . ."

"I am going to go farther," interrupted the visitor. "Vinland, I think. Unless the temple of King David is rebuilt."

"One day, my friend. Now, I value that bracelet at three ducats. To be honest, the workmanship is not good. That's for the metal and the value of the topaz insets . . ."

Later that evening Itzaak sent word to Marco Valdosta. Marco was trying hard to avoid politics and too much involvement with any faction, even the Strega. The boy still really merely wanted to heal the sick. But he and his wife had . . . connections. And if one duke could work iron with his own hands, there was no reason why another could not be a physician. Who knew? It would probably make him even more beloved than the Old Fox.

Milan

In Milano, Duke Filippo Maria dispensed orders to a man he hated . . . and yet needed and feared. "And that will be all that you need to know," he said, his prim, plump little mouth set in its usual false smile, which did not carry to his close-set little eyes.

"Perhaps just a little more information on what you require of me. I am a soldier, not an agent provocateur." So spoke the lean, scar-faced man staring unblinking back at him.

"A military provocation of the Scaligers. And the town of Nogara."

"We would be wiser to expand westwards," said his condottiere.

"I will decide on what is wise and what will be done," said Filippo Maria.

Carlo Sforza was relieved to be back in the saddle, heading away from the Palazzo Ducale. He trusted Filippo Maria not at all, and he had a good grasp of how the cunning, devious little man's mind worked. The duke was deliberately goading him a little. Testing his loyalty. Pushing his condottieri, playing one off against another. But Filippo Maria always did that. He was up to something more than his strategy of divide and rule.

Carlo felt the front of his tunic, felt the golden pilgrim medal that hung there. He remembered how it had come back to him and the message that had come with it. Damn Lorendana. Damn her. Even after all these years, she made him angry, and he was a man who had always been in control of his emotions. Unlike her.

He'd made mistakes . . . and this too was something unfamiliar. Sometimes, very rarely, he had been outthought, but even there brute force had seen him clear. Except against Dell'este. Her blood. Carlo would, at a time and a place of his choosing, possibly risk another throw against Ferrara's lord. Maybe. The Old Fox was neither that wealthy nor able to muster that large a force.

Carlo touched the medal again. He was much less sure about someone else he might have to face if Filippo Maria continued to prod Venice. The duke of Milan assumed that he was subtle in his maneuvers. But so were the secretive Council of Ten. This fencing in the dark could get messy, and there were certain things they should avoid messing with.

He had his own agents, of course, if not as many as either Filippo Maria or the Council of Ten. They kept him informed on the movements and actions of Lorendana's sons. Filippo Maria would be wise to avoid conflict with Venice, or the older boy, if the reports were true. Of course the duke only believed in magic when it suited him. But that was not the focus of his thoughts. Carlo Sforza wondered—as he had many times—about the younger boy instead.

His son, that one.

Who would, one day, almost inevitably come to kill him.

By the stories out of Corfu, and the stolen pilgrim medal he had sent back to his father, Carlo Sforza faced that prospect with a degree of respect bordering on fear, which was something he was totally unaccustomed to. There was a twisted pride, too, which was perhaps odd.

The snippets of information that had come to him, and the plots and plans that the duke of Milan was not entirely revealing . . . it all came together. Carlo Sforza was a man whose success rested on making quick, forceful and accurate decisions. He made one now. Francisco Turner was not a man he would lose easily or lightly. The man had a knowledge of ships as well as a grasp of several languages. His father had been an English sailor who had deserted his ship to stay on in Genoa and marry his light-o-love.

He'd left his son his name and a liking for beer. The rest of Francisco's skills had been acquired since then, mostly among the Barbary pirates who had once enslaved him.

"Francisco," he called the man forward. The rest of his men fell back. If the condottiere wanted to discuss matters with Francisco, they really didn't want to listen in.

It sometimes meant unpleasant things. Like bathing. Or purgatives. Francisco was a man of odd and dangerous ideas.

"I need you go to Venice for me, Francisco," said Carlo Sforza. "There is someone I need watched. I need them to trust the watcher. And that means it must be you."

Francisco nodded. He was not a man who questioned his lord's orders, even if this was not his usual role. He was adaptable, and, while he was no assassin, he could use a misericord and had an alarming knowledge of poisons. "Who, m'lord?"

"Marco Valdosta. And it will not be easy. He'll be watched by the Council of Ten's spies, possibly Ferrara's and almost certainly Visconti spies. We know how they work and will arrange a cover, but it is dangerous. And if rumor is to be believed he has divine guardians, too. Or at least magical ones."

"I understand," said Francisco, with a wry smile. "Well, m'lord, I'll do my best."

"He may be joined by his younger brother, Benito. That one is not a healer. If he arrives I need you to send me word. The barman with one eye at Marisco's will arrange it."

"Yes, m'lord."

"To make your life slightly easier, I believe Valdosta has been attempting to read Alkindus's *Quia Primos*. The translation, not the original. And not the Greek."

Francisco scowled. "The translation is dreadful."

"I thought I remembered you saying that, Francisco," said Carlo Sforza, with a slight smile. "I did have a fever at the time, though."

"You don't forget much, m'lord."

Carlo knew other people forgot things. He did not. It gave him an edge in what could be a dangerous profession. Many of Carlo Sforza's fellow condottieri were experts in the art of avoiding real conflict, unless it was a sure thing. They were good at noise and fury, and martial displays and soaking their employing cities and states. Mercenary soldiers preferred to work for pay and loot, and to avoid dying. Without a reputation for seeing to that aspect, a mercenary commander struggled to find the men who were tools of his trade.

Sforza was different. His men fought because the rewards were great, and worth the risk of dying for. With Carlo Sforza to lead them, they believed they'd get the rewards. His precise memory was one of the reasons they did. The other was his readiness to use overwhelming force. The Old Fox had the tactical edge on him. He also had the tactical edge on any of the commanders Carlo had met; but he lacked the brutal application of calculated force. When the time came, Carlo would exploit that. But Benito . . .

Benito would have been surprised to know just how much detail about his exploits had made its way to his father. It was especially the story of his conduct in the raid on the *Casa* Dandelo, when he had used the desperation of the slaves to apply overwhelming force on a superiorly armed and positioned foe; that kept coming back to Carlo's mind.

That was the way Sforza would have done it himself. And that . . . that made him a little afraid.

Chapter 5

Venice

Marco Valdosta sometimes wished for his old life back. When he had been Marco Felluci, with just enough money to put food on the table and a dream girl to see. The world had been a simpler place, then. He had been able to learn more about healing, work with sick children and ask for little else except the dream girl. Life was much more complicated since he had taken up the mantle of the Lion.

True, the dream girl was now his wife, and that had its blessings. True, old Lodovico no longer wanted him dead, and that too was a good thing. Of course a lot of other people had taken over that desire, some of whom were a lot richer and more powerful than Lodovico. But they didn't pursue the matter quite so relentlessly; and, besides, he had much better defenses.

There were so many conflicting demands on his time now. As the ward of Doge Petro Dorma, as the grandson of Duke Enrico Dell'este, as a person to whom the Strega turned, as a player in various power blocks and merchant houses of Venice, there was less time for medicine than he liked.

He peered down at the book, devouring the words hungrily. The *Quia Primos* set out the concept of precisely calculating the dosage of medication for treatment in fractions and ratios. It was an area that most practitioners of medicine had a hazy grasp of, at best. Here was a precise mathematical way of doing what had been trial and error...not that Marco minded the trial part. It was the error that he hated.

Old Alberto cleared his throat. "A message for you, milord."

The message from Itzaak, begging him to come to the Campo Ghetto just when he'd finally been getting into Alkindus's treatise, was not particularly welcome. Still, the elderly goldsmith was a good man, well thought of among the Strega. Not one to call him unnecessarily. He'd better go.

Marco and Katerina remained in the *Casa* Montescue even though he could have easily set up an establishment of his own now. He made his way from his study down to the water door. To be honest he hoped to avoid running into his grandfather-in-law. Not that he didn't like old Lodovico, but he'd inevitably ask when he'd be getting a great-grandson.

And that just didn't seem to be happening, despite plenty of effort by Marco and his wife. The fact that she still wasn't pregnant was worrying Marco. It was not good either for their relationship or for the future of Venice.

The Lion of Saint Mark needed someone that was of the blood of the four first families—the longi of the *Case Vecchie Longi*. Back then they'd been anything but noble, but only the families Lacosto, Terrio, Montescue and Valdosta could take up the mantle and become one with the great ancient power that defended Venice. The Lacosto had gone first, taken in one of the plagues that swept Venice periodically. Not even the Lion could prevent plague, it seemed. And the Terrio had followed, more recently, cut down by the same—which made Marco wonder, now and again, if this had been "just" a plague, or the meddling of something else, something working so subtly that not even the Lion had noticed. Of the Montescues, only old Lodovico and Katerina survived. And of the Valdosta blood—not name—only he was left. But the truth was, that was not what weighed with him, although he knew it should. It was that Kat wanted a baby...and to please her, so did he. He liked babies anyway; he'd be happy surrounded by a veritable swarm of them.

Marco was getting to the point of considering the various magical and medical interventions. Only...he was well enough versed in both to know that that area was full of quackery and fakery. He'd also postponed asking advice of the part of him he shared, willingly, with the Lion. The matter was...personal. Difficult even to talk about to himself, let alone something that was all of Venice and her marshes. It would feel like he was telling all of them.

He didn't manage to avoid Lodovico, but the old man was deep in conversation with his friend Admiral Dourso. They were sharing wine in a little reception room off the hall that led to the water-door, so he nodded respectfully at both of them, and tried not to make it appear that he wanted to hurry past them.

He must have succeeded a little too well. His grandfather-in-law smiled and gestured to him. "Ah, Marco. Come and join us. We were just discussing Alexius of Constantinople's likely reactions to the demands we made for reparations for his ships and their part in the siege of Corfu."

Marco shook his head. "The politics of Venice at home are too rich for my blood, Lodovico, let alone the politics of Byzantium."

"They're one and the same, Marco," said Lodovico, but he must have realized that the only reason Marco was down here was because he had somewhere to go. "Trade is our lifeblood. So where are you off to, young man? More sick canal brats?"

"Not this time, milord. A call to see an old friend. A goldsmith." Marco knew Lodovico would know exactly of whom he spoke, but he didn't want to spell it out to Admiral Dourso. The man was undoubtedly one of the masked Council of Ten that effectively ran Venice.

Admiral Dourso snorted into his wine. "Going to see old Itzaak, are you? Prod him a bit for information from those Strega connections of his about what is happening in Constantinople and Outremer."

"I try to stay away from politics," repeated Marco.

So much, thought Marco, for not telling him. The Council of Ten's spies were probably aware of what he had for breakfast and which page of what book he was on. For his own safety and good, no doubt.

"I'm sure it will be about some medicine or a new instrument for surgery. I try to stay away from politics, as I said."

"Ah, but will politics stay away from you?" asked the old admiral, straightening his stiff leg.

Somehow Marco doubted that it would, even though he wanted it to. He expected Itzaak to once again beg him to involve himself with the local Strega, which would be more politics. It was always politics. Plagues were simpler.

But when he got there, he found that the old goldsmith actually wanted to tell him about Constantinople. About gold coming from the territories allied to, or controlled by, Grand Duke Jagiellon, and the implications of treachery.

"I don't want to involve you in this, Marco. But I do need the Council of Ten told, without letting them know it came from me. The Byzantine emperor is getting gold, a lot of gold, from the east... since Corfu. It can only come from the monster of Vilna."

Marco knew a little of the old cabbalistic magician's background, enough to know that he'd been born elsewhere. The Campo Ghetto was a place of refugees.

"In Jagiellon's father's time, Jagiellon led the mobs that came to rape and steal and kill Jews," said Itzaak quietly. "It was politics, of course, but it was not necessary for him to do that in person. Orders were given and mobs went out. But it was his pleasure. And by all accounts he's delved into darker things since then, Marco. He must be opposed; hopefully, stopped. If Alexius is getting gold from Jagiellon, he is, without a single doubt, getting other things, darker things. Gold from the monster of Vilna always comes with so many strings attached that the man who takes it will become a puppet, whether he knows it or not. The man who sold me this gold was running again, and told me that I should run, too. But sooner or later we'll run out of space to run. I have found friends, peace of mind, and a little security here. I am not minded to lose them."

"I'll pass it on," said Marco. "But are you sure of this, Itzaak? The Council wants verifiable information, not just rumors."

Itzaak's long face grew longer. "Marco Valdosta, I give you my word, by the Temple of King David. My little talent never fails me. The gold the emperor Alexius is spending came from Lithuania. Recently."

Marco sighed. "Your word is good enough for me, Itzaak, but if I go straight back with this, they will know that the information came from you, and there are those who don't love the *stregheria*, or the Jews. You must realize I am watched. So at least I will buy a small gift for my Katerina. And then proceed to several other places, some of them where I will be quite alone. A few hours won't make that much difference, and perhaps this will make them think my news came from further-roaming creatures than you." *The tritons, the merfolk,* he thought. He would go and spend a solitary half hour in that water-chapel.

Itzaak shrugged. "Sometimes heartbeats do. But not this time, I think; I believe that you are right. And perhaps it would be best to—confuse the source. Now, I have some beautiful inlay work on these brooches here, Marco. Done in the Mussulman style, from Outremer. The craftsmanship is superb."

Chapter 6

Trebizond

Trebizond was part of a small semi-autonomous state, the sultanate of Pontus, which in turn was a vassal of Ilkhan Hotai the Ineffable. To make matters more complicated the city had a Venetian quarter, which had its own podesta and small garrison. Michael Magheretti had been delighted with his appointment to that post, three years back. Trebizond was vital to the interests of Venice, and time spent serving with distinction here would serve him well in his progression within the ranks of those who served the Republic.

He'd soon found that he was being tested by fire. There were far too many conflicting factions inside the Venetian quarter, let alone in the small city. And his authority was limited. The Doge had made it very plain that he was to soothe tensions, not exacerbate them as Commander Tomaselli had, in his short clumsy tenure as commander of the local garrison.

Michael sighed. "You wish me to settle a domestic dispute, Signor Gambi? That..."

"Please, Podesta. It is a small thing. But Nestor and I have been friends, business rivals yes, but friends for fifteen years. We're the bedrock of this community. A few words from you and the matter could be resolved."

"Tomorrow afternoon." Surely compared to the usual vicious factions all hiring Baitini assassins, and the inscrutability of the Ilkhan's emissaries, and the local Sultan's various relatives and cronies, it would be solvable?

Gambi frowned. "Your Honor, this really is a minor matter—if it is dealt with tonight. By tomorrow the families may be hiring assassins."

Something about the way he said it made the young podesta aware that this was not quite the domestic spat he had thought it was. Maybe it was the reference to "assassins." When families clashed in Trebizond, they usually employed bravos for the purpose. Thugs, certainly, even blades-for-hire, but not outright assassins.

Could Gambi be making a veiled reference to the Baitini? The sect was causing a lot of problems lately—even for the Ilkhan, whom they normally avoided antagonizing.

But there were factions there, too. There were factions everywhere in Trebizond. Spies spying on spies, assassins plotting against assassins. Michael was sure that at least three different spies were listening in to this conversation.

He sighed again. "I'll come and drink a glass of wine with you, signor."

So they walked the short distance to Villa Gambi. They were not unaccompanied, naturally; one never went anywhere here without guards. The villa was a handsome building—with suitable features for defense, as was the custom in the city. The podesta had been there before. Gambi was one of Trebizond's leading lights, and his support was valuable.

A window in an even more imposing pile across the narrow street flew open. *"Testa di cazzo!"* shouted the old man in a shrill cracked voice. "You try to turn even the podesta against me?"

"Please, Nestor, it's not like that. Can we not at least talk, old friend?"

"I am not your old friend," said the elderly merchant, grumpily. "But if you will come to my house, we will talk. The podesta can decide who is right. But you leave those thugs of yours outside."

Gambi seemed determined to make the peace between the two houses. "Please, Podesta. You will be quite safe with Nestor. I'll leave my men out here, too."

The heavy door was unbarred, and they went in, just the two of them. The doorman handed them over to a young woman. To his surprise Michael saw that it was Nestor Paravatta's bastard daughter, that Gambi's son—also here, far from Venice, from the wrong side of the blanket—was said to have insulted. She was the cause of the feud in the first place, but she didn't seem very upset about it all.

This smelled. Michael turned to Juliano Gambi, to ask what was going on—to be given a warning shake of the head. They walked on down the Turkey-carpeted flags and to a small room. Nestor was sitting there, showing no signs of his earlier outrage. The door swung shut with a dull clank. It was, Michael had noticed in passing, very thick.

Gambi pulled another, inner door, with layers of

fleeces nailed to it, closed behind him. He exhaled in obvious relief. "Sorry about our charade, Your Honor. They're watching us a bit too closely for comfort right now. But Nestor's inner room is about as secure as we can be."

"So...there is no feud?" asked Michael warily. "No insults between the youngsters?"

"Oh, many. They have a wonderful time at it," said Gambi. "And they'll have a nice noisy reconciliation, and maybe one or two more spats, when we've done. No, the matter is that three carracks bound for Constantinople were attacked by pirates off the coast near Ordu."

There were always a few astute merchants sending the goods of early caravans back before the holds of the fleet were full. There were good profits to be snatched. "I can see this could be a financial disaster, but well, was it a matter of faking a family feud to tell me? I mean piracy is a problem, and them daring to attack three ships..."

"Bless you, Podesta, they carried no part of our cargo. Well, I have a small share in a colleganza on one vessel, but not much. But it's the effort that they went to to stop the news of the attack that is of concern to us. There were only two survivors out of all three ships, and *they* were attacked by Baitini, here, within the walls, rather than let the men report it. It is not the piracy but the sheer number of attackers, and how they tried to make sure that there were no survivors that is worrying—and then the fact that the Baitini must have been actively waiting for anyone that escaped that would make it as far as this. This says the pirates are trying to keep their very existence quiet, planning something they don't want us to know about. And there is only one possible thing that it could be. They want the fleet."

That idea was enough to silence Michael. A large part of the wealth of Venice—and the survival of Trebizond itself—rested in the holds of the Eastern Fleet and the storehouses of Trebizond, waiting to load.

"Are you sure?"

Nestor shrugged. "Why would Baitini ambush the survivors—two common sailors—otherwise? And they killed the gate guards the crewmen spoke to, one of whom must have been the informant. One of the sailors got away, and found his way to the chapel of the Hypatian Siblings. He told their seniors his story. The Baitini attempted to silence them, too. But for a missed knife-stroke and a lot of luck we would have known nothing. And they were willing to murder all the Hypatians to silence that one man."

"That could cause a riot!" The siblings were not universally popular, but they had a strong following among the poor and the women. "How did they survive?" he asked in a kind of horrified fascination. The Baitini did not often fail, and the Hypatians were so helpless-seeming.

"The Baitini were caught trying to poison the water cistern." The older man allowed himself a grim smile of satisfaction. "The abbot sent to me that they had unfortunate accidents and fell from the roof. I did not enquire further. The siblings draw their members from all walks of life and are not all the gentle soft targets they appear. The Baitini were taken by surprise. And the siblings got word to us, and we, to you. So, Podesta, what do you plan to do?"

Michael wished he knew. The caravans from the east came in day after day, laden with the rich goods Europe craved. There were fortunes to be made . . . but plainly the pirate fleet thought itself able to capture the fleet. Since the Baitini were involved Michael would not rule out sabotage, infiltration and even suicidal murder for them to gain their ends. They—or at least the rank and file—were encouraged to believe in an afterlife in paradise guaranteed if they died fulfilling their appointed tasks. Oddly, the leaders of the sect did not feel this applied to them, thought Michael dryly. "What would you advise, signors?"

The two looked at each other. Eventually, Nestor said carefully: "Milord, keeping a fleet at sea for a long time is no easy thing. The time and day of the Eastern Fleet's departure is well known to all. They will not remain waiting offshore for another two months. This was a feeler, to blood their men, and to try our strength . . . and to stop vessels running across to Odessa and Theodosia."

"But do they need to? I mean the Baitini do not push against the Ilkhan. Surely if they're involved it means the Ilkhan are too? There are other ports and places."

Juliano Gambi chuckled wryly. "Come now, m'lord, you know as well as I do that the Ilkhan could ride in tomorrow and take Trebizond. The sultan's army wouldn't last an hour defending the walls, if they fought at all. Why should the Mongols do such a thing? They'd rather have the trade flourish and tax us. Besides they would fare poorly at sea against Venetian ships and seamen."

Gambi paused, and took a deep breath. "There is only one place such a fleet of raiders could be coming from—across the Black Sea. The satrapies and princedoms under Grand Duke Jagiellon's sway could build and man the massive fleet they would need, and provide port facilities for it, without it becoming common knowledge. No one else could do it. It's the only possibility. Those fifteen raiders were nothing. They were a patrol to keep vessels from venturing across to Crimea, as they do at this time of year."

Michael felt like the man who was called to help get a cat out of a loft, but who found a lion waiting for him instead. There was only one real answer—well, other than the fleet not sailing at all—and that would be to sail early. Before the ships were fully laden. That would mean a loss, but not, hopefully, a total loss.

"Gentlemen," he said with a calm he was far from feeling, "how much of your cargo can you have loaded and ready to sail in three weeks? Because that is when the fleet will be leaving."

The two men nodded together as if they were puppets controlled by the same set of strings. "There's going to be an almighty outcry," said Gambi. "But it is the only explanation for the efforts the assassins are making. And the Hypatians are to be trusted. I've spoken to the sailor myself. He's scared near witless, but he's telling the truth. I recognise him. Big ox of an oarsman."

"Maybe there will be less of an outcry than you think, my friend," said Nestor. "Merchants in a place like this are sensitive to unrest. And it's been reeking of it here for the last while. And if I know the Baitini, they'll try to foment more trouble. That'll play into our hands."

"If we live through it," said Gambi, with morbid satisfaction. "It's a good decision, though, Podesta."

Michael hoped the Council of Ten he would have to answer to in Venice thought so as well. They weren't here, where the streets smelled of fear.

Chapter 7

Venice

Poulo Bourgo, once a mercenary, and before that one of the bravos for the *Casa* Dandelo, the slave traders of Venice, had returned to the canals he thought he'd left behind forever. He did not return as a mere tool controlled from afar, however. The Black Brain had learned that such control was a flag of warning to the Lion of Etruria, the elder neutral power that guarded Venice. So Chernobog had instead used the flesh and mind of his sendling to imprint his general commands and desires onto Bourgo.

In essence, the Black Brain sent Poulo Bourgo back to Venice with a compulsion that overrode his logic or his fear. He thought himself to be still Bourgo, but he was not the man he had once been, in mind any more than in his appearance. He now carried a parasite-demon within him, a creature of magic and slime, that was inactive—but there, ready to do Chernobog's will. The parasite was also something of a protector, giving Bourgo the ability to recover quickly from almost any wound.

So Poulo was loose and free . . . apparently. His memory was clouded of just how he'd gotten back to Venice. But he knew where he was going despite the savage scars on his face, scarring that, along with damage to the cheekbones, changed the shape of the face, and left him with a permanent rictus. His hair, once curly, thick and black, was now a sparse white fringe around his misshapen ears. Until and unless people looked at his eyes they were inclined to offer the oldster a seat or charity. When and if they did look into his eyes, they went elsewhere in a hurry. If they could.

"Campo Gallia?" said the gondolier. "No, old man. That's a part of town that you should stay out of. I don't go down there myself. . . ."

He looked up into Poulo's eyes, then, and found that he'd changed his mind.

A twist of gulls flapped after them, as they might follow a fishing vessel.

Malaki Molados was a dealer in used furniture. And a fence, procurer, pimp, and a supplier of philtres and various drugs. He was not obviously associated with the now destroyed *Casa* Dandelo, but the linkage was there.

He was careful to keep it hidden. Venice was a fairly amoral society, and prostitution was barely considered a vice. The by-product of trying to retain family fortunes by restricting marriage to the oldest son of the *Casa* had created a large supply of affluent custom, and of course there were the infamous "nunneries" to which daughters of the noble houses were sent along with a suitable endowment, and often no desire to be a nun or to behave like one.

Some things, however, even went beyond the pale here in Venice. *Casa* Dandelo had trafficked in slaves, and were eventually destroyed for it. They'd paid well, though, and that was all that ever interested Molados.

He was always polite to a potential customer, even if they had apparently come looking for a spare cassone. Sometimes that was indeed what they wanted, sometimes to sell goods of questionable origins, and sometimes to buy...other things. How those customers got in touch with each other, and how they were able to recognize each other was a mystery to Molados. But they did somehow.

And sent customers to him. So he bowed to the scruffy, slightly ill-smelling fellow with the shock of white hair who walked into his shop as if he owned the place.

He was jerked upright by a harsh hand. "Didn't recognize me, did you, Malaki?"

He still didn't. But he had a sharp answer for anyone who took liberties. This was a bad neighborhood, but no one tried rough stuff with Molados. Word had got around. They left him alone and didn't get cut up. He had sewed weights and long razors into the edges of his short cloak, and more razor blades into the edge of his hat. He went for them now.

The white-haired man slapped Molados's hat off, and grabbed his wrists. "Even in these parts, Malaki, they'll kill someone who bought children off the Dandelos. Don't make me point that out to them. I know too much."

Who *was* this fellow? He was strong as an ox, despite his elderly appearance.

"I've got influence..." Molados tried to put a

ferocious edge in his voice. He had a bad feeling he'd failed.

"With your customers. Yes, you do—and I intend to use it. Now, who is still in business with the black lotos?"

"I don't—"

"Don't make me use your own razor on you. You'd wouldn't look good with an extra smile. You know who they are, and the addicts will never give it up."

Molados knew that one of the two of them was going to have to die, and he'd rather that it wasn't him. He talked, playing for time, knowing full well that when the rich and powerful people he'd betrayed caught up with him he was going to be killed for doing so.

He had to kill this man. He had a final hold-out, the razor in his boot top. He dropped and snatched it out, slashing.

Blood sprayed.

Only it didn't have the effect it normally had. The white-haired man slapped the blade out of his hands.

And as Malaki watched, horrified, the cut throat oozed a thick clear slime and knitted itself. The bleeding stopped.

So, very rapidly, did his scream.

The great winged Lion of Saint Mark was an ancient and powerful magical creature, and it was as much part of the Venetian lagoons and marshes as the marshes were part of it. It defended and watched over them, and, according to the compact with first four families, the four who had dared to defend the saint, it was a part of them too. Marco Valdosta wore the mantle now—and thus he was suddenly aware of a dark working, somewhere in Cannaregio. It had the reek of the North, of

Chernobog, about it. But how could such a thing have passed the wards of the Lion's territory? The Lion felt unease, which transmitted itself to Marco.

Marco had been in the act of making love to his wife, and the reminder that he no longer enjoyed any privacy was hardly a welcome one. But while the loving was sweet, there was, at this time of day, some desperation in it. They had been watching Kat's cycles carefully, and working on yet another worried attempt at conception.

His irritation was plainly something the vast otherness was aware of, and amused by. But there was a worry behind that amusement as well. The Lion wanted that child too, Marco realized. Was it his mother's blood, he thought wryly, with Benito and himself both trapped in relationships of three?

Kat touched his cheek gently. "What's wrong?" she asked.

A hard question to answer. While he was still groping, she said in a small voice, "It's me, isn't it?"

"No! A thousand times no." Marco said, hugging her, holding her. "It's just...well, something magical and evil stirred in the city."

"How...? Oh." She colored. "Doesn't he know there are times we need to be alone?"

"Um... The Lion is part of me, Katerina. Not something I can shut off at will." Marco felt awkward and embarrassed and not in the least like continuing what he had been doing.

Which, by the look on Kat's face, was just as well. She sat up, pulled the cover around her shoulders. "I love you, Marco, but..."

"If it is any comfort, the Lion really did not want to disturb us. It, er, wants us to succeed. But something very unpleasant and magical that should not be able to happen, just did."

"What?" she asked.

"Someone just died...but lived anyway. And no, I don't know why that was evil. I just have some idea of where it happened. I'm going to have to go and have a look."

"I'll come with you." She stood up.

"It might be a good idea if you put some clothes on first."

She grinned, the same widemouthed grin that had told him they were kindred spirits when he'd first seen it across the grand canal. "You too, Marco."

It was going to be difficult for Venice's most famous couple to travel anonymously. Not for the first time Marco wished that he was as at ease as his brother was, on the pan-tiled roofs. They were going, Marco knew, to one of the poorer quarters of Cannaregio, not somewhere that would draw their visit for any reason but charity. That was easily enough believed, although it would never fool the magic-user. Anyway, as Kat was with him, Marco wanted agents of the Council of Ten as bodyguards. He had the strength of the Lion to draw on, but they could both be physically killed, despite that.

Kat was taking no chances, guards or no guards. She checked her wheel-lock pistol and put it in her reticule, even before the task of dressing herself with Marco's help. He was at least deft at it, and a fair substitute for a lady's maid by now, he thought ruefully. By the time that they arrived in the sad, mean, garbage-strewn part of the Lion's domain, with a basket of goods for the local priest, where the Lion in Marco felt that this spell had been worked... it was gone.

The agent of the Council of Ten who was serving as their gondolier spat in the water. That briefly improved its quality. "Bad part of town, m'lord. Someone around here is trafficking black lotos. But we haven't pinned it down. It's causing a lot of stolen goods to move round here. If you hear anything, m'lord, in the course of your doctoring..."

Marco's heart sank. They'd never quite managed to eliminate the trade. And those who were addicted to it, would do anything, anything at all, when they needed it. Even the blackest of blood magic. And somehow one form of corruption always sought out another.

They went past the buyers of old furniture and on to the local church. The priest was a sad, rather beaten-looking man, stoop-shouldered and beginning to go bald. It was plain that the last thing he had been expecting this afternoon was a visit from the Doge's ward. His front parlor was a little untidy and he himself was rubbing sleep from his eyes. He was amazed, and suitably grateful and not a little suspicious and puzzled at the visit.

"I've seen several patients lately from this area," said Marco, by way of an explanation. "I was wondering...are there any problems? Above and beyond the normal poverty?" He probed delicately.

The priest nodded. "There are, m'lord. I think lotos. But really I can't say where it comes from."

Can't or won't? Marco wondered. The blue was fairly cheap and grew—or could be grown—in the freshwater parts of the marshes. It was only mildly addictive, and frequently provided rather unpleasant side effects. Oddly, it left more of a mark on its users than the black. Little things the observant physician could pick up, a nervous tic, bloodshot eyes. That wasn't something he'd seen a lot of here in the city, despite the availability and the price. This wasn't the sort of neighborhood you'd look to find addicts of the black. It was too expensive.

They talked a while of the medical problems, and the issues with water, and the poverty and—because they were Venetians—of the trade situation. But if the priest knew anything about practitioners of dark arts in his parish he wasn't saying. Marco did not wish to seem like the fanatical Bishop Sachs, seeing witchcraft under every bed. He knew Venice had its share. But he had thought—from his own involvement in it—that it was fairly benign.

They left after polite farewells and promises to see if anything could be done about the shortage of potable water.

Back in the gondola, Marco noticed that Kat was frowning. "What's wrong?" he asked.

"He wasn't pleased to see you."

"I don't suppose everybody has to be," said Marco with a smile. "You know I do have some enemies, Kat. Some even blame me for Benito. Recchia's family, the Capuletti. The Brunelli relations and by-blows . . . I don't try to be their foe but they are better at grudges than reconciliation. And this is Venice. Everyone is related to someone."

"Maybe that's it. But you're loved by the *populi minuta*, Marco. He must know that. And his house smelled odd."

"Odd? In what way, Kat?"

"Of fear, I think. It has a smell," said his beloved, seriously.

Chapter 8

Venice

The news of evil magic might be well hidden from Marco Valdosta, but there were a fair number of canalers who brought Marco the news that a new quack-healer had come to town.

They didn't see him lasting too long, though. "He doesn't know much," said Alfredo, scornfully. "Ignatius went to see him about that tightness of his chest, and he told him to try opening his windows. No potions or anything, and then he wanted to charge Ignatius a copper, too. You can imagine just where Iggy told him he could look for it. Mind, the fellow's got a shelf of foreign-tongue books. He looks the part. Just knows nothing. Everyone knows the air is full of poisonous humors, especially at night."

Marco had by now a good insight into the working of the minds of the *populi minuta* of Venice's canals. He'd learned, early, that people needed to believe, and to have something to hang that belief onto. He always gave a measure of help to that belief these days. Marco's patients often got better and that helped people believe...but so did some of the victims of the frauds and the charlatans that the desperate poor took themselves to. Even the better off and well-educated could believe in the most blatant fakery, and not all of the eminent and expensive physicians were anything but ignorant charlatans themselves. Marco had come to realize that the human body was a resilient thing, which would heal itself as often as not. Still. It was a wise physician who gave the mind something to use to work on the body with.

Marco had been inside Ignatius the pewter-smith's noisome little workroom. It sounded to him as if the new healer's advice might have been quite good. But he'd delivered that advice without the trappings that made it palatable, and thus to be rigorously obeyed. A cantrip on a scroll, which the patient was told needed to flutter in the breeze to be effective, would have achieved the same thing, and the patient would see the visible spell moving in the open window and feel that it was working. How not? There were the magic words, right there, clearing the air that passed them! Marco wondered about the books though. If the man thought to use props like that...

A few days later, another story about the new charlatan reached Marco's ears. The scornful verdict was that the new fellow was nothing but incompetent. "He wanted to know my cousin's weight, and then he went and peered in those books of his. A real doctor, like yourself, m'lord, knows how to treat a man's sickness. This one had to go and look inside his books and then weighed out some rubbish on a little scale, like one that the goldsmiths use."

In the minds of the ordinary folk, books were a powerful testimony to intellect. Using them was not.

Contrary to his informant's intentions, Marco was impressed rather than amused by the fellow's "incompetence," and had added two traces together. The man had showed up—admittedly not in the right part of town—at the time that the Lion had detected the use of some dark magic. He made a decision to look him up, and more importantly to see what these books were. Marco knew full well that neither he nor any other physician knew everything, and the weight of the patient and precise weight of the dose sounded like the advice in Alkindus, that he had been reading himself not two weeks back.

He found the man in his rooms above the Marciano *sotoportego*, customerless, with his feet up, reading, and drinking beer. Marco had not often seen the latter two things being done together, and particularly not in this part of town—and even more particularly reading a book that was not in Frankish or even a western script. The rooms were neat enough, and more than clean enough, and breathed an air of shabby gentility. More to the point, they did not stink, neither of chemicals nor of dark magic, nor of rotting things, and no more than was normal of the smell of the canals.

The man appeared more irritated with being disturbed in his beer and reading, than in need of customers or impressed by the quality of the person who just walked in. "And what might I do for you, m'lord?" he asked, lazily, not leaping to his feet to bow. Not in fact moving at all, his eyes going back to the book.

"Well, you could tell me what you were reading,"

said Marco, slightly refreshed rather than affronted by his behavior.

"Ah. You do not seek a love philter? That's a change."

Marco blushed. The thought of help with fertility was never that far from his mind these days. But he hadn't come for that reason . . . precisely. Though since it was never far from his thoughts, it certainly was possible that somewhere in the back of those thoughts . . .

Marco might be taken with the lack of formality and respect, but his escort loitering just outside on the stairs felt differently about the matter. The escort coughed.

"That's no real cough," said the man in the chair. "Go away and come back when you are really sick."

"I think it's a warning sign, not a sickness in itself," grated the gondolier who had brought Marco here. "The city of Venice expects more respect for its favorite son. I suggest you get up and bow and show some respect to M'lord Valdosta, before I toss you into the canal. And think yourself lucky if I just do that, *pizza da merda*. If I walk off and tell people about it, they'll treat you to drinking the canal dry."

The tall, slightly pot-bellied man stood up. He wore a well-worn sword, and didn't look overly worried, but he bowed. "My mistake. I am new to Venice. What can I do for you, m'lord?" Like his rooms, his clothing showed shabby gentility. Perhaps he was more interested in paying for books than cloth.

"I apologize for disturbing you," said Marco, both embarrassed and amused. The sword—Marco was of Ferrara blood, after all, and steel-knowledge was in his blood—was plain but of good quality. It did not match with the persona of a normal charlatan at all. An out-of-work mercenary—an officer perhaps?

"Not at all, m'lord. Alkindus can wait." He carefully put a marker in the book.

Marco grimaced. "It's been waiting long enough for me. But . . . are you reading it in the original?"

"Not the original, no. I'm not made of money. A copy merely. But in Arabic. Not as full of errors as the translations."

Marco was impressed. "You're a scholar, sir! I must introduce you to Dottore Felice at the Accademia."

But the man shook his head. "I wouldn't. I'd tell him he was a fat, useless self-opinionated fraud. I've little time for the likes of him. You can't learn a language just from books, any more than you can learn medicine just from them."

That was a sentiment Marco found himself in perfect agreement with. "So . . . you are a physician then, and a scholar?"

The man shrugged. "I'm someone who reads a bit, and has seen a great deal. I make no claim on being physician or a chirurgeon. I've done both as well as I can, when there was a need."

"Oh. I thought you'd set yourself up as a doctor. It appears you've been treating people and charging them a fee."

"I learned along with the smattering of medicine I have picked up, that most people regard advice as worth what it cost them. Besides, it helps to pay for the beer. People see the books and jump to conclusions. They assume either I'm a magician or doctor, and doctoring is something I have more experience of, and is safer to be taken for. I give them good advice, charge them for it, they don't like it and then they leave me alone."

"Doesn't that make paying for the beer difficult?"

Marco was thoroughly amused by now, and also very curious.

"It does. But by then I have picked up a few other jobs, teaching usually. And love philters sell at quite amazing prices and with great frequency. Ones that help for the smell of the breath even work sometimes. Now, m'lord, what can I do for you? What brings you here to my humble abode?"

"Curiosity," said Marco, not entirely believing him. The man plainly knew more about medicine than many an academic, simply by his choice of reading matter. He was probably a sell-sword, and a good one, by his attitude . . . but there was still the matter of the books. Caesare had been able to read, but had not done so by choice, and had certainly never chosen to read medical texts.

If this man was in fact doing so. He might be pretending in order to impress people. Marco remembered the opening paragraphs of the book well enough. "I have a translation of the book. How does it start in your version?" There, that was enough to tell him if the man had actually read the book, without sounding as if Marco was setting a test.

The man took a pull of his beer and intoned solemnly in a foreign tongue, and then in Frankish repeated the gist of the opening Marco recalled. He did it all without referring to the book, so his reading skills may have been unproven, but his knowledge was not. "I have read it too often," he said. "He's wrong about a lot of things, but I think he's right about precise quantities. After all, you use precise quantities of black powder for cannon. Too much will kill the cannoneer and too little won't throw a cannonball."

That was true too, but it was not the simile most nonmilitary people might have chosen. He'd been a soldier, of that Marco was certain. So what was he really doing in Venice? And how was it that he read Arabic, and medical books? He could claim otherwise, but he was a healer and cared about healing, Marco suspected. There was a little hint of irritation when he talked about people ignoring his advice. And yet . . . that black magic had come into Venice recently. Were black magic and healing even remotely compatible? Would a healer ever be desperate enough to use black magic? Best to keep an eye on this odd stranger, and if it was him, well, best to have the Lion close. "So, as you say that you teach, perhaps you would consider teaching me enough of the language to be able to read those?" asked Marco.

The fellow pulled a face. "I could teach you enough to start reading in Arabic. But it'll cost you enough to keep me in beer for a while. And it'd be years before you can read the language well enough for Alkindus. I'm not staying years, milord."

He was at least honest, it seemed. And less evasive than Dottore Felice had been when Marco had suggested learning Arabic. "Is it worth making a start?" asked Marco.

The man grinned. "To me it is. To you, m'lord, it depends on what you make of it."

The idea intrigued Marco, and it would enable him to watch this fellow. He wasn't sure where the extra time would come from, but it would have to be found. Besides, this was Venice, where even the slightest knowledge of another language generally had its uses.

Chapter 9

Trebizond

In Trebizond, the loading proceeded furiously. Sweating lines of porters carried tarpaulin-wrapped bales from the warehouses up the gangplanks into the roundships. The pace of loading and trade was frenetic. So was the intrigue.

The podesta, Michael Magheretti, realized quite soon that the Baitini were out to wreak havoc. Unfortunately for them, the story about them trying to poison the cistern of the Hypatian siblings had spread all over the city. The dead bodies on the steep stair outside their cloister, having fallen from the roof, and the gaff and the purpose it had been needed for, got talked about, and tied together. The assassins were feared, and used that fear to intimidate. They were discovering that intimidation only works when the victims believe that silence and cooperation will help them to survive. When that is not true—when you started poisoning water-supplies that would just kill everyone—that does indeed produce fear, but no cooperation, not even tacit cooperation.

It didn't help them at all that they'd attacked Hypatians. The siblings were known as gentle and tolerant near-pacifists, yet it was the Baitini who had died, not them. As he knew, the siblings were loved by the poor and the women . . . and, it seemed, by anyone who had come to them for healing and help. Resentment was growing by the day, by the hour, and the dead assassins were widely regarded as having been struck down by a miracle.

Surely, given that the Baitini had been the ones that had fallen, even their own fierce God could not be smiling on them? Had they gone too far?

The Baitini responded with characteristic violence, which had worked in the past. But what they had not realized was that in the past people had assumed that there was some logic behind their killing, and that something could be done to mollify the killers. Now people were swiftly revising their estimations and that, too, was making them angry. When you can appease something, you are inclined to do so. But when something is clearly operating from a position of intractable insanity—

"They've become mad dogs," Michael Magheretti said grimly. He sat, cross-legged, on cushions in the private audience chamber with the sultan of Trebizond and two of his advisers, sipping a spicy licorice tea. Or pretending to, rather. He really did not like the stuff and wondered if he could contrive to spill it.

"Maybe we fail to discern their reason," the plump sultan said. He had done considerable business with the Baitini before. Commerce had governed those transactions.

"Garrgh!" The more elderly of the two courtiers, who had slurped noisily at his small cup moments before, clutched at his throat, then fell forward struggling for breath, his lips turning blue and his hands clawing spasmodically.

The sultan gaped. His bodyguards, lounging in the doorway and around the walls, rushed forward and surrounded him. The podesta's guard did the same—tried to, rather. With only just two of them, it was more of a challenge.

A servant went running for a physician, as two others tried to help the dying man. But it was too late. By the time the doctor arrived, the old adviser was dead. A search of his body and clothing turned up a scrap of parchment someone had stuffed in a pocket. The scrap carried the mark of the Baitini. It was the assassin cult's custom to mark their work thus.

Magheretti looked up from the paper into the stricken eyes of the sultan. "I think, most exalted one," he said carefully, "That this is your answer. Things have gone quite beyond reason."

The assassins had intended to show the powers that ruled Trebizond that no one was beyond their reach. They had planned to set power against power, killing the Venetian in the sultan's palace. The wise assassin chooses his target and his place of attack very carefully. Only this time they'd killed the wrong man, in the wrong place.

The sultan of Trebizond was known as mild man, better at intrigue and politics than acts of violence. His major weakness was a love of falconry. His eyes now were as wide and wild as one of his birds, hunting, and it looked as if violence was a sure option. "Send a message to the Baitini," he said through clenched teeth. "That I want the ones who did this, and I want the one that gave the order and I want the people who paid for it. And I want them alive before tomorrow dawns. They'll answer to me under my torturers. They have killed the master of my hawks, and I will see the killers and their payers suffer for it."

"They will try to blame it on us," said Michael, his voice shaky. Thank Heaven he hadn't liked the tea! The poison had been so toxic—too toxic, really; the Baitini had overstepped themselves there too—that it had almost instantly slain the first of their party to drink it. "But I think that poison was aimed at me. They have gone mad. We need to get rid of them. Smoke them out."

"I think," said the sultan, grimly, "that this time they have gone their length."

The Master of the Blade sat with the Master of Poisons and the Master of the Garotte, in audience with the Master of the Hidden Hand, the new commander of the Trebizond chapter. They were far from the winds of Alamut and the scented halls of Damascus here. This had always been a busy post, but not a particularly religious one. Yes, the work was holy... but they had all known that money changed hands.

The new master sent from the Supreme Master in Damascus did not seem to grasp the realities of the situation here. "We are treading on dangerous ground here, Master. We..."

"We have orders from a higher authority," interrupted the Master of the Hidden Hand, his voice austere.

"You don't understand, Master. We could order some of the lesser hands to confess, suitably drugged. The sultan—"

"Is a man. His time has passed. It is our time now." The Master of the Hidden Hand of God said with absolute conviction. "We have orders, divine orders, to halt the sailing of the unbelievers' fleet until the normal day. If we have to kill all of them, it will be done. And we will make examples of those who try to go against the order. Do you dare to question that, or our Master's will?"

They did not, of course. But there were barely a hundred and thirty of them in the city. And they had lived and acted with impunity for many years. The local officials and soldiery feared them. Someone would always attempt to curry favor by giving the Baitini word of any move against them.

They were not prepared for the sultan's Mongol mercenaries, his personal bodyguard who were not in the least afraid of the wrath of Alamut. Three full companies of the mercenaries smashed through the doors of the house used by the Master of the Blade and several of the hands an hour later. The fighting that ensued was savage. Yashmad, one of the hands, escaped in the melee. Later, bloody, angry and afraid, he reported to his master, the Garrote. "Mamud and Ishmael are dead, I think. Malkis is still alive. They beat him insensible. They were dragging Amad. I don't know if he was alive."

The Master of the Garrote called one of his senior hands. "Send word to the palace. They are to release our people on pain of our . . . displeasure."

The man came back a little later, looking shaken. "Sheik Marawass has been taken to the torture chambers. Emblin has fled. The sultan is offering five hundred in gold for him alive and a hundred for his head. We'd better leave here, Master. Marawass knows too much."

Something hit the outer door with a thunderous crash. The Master of the Garrotte and the senior hand wasted no time, but fled out the back and over the roof. Someone in the street shouted to the soldiers—something neither would have thought they'd dare to do a few weeks ago. "Tonight we go killing. Them and those Venetian unbelievers," panted the master, angrily.

But first, they fled for their lives, knowing that the utter hold of fear they had enjoyed for so long was broken.

Michael Magheretti, podesta to the Venetian quarter of the city of Trebizond, tried to exercise both sympathy and patience. He had not previously been aware of just how many Venetian citizens had made their way to this far outpost of the commercial empire of Venice, only to find that the streets were not paved with gold. They'd found instead that it was easy to acquire a family and to live barely within their means.

"Please, Your Honor. You must help us," said the fifth supplicant for the day. "I have to get them out of here. They're all I have and I can't afford the prices the captains of the ships are asking, let alone the bribes."

"Bribes?" asked Michael. This was the first he'd heard of bribes.

"Yes. To get on the list. There's no space for everyone. So you have to pay to get on the list before they'll take your money as a passenger. And the price keeps going up."

Once—not long ago—Michael would have leapt to his feet and said: "I'll put a stop to that." But now he merely steepled his fingers and said: "I see. Who collects these payments?" he asked, his voice disinterested.

"Balbi. The boatswain from the *Pride of Chiogga*," said the man, before realizing that he might have said too much. "I mean, I have heard he might be..."

Michael nodded wisely. "You can't believe all you hear."

A little later he scheduled a series of meetings with various captains of the Eastern Fleet. And a boatswain. And the admiral of the Eastern Fleet.

There was considerable explaining. Also a boatswain who would be lucky if he did not hang. But it did little to counter the fact that three Venetian-quarter people had died the night before, and one had been a babe in arms. The ships were going to be full, not of their usual cargo of rare spices and delicate silks, but of people and a lot of the money they'd need to sustain themselves back in safer places.

Chapter 10

Constantinople

Hekate was, now and again, aware of the reach of Chernobog. After all, the people who lived along the northern fringe of what was now the Black Sea were the also descendants of the few survivors of the cataclysm when the gate had failed. Their blood had been diluted by many new immigrants and invaders, of course, in the long years since, which made the contact faint and far. Even the women no longer worshiped her, and that, too, diluted the sense of that dark power. Still. It was a shadow on her already shadowed world, and from time to time—like now—it troubled her.

She lifted the old bone harpoon, and felt its weight— far more than it should have been—in her hands. Not as heavy as it had been in days gone past but . . . heavy. There was still virtue in it, still some power, even if she had not been able to stop the Earth-Shaker, his tritons and their terrible conches with it.

Oh, she had punished them. They had suffered her wrath and desperate anger, but she had not been able to stop them, and still the sea had poured in through the tear Poseidon had opened in her gate, flooding and destroying the fertile plains around the great lake that had once nurtured so many...so many.

It was lost and gone, both her people and her love. And why should she do anything to aid these, these thin-blooded creatures who had deserted her?

Only the dogs remained, ever faithful. She lowered her harpoon, and Hekate turned back to the broken gate. Night had come. This was her time, and she walked the shadow-paths between spirit and mortal, seeing both, heeding neither. She walked through the streets of the city that those survivors had built on the edge of the chasm the Earth-Shaker had made, that the sea had torn deeper and wider, and, because of what she was, gates and walls and locked doors did not stop her. The city was still busy with the normal traffic of the night—whores, drunks, thieves and murderers. Hekate ignored them as if she did not see them, just as they did not see her or her dogs, because she willed it so.

All of them passed her without even a hint of recognition, her and the dogs...except for one man. He was not the kind of man Hekate, or anyone else, might have noticed. Of intermediate height, and very plain features, he radiated "ordinary" so effectively that even an old goddess was barely aware that he was there as she walked past. And then...

One of her dogs trotted after him and nosed his hand. He stopped. His hand instinctively went out to scratch it behind the ears. He plainly both knew and loved dogs and was not in the least afraid of them.

"Hello, Red-ears. You're out of luck tonight. I

haven't got anything to give you, boy." He sounded genuinely regretful about it.

Hekate stared, startled, as she had not been in a very long time. Looking closely now, she realized the man was using very powerful magics. She was, in one of her aspects, mistress of those. He had about him a "don't notice me" enchantment of such power it was unlikely that anyone would even remember his passage, not even goddesses—or at least not goddesses who had not focused their power and will on him. As she would not have, had it not been for her dog. Now that she looked, aware of the enchantment, he was not quite as ordinary or nondescript as he wished to be seen as. And he could see and, more to the point, interact with her dogs.

She stayed in the shadow, where her power was strongest, watching. She was both a little angry and very surprised. It had been years since anyone had seen her dogs, and then only when they were very close to death. This man showed no signs of that being the case. She could always make it so...

But he petted Ravener, now scratching around the ears, and under the jaw. Her dog leaned up against his hip, quite as if his name was Faithful and not Ravener. His sister looked on, not knowing quite what to make of this.

He plainly saw the other dog too. "Looks like you have a whole litter of brothers and sisters, Red-ears," he said conversationally to Ravener. "I wonder just what your mother was associating with. You're not like any breed of dog I've seen before."

The dog slowly, gravely, wagged his tail.

The man sighed. "There are always too many strays.

I wish I could take you home, boy, but home is where I seldom am, even if I could take you along. Mind you, you look too well nourished for most strays. I'd probably be stealing someone's rare breed of hunting dog." Then, he chuckled a little. "Although that is not likely in this part of town, eh? Still. You look like coursing hounds to me. Could be you're out on a run, and you'll go back to chopped steak in a gilded bowl."

He held out his hand, back upward, for Ripper to sniff. The bitch, Ripper, held off from being petted but the growl died in her throat and her ruff went down. Ah. He was using powerful magics there too—on her dogs! Hekate shifted her grip on the harpoon, torn between outrage and growing, if reluctant, curiosity.

He straightened up, gave Ravener what was plainly a farewell pat on the head. "Go well, dogs. I'd better be about my business."

Hekate was almost startled enough to drop the harpoon. That was a powerful good-wishing he'd given her hounds. And, she realized at last, he'd *not* been trying to bespell them. His beguiling was altogether unconscious. He just liked them and had been reaching out with his power to bring them closer to pet, as any lonely man might. He'd sought to give love, not entrap or bespell her holy creatures.

She almost called after him. Briefly she was distracted from mourning her lost children and her lost land. Here might be one—

But the scent of the sea carried by an errant night breeze brought it all back to her, and she turned away from him, her head bowed beneath unbearable grief once again. She would wait, and weep for them and then, when the dawn came to the great crossroads, she would choose her way—between east and west, life and death.

And as always, she would take the third way.

And her dogs would follow her down.

Antimo Bartelozzi went on his way, observing, making notes, looking for information to use in what he was sure would come, and come soon—his master and Venice moving against Constantinople. There was a little nostalgic smile on his lips. He had a soft spot for dogs. He'd not had one of his own since his childhood, and the lack of a faithful companion sometimes gave him an ache. He usually found one to pat, and even the most vicious of guard-dogs would come to him. This was useful in his line of work, granted, but it didn't alter the fact that he *liked* them, for themselves. And he often wished that his life had room in it for—not just one, but a pack. Dogs were happier in a pack. Come to think of it, so were humans, more often than not. And while he did not much care for human packs, dogs, now...

Old age and a peaceful retirement were not something he'd ever thought much about—neither were things he was likely to enjoy. Spies and assassins rarely got them. But he would like a nice quiet place in the mountains with a few dogs, if it ever happened.

It was...a lovely thought.

Chapter 11

Trebizond

"The chamber-servant to Lady Hooli is to open the door to the women's quarters at midnight," said the Master of the Blade to the three of the hands he had designated to the task. "Amud, you and Ishmael will go to the Hypatian chapel for the matins prayers for the few who attend their early rituals. They are at the root of this defiance."

More orders, another night in Trebizond, more killing, and more terror. It was getting harder, though. The sultan had instituted a dawn to dusk curfew, and not all the strikes had been successful—inevitable with the haste, and the pressure, and the tense watchfulness of the people. But even with help of the drugs, some of the hands had failed as well. Been taken alive, and talked under torture. Moreover, they had been betrayed by others, repeatedly.

And killing some of the people they'd suspected of informing had swung around to bite them. Servants, slaves, women, these had always been easy to pressure into cooperation before. They were, themselves, safe from the Baitini by virtue of being of no account, and often bore a grudge against their masters. Only now they were deathly afraid for their own lives, and clung to those who they thought might protect them. The houses of the wealthy and powerful in Trebizond were little fortresses anyway. And the Venetians—well, they'd banded together, and many of the women and children were sleeping on the ships. The sailors and officers who would normally be enjoying the comforts and pleasures of the city were on board, too. They were angry, and had neither fear nor respect for the Baitini.

The tavern keepers and whores were bitter, too. The Masters of the Hands would have killed the alcohol sellers long ago, but the Ilkhan had let it be known that he would hang the masters, and destroy Alamut totally the next time they overstepped certain bounds. And that was one of them.

But now, the restraints were banished. The Master of the Blade of Trebizond had heard from a fellow Master in Sinope that they were wreaking havoc there too. Privately—very privately—the Master of the Blade wondered if the Supreme Master had finally gone mad. They were still too few, and the Mongols were not that weak. The Hand mocked the Mongol overlords, called them dissolute and degenerate. But the rest of them still feared the Mongols, and with good reason.

He wondered what the Old Man of the Mountain in Alamut thought of all of this. But that was not his affair. His role was to do the killing. Tonight seven of them would descend on the merchant Giuseppe Di Colmi. The man thought himself and his family secure. But there was a cellar, and patient digging had made an ingress from next door. This would shock the Venetians into slowing down their loading of ships, as the Supreme Master had ordered. Nothing else seemed to have succeeded so far.

The woman brought the food. The master could see fear in her eyes too, as she set out the bowls for the hands to eat, before the cleansing and the holy rituals. The woman left and the hands ate.

The poison took effect two hours later. The drugs of the ritual had dulled their senses until it was too late. The Master of the Blade found himself lying in the narrow crawlway, vomiting blood. He did not have the strength to move. The Baitini were not the only killers-for-hire available, and their digging had not gone undetected after all.

The servant of the Lady Hooli did not fail, and the woman and her husband and child were found dead the next day. But the Hypatian chapel was not nearly empty, as had been expected, Instead it was as full as it could hold, mostly with crewmen and soldiers, on their knees, heads bowed.

The hands had their orders: Kill the monks first, and then as many of the worshipers as have not fled. Independent thought was not encouraged, and the rituals and drugs made doing so difficult. The drugs banished fear and stifled pain, but they drowned thought as well.

Besides, even if their mazed minds had been capable of fear, the hands were far more afraid of the punishment meted out by their own people for failure than they were of anything else. So, ignoring the crewmen and soldiers entirely, they ran forward screaming the name of their God, blades out, toward the nave and the cross and the two Hypatian siblings leading the service.

The unarmed white-haired woman faced them with a kind of terrible calm dignity that almost, but not quite stopped them. But they'd come to kill. Paradise waited on their deaths in the service of the Hidden Hand. It was written and ordained.

They cut her down in a flurry of wild stabbing.

The other sibling was younger and less courageous, perhaps. He was trapped in the nave of the small chapel and clung to the feet of the figure on the cross that hung there. The celebrants—at first shocked into immobility—were now scrambling to their feet. They were big strong men, mostly oarsmen, and the front row had grabbed the heavy pew and used it as sort of broad shield, penning and pushing at the wild-dervish assassins. The pew was too wide for the nave and struck the round wall just as the lead Baitini swung his knife at the surviving Hypatian sibling, screaming: "Die, unbeliever!"

The cross the sibling was clinging to fell off the wall, onto the assassin with a terrible crash.

There was a moment's silence, before the celebrants surged forward. They were not drug-fueled or trained particularly. But they were many and they were angry and afraid. They'd come to celebrate a final mass before setting sail. The sea was a perilous place, but not, it would seem, as dangerous as Trebizond.

Anger and fear and many big men, who all carried knives as working tools—who had just witnessed what many took for a miracle, not perhaps extra weight on old mortar—and the half-dozen Baitini found themselves overwhelmed. Once they were down they were kicked and slashed and trampled.

The violence was only stopped by the surviving sibling somehow hauling the heavy cross upright, off the fallen Baitini and yelling: "In Christ's name stop!" He was probably in shock, and that lent volume and fury to his voice. "Hold back! This is a house of worship, not murder. Holy Saint Hypatia preached tolerance and forgiveness of our enemies. We have no need of violence here in God's house, because his rod and his staff protect us."

He pointed at two of the sailors, about to crush a stunned Baitini with a pew they hoisted between them. "You will put that pew back! As for these men, if they are still alive, bind them fast. And bind their wounds, too. We must see to Sister Eugenia."

But it was too late for the other sibling. They carried her to the altar, where the male Hypatian still stood, leaning on the cross he held upright. "Hold the cross," he said to some of the sailors. Two of them took it—it was heavy and they staggered slightly—as the sibling knelt and prayed over his departed sister. The chapel was silent except for one of the Baitini, who was hastily muzzled with a rough hand and then gagged. The sibling stood up, not hysterical now, no, and not in shock. Perhaps the strength of his elder had passed into him. That was likely how it would be told, later. "Lean the cross against the wall. I will need someone to assist me with Mass."

"But they've killed her, Brother..." said one the Venetians.

The sibling straightened, stern, strong. The Venetians took comfort. "Yes. She died in the service of the Hypatian Order, in the service of Christ in the House of God. People have come here to receive a last communion before the ships set sail, and she was a willing sacrifice to see that was fulfilled." He took his place behind the altar. "Thus, in her name, in the name of God and of Saint Hypatia, it will happen."

"And these?" Someone pointed at the Baitini. Two were still alive and conscious. They were in a poor state—their clothes ripped and bloody, and plainly several of the others were dead.

"Let them watch," said the sibling. "They may receive the sacrament if they choose to repent and accept grace. If not, when we are finished they will be taken out of the Church they have defiled with their actions, and they will answer to the sultan himself. And may God have mercy on their souls, for the sultan will have none."

The Eastern Fleet sailed that morning, the winged lion flags fluttering bravely in the brisk breeze and the broad sails of the round ships belling with it, carrying the ships away from the shore. Ships laden with children and women, and not their usual cargo.

The traders that remained forted up together. The late caravans would be rich pickings, but money could not buy life.

And the sultan of Trebizond sent a message to the Mongol satrap of Erzurum, asking for help.

Chapter 12

Venice

Benito was surprised at how much he was longing for a sight of Venice, of his brother . . . even of Kat. He grinned. She'd been right about what he should have done about Maria too, the vixen. But his desire to see the city on the horizon was thwarted by the sea-mist clinging to the lagoon, a harbinger of autumn. As a reminder of what was to come between him and Maria, it obscured everything. The vessel had to creep through the Lidi channel under oars, the leadsman calling depths as it moved out of the Adriatic and into the waters of the Venetian lagoon.

And then, as if swept by a down-draft from the Wing of the great Lion of Saint Marco, a breeze off the sea stirred the mist, roiled it and rolled it away to reveal the city in the gold of morning sunlight, coming up out of the last clinging mist on the water.

"I'd forgotten just how beautiful it could be," said Maria from beside him. "It's best seen from out here. It hides the bits you'd rather not see."

"And you can't smell the canals from here either,"

said Benito, with a grin. "To think I dived for Kat's Strega stuff in that water, once."

"Huh," said Maria smiling back at him, "And nearly drowned her, from what I heard."

Benito shrugged. "Well, I was young. Inexperienced. I had to get her blouse wet somehow. I thought pretending to hide in the water from the Schioppies was pretty clever back then. And she nearly pronged me with a boat hook."

"Not surprising, really," said Maria, tartly.

"But I am reformed now," said Benito, suggestively patting her behind.

She rolled her eyes, still smiling though. "You aren't. But I love you anyway, Benito. It will be good to see them again, even if I don't tell Katerina you were ogling her breasts."

"Whatever you do, don't tell Marco. He's got no sense of humor about that sort of thing."

"Now I have something to keep you to good behavior," she said, hugging him against her hip. Obviously she too was feeling the closeness of autumn and parting.

Marco Valdosta was at his daily clinic, in one of his favorite places, the chapel of St. Raphaella. And he was a worried man. This was the second patient he'd seen—in a poor quarter of town—showing the signs of addiction to black lotos. Denying it of course, but Marco could not see what else it could be.

But... black lotos was expensive. Always had been, and since Petro had become Doge, and had tried to destroy the trade, more so. So what was it doing down here? And what sort of havoc could it wreak among the poor and their families?

He was faintly surprised to recognize the priest he and Kat had met in Cannaregio, accompanying a woman who was wringing her hands in despair.

"M'lor' Valdosta," said the priest humbly, "I hope I do not presume too much on having met you that once, but I need some help with this young woman. She is, er, rather beyond me in class and breeding. But she has no one to turn to and I wondered if you could help her in any way."

The woman bit her lip and looked down. "No one can help me," she said in a sad small voice, "My Mia is gone. I've lost her."

She wore worn and somewhat threadbare clothes with neat darns, but her accent spoke of education and a wealthy upbringing. She walked away, almost as if blind, to stand in front of one of the small tryptichs in the chapel, the one showing Mary with the baby Jesus.

"She, um, is the bastard daughter of one of the *Case Vecchie* families," the priest explained. "The *Casa* Brunelli. They saw to her education and welfare, until, well, the attack by the Milanese, when Brunelli fell from . . . prominence."

Marco knew that he was largely responsible for that fall. That there might have been innocent peripheral damage had never occurred to him. "Oh . . ."

"She found a place as a governess to some very young children in the house of one of the *curti*," continued the priest. He scowled. "The master of the house seduced her, got her pregnant—which was more than he could do with his second wife—and she, jealous woman, said she had to go. But he provided for her and the babe . . ."

"The baby got sick and died?" asked Marco. He'd dealt with that melancholia before.

"Worse. The child disappeared. She can't find her or any trace of her. Swears she never took her eyes off her. She was a lovely little girl."

The priest sighed. "But around here it would only be a few seconds and the child is into a canal. Anyway, the merchant swears she neglected the babe, and won't pay her keep. And she is so upset she can't look after herself. I've been trying to help, but mine is a poor parish. And she's gently bred. So . . . um . . . I just wondered if you could put out some feelers. If she could find work with some children again—it's only with children that she seems to be herself. She needs help, m'lord. She needs to be back among her own kind. And she loves children."

"I'll see what I can do," said Marco, doubtfully. Guilt combined with sympathy here, though. He and Benito had been poor and protectorless on the canals of Venice. His brother had been good at living like that, but he had not. And he had not had the terrible melancholia to cope with too. She was a pretty little woman, despite the signs of distress. "I'll find something for her."

"Thank you, m'lord," said the priest earnestly.

"What is her name?"

"Marissa di Pantara."

Marco knew of the family. They had had money, once. Like so many, the trade that made Venice wealthy was not kind to everyone, and Fortuna could not smile upon all.

Benito found that time had not dulled Venice's memory when they stepped ashore at the Fondamenta

Zattere Ponto Lungo. He got waves, catcalls and whistles ... and a few fluttery eyelashes and blown kisses and more waves from upper-story windows. Maria glared at them, hard enough to cause a few windows to be hastily closed.

"Here you are, with a wife and baby, and they still make eyes at you! Shameless!" She glared at him from under lowered brows.

"Ah yes," said Benito, waving back—and ducking. "Makes you wonder what sort of woman could make me leave all this and go back to a war, living off boiled roots and Kakotrigi wine for her, to say nothing of breaking into a besieged fortress or two."

Maria looked away, a bit guiltily, and shook her head. "You really can take the wind out of a woman's sails, Benito. But they'd better stick to waving."

"They'll have to unless they plan to go to Constantinople. Waving goodbye is all the opportunity they'll have. Now let's take a gondola to Marco and Kat. I spoke to Captain Parosos. He'll have our baggage sent there for us."

So they found a gondola.

The women—and men—still waved and grinned. Some shouted "Keep him off the bridges!"

"Seems like they remember young Benito," said the gondolier to Maria.

"They'd better not all be remembering him," said Maria tartly. "And stop smirking."

As the gondola poled on through the familiar canals of Venice, nostalgia and remembrance tugged at both of them. "I'd forgotten how much I loved and hated this place, 'Nito," said Maria quietly. "I don't think I even knew back then that I felt that way away about it."

"Loved, I understand," said Benito, holding his daughter. "But hated?"

"Well, the cold in winter. And being wet and just never being able to get really warm and dry."

Benito nodded. "Being hungry, being scared, too. I suppose that that could have happened anywhere though."

"But it did happen here. And the buildings and the water bring it all back to me. I wouldn't mind poling a boat again, though. Not in the rain in winter though."

"Ach, your old boat's still on blocks at Similano's yard," said the gondolier.

"I told Rosa to sell it," said Maria.

"I reckon she thought you'd be back and need it," said the gondolier, spitting in the water. "La Serenissima never lets go of you, really. I was Outremer and in Trebizond for nearly ten years."

"The other thing about Venice is you can never be alone, and without someone knowing what you're doing," she said acerbically.

"Yes, I missed that, too," said the gondolier cheerfully. "Here we are. The *Casa* Montescue."

The *Casa's* staff was of course overwhelmed with excitement and delight with the arrival of Benito. So was Kat. Marco was out helping the sick, as usual. A runner was sent to find him.

Benito had enough faith in his brother to know he'd be delighted to know that he and Katerina were to be Alessia's wards. Delighted? That was putting it mildly. There would be a baby in the house at last. And maybe...maybe the presence of one baby would make enough magic to bring another.

Chapter 13

Venice

Like dark tendrils the poison that had crept out of the *Casa* Dandelo, the trade in slaves, had corrupted everything that its vileness had touched. Slaves had been ideal for those who desired such flesh. Slaves had no one—at least no one who could do anything. And if the price was right, the *Casa* Dandelo would sell. And with the illegal trade came other things. Black lotos. Murder and kidnapping. And, of course, extortion and the treason it could buy. The old adherents and customers of the *Casa* Dandelo still had ties to the Montagnards, and to Filippo Maria of Milan.

That worked very well for Poulo Bourgo. His new master had nothing magical coming into the bounds of Venice. But other places were a different matter. Ordinary messages could travel down the same channels to Venice as were used by contrabrand and the flesh-trade.

And thus came the news of a little girl arriving in Venice—much younger than most of the victims the network traded in. A victim his master in Vilna wanted the duke of Milan to get.

The duke wanted her as a hostage and not for their usual reasons. But snatching and transporting children was familiar enough to Bourgo's associates.

This group of people had no more love and respect for Benito Valdosta than most of society had for them. They feared him, though. That was apparent during the meeting the former mercenary found himself at, with various conspirators—all in various attempts at disguise. Of course Poulo recognized some of them. "We need someone on the inside," said the man from Milan.

Poulo Bourgo had never actually met Carlo Sforza. But the man's tallness and forceful nature were well known. He had seen him in the distance and now his profile betrayed him. Poulo had had occasion to run into several of the officers of Sforza's mercenaries. He'd been looking for work at the time, but their commander had not been there, or hiring. Sforza had been able to pick and choose in those days. He'd come down in the world since then. Not far down, but down.

It was surprising that he'd attend the meeting in person, but that was Sforza's reputation. Direct, forceful, in personal control.

"Let your master know that has been arranged," said Poulo.

"For maximum effect you need to wait until Benito Valdosta has left Venice," said the tall man from Milan.

Several of the others nodded fervently. That was not the only reason they would be pleased to wait until Benito was far, far away. They did not want to face what would come when he learned his baby girl was taken. And when Benito returned, as he would?

They planned to be just as far away as their money could take them.

At that moment, Carlo Sforza was actually on a hill just beyond Nogara, watching as the Scaliger mercenaries prepared for battle. The former allies were not much of a challenge. In fact their condottiere, Marcus Baldo, was about as far back from the lines as it was possible to be without hiding in a privy outside one of the villas they were attempting to use as a defensive position.

The villa had a straw roof, too. Had the fool never heard of fire?

Milan

Filippo Maria Visconti, the duke of Milan, was the driving force of the Imperial Montagnard faction in Italian politics. The name was something of a misnomer, and had been for decades. The Holy Roman Empire had long since distanced itself from the Viscontis and their cause, and made clear that it wanted no part in the endless small wars of Italy. The dukes of Milan retained the formal pretense of serving the interests of the great power across the Alps simply because it sometimes enabled them to act more surreptitiously than they could have otherwise.

This was perhaps one of those times. The well-known fact that the Milanese dukes and their relatives conspired constantly in the Montagnard cause might disguise the fact that this particular conspiracy had a very narrow purpose.

The duke beamed on his second cousin, Count di

Lamis. Di Lamis was a tall, assertive-seeming man, but not one who had turned that appearance to martial endeavor. Rumor had it that he was scared of blood. Filippo Maria had sent him to the meeting that the surviving Visconti loyalists of Venice had requested for two reasons. First, he was expendable if it proved to be a trap. Second—you never knew, and the duke believed firmly in serendipity—he might be mistaken for Carlo Sforza, which could prove handy. The count bore a certain resemblance to the condottiere.

"So just who is this fellow, Augustino?"

The tall count shrugged. "He calls himself Poulo, and he's elderly looking with white hair. His accents suggest he's fairly low-born—but he's effective. It seems he has a finger in a fair number of criminal matters, but he supports us. Or at least he wants to see the back of Petro Dorma."

Filippo Maria steepled his fingers. "What does he want from us?"

Augustino di Lamis looked faintly puzzled. "Nothing much, now that I think of it. Not the usual demands for money or weapons. Or even the assurances of titles and lands. All he asked for was a squad of cavalry stationed at or near Villa Parvitto—to carry the child onward as fast as possible, when they have captured her."

"Villa Parvitto? Where is that?"

"Technically, in Scaliger territory. Now in Veneto, in the borderlands. It appears to belong to one of his confederates."

Filippo Maria allowed a faint frown to shadow his face. He was wary of traps. "Why my soldiery?"

Augustino smiled toothily. "He was laboring under

the delusion that I was someone else, and seemed to assume I'd send soldiers." It wasn't the first time this mistake had happened.

"Ha. Excellent!" Filippo Maria rubbed his plump hands in glee. "Perfect in fact. Couldn't be better. At a stroke we implicate Carlo. If things go wrong and this fellow is caught and the *Signori di Notte's* torturers squeeze this information out of him, Sforza will get the blame. He's campaigning in Scaliger territory, doing quite well, so it looks likely to be him. It'll inflame old wounds between him and that bastard son of his, so when I disown him for this deed, he won't go to Venice. And wherever he does end up he'll take the enmity of the Valdostas and probably Dell'este with him."

"Yes, but what if this Poulo succeeds? He seemed well in control, and very familiar with the whole process of kidnapping children."

Filippo Maria shrugged. "Then we have a hostage. It's not going to make Venice and the Valdosta clan any more or less my enemies than they are already. And we'll see that this Poulo fellow is betrayed and rats that it was Sforza who organised it. Carlo is bound to me by need then."

Venice

Back from his meeting of conspirators, Poulo Bourgo moved to take complete control over the shadowy network of black lotos and the even more secretive world of those whose tastes ran to very young victims. There were certain brothels that catered to that trade, too. On his way to pay a visit to one of them, Poulo was surprised to see one of Carlo Sforza's closest confidantes, and someone he had once met himself, talking to none other than...Marco Valdosta.

So. Sforza was up to something. Maybe treachery—but that was not really his reputation. Direct force was, and this looked like he was preparing a direct route to deal with one of the main problems Venice posed to the Visconti, and indeed to Chernobog.

Killing Valdosta would certainly be one way of doing so. It was a very risky option, however. Lurking within the innocuous-seeming young Valdosta was a vastly more powerful creature, here in the lagoons.

Perhaps Sforza's aide planned to take the child?

Poulo waited. It was imprinted onto his very being that he should stay away from Marco Valdosta. When the willowy Marco left, with a cheerful wave, Poulo followed Sforza's man up to a set of rooms above the *sotoportego*.

The man was seated, door open, feet up. He had a book opened at a place-marker already, but Poulo was not fooled. He wasn't reading. Too ready...Poulo knew, these days, he could kill the man, but that was not his purpose.

"And what can I do for you, signor?" asked the fellow, coolly. He plainly did not have the vaguest idea that Poulo had met him before, which was not surprising. "There are pox-doctors and sellers of love-potions and enhancements to your virility elsewhere. I can't help you with that sort of thing."

"More like what I can do for you. We're on a similar task for the same master. If you get her and find things are a bit tight, make for the Villa Parvitto." That was intended as something of a trap—or a signal. After all, Sforza would have provided the waiting escort there. This man would know.

"I think you have the wrong man. What is 'Villa Parvitto'? Do they have good beer? That's my next task. The beer here is barely worth drinking. And I don't work for any master, my friend. I am what they call self-employed. A gentleman of fortune. Now, I have a book to read. Go away."

Well, if he wanted it that way. Still...

"Just into Scaliger country. Remember that if you need an out."

"Who are you?"

"If you don't know you don't need to know," said Poulo, and turned on his heel and left.

Chapter 14

Odessa

In Odessa a very frightened little man made painstaking notes about the numbers of troops passing beneath his window. He was unsure how or even *if* he would get the information to his paymaster. But if he had nothing to sell, he would never have enough money to leave.

Vilna

Jagiellon was wise to the workings of agents and double agents. Spies and betrayal were meat and drink to him. The workings of economics were not. The Black Brain knew a great deal about several planes of existence. If anything, he knew least about this earthly one. Trade was something Chernobog had always understood poorly. Power meant that you took what you needed. The only purpose of trade was to corrupt and to move spies into the territories of those who did not understand absolute power. Right now it was more important to keep them out of his territories than to send them out. He had solved the potential problem of spies by closing the port. Odessa was slowly starving. People even dared to mutter against the voivode. At this stage it was still merely frightened resentful mutterings. It would have to get a great deal worse for the utterly cowed population to even contemplate rebellion.

The voivode of Odessa also poorly understood his overlord. He thought he was merely a cruel and monomaniacal man who could possibly be reasoned with.

He screamed. His arm, raised in supplication a few moments before, was definitely broken, and Jagiellon had merely brushed him aside as a man might a beetle. "Grand Duke," he gasped. "Agh! I . . . do but fear that if they get any sign of outside sympathy or support . . . they may rebel."

"And where would that come from?" asked Jagiellon, seemingly unaffected by the clenched-teeth whimper of his vassal.

"There . . . there are some of mixed blood. Mongols. The Vlachs too . . . agh."

"The Mongols we have dealt with. The Vlachs are a slave race, by and large. Go. I have other affairs to attend to. Do not waste my time again." The kneeling voivode struggled to his feet, trying to support his arm, and, not daring to do otherwise, bowed and fled from the throne room.

The Black Brain had, however, been aroused from the affairs it pursued in nether hells. It turned its attention to the progress of the fleet and the thrust to the south.

Jagiellon had had reports. But he preferred to hear about it from the source. And he had puppet emissaries—those who were literally his eyes and will. He would have had more, perhaps even that foolish voivode, had it not required no small expenditure of power and time. They had also proved an ineffectual way of command. Vassal generals and princes often did better driven by their own greed, fear and will. Of course he always had to have some control over them. It was in his nature.

A little while later a blank-eyed man roused himself from where he lay, rather uncomfortably, in a supply tent. He was cold and stiff and walked with a jerky and unsteady gait, as a result. No one spoke to him as Jagiellon looked around the shipyard. Most of the workers there were aware of what was looking at them. Neither Jagiellon nor Chernobog knew very much about shipbuilding. Jagiellon had never chosen to interest himself in such mundane tasks before he encountered Chernobog. Ships such as these that plied mere oceans of water did not occur in Chernobog's normal realm. However, both of them could recognize the signs of industry. There was plenty of that. Rigging and ratlines were being strung on some of the vessels already. Others were still being clad with their outer planking. That ran to plan, too: if they were going to be forced to wait for another season, they may as well build more vessels.

Chernobog left the human vessel right there. Someone would take it back to the tent. Instead he occupied the body of a cavalry commander and looked out onto the vast parade ground. Levies from across the lands that gave fealty to Prince Jagiellon were engaged in drill. In part Jagiellon had already known this. The Black Brain kept a far closer grasp on military matters. It was a necessity. The levies came from several linguistic groups. Many of them were hereditary enemies. To a greater or lesser extent the Black Brain managed and controlled their officers. It required a vast capacity. But then Chernobog had that, even if it sometimes poorly understood the abilities and limitations of mere human soldiers.

The army being readied for the round ships—some forty thousand men, now—was but a small portion of the force that Jagiellon was mustering. He would have to strike in the north and the center, once he held the gate to the Mediterranean. For the last few years he had kept up a slow war of attrition, without any major attacks, while building more reserves. He'd learned that it would take large numbers to bring down Europe under the leadership of the Hohenstauffens.

This time they would feint north. The war-hardened Holy Roman Empire, led by the Knights of the Holy Trinity, would stop the attack, as they had many others. But the underbelly of Europe was distinctly soft and unprepared. With any luck, whoever succeeded the now dead King Emeric of Hungary would attempt to take advantage and attack either Italy or the Holy Roman Empire—not realizing that this would leave him vulnerable on his own eastern borders. Jagiellon would settle for a bridgehead into the heart of Europe through Hungary. The part of Jagiellon that was the Black Brain, Chernobog, cared little for these geographical conquests, normally, but these were physical prizes that were not without value in the spiritual world. And besides, pouring across the northern Carpathians from the lands of the Kievan Rus would allow Chernobog to seize the physical earthly holdings of an old enemy, Elizabeth Bartholdy, who was also killed in the upheavals in Hungary. There would be a certain satisfaction in that.

Venice

Benito Valdosta had no such advantages. All he had was a stack of maps, the foremost tactician of the age to stare at him from under beetling brows if he said anything stupid, and a small dribble of information.

"One positive thing to come out of Odessa being as tight as a duck's vent is that some of Jagiellon's channels have dried up, too."

"Don't gamble on it," said the Old Fox. "Remember Caesare. He has puppets and means denied to good men."

"Even denied to us," said Petro, with a quiet smile. "I believe Patriarch Michael and Eneko Lopez when they say traffic in that sort of thing is a peril to the soul, better done by those properly protected, and best avoided entirely. But it is my task as the Doge of the Republic to keep the body and soul together for as long as possible. A few eyes in the lands of our foes would help a great deal."

"Part of the problem, besides the vulnerability of any such ventures to the spirit of the traveler," said Marco Valdosta seriously, "is the sheer vastness of the world. There are lands beyond lands and people beyond people. And the power in the east has made anchoring to any fixed point there difficult and dangerous. It would be easier to find an individual drop of rain that fell into the ocean last week."

"It's sometimes easier to do things the hard way, in other words," said Benito. "I just wish I wasn't trying to juggle so many uncertainties and possible variables in my head. All I can be sure of is that we'll be ready to sail in a month with less of a fleet than I would have liked, but better than we expected, once the vessels from the western convoy are included. The lists are up in San Marco, and they're filling up fast. I would have thought Venice had had enough of war."

"Ah, boy," said Lodovico Montescue. "But they haven't had enough of you."

"That'll change," said Petro Dorma, smiling faintly.

"Just make sure they are all on a ship first," said the Old Fox slyly, "before they find out quite what you plan for Constantinople."

"It's the part where the admirals discover that he has hijacked their fleet that I look forward to. Especially as I will not be there to listen to it," said Petro Dorma. "Admiral Dourso guesses, I think. But the others from Genoa do not know you yet."

Lodovico cracked his old knuckles. "The joys that await them."

"And me," said Benito. "They look at me and say that I am still wet behind the ears. And the worst of it is that I know they are right in some ways."

"It is a good thing," said Enrico Dell'este, "That I am coming along to provide a certain gravitas. Not to mention gray hair."

"You. But . . . Ferrara?"

He shrugged. "Is as secure as I can make it in terms of Italian principalities. I have two heirs. A great-grandchild, too. If Venice and the Doge stand, Petro here has given me his word that they will inherit

my seat. I am old. Respected. I may not go to war
again. I would have a part of this one. If this fails . . .
I think the West may fail too. Even if that is not
true, the relative peace we now enjoy will be over."

"I think you are reluctant to let your grandson go
off on his own," said Lodovico. "Not that I would not
like to watch, but he has proved that he is capable
of looking after himself, and Venice, too. As long as
there are no dancers and public bridges."

"It's that part that I promised I would prevent,"
said the Old Fox, cuffing his grandson's head gently.
"He is his mother's son, sometimes."

"I do trust that you are letting it leak out that we
will overwinter on Corfu?" asked Benito, feeling more
than a little uncomfortable.

"I have very carefully, in the strictest confidence, told
a certain lady," said Lodovico, grinning like someone
only a third of his age.

"You need a minder too," said the old Fox, shaking his head.

Chapter 15

The Black Sea

The Eastern Fleet sailed out of Trebizond, into the Black Sea.

Admiral Lemnossa set an atypical course, bearing away from the coast they normally hugged, taking advantage of a stiff southeasterly breeze to bell their sails and carry them away from the sight of land. Land had watchers and in the open ocean they only had to scan the horizon to know if they were being pursued. On the southern coast of the Black Sea that meant a long way offshore as the steep coastline gave more than the normal eight miles of vision to the horizon.

They had not been at sea for four hours when it became obvious that at least one vessel was trying to stay in visual range. A lateen-masted fishing boat heading down the same course seemed unlikely in the extreme. Lemnossa ordered two of the light galliots to drop back. Running as the fishing boat was before the wind, it had limited options in using the wind to outrun the galliots under oars.

"So what do we do if we catch him, Admiral? Sink

the *testa di cazzo*?" asked the young captain. This was his first command, and he was ready to dash in where even angels—or great galleys arrayed for war—would go in cautiously.

"It's tempting. We'll shift course a few more points to windward when you engage. If he tries to fight— that's their look-out. If they try to run, catch them, and bring them along. If they come to meet you, it might be that they have that young woman with a baby on board that you thought you'd left behind."

The light galliot's captain grinned. "Then I'll just have to sink them. My other girlfriend is waiting in Negroponte."

"Probably with the same little present for you. Go and deal with them."

They did. And the fishing boat had tried to run.

A little later the galliot, running with the wind so that the tired rowers could rest, and now accompanied by a lateen-rigged fishing boat, rejoined the fleet.

"They tried to pretend they were just fishermen. But those two never caught a fish in their lives," said the young captain, pointing to two angry-looking prisoners trussed up in enough rope to anchor a round ship in a gale. "I spotted their nice soft hands—and the real fishermen were terrified of them, you could see. So I gave the nod to some of my boys, and as we questioned them, Julio and Rupe hit them over the back of the head with marlin spikes. They had all sorts of nasty toys hidden on them. Knives and potions. When we'd dealt with them the fishermen tried to tell us they'd been forced into this. But they had a fair amount of silver on them for that story. So, do we feed them all to the fishes?"

"I reckon keelhaul them," said his mate. "Baitini bastards. They're good at sneaking around and killing people. Let's see how good they are at bleeding and breathing water."

"I have always wondered," said one of the lieutenants, as the admiral looked on thoughtfully, "how an assassin without hands manages?"

"Wouldn't do much good," said the captain. "This lot kills their own. Got no loyalty." He spat overboard. "Worth as much as that spittle to each other."

The admiral looked at the two trussed prisoners. Looked at their eyes. "Take that one away." When they'd hauled the smaller of two away, he cut the gag off the remaining man. Who swore at him out of gratitude.

Admiral Lemnossa raised an eyebrow. "I'm a sailor. I've been at sea for more than forty years. Is that the best you can do? Try a little harder, man," he said testily.

The assassin had expected torture or death. He was braced for that. Not for disdain.

"You will all die for this," he said sullenly.

The admiral yawned. "By whose hand? You are at sea, and if we tossed you all overboard no one would ever know how your fish-eaten corpse met its end."

"The masters know..."

"They know you set off to sea. No more. The sea kills more men than your kind ever have, or ever will. So what do I do with you?"

"Kill us. Torture us. It's what you plan to do. We will have our reward in paradise!"

"Then it would be in our best interests to keep you alive and unable to receive it. Or if you die to make sure that you die defiled," said the admiral, who had manipulated angry and drunken sailors to his will before. "Or I could let you go . . . if you convinced me that your retribution was sure."

"The fleet that comes is greater than yours. Forty great galleys!"

"Impossible. And how could one such as you know?"

Bit by bit, with a combination of apparent boredom and the mention of unclean animals, Lemnossa found out just what the rank and file of the Baitini knew . . . or thought they knew.

He then repeated the process with the other fellow, who was less pliable, but Lemnossa had the bait of what he had extracted from his fellow Baitini. He had, of course, no intention of killing either of them. They were too valuable for that. He knew, now, that the fleet from the Dnieper was, at least in part, at sea. He doubted it was the size these men believed, or that it was coming to liberate—from their point of view—the caliphate from the Ilkhan's persecution.

To the Baitini, Mongol oppression seemed to constitute not letting them kill anyone who offended them. Even worse to them was the fact that the Mongols were in a position to do this to the sect that had controlled much of the land that the Ilkhan conquered. The admiral found himself in sympathy with the Mongols, and wondering just why they'd left the Baitini in existence for so long. Lemnossa was sure of one thing—that fleet was going, not to the lands of Ilkhan, but to Constantinople and points west. And it was set on stopping his fleet from reenforcing the ships and crews of the Venetian Republic.

That was something Venice needed to know. But of course he had to get there first. The assassins could be fed some misleading information too, and let loose. They were spear-carriers, not big fish. Nasty spear-carriers that he'd prefer to hang out of hand, but still. He had near on seventy leagues of possible trouble before they reached the Bosphorus; he could not keep these two aboard, and they would serve a better purpose being turned loose than serving as fish-food. While fast ships raced from Crete to Venice with the new wine in a mere twenty-two days averaging six leagues in a day, his laden round ships and their escorts would be hard pressed do much more half that speed.

Normally, they'd wait out any bad weather, and would stay in sight of land. Now . . . that wasn't an option.

That night, around midnight, the taller Baitini captive heard his tiny cabin door being quietly opened. There were two men with a shuttered lantern. He was still very thoroughly tied up and his captors had had scant regard for his physical needs—food, drink or relieving himself. He had not been gagged again, but he expected the worst. He was prepared for it now.

"Shh. We've come to rescue you," whispered one of the men who came in, in the bastard Greek of the southern Black Sea coast.

"Cut me free," he said, distrustful.

"We'll cut your feet free. If we're caught we need to claim we're just taking you to the heads. Now, remember this. It's Phillipo Pelluci and Julius Malacco, see. We let you go. You tell your people we let you go. If you'll do that, we'll get you onto a boat, and let you go free. Will you?"

His first inclination was to get these fools to cut him free and then to kill as many as he could. But his task had been to report back. "Where is my companion?"

"Fish food. He died when they put him to question. They'll do you in the morning."

"The admiral thinks he can fool your lot by going to Theodosia and then Constantinople, and not along the coast. He's mad. The Genoese won't help us," whispered the second man. "Now we must go, quickly. Before the watchman comes back."

"Only if he agrees," said the other Greek-speaker.

It was written that the defenders of the faith could lie to unbelievers. So Malik nodded. "Yes. You will be spared. And given much gold." They were driven by greed, these sons of Iblis.

They cut his feet free. One of them sneaked ahead and the other escorted him to the fishing boat tied alongside.

It occured to him then that his sailing skills were nonexistent. "You must come with me," he said.

"No. If the ships get through, we get home. If not, your people spare our lives. That's the bargain," hissed his escort. "Or we take you back. And kill you right here if you try to scream. If they catch you out here they'll kill you anyway."

"I cannot sail."

"The wind will take you to shore, even drifting. Go." He was pushed to the rail, and the other sailor came and helped to lower him, hands still tied, down onto the bow.

One of them tossed a knife down to peg in the planking beyond. The other cut the boat loose. Malik wondered if he should shout now...it would serve them right. But he was free, and retribution would wait. Their plot would have worked. The fleet was not going to be watching Crimea across the ocean.

He barely knew where Theodosia was, or the likewise accursed Genoese. Godless foreigners, just like the Venetians. But it was not where the fleet would be expected to go. They would have been waiting for them off Samsun. The Venetians setting their fleet departure forward had merely changed the timing, not the plan. He made his way to the knife, and began work on cutting himself loose as the fleet, dark and silent on the water, grew more distant.

If he had been a sailor he'd have wondered why no one on watch noticed him and gave the alarm. Or why the little fishing vessel had been moored so that he could be dumped aboard. But he was not. He was barely able to hoist a sail and head toward the distant shore. He was not there, three hours later, to see the admiral ordering all sail made. They weren't heading out across the Black Sea for Crimea. They were, hopefully, going on a leg that would see them in sight of land somewhere near Sinope. From there their course would be a lot more predictable, but also hopefully the news would be too late.

The admiral would prefer to avoid battle if he could. This was a commercial fleet, but, when need be, Venetian sailors could be relied on to fight. Most of them had shares in what cargo there was on board the vessels. He just hoped that the Baitini and their backers had no real grasp of the rivalry between Genoa and Venice. They'd be as likely to shut Theodosia up and range their cannon on Venetian vessels as to offer them shelter. At sea they'd avoid each other. Or accuse each other of outright piracy, of course.

❧   ❧   ❧

Two days later, the early morning was broken with a yell from a topmast lookout. "Sail! Sail ho! Northeast."

The captain himself went up the ratlines to the basket. He came down, looking thoughtful. Admiral Lemnossa was waiting. "It's Genoese vessels, Admiral. Seven of them. Round ships. They seem to be bearing down on us."

"Can we outrun them?"

"Probably. It'd bring us back toward the coast. But seven vessels...they're no threat to us, m'lord."

"Except to carry word of us, no." He sighed. "Let's hold our course."

"We can always sink the bastards."

"Tempting though it might be, it'd cost us, too. And they might not be that easy. Those ships of theirs are big," the admiral admitted grudgingly. The Genoese had pursued size over numbers in the last few years. The bigger vessels were harder to maneuver, but they carried more men. That counted for a great deal, in boarding actions.

So they held their course...but on the convoy, men began readying their gear for conflict. There were two men up in the mainmast basket on the flagship, watching. One came hurrying down the ratlines. "They've got the Venetian Lion flying along with their red cross. And a white flag."

"Parley." The admiral pulled a face. He knew Genoese pride ran as deep as Venetian, and they were good seamen too, although you'd be hardpressed to find a Venetian who would admit it. If they were heading for a parley with Venetian vessels, then they were heading away from worse.

❀ ❀ ❀

And that turned out to be the case, when the senior Genoese commander, Captain Di Tharra, came aboard. The vessels were showing signs of conflict, so Admiral Lemnossa was not surprised to hear that they'd been attacked.

"Mostly galleys, m'lord. From the north somewhere, by the look and garb of the crews. Maybe forty of them. We were lucky we hit bad weather. They're not sailors. But there are plenty of them. Like lice."

He took a deep breath. "We lost five ships, M'lord Lemnossa. We came to ask...to beg to sail in the convoy with your vessels. We were attacked sailing west...we fled southeast under cover of darkness. We were making for Trebizond to petition the Venetian podesta... but you're already at sea. Safety in numbers, m'lord. We beg you out of Christian charity to permit us to sail with your company." He looked as if he were swallowing something unpleasant. "We could pay."

"No, we will not ask a fee. Not this time." Lemnossa knew if word of that got back to Venice, they'd be wanting to know why he hadn't skinned the bastardos, but it fitted. It fitted too well with what the Baitini had said. And the Genoans too were at sea early. Theodosia was the leading slave-port of Europe. The seasons for human traffic were different...but they also carried cargos that came from farther afield, across the scattered khanates and fiefdoms of central Asia, silks and treasures from as far as fabled China. Instinct said that next time it might be his fleet, and that it might be that all the ships they had were not sufficient.

"We plan to make port at Sinope," Lemnossa said.

The Genoan scowled. That city had been a Genoan trading post until recently. Unfortunately, the Genoese had 'fallen out with the bey of Sinope and his master the sultan of Rum. The parting had involved some burning of fortifications and a partial destruction of the quays and the town. The Genoese flag would be greeted with cannon-fire these days.

The admiral took a deep breath. He was an old man, and there was much in the way of punishment that the Venetian senate could mete out to him. On the other hand, less than they could do to a young and ambitious captain. And Lemnossa could see the scars of combat on the Genoese vessels. They'd lost comrades, been lucky, and come crawling to an old enemy. "You can sail under our flag," he said gruffly, wondering why he did this.

By the look on the face of the Genoese captain, he did too. But the admiral had a fleet full of refugees, and still had a Baitini prisoner below decks. "We may need extra strength. There has been some hint of trouble. We'll reprovision, water the vessels and sail. The merchants and the whores are going to be very unhappy with us, Captain. A good part of the fleet will stay outside the port. Unsettled times. We can part company once we're in Byzantine waters."

"Thank you, m'lord. We've . . . we've got a fair number of wounded aboard. And some damage." The captain swallowed. "We could pass some of your ships through Byzantium under our flag. It would save you a great deal in tariffs."

"That way our respective masters who are far away and safe might just be more understanding," said the admiral. "Is there any other help we can render?— seeing as we're both probably going to have to explain our actions. Me to the Senate, and you to your duke."

"And his council," said the captain, sourly. "Well. They'll be angry enough about the loss of the ships and cargoes. My thanks, m'lord, we've got a chirurgeon, and work on the ships may have to wait until we have a safe port. We've done what we can, and just hope we have no more storms or encounters with these ... pirates."

The admiral noted the pause. "Ah, so you think not, then?"

"There were too many of them, and their vessels were too alike. In Crimea the Mongols pay tribute to the north. We've been trying to make a treaty with the voivode of Odessa to allow us to trade up the Dnieper ..." He realized that he'd said too much and shut up.

"But no deal, eh?"

"No. Not even vessels into Odessa," said Captain Di Tharra.

The admiral knew the Council of Ten in Venice were very pleased that they had a spy in the city of Odessa. It hadn't seemed that valuable to Lemnossa before. Well, he'd been wrong. And he wondered if Venice heard from their man, and how?

The two fleets proceeded together. Two days later they sighted Cape Sinope—a triumph of good luck over navigation, the admiral knew, but he was willing to take the credit for it. It helped to have the sailors believe in his ability. The Genoese vessels had struck their colors and now flew the Winged Lion of Venice. The admiral didn't ask how come they had such a flag. After all, he had a Genoese red cross in his flag locker.

Lemnossa had the remaining Baitini prisoner brought up to him. The man had apparently been very seasick. He still looked ghostly pale. "Do you want to go ashore?" the admiral asked, as if the prisoner was one of his captains, and this was just a casual question.

The prisoner tried to gather spittle.

"Now, now. I made you a perfectly reasonable offer. We let your companion go when he accepted it. And, as we have not been attacked, he kept his side of the bargain. We did explain you would be . . . dealt with if he failed us. He must be fond of you."

"You lie, unbeliever."

The admiral shrugged. "We will let you go when we leave port. All you have to do is as your friend did: tell them we make sail for Theodosia, and then the shipyards in the Dnieper." It was unlikely that this minor foot soldier would even know where those places were.

"Why are you telling me this?" demanded the Baitini, suspicious, his voice harsh.

The admiral raised his eyebrows. You really didn't have to be very clever to take orders to murder. In fact, being clever was probably a disadvantage. "It should be very obvious even to you. We're not. If you tell your people that, we let you go. And we will free the crew of the boat that carried you, if you keep your word." The admiral knew just what value the Baitini would place on those fishermen's lives. He gambled however that the Baitini would not know that he knew. "They helped you. It would be fair and honorable."

The assassin took a second or two to grasp all this. "Very well. You will let them go?"

"What use are they to me? They will complain to

the sultan if they get home, but I will be far away. I'm not coming back. This is my last convoy."

"I will do this," said the assassin with his best attempt at looking sincere.

The admiral wondered if he'd taken to religious murder because he was a failure at selling unsound horses. But he said nothing, and had him taken below.

"What was that about?" asked his captain, when the man was back in the tiny cabin they'd kept him in. It would take a while to clean it, after the Baitini had gone, they both knew.

"Well, he'll run to his masters here in Sinope, and tell them what he knows—which is nothing more than they know—we're here, we did not take a heading out across the Black Sea. At the very least, he'll end up having his companion killed as a traitor. At best they won't be expecting us to do a dog-leg to sea—towards the north. When and if they work that out—they obviously have some way of communication with the pirates—they may conclude we really are heading for their lairs and boatyards. It's an outside chance, and they may wish to send vessels back to defend them. Whatever. We lose nothing, and we sow a great deal of distrust about the value of their information. Eventually that'll help us."

"You should be directing the Council of Ten, m'lord."

The admiral smiled. "If they don't take my head, if we get back in one piece, I hope I'll be allowed to join them one day. It might be less tricky than this. Anyway, how goes the re-watering?"

"Fast, m'lord. We'll be ready to sail by tomorrow. The bey doesn't like the way we're doing things, though."

"Then I shouldn't be surprised if I am summoned to an audience. Probably tomorrow. It would be today but I must be ignored for a suitable amount of time. And I expect some of the Baitini will try to kill me. So I would like you to know what I have planned."

"We should be ready to sail tonight," said the captain firmly.

The admiral smiled. "While I don't believe you, let us do so. We can cope with less water for a day or two. I'm a little behind on confessions and penances, and I'd like the opportunity to sin a few more times before my final reckoning is made."

PART II
October, 1540 A.D.

Chapter 16

Constantinople

The dogs of Hekate lived, as she did, in a place between, where time has little meaning. She walked the world at the crossroads, her dogs at her side. There were many crossroads and she could choose to walk any of the roads away from them. She only ever took one way—to the place between, which is not below but is down. The place between there is neither life nor death. The place where everything and nothing is possible, the place of shadows. The place where there is nothing to long for. No want.

Or hunger.

But . . . although they were not mortal dogs, hers partook somewhat of the nature of all dogs, and dogs are by nature hungry. A cat will turn up its nose at food unless it is what it wants, but a dog is always willing to eat. But in that half-world of shadow and nothing that she had kept to, they had perhaps forgotten that part of themselves, as she had forgotten so much but grief. It had been many years since her faithful hounds had eaten, until the mortal at the gate had fed Ravener. It had been many years too since Hekate herself had noticed food; perhaps that was why. Her power was, in a way, a reflection of her dogs' devotion; their care was all for her, single-minded, and when she forgot things...so did they.

Yes, there were cults that worshipped her name, in darkness and secret. But that was not the lady of the gateways and crossroads, of the three faces. Such cults worshipped her because she was believed to be powerful in magic. This was true, but they misunderstood her power. And their homage added nothing to her. But the love of her dogs did, and she gave back to them, in full measure. Her needs were theirs; theirs were hers. And now...

They were hungry. She was too. And she was stirred to give back to them what they wanted, even though they did not, precisely, *need* it.

So she went back to the crossroads. To the gate that failed. To the great city that even though it was a long way from its former glory, never quite slept. It never occurred to her that she might not get from the mortals here what she wanted. True, she might be forgotten, but when they saw her, they would know her, and remember her. They would know what was owed to her. They would give her food—for her and the dogs. They had always given her sacrifices. It was her due.

So she came to the gate, and passed through it into the world of mortals. And found that having exerted her power at walking unseen and untouched for many generations meant that it was very, very hard now to be seen or touched. A drunk lying in an alley saw her. But he cried in fear, and fervently hoped that she was an illusion. The face he saw was not a kindly one. No one else noticed her. She paused. This could present a problem. She could not *take* food; it had to be given, sacrificed by a willing mortal. Those were the rules, the ancient rules by which her kind lived. Mortal things for mortal creatures, unless they gave these things willingly.

So Hekate went in search of the man who had fed Ravener, or at least she set her dogs to the task. There was nothing under heaven, or under the earth, that they could not nose out for her if she wanted them to. They sniffed the air and found the scent...their ears perked, and they quivered with eagerness to speed away. Ah, how they loved the chase. She'd forgotten that. Forgotten so much in her anger and bitterness. She had been queen of the hunt long before Diana, once. Now, as then, she loosed them, and followed, fleet of foot and unhindered by her robes.

They ran him to earth, of course. They had the essence of the man, from the well-wishing he'd put on them, and that was far more pervasive than mere scent to Hekate's dogs. She called them off, as soon as she saw him. They liked him, yes. But they were hunters, and they had been hunting, with him as the quarry. They needed to cool a moment so they might remember again he was a man that they liked, and not the prey to be pulled down.

He was with two men in a rather noisome alleyway. They did not see the dogs, but he did. She stepped back around the corner—there was always a corner where she wanted one—and she called the dogs back to her. That was politeness. He had not insulted her, he had given her dogs respect and well-wishes. She could be polite. Besides, she was curious, and that was something she had not felt in a very long time.

She was almost sure he hadn't seen her. He'd been busy handing a small pouch to one of the two men. A small, heavy pouch, by the looks of it; that meant *money* in her experience of mortals and money in dark corners generally meant trouble. They looked like warriors. They carried swords of iron. She willed herself to hear what was being said. It would do little good to her dogs if the only man who seemed to see them was killed; they were hungry now.

"That of course would be the initial payment. A token of our trust. You can check that the rest is held by Isak ben Telmar, at the Rialto bridge. He will give it to you when you present him with the whole amulet. And don't even think it, Captain. I don't have the other section of it. You'll be given that when your side of the bargain is kept."

It didn't sound like murder to Hekate. Murder was no stranger to her. Crossroads were a good place for murder, and one of her three faces looked often on death. But the man sounded cool, unperturbed. And she did have some idea of the power he wielded. The other two warriors probably did not. She thought, all in all, there was no cause to worry.

A little later she wondered if she had been wrong about that. He bade the warriors farewell, and walked down the alley to where she stood, her cloak of darkness gathered around her. His hand was on his knife hilt, as if he expected trouble. Trouble—from the place where she stood. It was a steel knife, and her power was stronger over bone and stone. Her people had not had much bronze, and no iron when the Earth-Shaker had broken the gate and flooded her lands.

He was a creature with bone within him, of course.

Steel knife or no, she could kill him without effort—but that would rather defeat her purpose. She allowed him to approach, and he peered into her corner, into her shadow.

He seemed rather taken aback to see her there with her dogs. He plainly recognized those. "Lady. I . . ."

If she'd been a man, by his posture, he would have had that knife out and thrusting. Well, if the bitch Ripper had not growled at him, which she did. But she was not what he had been anticipating, not at all, and the presence of the dogs he knew set him further aback.

He gathered himself. The hand was still ready, but he had plainly decided to talk, or at least talk at first. "Your dogs, lady?"

She nodded. It had been eons since she'd last spoken to anyone.

"I've met them before. I thought they looked too cared for to be strays."

She was indignant. That startled her into speech and nearly into action. "Of course they are not stray animals! How dare you!"

He seemed to have missed the threat, or at least the indignation, and was reaching out the back of his hand toward them to be sniffed, and Ravener, the faithless hound, was wagging his tail. "I'm glad. Dogs need people."

That was true, too, she had to agree, and she softened to him a little. Well, she needed them and they needed her. "They are mine, and mine only. They may wander afar, but they always return to me and always will."

He looked at her, and then at them, his face inscrutable. Reaching a decision suddenly, he said: "This is not a good part of town, lady, dogs or no dogs. There

are people here that'd kill them for stew, let alone
what they'd do to you. Let me escort you back to
your home, or at least a better part of town. I mean
no harm. Ask your dogs," he said with a smile.

"I am Hekate," she said, putting him firmly in his
place. Harm? Him or any other mortal? The Earth-
Shaker Poseidon had not been able to harm her. He
had destroyed all she loved. Taken her children, yes.
But not harmed her.

All that plainly meant nothing at all to him. And
he was absentmindedly petting her dog. "Where do
you live?"

It had been alarming enough to realize that he
was being watched.

Antimo had always known—a prickling at the back
of his neck—when he was being spied on. He'd learned
to act on those instincts. And paying off a captain of
Alexius's mercenaries was not a good time to be watched.

He'd come back this way to kill the watcher.

And found firstly that she was a woman. A very
odd looking one. Antimo had an eye for detail. He
had no interest in women's fashions, but he could
describe precisely what they were wearing.

He'd never seen anything quite like her robes; they
looked like something he'd have likely seen on an
antique vase, and who wore that sort of thing, even
in Byzantium? Well . . . the women did wear a sort of
all-enveloping garment that wasn't a cloak, sometimes,
but not the fashionable ones. Nor did women wear
what—in the moonlight anyway—looked like the gold
and jet jewelry that she was wearing; heavy, simple,
somewhat crude by the standards of Constantinople,

where the goldsmiths prided themselves on the delicate granulated-gold work even the least-skilled could produce.

Then, there were the dogs. A man might walk abroad with dogs to protect him; a woman, never.

There might be whores working this alley. But they weren't wearing gold, or being guarded by red-eared dogs. These dogs liked him ... but he knew, instantly, by their posture that these ones would defend her, or die trying, even against someone they liked. But who was she, and what was she doing here, watching him? She seemed to think he'd know who she was.

"We came to seek you out," she said. "I am She of the Gateways and these are my hounds."

If that was a name for some particular district here, he didn't recognize it. Could there be a Great House here known as The Gateways?

Her hounds ... They were hunting dogs of some kind, he was sure, looking at them again. Some breed of coursing hound that he just did not recognize. Strange looking animals. Hungry ones, too, by the way the one was sniffing at his bag. She looked at him through slightly narrowed eyes, plainly waiting for a response. Unfortunately, he had no idea what she expected. So he smiled and patted the sniffing dog again. The other had also come forward, stretching its head and nose towards him. Yes, he knew that one too, the female, more suspicious than her brother or mate, whichever he was. The fur on her back was still slightly raised, but that was almost a wag of her fur-feathered tail.

"Who are you?" she asked, as the second dog came closer.

She'd just said she'd been looking for him...how could she not know his name? But he spoke, without meaning to. "Antimo Bartelozzi, of the city of Ferrara." As the words came from his mouth, he started. What was he doing? He never gave his name, his actual name, when he was out working, let alone where he came from. What had come over him?

This was all something of a rude shock to the guardian of the crossroads. Firstly, the mortal did not know just who he was speaking to. She had been *sure* that once she spoke her name, he would know her for what she was! That even if he did not worship her, he would at least know to give her respect and her due!

She had no grasp of how many eons she had been mourning. Time had not touched her, and as a goddess the changes of such things as language were of no consequence. She knew, vaguely, that she had no true, direct worshippers except the dogs now, that she only retained her power because in between, nothing decayed, not even grief. And the loss of power given by worshippers had meant little to her in the face of her terrible grief.

But to be forgotten, completely?

Oh, she had *said* that to herself, made it all part of her litany of mourning, but deep down she had not believed that she could ever be forgotten. Not really. Certainly not here. To find that she really was...

She needed to know more. She had exerted her will on him, and he had answered. But it meant little to her. Where was Ferrara? And he seemed to have no ideas of the worship or sacrifice that a god required. Was owed.

Well then. She would make her demand more ... forceful. Not so as to harm him, but to compel him to give that which he was not aware was his responsibility.

Her command: "My dogs are hungry. Feed them," was interrupted by the arrival of a group of men. They had a hint of the prowling pack, in the way they walked.

Antimo took one look at them and said something half under his breath. She could feel his desire to be barely noticeable, to be small and ordinary, exerted.

It was the wrong message for this pack. They liked that type of prey. They surged forward. Of course they did not see her.

"You'd better gather your skirts, lady," said Antimo, "and run. This is more than your dogs can deal with." He brought a blade into his hand and turned to face them.

She drew her cloak of darkness around herself and her dogs. And him. Her power might be lessened, but it was not gone. Oh, no. "I am still Hekate," she said. "Let them dare to approach."

The moon had lit the alley, moments before. Now Antimo found himself in darkness so Stygian as to make him wonder if he'd just gone blind. He knew he wasn't alone in it because of the cursing at the mouth of the alleyway.

"Black as hell in there," said someone. "I could see him a moment ago."

Then a second voice, tinged with uncertainty and the fear he himself had felt just a few moments before: "It's a trap. Let's get out of here, boys."

That was followed by the sound of their blundering departure.

This was not what Antimo had expected. These gangs were something of a feature of the back streets of Constantinople, the blues, greens and reds—descended from the long ago supporters of various chariot-racers, he'd been told. Now they were a law unto themselves, each absolute in their own districts. The emperor was too weak and too uninterested to rein them in. So the merchants hired guards, and paid for protection, or paid the gangs to *be* the protection. Decent citizens locked their doors and tried to stop their sons from becoming involved.

They were the sort of thing Antimo was normally good at avoiding. He'd have heard them coming, if it hadn't been for this odd woman. Hekate? The name brought vague associations of witchcraft to mind. Antimo kept clear of magic and its practitioners as much as possible. Of course many were frauds, but he had reason to know that some weren't.

But this woman and her dogs must be the real thing, and, compared to what he had seen, powerful. He was not a superstitious man, or one who believed he had much chance of Christ's favor, but he muttered a prayer anyway. Whether it was the prayer or the fact that the gang of greens—this was their territory—had gone hunting elsewhere, the darkness lightened.

"I think we will take this way," she said. There was a narrow, twisty path between the buildings he had not noticed earlier. She and the dogs led, and despite his first rational idea, which had been to run the other way, his instincts led him to follow her along it and into the wider thoroughfare beyond. A lamp set in a window-sconce to show its owner's wealth and power shone out into the street, and he could see her clearly now. That was definitely gold she was wearing around her neck and in hoops from her ears. Heavy necklaces, hung with black uncut stones, gleamed. And yet... he knew that she was probably a lot safer in the back alleys than he had been.

He took a deep breath. "Lady, you said your dogs were hungry. As it happens I have the makings of my own supper here. I could give it to them."

She nodded, regally. So right there he took the piece of bacon and the bread and soft cheese out of his pouch, cut them up and fed them to the dogs. He kept the onion. It was a habit of his, when he carried money, to put humble food on top of it. Exploring fingers tended to recognize the shape of onions and feel of bread, and give up without finding the hidden section below that.

The dogs—having wolfed down all that there was to be eaten—looked hopefully at him. The bitch, who had been more wary before, went as far as to lick his hand. "That's all I have, Red-ears."

"They are called Ravener and Ripper," she said, and turning away, began walking. The dogs followed almost instantly, without being called... and then they were gone.

He really wasn't sure just where to.

He couldn't find the narrow gap between the houses she'd brought him out of, either.

Antimo didn't like being out of his depth, he didn't like uncanny things, and he didn't like things with the heavy smell of magic about them. But he liked her dogs. And he had come to no harm—in fact, thanks to this woman, he had avoided harm.

"All's well that ends without needing to clean your blade," he muttered to himself, and decided to forget the woman for now. Whatever her business with him—well, it seemed mostly to have been done when he'd sacrificed his dinner for her hounds. He had done good work for Ferrara and his duke tonight. He would find something else to eat, to go with that onion.

It had been a very long time since Hekate had last thought of anything but her sadness. A very, very long time. Much had changed, it seemed. She was unsure about it all; she did not like, in the least, that she had actually been forgotten. She did not like these streets where killers hunted with impunity. But her dogs liked the man . . . and he had given to her what she was due, a sacrifice, though he had not known why. All in all, this encounter had left her feeling . . . unsettled. But somewhat less deeply wrapped in her grief because of it.

And more awake than she had been for a very long time indeed.

Chapter 17

The Black Sea

"I suppose," said Admiral Lemnossa, looking at the sails on the horizon, "we're lucky to have avoided them for this long. I hoped that jig out to sea would avoid them entirely while they searched the coastline for us. Still, we're not more than a day's sailing from Herculea. It's to be hoped that we might see some Byzantine vessels if we get in sight of the port. Not a very large hope, I admit. In the meanwhile we'll sail in as close a company as can be managed. I leave you to the thankless task of getting them into some kind of formation, Henri. And get the cannon loaded and the men armed. It'll be a fight. I'm going to sit here, and do some thinking and praying. That's a fair number of galleys out there."

He said it all with the sort of tranquility that had made the admiral a byword in Venice. He was not a military commander, as he had assured them repeatedly. He was a Venetian who liked to see his cargo safely landed. Sometimes that meant sinking a few interfering vessels, or some fighting.

Soon there were men with crossbows, pistols and grenades up in baskets on the masts, and barrels of seawater were being filled to deal with potential fires. Men strapped on swords, women and children went below—but their very presence lent steel and anger to the resolve of the Venetians. The pursuing galleys were being rowed hard, and were gaining on the round ships. That didn't stop the Venetians from looking at them with disdain. Scows compared to their own galleys. The Venetians swung their fleet to run toward the land, which brought the attacking galleys almost at right angles to them, and having to row into the wind. Soon the cannon fired some ranging shots. And then, all too quickly, battle was joined, with a return of cannon-fire.

Only it wasn't quite as simple as it seemed. The broad spear of the oncoming galleys continued to run at the flank of the fleet, roughly five wide by six deep, not so much in a formation as riding in the wakes of the front-runners. They were war-ships—galleys under oars and some sail and much faster than most of the fleet of trader-vessels. The Venetian and Genoese round ships under sail lacked their speed or maneuverability but had size, height and also broadside cannon—mostly smaller caliber cannon, true, and very inaccurate. The chasing galleys had only stern and bow cannon. That was something Admiral Lemnossa had gleaned from his conversation with the Genoese from Theodosia, and on which he had based his strategy.

Looking at the way the enemy attacked, he'd bet they'd struggled to find sea-captains with battle experience.

"The *testa di cazzo* are idiots!" said his captain incredulously, looking at the oncoming ships. "Most of them can't fire without bringing down the masts of the ships in front. Did no one ever explain line abreast to them?"

"They're trying to fan out in the front. Give the signal, Captain. Let's go about."

The admiral had gambled that the Venetian and Genoese sailors could still work the sails while the air was prickled with arrows. It wasn't much of a gamble. He knew his sailors. The oncoming raiders were approaching the flank rowing hard almost straight into the wind. It was not a very strong breeze, not enough to hold the rowers back.

The raiders had expected the fleet to turn away and try to run. What they hadn't expected was for the prey to turn towards them at the last minute, using all of that slight wind. Instead of striking a running fleet in the flank, their own flanks were now exposed. Their bow-chaser cannon were no use, whereas the cannon on the broadsides of the round ships could fire into the mass because they were bunched, and they could not turn without hitting the oars of other ships in their fleet.

From the castles, and from the baskets and barrels on the masts, fire poured down on the attacking galleys. The attackers became the attacked. Boarding had been their plan of attack and that still happened here and there. But the battle had become something of a melee, and the initial shock and damage of the broadside fire had been quite decisive. So had been the fury of the Genoese and Venetian sailors.

The other factor, of course, was the slave-rowers. The four Venetian galliots had freemen-rowers. They could and would fight. The slaves on their opponent's ships took up space that could have been used for fighting men.

What had been planned to be a vicious butchering of a merchant fleet turned into a fight, and one in which the attackers lost vessels and a lot of men even before the enemy had been engaged. As the battle raged on, a number of the galley crews decided that it was a choice of sink, be overcome, or flee. Some didn't get that choice, but the numerical odds shifted rapidly away from the galleys to the Venetians and their Genovese allies.

Less than three hours after it began, the battle was over. The Venetian and Genovese fleets limped their way onward—not unscarred, but comparatively unscathed. Of the thirty attacking galleys, some seven had been sunk, four captured, and the rest had fled.

The freed oar-slaves provided some more information. This was only part of the galley fleet—the admiral's feints and ruses had drawn off some of the attack. But that wasn't all. They'd seen large-scale shipbuilding on the Dnieper. But the numbers of vessels was unclear and the intent of the project remained unknown.

The fleet sailed on toward the Bosphorus, with some relief.

Admiral Lemnossa buried his flag captain with honor, and sadness. "The young should outlive the old," he said as the cold water took the captain's body.

Venice

Benito had discovered that he loved the Arsenal. The last time he had been here he'd worked desperately to avoid thinking about Corfu and Maria. The work had been a catharsis even if it had driven Admiral Dourso and the senior masters a little mad. But he had not realized how much he had missed the work, the place, the smell of woodworking, pitch, new cordage—and, by the cheering, how the place had missed him. They carried him around on their shoulders, and even the masters had a good word and a smile for him. That would wear off, soon enough. In the meantime he would take advantage of their goodwill to get things done. Benito knew that there had to be spies, agents of Jagiellon, Milan, Aquitaine, the Holy Roman Empire, and probably agents of Alexius in Venice, and possibly even here in the Arsenal. There was no way that they could keep progress a secret, although there would be no harm in trying. But really, speed was of the essence. The forces marshaled against them could do little about that. And once the fleet was at sea communication with their principals would be more difficult.

He could only hope that these feints within feints would work. Benito knew that lives rested on that. Some of those cheering for him here would not come back. It was not a light responsibility. He preferred risking his own neck. At least he knew his own skills and his own limits.

He'd even talked it over with his brother. Marco, normally soft and gentle, shook his head. "Stop being a fool, Benito. Some men will die, yes. But if the evil that is Jagiellon, and the thing behind Jagiellon, got loose in the Mediterranean, many more would die."

That was the Lion of the Lagoon talking, the magical guardian of Venice that his brother shared his life with, Benito knew. It had more steel than Marco. And it was right. Soon he was discussing the casting of forty-eight-pound bombards, and how best to put these into the ships—something to which they were as ill-suited as the ships were. Some had been put into vessels as bow chasers before, but they were hard on the ships' structure, and the masters at the Arsenal had put a stop to it. They were devastating . . . to both the ships they hit with their cannon balls and the ships firing—and they were not accurate.

"It's just not practical," protested master Giobrando. "It's going to strain every plank and every seam and every strut on the vessel. If you must have more cannon, keep them to twelve-pounders."

"What do you suggest that we do, Master? Bombard them from the beach?" said Benito.

"It would work better than putting those cannon on the ships," said the master, stubbornly. "You'll just sink the vessels. On land at least the crew won't be drowned."

Benito sighed and rolled his eyes. He hoped it was with a suitable display of long-suffering exasperation, a show that he hoped was being appreciated and noted. "And what would we be doing on land? But if that is your opinion, then you'd better make it possible for us to unship them easily. But still so that they can be fired from the vessels." Brass cannon were expensive, and Benito hoped that that alone, plus the performance about putting them on the ships would convince the spies and those who they reported to, that Venice planned to reduce the walls of Constantinople from the sea.

By the venomous look that he got from the master shipbuilder, Benito was fairly certain that the man would be telling everyone who would listen, just what an idiot Benito Valdosta was being this time. "I will make sure they can be unshipped. And if you'd take my advice Milor' Valdosta, you'll make sure that they are."

Benito put on his most annoying smile. "I'll ask for your advice if I need it, Master Giobrando. We are making certain magical preparations to strengthen the ships."

Giobrando's snort was the only comment of what he thought of the efficacy of such magic. All he actually said, again, was, "I'll make sure that they can be unshipped easily."

Benito shrugged as if the idea was simply irrelevant. "Whatever you like, Master Giobrando."

"I'd like to leave them here."

"That is not an option. We're going to need those cannon."

Benito did not say what they were going to need them for. He just went to talk with the apprentices pushing tow into the chinks in the timber-cladding, and to join them at it, falling into the pattern of working while he talked as naturally as if he not been away from the Arsenal. Benito knew he was playing a dangerous game. He really didn't want Giobrando as a lifetime enemy. But a deception works best if you have a truly believing shill. Besides it gave them something to talk about beside the horse transports. There was nothing that unusual about horse transports. Though slow and unwieldy, they were still often used.

Chapter 18

Venice

It was wonderful having Benito back, Marco found. He hadn't realized quite how easily he bonded with his half-brother. He knew how much he'd missed him, of course; almost every hour he'd found himself wondering how Benito would react to something, or what Benito would have said. But Benito and Maria stepped back into their lives as if, somehow, they'd never left, or had only stepped out for a pole around the canals.

And as for the little girl...

Marco shook his head. Maria had thought that the reality of little ones might put them off wanting one of their own. There were aspects of parenthood that were going to be a challenge, yes, and having a child right there, demonstrating those aspects was sometimes daunting. The occasional tantrum, for instance—or the absolute refusal, one night, to go to sleep. But Alessia had wormed her way right into their hearts. It was harder now than ever before that they had not yet managed to start one of their own.

The last time Benito had been in Venice he had been driven by a need to get back. Marco had not been fooled, nor had anyone else. Benito had been driven to get back to Maria, not Corfu. The time before that, he had been miserable because of Maria...because he had lost her, and had no prospect of getting her back. Now, back home in Venice again, with her, underneath it all he was dreading the inevitable winter of his bargain perhaps, but now at last he was *with* Maria. And he had changed, he'd grown. He was more of a man now, and less of the wild boy that he'd been. That was partly Maria, but also, seeing him with his daughter, Marco knew it was because of Alessia as well. And who could doubt now that she was Benito's child, especially when she smiled or looked up at you with curiosity, to see what this exciting adult would do next, head slightly tilted, eyes bright? Benito might never realize it, but being a father had been good for him. It had given him stability that nothing else could. And the need to think, because he was no longer Benito alone, who could risk any mad thing. There was a small one depending on him. Who would be left helpless if something happened to him.

Marco saw that stability, that—call it what it was, *maturity,* and he was even more determined to get there himself. Finally it had driven him to the point where he had steeled himself to ask Francisco about it during their next language session. The fiction that Francisco was not a chirurgeon, or at least as skilled in medicine as most of the learned Dottores at the Accademia, had not lasted very long. His skill was undoubtedly in field medicine and plainly learned, by the examples he gave, in the tail of an army, if not in its van. But that was hardly a bad thing. Marco would take practical medicine over bookish speculation without a second thought.

Besides, the books all too often contradicted each other.

For a while now Francisco had been coming to the *Casa* Montescue, rather than Marco going to his shabby rooms. It was less restrictive for both of them, and Marco was less likely to get irritated by the Council of Ten's watchers. It was bad enough having the Lion as part of himself, knowing far too much of what he was thinking, without having to bear the constant observation of others, who were all too mortal and would not know what he was thinking and would speculate and speculate without actually *asking* him.

"Francisco," he said, a bit hesitantly.

The soldier-doctor-teacher stopped drinking beer and looked enquiringly at Marco, who had been attempting to read a simple Arabic passage aloud. Marco blushed. "The fertility of men ... and women ... How does it work? How can you ... aid it?"

Francisco took his time in answering. And when he did it was with a wry smile. "My experience has tended to be with people who wanted the pleasure, not the results, m'lord. There has been some writing on the subject, but I think most of it is worth less than the paper it is written on." He put his beer down, and gave Marco a direct gaze. "Look ... it's typical for a man who wants an heir to blame his wife. But, well, you can't grow crops if the seed isn't good." He looked Marco up and down. "But most of the lords I've heard of having this sort of trouble tended to be elderly and on the corpulent side, and fall into bed blind drunk, and then wonder why nothing happens or why the baby looks like their groom. You're not a heavy drinker. What sort of exercise do you do, m'lord? I mean something that makes your heart race, and your chest heave, and your breathing rapid, not a stroll to the plaza."

The idea was rather odd to Marco. Military men trained at the arts of war. Other working people did what they had to do, be it pole a barge or carry bales. But that was really not something the masters or the mistresses of the *Case Vecchie* did. One walked sometimes. Those that had estates outside the lagoon would go riding or hunting there. Some would go and fence in a salle. But none of these had really appealed to Marco. "I can't really think of anything. I walk a little." The only other exercise he could think of doing wasn't having the desired result.

Francisco nodded, as if he had expected something of the sort. Venice was not the sort of city that lent itself to vigorous exercise. "Well, maybe you should consider doing something. You're starting a little pot-belly, m'lord. A really brisk walk or something at least a few times a week. I like to ride or run, myself. I go across to Chioggia twice a week. More often would be better, but that is all that is practical right now."

The agents of the Council of Ten had actually told Marco about Francisco's "excursions," finding them worrying and strange. It was nice to have that mystery cleared up, although Marco doubted the Council of Ten would grasp the idea very easily. Now that he thought about it, he remembered Kat had telling him that Francesca used to walk briskly for exercise every day. He'd thought it odd then. Maybe it wasn't so odd, after all.

"The body is all part of one machine, m'lord. Making one aspect stronger may stir the juices in another."

"Running?" Marco asked. "Really?"

"It's useful. If I'd been faster at it once . . . well, that was long ago. As a boy I was entered into foot races by my father. He bet on me, so he made me practice, and I discovered that I liked the exercise." He shrugged. "Otherwise beer makes me fat. So that's one idea. Perhaps both of you should get exercise, and sun, and air that does not stink of canal water. It cannot hurt, and it might help. And the reality is, there are those women who do not have children. No matter how often they try, or with how many men. You might have to accept that, m'lord."

Well, that was disappointing. He'd hoped for a potion, or . . . well, something. Still. It was practical and easy, and as the man said, it would do no harm, this exercise.

They went back to Marco's attempts at reading, and, when that was done, Marco asked about something else that had been troubling him. He knew, by now, that Francisco had been a slave of the Barbary pirates for a time, and that was where he had acquired his linguistic skills and some of his medical knowledge. It was an area from which black lotos was still smuggled into the lands to the north. And not two days ago he'd been called to help with a woman deep in the hallucinations the drug could cause.

"Black lotos . . . did you ever have to treat anyone with addiction to it?"

"No. I have seen a few, over in Icosium," said Francisco. "Until I started teaching I spent my time with mercenary companies, m'lord. There are drunks, in mercenary companies, but not many with such expensive tastes. That's for the nobility. And a mercenary company doesn't keep such men, anyway. Drink is one thing, but black lotos? Makes a man useless for fighting. I know of no drug that would stop men craving drink, and I doubt if there is one that'll stop them craving lotos. Only desiring to do so more than desiring the drug can do that. And that, m'lord, is a truly powerful desire." He rubbed his nose. "Mind you, we did have a bombardier once. The drink was the death of him in the end... but the condottiere needed him in the siege. He was a genius with cannon and a fool with burned-wine. We kept him going by giving him just enough. While he was in that state you'd hardly know he was enslaved to the stuff... except he'd do anything to get more."

Marco sighed. "I was hoping there'd be something in the Arabic medicine books."

"There is no easy way out of it, m'lord," said Francisco sympathetically. Clearly he wondered why Marco was asking—and clearly, he was not going to ask.

"I've heard the ink cap—you know, the mushroom, can make a man dislike alcohol, or rather alcohol dislike the man." Marco offered that in hopes that it might trigger a similar memory.

Francisco chuckled a little. "Ah. Tippler's bane. Makes them feel as if they had the hangover to end all hangovers. But I've no knowledge of it working on anything else." He shook his head. "And it doesn't stop a man wanting to drink, just stops him from keeping it down. When it comes to a man's addictions, m'lord, whether it be drink or gold, there is never an easy answer."

❖　　❖　　❖

Maria watched how tenderly Kat held Alessia. The tentativeness had gone now, and there was...almost a hunger in the way she looked at the child. She didn't want to ask—but really, she didn't need to. She'd seen the same hunger in other would-be mothers coming to worship at the shrine of the Mother. The difficult part would be talking about it. Not that Kat wouldn't want to talk; Maria knew that, she could feel it—perhaps yet another gift of the Mother, that she could tell these things now. Just...the problem was, how to start.

At least she could be sure Katerina would give Alessia real love, not in the *Case Vecchie* style of handing the child over to a nurse to care for. So when she went to the Underworld, as she must, her baby would not just be in good hands, but in the best. A little of her ever-present anxiety eased. Kat would be as much a mother to Alessia as if Maria herself was there. Kat would keep her safe.

Besides, no one could ever imagine Marco Valdosta mistreating a child; the very opposite, in fact. To judge by their first few days in Venice, Alessia was going to be a thoroughly spoiled little girl, pampered by everyone from Milord Lodovico to the lowest chambermaid. Marco was already talking about hiring some extra servants. Some people of real quality, he'd said. Well, she'd have to meet them first. If there was time... She knew Aidoneus would find her anywhere. There was no point in running away. Anyway, that was her bargain, and she'd stand by it.

Marco came in, fresh from his language lesson with what Maria guessed to be an ex-soldier, who was apparently teaching him to read Arabic script. The idea of learning to read not only another language, but other letters made Maria's head hurt. Her grasp of the ordinary alphabet, which started late, had been hard enough, although it had grown easier with practice, to the point where it was no longer an effort to read Kat's letters, even it was still a labor replying to them. His arrival did put the damper on speaking to Kat about fertility... and the Mother-Goddess. Men were entirely too sensitive about these things. Or squeamish. Besides, he might take it all too personally. Most men would be inclined to blame their wives; Marco would be inclined to blame himself.

"Francisco has persuaded me I have to do more exercise," said Marco cheerfully, picking up Alessia. "I am getting fat."

"You are not!" said Kat, flying to his defense. "You were too thin before."

Privately, Maria agreed with both of them. Marco *had* been too thin, back in the old bad days, but now... the good life was perhaps a bit too good. He was getting soft.

Not like Benito. Benito was and would always be a restless soul, who found it difficult to sit still and who enjoyed fencing with his arms-master, or chasing game on foot in the rugged folds around Pantocrator when he could get away from his desk. And he'd throw himself into doing anything physical. Marco wasn't like that, which probably made him more peaceful to sleep next to, but also was likely to turn him into one of those round little scholars with white hands like a woman.

Marco wagged his head at his wife. "No, I think he is right. And I've made up my mind I have to do something. For . . . reasons. Anyway, my problem is just what to do. Even taking a walk is impossible. People want to talk to me. The agents of the Council of Ten surround me. We both know I am a disaster at poling a boat. Dancing . . . no. And I really do not enjoy fencing. What do you suggest?"

"We could go over to the old villa on the mainland and you could ride. We could both ride, together." Kat actually sounded as if, now that idea had been broached, she thought she might enjoy that.

"Isn't that the horse getting the exercise?" asked Marco with a smile.

"No," said Benito from the doorway. "Trust me on this one, Brother. I would rather spend all day climbing ratlines, than spend an hour in the saddle. Or in my case, on and off the saddle. Perdition! A horse is a thing created by the devil, I swear."

"Benito! Have you finished with the admiral?" said Maria, running to him.

Benito grinned evilly, hugging her. "I think I have nearly finished him off, yes. So I decided to spend some time with my wife and baby, while I still could. If I can ever get either of them away from my brother and his wife."

Chapter 19

Constantinople

The narrow waters of the Bosphorus had seemed like a refuge. The admiral of Eastern Fleet had relaxed when they had entered them, with the wooded bluffs seeming like shields.

Now, with the sunset red-hazed by the smoke hanging in the still sky above Constantinople's walls, Lemnossa realised that it was no sanctuary. The great chain was being raised—you could hear the huge windlasses creak and rattle in the Megalos pyrgos in the Galata citidel even from here, a good mile away. It was, in these almost windstill evening conditions, too late to flee. They were trapped in the Golden Horn anchorage. It did not look good.

Normally the little oared lighters and schifos pulled out from the shore like flies as the fleet sailed in, toward the wharves below the Venetian quarter. Not this time. All that approached was a solitary Byzantine Empire fusta, which rowed to the admiral's flagship. The officer who climbed up onto the Great Galley plainly had no love for Venice or the Venetians. His bow was a bob, so perfunctory as to border on an insult, and he certainly was not going to salute the admiral. "You are to provide us with your manifests. Charges to the value of half your cargo will be levied before your vessels are allowed to proceed."

Admiral Lemnossa sighed. "What's your name, son?"

"It's of no concern to you. And I am no son of yours, old man. Those are orders from the emperor Alexius himself."

"They're also a direct breach of the Treaty of Tarsus that your emperor is signatory to. So, if they're his orders you'd better bring us proof of it, signed and with the Byzantine Imperial seal, or when the Venetian fleet arrives your emperor is likely to offer fulsome apologies, offers of restitution and your head on a platter. And if you didn't know that you'd have been happy to give me your name and style," said the admiral, calmly.

The calmness jarred the young officer briefly, but his bombast and arrogance reasserted themselves. "The emperor repudiates the terms of Tarsus. You have until sundown tomorrow to comply, or the cannon on the wall will be brought to bear on your vessels."

Under the circumstances Lemnossa decided that they would be wisest to lie off, rather than come in to the quays. They were still under the guns of the city and of Galata—just off the Venetian quarter, and the little quays in the bay they would normally have made for. A little later a small boat came over from the Genovese Fleet. Lemnossa took a look at the Genovese Captain Di Tharra, and held up a hand. "Wine first." The captain's face was the color of the purple-red of the wine from the vineyards of Masceron.

The captain tossed it off in a masterful fashion, and did look a fraction the better for it. He was plainly near incandescent, still.

"The *testa di cazzo* wants half our cargo. Half! He said as we sailed in here with Venetians, we could be treated like them." He looked enquiringly at his host. "I assume . . . ?"

"Yes," said Lemnossa.

"So what are you going to do?" asked Di Tharra.

Lemnossa ground his teeth. "Pay, I expect. I do not expect my crews or my officers are going to be very happy to do so. But we're not in the best of positions to refuse. We'll need guarantees, though." He jerked a thumb at the walls of Constantinople. "Alexius must need the money desperately or he'd have tried sinking the fleet anyway. We're trapped and while we could inflict quite some damage it's obvious we're not equipped for war but for trade. That won't be the same next time we come to Constantinople. He must know these vessels will be turned against him, and that this must mean war."

The captain nodded. "The duke of Genoa is going to be, shall we say, spitting hellfire. We negotiated a trade-treaty with the emperor Alexius only last year!"

"He may have acquired other allies since then," said Admiral Lemnossa, thinking that the pieces fitted all too obviously and well. He just had to hope the Ilkhan Mongols were not part of the scheme.

The Genoese captain snorted. "Alexius? They must have a rare taste for incompetence and treachery."

Lemnossa nodded. "They will pay him back in kind, at least with the treachery, of course. But Alexius has never been able to see that far into the future. Today is far enough for him."

"Which brings us to what we do tomorrow, m'lord. We cannot stand off against the fortress on our own. And if we do somehow break through the chain, we still have the Hellespont."

"So we will pay up. Alexius is correct on this one. More and we might have balked and taken our chances. We can try to negotiate, of course."

They sat and talked, trying to find an alternative and not succeeding. Night fell and a seaman came to interrupt them. "Admiral, there is a man to see you. He's just come from the Venetian quarter with a message from the ambassador, he says."

Admiral Lemnossa looked at his Genoese guest. Shrugged. They were in trouble together. "Bring him up."

"I could leave, m'lord."

"I'd probably just have to get someone to row me over to your vessel to tell you about it."

The man who came up was a fairly hard looking fellow, who walked like a sailor, not like the messenger of an ambassador. He handed over a sealed parchment. "Had to come down the wall on a rope, m'lord. Signor Porchelli is bit old for it."

"Can we take a few hundred men back that way and go and hang the emperor in his own throne-room?" asked the Genoese captain.

The messenger did not take it as a jest. "No, m'lord. We had to bribe the guards on the wall to let me get up there. There are some schifos tied alongside the quays and I took a small one, muffled the oars, and rowed out here. The Venetian quarter is sealed off. Guards on the outside, barricades in the streets. We're expecting trouble. It's been building up for a while. The emperor blamed it on the demoi—the street-gangs. The blues, the reds and greens...but it's more than that. We were told the guards were for our safety, but they don't stop them. It's us they're guarding, stopping people defending themselves and stopping us escaping, or at least escaping with any of our goods."

"Do you mind if I read this, Captain?" asked Lemnossa, cracking the seal.

"Of course not, Admiral."

Lemnossa reflected that a few cannonballs and pirates, and the emperor Alexius had done more for Venetian-Genovese relations than a hundred years of diplomacy had. The letter was brief and to the point: the Venetian merchants in the city had suffered depredations and violence, and if reliable informants were to be believed, crippling taxation was about to be enforced on them. As the Venetian quarter was Venetian territory, that was not something that it had been subject to before: a fact that embittered a series of emperors. The ambassador had approached the emperor on hearing that the fleet was in the Bosphorus, as to opening the wall-gates to allow normal trade. He had been lucky to escape with his life. The fleet must proceed without delay to Venice and lay these matters before the Senate and the Doge. The city lacked as adequate a defense as it might have, as there was a revolt underway in the Opiskon theme, the region that faced onto the Hellespont. Once the ships had passed Constantinople, they were unlikely to be interfered with.

Only they were on the wrong side of the chain. Lemnossa sucked breath through his teeth. There had to be a way of salvaging as much as possible from this wreck. "I think," he said slowly, "we'll need some leads-men on the bow. We need to move these vessels deeper into the Golden Horn. Then they can't bring cannon to bear on us from both sides, and, if we fire back, we won't hit the Venetian quarter." He looked at his companion. "Or the Genoese. It is closer to the chain, anyway."

"The Genoese are in big trouble," volunteered the messenger with some satisfaction. "They tried to protest about the control of their gate. Alexius had five of their leading merchants crucified."

Captain di Tharra of Genoa stood up. "I thought it might just be pique, that we'd sailed in company and could not be turned against each other. But it goes deeper than that, m'lord. I'll move our vessels with yours, although we lack the sweeps to move them easily."

"We'll see to taking lines across. Your round ships are good for defense, with those castles of theirs. We'll get ourselves into as good a negotiating position as possible. Make cooperation contingent on access to our people." He grimaced. "It's likely that Alexius plans a wholesale looting of both Venetian and Genoese storehouses and assets, given his actions here. If we negotiate wisely we can let him believe we plan to replenish those. He's mad enough to think he can get away with robbing us there, too. If we play it right, we can do the opposite. It'll not help our crews and our investors, but my Senate and your duke should be grateful. And we'd be no worse off for doing it."

"You're a master strategist, Admiral," said the senior captain respectfully.

"I wish I was. We would not be here if that was the case. Now let us use the night hours."

The morning found the fleet lying at anchor nearly a mile farther up the great Golden Horn, anchored bow and stern to offer their narrowest, strongest profile to the seawall and effectively out of range of the cannon on Galata. The Byzantines could hardly have been unaware of it, but had taken no action. The day was well advanced before a Byzantine fusta came out to the fleet.

It was a very different officer aboard her. He saluted respectfully and delivered his message. "My Lord Admiral. My commander, the Megadoux Laskaris wishes to know why you have assumed formations as if for war. You are to proceed to the usual wharves given to the Venetian trade offload, or we will be obliged to take action against you."

Lemnossa laughed softly. "Oh no, young man. I'm not one to stick his head twice into the same noose. Yes, we're trapped in your harbor—but that does mean that those masts over there, which are your fleet, are trapped in here with us. And no other vessels to trade or aid are able to come in. The Sea of Marmara coast has currents bad enough to make it a risky landing place, and risk is expense. Now, let us negotiate in good faith. I am reluctant—but willing—to agree to a slightly elevated duty to the value of some small part of our cargo, as the expense of putting down the uprising in Opiskon must be considerable and would endanger us too. There are merchants in Constantinople hungry for our goods. Your emperor can extract some tariffs from them."

The officer swallowed. "Ah. Let me carry word of this to my seniors. How did you know about Opiskon?"

The admiral shrugged. It did no harm to sew a bit of disinformation, and perhaps a lieutenant would learn that good manners had value. "Shall we say that I was informed. You think just who I have seen since we entered the Golden Horn." He waved a hand about. "A naval encounter here in such closed quarters would be messy. Merely a hand-to-hand melee. We're carrying extra crew as we've had pirate trouble. We sank quite a number of their vessels."

Before the trouble started, Antimo Bartelozzi had moved himself quietly out of the Venetian quarter, into the rundown trading district that had once been granted to the duchy of Amalfi and was now more or less the whores' quarter. In a city with such a heavy dependence on mercenaries and the emperor's two remaining tagmata, it was going to remain the part of town with the freest access. Yes, he might be mistaken for a pimp, but it was better than what he saw coming to the foreign trading quarters. He'd be leaving shortly. He'd hoped to buy a passage on a vessel of the Venetian Eastern Fleet, but if his information was correct, they'd be lucky to sail out of the Golden Horn, let alone be allowed contact with the Venetian quarter.

He knew that the fleet had come in, and at first light had quietly made his way up the third hill to a building with a suitable flat roof. He'd secured the use of it some four months before, and had done considerable mapping from up there. And from here he could see that the Venetians—and by the shape of the vessels—some Genoese ships, had not played the game according to the plans of the Byzantines.

That was good, but he would still make his way overland to a small port farther west. Possibly Aenus—a small place far enough away to avoid any shred of suspicion or close examination of the baggage of maps and information he had to transport. He wanted to look at its defenses anyway, although a land-battle across Byzantium was probably a less-than-wise strategy as a way to capture Constantinople.

He went back down the narrow stairs to gather more word from the streets. They got it wrong, as often as not. But put together with the diverse facts at his disposal Antimo could make an educated guess.

He was unaware that he was being watched. That should have been of concern to him. But then Hekate had means denied to Alexius's spy-catchers. She had understood how he knew she was watching him at their first encounter, and taken steps to counter his powers. She was, after all, a goddess.

It took three days to hammer out a deal, and a great deal of shuttling to-and-fro. But Alexius got less than he'd hoped for, and Admiral Lemnossa got exactly what he hadn't wanted, but had expected: more refugees. And the relief of putting Constantinople behind him.

It did nothing for the fury of the ship's crews though. Every man on every vessel had lost money. They'd inevitably clubbed together with their friends and relations to buy a share in one of the colleganzas. Inevitably, too, they'd dreamed of the best possible profit—most of which had just disappeared into Alexius's coffers. And now all they wanted was some of that loss back out of his hide. That played along with the worry and anger of the refugees, who were mostly only going as far as Negroponte as the next safe Venetian outpost. When the admiral considered how overloaded the ships were with humans and stock from Constantinople, he was glad to be offloading some of this lot there.

The lightening of his vessels could not come soon enough.

PART III
November, 1540 A.D.

Chapter 20

Venice

Benito had long since decided that he could deal with almost anything better than goodbyes. This one was far worse than any other. Yet there was no way he could leave without saying goodbye to Maria and Alessia. Life was too short and fragile and precious for that. He knew that the task ahead was fraught and that Maria would be going to Aidoneus' shadowy kingdom soon. It was almost enough to make him put his daughter on the ship with him. But at least there was Marco here in Venice, and Katerina as well. Marco and the spirit of the Lion of Saint Mark. And although there were differences between the brothers, there was no one Benito knew he could trust more, and a child would not be safe on the ship. Not where he was going. And she would be even less safe alone in Corfu. The time was coming.

The fleet was almost ready. The fast galleys that had sailed out of the gates of Hercules had returned and were in the final stages of refitting. Word was in from Genoa that their vessels were ready to sail

within three weeks for the meeting at Corfu, along
with the Aragonese. Little did they know that they
would not be overwintering there. A winter expedition
was madness...but such was the reputation that sailed
with the fleets, that there was no shortage of madmen
willing to gamble on the weather. The first relief had
come to Corfu in winter despite the weather.

Benito had no intention of gambling. He had
instead the intent of gathering some aid. Reluctant
aid, maybe. But aid anyway. He went in search of
Marco. He expected to find him in the Church of
St. Raphaella, which was fine as it was where they
needed to go. Instead he ran into him, smiling, on
the stairs leading up to the Doge's palace. "The
fleet's been sighted. The fleet from the Black Sea.
Maybe there will be no need of all this."

Marco always hoped to avoid war. Well, the part
of Marco that was Marco-the-healer did. The part
that was Marco-the-lion did not. Benito had decided,
when he was still a boy, that if a fight was inevitable
anyway, you might as well get it over and done with,
on your own terms. He doubted if the fleet's return
meant anything good. But there was no sense in
dampening Marco's hopes. He'd bet the news from
the fleet would do that anyway.

And Benito was not disappointed; a wise man had
once told him, "a pessimist is never unpleasantly surprised," and when it came to war, he supposed he must
be a pessimist. He was allowed—a rare and doubtful
privilege—to sit quietly behind a screen in a discreet
private salon in the Doge's palace while the admiral
of the Eastern Fleet reported to the Council of Ten.

"Monsignors, Doge Petro," said the admiral. "We

have two-thirds-empty holds, and we have several vessels barely fit to sail. We abandoned two at the little Arsenal in Corfu—although we have brought home a few prizes from the attack we suffered. They're not worth much, though. There's trouble brewing, big trouble, with the eastern trade. Emperor Alexius demanded a high toll for our passage. Half our cargo, and the vessels were less than full anyway."

"That's a direct contravention of the treaty of Tarsas," said one of the Council members. They were masked, as usual. But Benito had a good idea who it was by the voice and intonation.

"The Venetian ambassador, Signor Porchelli, made representation to the emperor. He was lucky to get away with his life, monsignors. The emperor has gone completely mad, we think. He said he did not care. We could pay and go or stay and be sunk. He said that he has no need to fear Venice anymore. Constantinople is restive and afraid. They prepare for war. The Venetian quarter is sealed off. Our people there fear a massacre."

"They surely would not dare."

The Eastern Fleet admiral shook his head. "I think the Byzantine generals are reluctant, monsignors, but Alexius's mercenaries...they see the prospect of rich loot. We paid and brought many of the women and children with us. Also some of the reserves of goods and gold our traders there held for their houses."

Benito knew what that meant: very, very scared merchants. Without much gold, or stock, their ability to trade would be severely curtailed, and for a Venetian merchant house, death was almost preferable.

"The fleet is early, and you left Trebizond early.

Without full holds, to judge by your statements." That was Petro. Benito knew the voice too well to be mistaken.

"Yes, monsignors. We had little choice. The Venetian podesta there made the decision, and it was a wise one, as events proved."

Peering from behind the screen in the dimly lit room—the Council preferred it so to preserve their anonymity, which kept them from undue influence and, of course, assassination—Benito could see the admiral of the Eastern Fleet tugging his beard nervously. The Council did not like rash admirals. They liked over-cautious ones even less. Lemnossa was a wily old bird by all reports, but the Council could be judgmental and vindictive. And the Venetian Republic had lost money.

"We have had trouble in Trebizond, monsignors. The Baitini have moved against the local satrap. So far the Ilkhan has done nothing."

"Baitini?"

"A sect of the worshippers of Mahomet, considered by many of their co-religionists to be heretical. A dangerous sect the Ilkhan all but crushed nearly a century ago. They were the last major force to stand against the Mongol in Damascus and their other secretive great fortress, Alamut. They ruled by fear and assassination, rather than by overt power. They were the power behind the throne. They believe they have a special relationship with God."

"Don't all sects?" said someone.

"These are very fanatical, monsignors. They were suppressed, but lately the Venetian merchants in Trebizond say that they have become more open in their extortion and murder. The city is in ferment. The Venetian quarter is an armed camp. Trade is severely curtailed, with caravans from Hind reported as going to other ports. A small fleet left early, as some do every year. They never returned."

"What?"

"It appears they were attacked by another fleet, monsignors. A fleet of galleys coming from Odessa, judging by sail-setting and their garb. Two sailors survived, clinging to some flotsam, and made their way overland, back to Trebizond. One of them was murdered, in the streets of Trebizond. The Baitini are working in concert with these raiders. They tried to kill both of the sailors, and it is only by the grace of God that one escaped the murderers to tell us his story. But even given that the man who survived was traumatized and just a common sailor, we knew that the size of the rover-fleet was substantial."

"It appears that the duke of Genoa will have his pirate problem."

"Yes, monsignors. I had not got there yet, but seven vessels of the State of Genoa—well, we met them several days' sail from the port of Sinope. They signaled us, and as we outnumbered them and outgunned them, we allowed a small boat to come across to us. They sought to join our fleet, seeking protection as fellow Christians from the pirate fleet that had barred their way. They had been driven out of Theodosia, and lost five vessels, and suffered considerable loss of life. We—out of Christian charity and to swell our numbers—allowed them to join our fleet. We encountered their attackers in some force a day out of Herculea. We were prepared and ready for the conflict, and the attackers were . . . shall we say, unskilled, monsignors. Bloodthirsty but unskilled. There were only some thirty galleys, and so with our allies we outnumbered them, and they were tricked into allowing us to fire broadsides at them. Their ships are merely equipped with bow and stern chasers, and they're poor gunners. The long and the short it is we beat them off with some loss of life and damage on our part, but not a vessel lost. We sank seven of them, and captured four, although we scuttled one as she was in no state to be sailed at any speed."

He paused and took a long drink from the goblet of wine that was given to him. "We had no trouble from there to until we entered the Bosphorus, although vessels were sighted. We were a goodly company. And we were glad of it, monsignors. It's time the pirates and Byzantines were taught to respect the ships of Venice."

"And, by the sounds of it, of Genoa."

The fleet admiral laughed. "You should have heard the Genoese senior captain's reaction when the emperor demanded half of the Genoese vessels' cargo too. They're used to Byzantines trying to play them off against us, not being treated like us. Alexius would have it that if they'd sail with our fleet, they could be taxed with us. I hear he was uninterested in their suggestion that he deploy his navy—not that it's up to much—against the pirates in the Black Sea. They're too organized, monsignor, just to be a rabble fleet. We need to take steps to see to our trade."

"We plan to, Admiral. We plan to return to Constantinople long before spring with a sharp rebuke for a little emperor for breaching the terms of our treaty. It's a pity that the rebellion in Opiskon appears to have fizzled out."

Peering around the screen again Benito saw the Eastern Fleet admiral nod approvingly. "Not a moment too soon, monsignors. You'll find our crews keen enough to join the expedition. Emperor Alexius hurt our pride, and worse, our profits. Many's the colleganza that'll be cursing him tonight. Give the men a week ashore..."

That was what Benito needed to hear: The admiral's assessment of the response of the men. Benito realized he should have guessed how far astray Emperor Alexius would let his greed lead him. It was not just the wealthy of Venice who traded Outremer. Even the lowliest seaman had a small share in a colleganza—a trading collective. A canny man could make himself a good profit—five times his investment—if he chose his goods and traders well. Those ordinary seamen would have lost money. Their retirement money for the older men, their weddings for the younger. The *populi minuta* would be angry and ready to put to sea again, despite the fact that it would be cold and wet at this season. He made a mental note to see what he could do to improve conditions on board. Half-frozen rowers on the galleys would not help their need for speed at all. Petro would complain about the money for oilskins and woolen hats, but not too much. Swords, powder and ball, arrows...no one quibbled about the need for those. But Benito had already heard Admiral Dourso in the Arsenal, who skimped nothing for his own comfort, attempting to cut corners on the well-being of his crews. That would not stand, not on Benito's watch.

The interview with the admiral of the Eastern Fleet continued for some time, refining details and clearing

up points. Benito listened. And began to calculate
on how many ships Venice could put at sea. He was
pretty sure the lists in the Piazza San Marco would
be filling up within the next few days. Men would be
signing up to join Venice on a punitive expedition to
Constantinople. Benito had his name at the head of
those lists. That would be popular. He also—and this
would be a lot less popular—did not want to cripple
and loot Constantinople. By the sounds of it they
might need a bulwark against the east if these Baitini
succeeded in their plans to subvert the Ilkhan's empire
from within. That sort of thinking was not likely to
appeal to men who had just lost the little they had.

Later he set off in search of Marco. One look at
his brother's face told him that the admiral of the
Eastern Fleet's news was being carried along by hundreds of lesser channels. He also had that impatient,
almost fevered Marcos-the-healer look. So the ships
had brought more than just bad news.

"What is it, Benito? I need to get down to Fondamenta Zattere Ponto Lungo. There are some sick
children. They have been very crowded on the Eastern Fleet vessels, with everyone trying to get out
of Constantinople and Trebizond. They left some at
Negroponte and at Corfu, but they were still crowded."

Benito came straight to the point. "I need you and
Brother Mascoli to take me down to the water-chapel.
Where you took me to meet the water-people."

Marco nodded, quite as if he had expected this.
Perhaps he had; who knew what the Lion whispered
in his thoughts? "This evening? I really must go right
now. I'd rather treat sick children immediately than
let them scatter into the city and spread diseases

around far and wide. Bring your daughter with you. Her godmother should see her."

That, Benito had not expected. "I want to ask them for aid—again—in getting a fleet to Constantinople. Do you really think I should bring Alessia?"

Marco nodded. "It will do no harm to remind them of the bond between you."

Benito pulled a face. "I don't think they take very well to blackmail."

But nonetheless he had her and Maria with him that evening when they made their way down to the consecrated water-chapel below the chapel of St. Raphaella. The undine Juliette and the triton Androcles came, as they waited. Benito saw the raised eyebrows of Juliette the undine, as she saw him holding Alessia. *"I see she has found her father. We'd heard about that."* Then she saw Maria, who had stayed back a little. She bowed with profound respect, disturbing the hair that cloaked her ample bare breasts. *"I could wish we met again in better times, Lady of the Dead."*

Maria had wanted to properly thank the merwoman who had stood in for Umberto's sister at the christening of her daughter. She still had some of the canal-woman's fear of the below-water dwellers, but her time as an acolyte of the Mother Goddess had broadened her perspectives a little.

But she still had not expected this nonhuman, so far away from little Corfu to know that much, or to call her by a title she did not really relish. "What? How—"

"He follows you," said Juliette. *"We can see. He longs for you, and for your strength. He comes. Soon."*

Maria felt the tears prick her eyelids, and fear

gnaw at her belly. Fear of leaving her daughter. Fear of leaving the man she loved. Not fear for herself... but also fear because the last time she'd felt this sick she'd been pregnant. And she was just a little late. She hadn't told Benito this small fact yet. He had enough to contend with.

She looked at Benito. He was studying the merpeople in a way that she'd learned meant he was looking for an angle to use with them. And plainly not finding it as easy as he usually did. "I need help," he finally said.

A direct admission from Benito? He must be more worried than he'd let on.

The merfolks' eyes narrowed, but not with dislike, more in the manner of a shrewd merchant about to bargain. The triton spoke, "Not something we give easily or for no reason. Or for free, fire-spirit."

Benito nodded. "I thought that would be the case. You remember the magical creature that tried to kill Marco. That attacked the ships."

"Lamprey. Magical. Something we'd rather stay away from," said Androcles, sinking back down into the water.

Benito spoke quickly, before he could move too far away. "I think more are coming. Or at least the monster's master comes. He likes using the water for his servants." That arrested the two merpeople, who had plainly been about to depart.

Now their eyes narrowed again, but with slow anger. Not for Benito but...yes. He had them. *"What do you want?"* Juliette asked.

"To destroy it forever so that I can have a better world for my daughter," said Benito, lightly. "That's what I want, but it is not what I'll get."

Androcles was amused now. "And what do you hope to get?"

"I need to take a fleet all the way to Constantinople. In the teeth of winter. That is neither wise nor easy. But I believe it must be done. So we will do it. But I could use some help with the weather."

Juliette snorted delicately. *"Try gods."*

Benito ignored the comment. "You are more weather wise than we humans are. And I have heard tell you can communicate over long distances."

Androcles wagged his head a bit. "It would be hard to be less weather wise than humans. And sound travels well underwater. We can hear sounds ten or twelve leagues away."

"There are ports along the way, or at least sheltered anchorages we can use—if we are not caught too far from them. What I want is some kind of advance warning."

"It's not wise to cheat the sea of its prey," said Androcles, with the air of someone testing waters.

Benito shrugged. "Please. This is me you are talking to. I'm not wise."

"He even cheated the Lord of the Dead of his bride," Juliette reminded all of them. With cautious admiration.

Benito squeezed Maria's shoulder. "As much as I was able."

"More than most humans," said Androcles, but he nodded. "Very well. Something can be arranged. But there is a price."

"If we can afford it, it is yours," said Benito, sounding as if he was one of the best bargainers on the canals. He probably was, thought Maria, with an inward smile to herself. He'd started hard and young, no matter where he'd risen to.

"Ah. Nothing you cannot afford. A drop of your blood on the water when you wish to call us, and a little something that Venice can afford. Besides the fact that we owe the healer, it seems wise to be on the right side of you," said Androcles disarmingly.

"And he is my god-daughter's father," said Juliette, coming forward to touch Alessia.

"What is it that you want?" asked Benito.

"A piece of water to call our own. A place where no one fouls and no one fishes. A couple of acres here, within the Lion's shelter, that we can call our own. If ill times are coming, we'll need it." By the sudden sober look on the triton's face, this had been something the merfolk had long desired. Maria understood. Sanctuary, under the shadow of the Lion . . . valuable. Worth, to them, more than pearls. If they could not be safe with the Lion to guard, they could not be safe anywhere.

Benito nodded. Maria knew it would not be easy to police, although Doge Petro could make it legally so at the stroke of a pen. She was a canaler. You could hardly be that without knowing that the writ of the law as to fishing rights was often trespassed on, and the offenders were seldom caught. And she had a strong feeling these were not folk you could casually give your word to. So she said so.

"We'll tell you who breaks the bargain. There are always some who will go too far for fish." Juliette looked pointedly at the triton.

He grinned, showing sharp teeth. "It will be up to you landfolk to punish them. We will know if you do not."

Benito nodded. "I will talk to Petro about it, but I think I can safely promise it. He knows the value of sanctuary—and allies."

Maria planned to take it a step further. She'd talk to the canalers about it. There'd be enough of them heading out with her Benito. It was not a deal to be turned down. The canal people were superstitious enough to keep each other out of the protected water, just in case.

Marco, who still practiced most of his medicine among Venice's poor and probably knew them as well as Maria did, obviously thought likewise. "I will talk to the canalers. Keeping their loved ones safe from the ravages of the sea while on this voyage is a bargain they'll find hard to refuse, I think. And if they agree... well, their word is good. With all respect to Petro, it would be of more value than any piece of pap—"

They all felt it then. A cold that had nothing to do with temperature, the shiver down the spine, the touch at the back of the neck. And the power, oh yes, the power. The two merpeople vanished. Slipped away under the water like ghosts. Someone else had entered the water-chapel, although the door was still closed. They could all feel his cold presence behind them. Maria was chilled to the bone, and she held tightly onto Benito and her daughter.

They turned, slowly, to face Aidoneus, lord of the cold halls of the dead. Once again, Maria was struck by his beauty. How could a thing that ruled the dead be so handsome?

He inclined his head, unsmiling. "My bride," he said.

She had known this was coming. She just had hoped for more time. But he would come when he would come, by his own calendar—and by his calendar, winter was about to begin.

Maria felt Benito tense. "For four months," she said calmly, squeezing Benito's shoulder. "That was our bargain. I honor my bargains. Benito will honor his."

Aidoneus nodded. "I will keep her safe. And keep my bargain."

Maria took a deep breath. "And him. Now...I need to bid them goodbye." Her voice cracked slightly. She had meant to keep her self-control. But...four months. Four months of no Benito. No little 'Lessi... Four months among the dead, four months being the sole living creature in those cold, silent halls...already she ached fiercely for them, and she had not said goodbye.

"If you don't want..." Benito began.

Maria shook her head, fiercely. "A bargain is a bargain. I keep mine. And I'll be back in the spring. I promise."

Benito took a deep breath. "Or I'll be there to fetch you. And this time..." He left the threat unspoken.

"I will keep my bargain, too," said Aidoneus to Benito, gravely, and with no sign of insult. "Not because that is my nature, but I would be foolish not to. She is not someone to anger lightly. And I need her. She brings life to my lands. That is no small thing."

Benito grimaced, and being Benito, could not forbear but try for a joke of some kind. She understood why. The cold...it froze a man's soul. No wonder Aidoneus wanted Maria's fire. "And she throws plates. And anything else she can get her hands on. And she has a temper and a voice that will probably blow those mists of yours away. Very well. I accept it. But I don't have to like it."

Benito turned to his wife and folded her in his arms, a stocky, short man, with muscles like rope, binding her. She could feel his anger and his sadness. And she could feel that he loved her, that if he could he would take her place, that he would go again to the land of the dead to bring her out.

"I've done it once," he said quietly to her, confirming what she felt. "If need be, I'll do it twice."

She hugged him, unable to speak. She kissed and cried a little over her baby. And then she put her child in her father's arms, and turned away and walked beside Aidoneus into the misty archway that had opened ahead of them. It was quite the hardest thing she'd ever done. If she'd turned back to see him and their daughter standing there beside the greenish water of the water-chapel . . . she knew she'd fail.

But she had a bargain to keep.

Chapter 21

Milan

Filippo Maria was delighted with the new conduit of news coming out of Venice. Details of the forty-eight-pounders ordered, and how they were being fitted—along with the Arsenal guild masters' varied reactions to it. The coming spring campaign was enough to make him chortle to himself. First, because by spring he planned to be ready for a fairly bloody summer—with a lot of Venice's soldiery away. And second, because his engineers had laughed at the bombards. The duke of Milan had nothing but disdain for the emperor of Byzantium and his rapidly shrinking and collapsing empire. But he must send Alexius word somehow. The news that Venice and Genoa would be engaged in faraway wars was a good thing. They had territory that would be lost by the time they got back. And it fitted so well with his plans for Sforza.

Carlo Sforza read the report carefully. It was not why he had put the man in place, but it was still extra information, and valuable. Not for the first time

did he ponder his future. A great condottiere had to
keep winning. Not only did his mercenary soldiers
need the loot and the morale boost, but his employ-
ers tended to have strong ideas about what they were
paying for. Many of his peers were good at playing
the part. Sforza had been good at doing the deeds.
Now... Now he knew his employer wanted him to
challenge Venice again.

And he did not wish to.

Vilna

Jagiellon sat on the throne, motionless. Someone more
ignorant than the tongueless slave that brought the
message might have thought the grand duke deep in
thought. But by now the slave knew better. Someone
was going to die. His master used blood rites in that
chamber down in the dungeons. Blood rites and dark
magics feared even here in pagan Lithuania.

The slave was correct. "Fetch me Count Tcherkas."
So he did. The count, like many of the nobility here,
dabbled in magic. He was not in the league of Count
Mindaug—but then Count Mindaug had gone to great
lengths merely to seem an ineffectual academic. But
the rituals the grand duke and the demon Chernobog
used needed participation. And needed terror—both
from the victim and from the perpetrator. Jagiellon
was too far gone to feel human emotions. Tcherkas felt
fear, revulsion and...eagerness, in the blood sacrifice
and skin eating. It helped to penetrate the veil—not to
Venice, but to Milan, deep within the western lands.

From there the news he could glean from Venice—
where Chernobog dared not venture, not even in

spirit—and other points of the Mediterranean was that the West was readying itself for a spring attack on Constantinople.

"Spring. By then it should hold, until the fleet from Odessa reaches there, even if the Venetians have somehow managed to work out a way to fire massive forty-eight pound bombards from the decks of their vessels without sinking them."

Jagiellon turned to the count. "Send word. Alexius must be warned of this. The Byzantine emperor should concentrate his guns on the seaward walls, on the walls facing the Sea of Marmara as the great chain will keep the vessels out of the Golden Horn. That will keep them out of effective range."

The count, still gagging from his meal, nodded.

Jagiellon went on as if he had not engaged in torturous blood rituals a scant hour before. "If Alexius can be kept from alternating between his depravities and total panic, he will hold the city. He is a weak reed, but at least that means that he is corruptible and malleable. I also want some men and weapons sent with the raider fleet to the coast of the sultanate of Pontus. The Baitini are squalling from Ilkhan lands."

The demon was somewhat more concerned about this leg of his plans. It appeared that the laissez-faire methods of Mongol rule were changing in response to the Baitinis' attempts to instill panic and terror. Not—as they dreamed—cracking and disintegrating. He might have to spare some troops there to take Mongol pressure off the borders with Alexius's Themes in Asia Minor. They would read great things into a small landing somewhere, and redouble their efforts. The demon did not care if they won or lost.

He wanted westward geographic expansion for reasons that were not earthly.

Constantinople

Antimo quietly locked the door. The first two sets of his maps and coded notes had already been dispatched. A good spy also had to be a good scribe, and a patient copyist. He could lose six months' work by not making multiple copies. He could lose his life by traveling with them. Nonetheless, he had copies of his notes. Not hidden in the obvious places like the soles of his shoes or lining of his bag. The church might not be forgiving if they read the Latin text of some of the Bible he carried. With luck, which had favored him in the past, they would never see it and neither would anyone else.

Leaving at night was a risk—it meant getting over walls and bribing guards, and there was no need for that yet. It was, outside of the foreign quarters, still business as usual in Constantinople. Yes, trouble was coming as sure as sunrise, but not until springtime. A lifetime away. In the morning he'd be leaving quietly with a group of minor merchants going to a cattle sale some miles away. He wouldn't be coming back with them. There were just a last few things to be arranged tonight.

He was unsurprised to see Red-ears and his sister there, tails wagging. He'd met Ravener and Ripper so often on his nightly walk-abouts that he'd taken to carrying a tit-bit or two with him. Dogs—they were always hungry. He'd been like that as a boy himself. Maybe that was why boys and dogs had such an affinity.

He hadn't met their mistress again. Somehow he felt that was just as well.

But she was there, standing in the shadow.

He was plainly leaving the city. Hekate had watched him obsessively, she had to admit, for the last while. He intrigued her; he brought her out of herself. For so many centuries, she'd been wrapped in her grief, mostly oblivious to the marchings of the mortal world. That grief had not left her, and it never would. But now that she had begun to shake free of the total absorption of it, she was aware of so much that had changed. She had been peripherally aware of it, of course. But she just hadn't cared enough to pay any amount of attention to it all.

The world had become a very strange place to her; she was forgotten as a goddess, and mentioned only obliquely. She had been so forgotten, in fact, that only the drink- and drug-addled and the mad could see her. And... those who still had magic, which were few, very few here. The only point of connection with this new world she'd found was the silent magic-user and his strange business.

What was he doing? It puzzled her. There must be some form of magic involved, she had at first concluded, what with the pacing, the writing, the complex diagrams. She could not imagine what else it could be.

But magic was something over which she had had some power, and which was a part of her, and she saw no trace of it in these workings of his.

Had that too gone from her?

No. Impossible. She still walked in the shadowed

paths, she still, when she chose, could easily, trivially, work bits of sorcery that were beyond all but the most powerful of mortal magicians.

Was he in the service of some other god or goddess unknown? Was that why he did what he did? Were these some strange rites she did not recognize?

And now—now he was leaving.

She was Hekate. What did she care if one mortal moved away?

Yet she did. And the dogs would miss him. She parted the shadow so that when she spoke, he would see her.

"Where are you going?" she asked.

He turned very cautiously. "I didn't see you there, lady. Just out."

She shook her head, denying his words. "You are leaving the crossroads. This place."

"I was trying to make that less than obvious. Yes. I have to go. You'll take care of my friends here, will you?" He petted them, scratching behind their ears, then said, looking at the dogs, "I think you should leave here, if possible, as soon as is practical. There's siege and war coming, probably sooner than they anticipate. That's not kind to dogs or women."

She knew that. Oh, how well she knew that. "Will you be coming back?" she asked, remembering. Remembering far too much. This man was . . . kind. Unexpectedly kind. He was warning her.

"It's possible," he said, cautiously. She sensed why. He did not want to lie, nor to promise what he could not do. "I go where I am sent. I may come back here to finalize things."

She was moved to a generosity of her own. She moved her power and set it lightly on his shoulders.

"Hekate's blessing goes with you. You will walk safe and silent in the darkness. It will cloak and hide you. And at the crossroads, the moon will light the right pathway for you, if you call on me."

He seemed taken aback, perhaps at the generosity. "I can help you to get out."

Now, she was touched. He did not need to do this thing, to offer safety to her, as he understood it. And he was not offering, thinking he would gain carnal favors of her. He did so because he—he liked her dogs. And thus, her. And he would do both of them a kindness.

But of course, he still did not know to what he spoke. "I am Hekate," she told him, gravely. "I choose my path."

Antimo Bartelozzi did not know what insanity had overtaken him. He'd seen enough sad sights and victims, and indeed, beautiful women, for the lifetimes of ten men. He'd never let that impair his judgment or distract him from his task. Why was he telling her all this? And offering to get her out of here? Had he been poisoned and was he in some kind of hallucination? That might be why her image was so strange. She seemed for an instant, to be the night itself. He shook his head, desperate to clear it. He wanted a goblet of wine. Badly and right now. But she wasn't going away. She wasn't, somehow, the kind of woman you could brush past, or merely excuse yourself, saying you had to get on with things. "Um. Can I offer you a glass of wine?" he said, awkwardly.

She nodded regally. "That would be acceptable."

Libations and sacrifice at the crossroads were her due. It had been many years since anyone had done so much for her.

"We could go to the taverna on the corner I suppose. Just...ignore anything they say to you. It's not really a place for...ladies."

It was at a crossroads. It also reminded her why she had always had the sky as her temple. Darkness was not something that She of the Night disliked. The stale smoky dimness of this place was less appealing. No one saw her, or her dogs. There were other women in the place. One of them even attempted to come and sit in the alcove near the back of the smoky room that this Antimo had led her to. Ripper growled, and she backed off, looking a little confused. "Two goblets. Of the good mavrodaphne," said the celebrant to the servitor who came to ask what he'd have. He must be a celebrant, who had come to enact the ancient sacrifice and act of making a libation. That strengthened her, slightly. It had been many years since she last had had any true worship from humans.

"Two? You want some company, mister?" asked the servitor.

"No," he said, his voice seeming harsh, almost angry for a second. The servitor looked at him, as if seeing him for the first time. It was possible, considering the magic Antimo wove about himself, that this was true. He did not see Hekate at all, but that was how she desired it.

He brought the two goblets, and set them in front of Antimo. Wooden goblets, as appropriate. Antimo pushed one across the table to her.

Was that it, nowadays? No prayers? No songs? No respects?

"It's surprisingly good wine," said Antimo, reassuringly. "Taste it. I know it seems hard to believe coming from a place like this."

She did. It was indeed good wine. Rich and full of fruit, full of the summer. It was the first thing that she had tasted for many generations and it brought back a flood of memory. She had always been associated with the fruits of fertility. With harvest and the birthing. There had been feasts under the harvest moon, and the best wine offered....

It wasn't really a whine. Just a sort of *well, what about us?* comment from Ripper, accompanied by a nose against his elbow.

"Gently, hound. I could have spilled that," said Antimo. "I wouldn't eat here myself, but dogs have a tougher digestion than most people. I suppose it is unfair at least from your point of view, eh?" He called the servitor over again. "I'll have two bowls of stew."

"Two. To keep the other goblet of wine company, mister," said the fellow. "Well, you're paying." He brought two shallow bowls of meat and vegetables from the black pot hanging on a chain at the fireside. Antimo set them down. Hekate's dogs didn't even wait for them to get to the floor. Hekate did not say she wouldn't have said no to the food herself. She did not, strictly speaking, need it. But this was the closest she had come to being part of the mortal world for a long time. Antimo seemed content to sip his wine, however. So she did likewise, working her magic on it.

"You will take some of this wine with you on your

travels. Pour some out at the crossroads and call on me." And then feeling a little odd—perhaps it was the wine after so many years—she stood up. "You must come back. My dogs and I will wait for you."

This time, he made the pledge. "I will."

She swept the night around her like a cloak and called Ripper and Ravener to her, and went out, to the third way. To her place.

Antimo sat looking into the gloom at the empty seat. What was all of this about? Why was he doing this? Was it all some kind of hallucination? But the bowls, when he picked them up, were empty and so—when he reached across and took it—was the crude wooden goblet. Only . . . it was no longer just a crude wooden goblet. Someone had carved into it, with artistry that was plain even in this poor light, a frieze around the body of it. A complicated scene of the chase, by the looks of it. Antimo quietly slipped it into his cotte, put a copper down to pay for it—or for the servitor's pleasure, and left. Someone was complaining about how dim the taverna was.

He was a little afraid. He'd often been scared and in real danger, and he was used to controlling that fear. But this, this was something different and alien. He remembered the silky softness of the dogs' ears and was somehow comforted.

He left town the next day as planned. But he had a wineskin filled with the wine from the taverna.

Two days later, at dusk, he left the group of cattle buyers and struck out on the back roads. He was seeking a port to find a ship to take him back to

Ferrara or, as his master had instructed, at least as far as Corfu, when he came to the crossroads.

The other three travelers had all stopped a little farther back and were eating a simple supper. Antimo was a little wary about them. They were chance-met companions of the road . . . apparently. But two of them were even more vague about where they came from and where they were going. The other man was a farmer heading for the coast to buy a horse. He'd had a good harvest, and never owned a horse before. There were bargains to be had down at Echinos. He spoke of it as if it was the big city and not just a coastal village.

Antimo told them he was going to relieve himself. When he got to the crossroads, on the spur of the moment he pulled out the wineskin and spilled some out onto the ground. "Hekate."

The moon peered over the lip of cloud and seemed to brighten the left-hand path.

"What did you say?" It was the young farmer.

He'd plainly overheard exactly. "Hekate. It's . . . it's an appeal for good luck and wise choices on a journey. An old superstition from my village."

"Oh. I thought she was the witch-goddess of the underworld."

The last thing he needed was a witch-hunt. "No. Just an old superstition about crossroads. I'm going to walk on a bit."

"Oh. Yes. I don't like those fellows. I'll be getting along, too. We can't be that far from Echinos."

Antimo noticed that he lingered a moment behind and spilled a little out of his wineskin onto the ground, too. And that the other two had also got to their feet and were hastening to gather up their things and go after them through a dusk that was thickening, and shadows that seemed darker than usual. He and his companion quickened their pace; the road ahead seemed brighter, lit by moonlight that made the shadows behind all the darker.

He expected at any moment to hear the footsteps of the other two catching up with them. And, truth be told, felt for his knife, expecting he might have to use it. The farmer had been a little too open about the money he carried with him, and Antimo had a pack that might contain, well, anything. He didn't want a fight; the farmer would certainly be useless, and two against one were never odds he liked.

But somehow, they must have taken the other track.

Chapter 22

Corfu

The Venetian fleet sailed on the first day of November. Not a good season for sailing, but Benito had his weather information. All he had to do was persuade the nervous sailors, and particularly the ships' officers, that he was right. The sailors...well, word had got around that he had help. The sailors of Venice had a rather ambivalent relationship with the merpeople. There was a fair amount of fear. But a grudging respect, too. There were stories of those who been helped, or struck deals or friendships with the dwellers in the deeps. There were a few interesting sexual fantasies, too. At least, Benito hoped they were fantasies. You never could tell with the nonhumans.

The sea was cold, wet, and tossed with small whitecaps. But there were, so far, no winter storms.

Still Benito was grateful to see Pantocrator looming on the horizon. At the same time it cut him to the quick to know that Maria and 'Lessi were not there, waiting in a world that had become his.

Neither was the other thing he had been hoping

for: word out of the lands of the Golden Horde. "Your kinsman sends word that Prince Manfred and Erik arrived safely, and left under a Mongol escort. With the envoy flags a-flying," said Giuliano Lozza. "But nothing has come back out."

Benito swore colorfully. Lozza shook his head. "It's consorting with sailors, Benito. Now, a man dealing with olives and grapes has to learn to moderate his tongue. By the way, I was told by my dear wife to give you this invitation to come and dine with us, to celebrate our harvest. She wrote it herself," he said proudly, handing Benito a small roll of parchment.

Thalia had been illiterate, a peasant woman, and had felt her station precluded her marriage to the swordsman landowner. So she was taking steps, was she? Well and good. Being able to read and write broke a lot of other chains. He'd seen it with Maria. One day, perhaps, all children could be taught.

He unrolled the parchment. The care—and a slight unsteadiness still in one or two of the letters shone out of the script—a simply worded invitation in a childlike round hand. With the seal of the House of Lozza and two thin strands of silk in the colors of the tassels on Benito's sword scabbard. The colors of Ferrara.

"Thank you," said Benito, looking at the script again. "I will be there. And I will treasure this," he said, touching the invitation.

"And so you should," said Lozza gruffly. "She only did it fifteen times."

"You must be proud."

"More than you can imagine, my friend. And more than grateful to you for pushing us to take that last step." He paused. "We'll name that first boy for you. And we have reason to believe," he said, beaming, "that that may happen as soon as the springtime."

Benito clapped him on the shoulder. And then embraced him. Lozza had been scarred by the murder of his first wife and their babe. Thalia had started the healing process. This, he hoped, would continue it. Some men are naturally suited to leadership and deeds of war. Giuliano Lozza was naturally suited to growing olives, and raising children. He also happened to be good at leading men and using a sword, but those skills were irrelevant asides so far as he was concerned.

"You do realize that my name may lead him into trouble and fighting?" said Benito, grinning and flattered.

Giuliano nodded and tried—and failed—to assume a serious expression. "Ah, but not as badly as the second boy. It will be hard for a good Corfiote boy to be called Erik. We will see you tonight, then, m'lord."

That left Benito several hours at his desk to try to catch up on the work that had accumulated in his absence, and to wonder about the message in those threads of silk. It was not the expected place or a suspected place. Therefore . . .

He was hardly surprised that evening to be taken to the family chapel to meet a nondescript monk praying there. A man who had a passing resemblance to the House of Ferrara's chief agent, Antimo Bartelozzi. The one who dealt with Family matters. "Convey my respects to Duke Enrico. I thought it would create undue suspicion to meet both him and you. I had heard you speak of Lozza, and I knew his father well. I have news from Constantinople."

Antimo had more than news. He had a detailed report to send to Duke Enrico. Reports of troop numbers, of supplies, of amounts of gunpowder, and maps. Detailed, measured maps. Most of the maps Benito had seen were little more than drawings from memory. These had been done to scale with a great deal of precision. Looking at them, Benito understood just how his grandfather had acquired such a towering reputation for strategy. Good staff work was obviously a major part of it. There was also a sealed package. "For the duke's eyes only, M'lord Valdosta," he said apologetically. "Money matters. And contacts. If you would pass on to the duke that I shall shortly be returning to Constantinople, overland. I will attempt to be outside the walls when you arrive." He coughed—more clearing his throat than anything else. "M'lord..." there was an odd tentativeness to his voice. "I have reason to believe you'll...um, have a lot of influence with both the soldiery and the sailors. A sack is always a grim thing. I...I have a request to make. If you could advise....tell the troops there is a woman in the city, always accompanied by two large hunting dogs with red ears. She's been of help to us. To me."

"There are lots of women in every city," said Benito gently, thinking he understood, and being a little surprised. "I'd get her out, Antimo. Troops...well, they get out of hand."

"There are no other women who always have those two dogs with them. I tried to get her to leave, m'lord. She's...strange. She's no leman of mine," he said hastily. "Just a very strange woman, with very strange dogs. Her name is Hekate."

❈   ❈   ❈

Benito sat with his grandfather and then, once he was seated, and armed with a glass of wine, handed over the parcel from the duke's spy. Considering just what the agent had told him, he was intensely curious about that flat little parcel.

The Old Fox raised his eyebrows. "Antimo. Well, well."

"He was afraid you'd be watched."

"That's not stopped him in the past," said Duke Enrico, looking just like a wary fox for a moment. "He is . . . unusually good. He nearly killed me once, you know."

"You've mentioned that." Normally Benito would have pressed for the story. He'd yet to get it out of his grandfather, but they had become closer with time spent together during the voyage and in Venice. "What's in the parcel? He gave me a detailed report of the situation in Constantinople and of the areas of Byzantium he crossed, and quite a few exceptional maps of the city and its surrounds."

The Old Fox smiled. "You don't even want me to keep a few secrets, boy?"

"No. My curiosity has been killing me for half the night. He was out at Lozza's estate."

The duke laughed and opened the packet. It appeared to be nothing more than a tangle of string. The duke shook it out carefully. It now appeared to be a shawl of knotted strings, all hanging down from a single cord. "Now you know. And not a bit of use feeling it through the covering has been to you, young man. Usually he attaches it to a carpet."

"A code in string?"

"The knots are numbers. It'll take me a while to

read it, but they correspond to letters, and the letters give us the names of the mercenaries within Constantinople we have reached an accommodation with."

"And?"

His grandfather scowled. "And the amounts of course."

"Ah. Cheaper than a long campaign though."

"So, where is Antimo? I'd have preferred to talk this through with him."

"He said he was going back. He would see us there, hopefully outside the walls." Benito hesitated for a moment. "I think he's involved with some woman there."

"Antimo?" Enrico was plainly surprised, and intrigued...and perhaps a little perturbed. "It would be the first time I've seen any signs of it. He pays more attention to dogs than to women."

Benito shrugged. "This woman, it appears, has the dogs. Two of them with red ears. The only other thing I know about her is that her name is Hekate, and he's worried about her. Now, I'd better finish this wine and go and chase a few people down at the little Arsenal. They may not really believe we plan to sail within the week."

"They'll change their minds about that. After you have done, come back. I'll have had time to interpret this, and to look at the maps."

"He is an exceptional mapmaker," said Benito, mildly envious.

The Old Fox nodded. "And an exemplary agent. He seldom fails. But he could not find you for some time."

"That may have been more luck than judgment," said Benito.

"Or divine intervention," said the Old Fox, smiling wryly.

Benito and the fleet were able to sail, much to the shock and surprise both of the people of Corfu, and the ship crews, two days later, to meet the fleet of Genoa and a token five ships from Aragon, sailing for Corfu.

He had had news from the tritons of a huge storm.

Venice

The addition into his household of a lively, inquisitive toddler was a not-unmixed joy, Marco found. It was true that she had an infectious laugh and craved being cuddled, it was true she was *not* what you would call anything like "naughty." She was tenderhearted to a fault, and had cried so much over a dead bird found on the balcony that they now let her feed the birds from there. Her giggles rang through the halls, and made even the grimmest servant smile.

As for Kat, well, Kat adored the child. And at first it had been hard to get her to part from the little girl. But now that she had settled in, her presence was also not an unmixed blessing. 'Lessi liked being with him most, Kat second most, and if possible, both of them. She was often found glued to their sides. Yet she was perfectly capable of vanishing the minute he turned his head.

And she was into everything. "Like a monkey," one of the servants had sighed, and Marco was inclined to agree. She could not see a drawer or a cupboard without wanting to open it, and if possible, play with what was inside. *How* she managed to do that, as little as she

was—at least once, he'd found that she had patiently
pulled out all the (now emptied) drawers beneath the
one that was out of reach, and used them as a sort of
staircase to get to the one they had fondly thought was
safe. He was strongly considering finding a way to tie
drawers and cupboards shut. As much of a nuisance
as it would be if someone wanted something, the consequences of her getting hold of something that could
harm her were not to be thought about.

And everything went into her mouth, which was the
other problem with her constant rummaging. Books
too! So far she hadn't actually ruined anything but
there were a few leather-bound volumes that now
had gummy corners.

Then there were mornings. Ah yes, the mornings.
She got up *very* early and her idea of a good time
was to slip out of her nursery and creep into their
bed, squirm in between them, and giggle. And wiggle.
And twist and turn and pat her hands on them and
sing to herself. And her little feet were never still. She
was as restless a child as her father was as an adult.

It was hard to grasp just how the addition of one
very small person could add so much extra effort to
life at the *Casa* Montescue, but certainly the servants
seemed to have twice as much work now, and he and
Kat half as much time.

And yet…and yet…No one could bring themselves
to actually complain, not when she would come up
to you and tug at your sleeve and when you looked
down at her, she would put up her arms and lisp,
"Tiss?" She was very good at bringing all of them—
from Lodovico to the scullery maids, around her very
small thumb.

But something had to be done, and Marco knew it. Rescue came at last from an unexpected quarter. Marco had forgotten the priest from Cannaregio, and his promise to look for some form of genteel employment for the woman who had lost her daughter. When Old Pietro came to his study—where Alessia was attempting to open drawers, many of which had surgical implements in them—and told him Father Gotaro begged for an audience, and had a woman accompanying him, he felt very guilty indeed.

'Lessi of course did not let him go alone. They went to the small drawing room off the main hall, where Pietro had put the visitors to wait—It was raining outside, he could scarcely have left them on the step, he later explained. Marco set his niece down and opened the door and she toddled in.

The priest bowed...but not the woman. The woman instead squatted down, ignoring Marco, her face transformed, tortured lines eased—hands outstretched to Alessia—who, being the child she was, trotted cheerfully up to her.

"Ah, m'lord." The priest bowed again. "What a lovely child. I just wanted to press the matter," he jerked his head slightly at the woman entranced with Alessia. She was smiling, looking like a different person. "It... does her so much good to be with the little ones. She's hard to get to eat properly. But local mothers..." he shrugged. "I suppose they blame her."

Marco could understand that, even if it wasn't logical. He could also understand just how easily a toddler could disappear into the canal. Of course not here in the *Casa* Montescue—the door handles were out of reach, and there were servants about to find and watch. But...

And that was when he put two and two together and realized that this was the answer to both problems. They could use some help with Alessia. This woman wouldn't be alone, and the priest was right, she clearly adored children and was good with them. The priest vouched for her. With all the servants here, he could simply tell them that rather than interrupting their own work to be running after the child, all they needed to do was to keep a discreet eye on 'Lessi and her nursemaid, just in case something was needed. It would do the woman a great deal of good. And it would assuage his conscience.

He cleared his throat. "Well, actually, Father, I hadn't actually found anyone yet—but as you see, we've acquired our little niece temporarily. It occurs to me that we could give her a trial with Alessia. It would be a temporary thing—until my brother and sister-in-law get back. I'll talk to Katerina about it, this instant."

Before the priest could thank him, he got Pietro to go and find Kat.

Kat was less than sure, when they spoke in the hall. "I mean, Marco...we don't know her at all."

"We could try it out for a day or two. Alessia's interests must come first of course. Just mornings. They will stay inside the *casa*. There are always servants too—and us." It was obvious—at least to *him*—that they were going to have to do something of the sort. They hadn't had enough hours in the day before 'Lessi; now...now it was very difficult to get anything done.

And he and Kat had *no* privacy.

She seemed to be mulling all that over in her mind. "Well...let me meet her. I really didn't like that priest."

They went in, and rather than standing on her dignity—the potential employee was sitting on the floor, playing peek-a-boo with a laughing Alessia.

A better way of persuading Katerina would have been difficult to find. The woman stood up, curtseyed—still being held onto by Alessia. Her voice was quiet and sad and her accents refined.

By the second day the new nanny Marissa was an essential part of the household. Not only did she get in very early, but her only task was to entertain and watch 'Lessi. Which she did with an obsessive care. She talked to her, listened to her, carried her, fetched toys, fed her . . . "Makes life a lot easier," said Marco, listening to the laughter as they sat in bed.

It did. It was a few hours which were now miraculously and deliciously less full of a small child. You couldn't not love 'Lessi—she was just rather a dramatic and chaotic change in their previously childless lives. Marco began planning on getting to that less sedentary lifestyle. Of course Marissa was only a support, and there to help while they were home, and while they had temporary custody of Alessia, but perhaps later . . .

Well, at this point, who knew what the future would bring.

Chapter 23

Baghdad

In his magnificent palace in the great city of Baghdad, the Ilkhan, Hotai the Ineffable, glowered at his grand vizier and the four assembled generals. He had moved far from his Mongol origins in dress and indeed in habit, but not in traditional diet. And he ate as if he spent the same number of hours in the saddle or at war as his distant cousins. Sheep meat and good wine, if not qumiss, had not been kind to him. It had made him rotund and lazy, he admitted to himself. But he was not a fool, and he managed his empire, and his large court, and even his harem, well.

Running the empire had kept him here...sedentary, being an administrator. But that was why he had generals running each of the fronts of the empire, unlike his father who had liked campaigning himself and lived to eighty doing so, forever crisscrossing the empire and dragging his court around.

However, the news that brought his generals and his vizier before him was nasty hearing, and made the old warrior blood in him rise and demand that something sharp and pointed be brought to bear on the problem. "What do you mean, they are everywhere? These Baitini are not spirits! We know where they come from! Take punitive steps. Alamut must be destroyed. Bring its master to Baghdad in chains."

"I was alerted to just what the problem was by the Old Man of the Mountain, in Alamut," said the grand visier, with a conciliatory wave of his hand. "This time, it is not the Old Man's doing. It appears that the group no longer takes orders from there, and destroying Alamut would be counterproductive." He coughed. "They have actually always been part of the local governance. They made reliable . . . agents . . . and once we bought them, they were relentless. It was the way they worked, and they're good for solving . . . problems. In fact, we have used them a great deal, Your Ineffability. Only, now they have turned against us—or some of them have, at any rate. We, um, had no idea of their numbers or how high they had risen in certain administrations. We have identified some of them, of course, but we don't know who all of them are. But there are several satrapies that are effectively being made ungovernable by their actions. And what worries me is that I don't know why, or what they plan."

"We need to make an example," said General Quasji, of the northern march. "I propose that we sack their principal cities."

The Ilkhan eyed him unfavorably. Normally such interviews were conducted with the entire court. The grand vizier had not called for this meeting to be private for no reason. Plainly he had chosen these men for loyalty and to ensure secrecy in this council.

But this fool general was playing as if to the gallery. Playing for future power. "They are *our* principal cities, Quasji. Our sources of taxation and income. Why would we sack our own cities and destroy the livelihoods of our own subjects?"

"Besides, they seek to make a religious schism in our troops," said General Harob. "We have no small number who have gone over to being followers of the Prophet Mohammed. While the great majority of the Moslems in our domains do not share the sect . . . they have put it about that we are the enemy of Islam."

General Harob was in control of the campaign in Cicilia. Hotai knew him to be a devout Nestorian. It was why he'd been put in Cicilia, to keep the war there from being perceived as a religious one, to draw in allies against the Mongol from the Christian lands to the west. The Ilkhan played a slow game in Asia Minor, gradually nibbling away at the kingdoms there. Actually Hotai had no vast appetite for conquest. But it was a Mongol tradition and it kept the army in a state of readiness. "If we were to persecute our own people in the hopes of destroying these Baitini, we would appear to actually *be* the enemy of Islam."

"I think a show of real force might be in order," said General Malkis. The elderly campaigner was effectively retired from the campaigns in Hind, but still wielded a great deal of influence. He had been a loyal friend of Hotai's father, and it had been his support that had made it clear that there was to be no dynastic squabble when Hotai had become the Great Khan.

"That must be done," said the Ilkhan, "Assuredly. But what? Throwing ourselves against our own people is like skinning the sheep to get the wool. True, you have wool and meat and skin, but only once. Then it is gone forever."

"But we do not wish to show any sign of weakness to our foes. We'll have invasions and insurrections," said the grand vizier. "There is unrest in many quarters already."

Hotai knew this was all leading somewhere, and not towards his dinner. "What do you propose then?"

"A royal procession, Great Khan. With attendant troop maneuvers and parades and displays of force. And a few salutatory lessons, perhaps. Especially if we can capture some of these Baitini. We might bring back the polo game using the heads of the condemned, perhaps." The vizier pulled at his lip. "The general populace would enjoy that. They fear the Baitini, I am told."

Unlike his father, Hotai had not left Baghdad since being raised to being Ilkhan to the Southern Horde. He blinked. He had traveled as a young prince, of course. Just to move the whole court was...

Actually, a pleasant idea. It would do some of them a great deal of good to have something other than debauchery and intrigue to deal with. They'd like it less than he did. "Plan to make it so, Grand Vizier Orason. And I think we need a few visitations of troops to areas which have had particular problems. Just our being there will be a reminder for them. So: where shall we go first?"

"West or north, Great Khan. There are more problems there. The Arab tribes are restive, but we have more troops there anyway. And they have little more than sand, goats and banditry to the southwest."

Hotai smiled and made up his mind. "We will proceed first to Mosul. And have proclamations read in the cities of Aleppo, Tabriz and Damascus, so that they are to prepare. We will visit them as well."

"But . . . they are, well, in opposite directions, Great Khan," said the grand vizier, plainly wrestling with the idea of explaining geography to his overlord.

He nodded. This was part of his plan. Altogether, he was cautiously pleased with it. "Precisely. We will not say *when* we will visit them." They would be in a froth, a frenzy of preparation and worry. They would also have great motivation to root out these Baitini themselves, to have prisoners to present to their Khan.

That drew a smile and an acquiescent nod. "It shall be done, Great Khan. There is also the matter of requests from several of our subordinate states. It is an opportunity to draw them more under our control. They're asking for help."

He made a gesture of agreement. "It will of course be our gracious pleasure to render it. And now you are dismissed from my presence, except for you, General Malkis, and you, Orason."

When they had paid their respects and left, and the tongueless guards were back at their stations at the great closed doors, the Ilkhan cleared his throat. "And now. We need to discuss how we rid ourselves of this canker within."

The grand vizier scowled. "I have been compiling lists, Great Khan. The problem is, well, they are well suited to spying and gathering information. It is difficult to know who to trust. Several of them are in high positions. And they have been loyal to the Ilkhanate for a century. We thought them loyal, at least. But it appears that they have been like maggots beneath the skin of a sound-seeming apple. It is only their numbers that hold them in check at all."

"Not so in the tumens," said General Malkis. "We are Mongol."

The Ilkhan knew that this was not really so. In theory, the military were Mongol. Of course in practice this had not been so for many years. The noble Mongol were still largely of Mongol blood, but intermarriage, especially with the Turkic tribes whose way of life was similar, was normal. And of course skilled military engineers had always been welcome in the army of the Khans. They had received many honors and become part of the nation.

The general correctly interpreted the look his overlord gave him. He had known his father well, and Hotai had been told he shared many mannerisms with the late Great Khan. His father had mostly been a distant man, often away and at war, so Hotai really could not say. "They are Mongol in loyalty at least. Your great-uncle the Ilkhan Hulagu decided the 'shmaeli made poor soldiery. He disliked and distrusted them and put measures in place against them."

Hotai's great-uncle had been an erratic and occasionally brutal ruler. But his legacy had been a secure empire, and, it would seem, had kept the enemy within out of the military.

"There will be a few. They're allowed to lie to unbelievers in the name of their religion. Still, it is a strength. But it will draw the army away from its usual work."

"What effect will this have on our campaigns?"

The old warhorse shrugged. "Great Khan, we fight

many small wars all the time. I think our enemies scattered, and unlikely to ally...but they will push back in places. Or find relief and regroup. Cicilia is one such front. Hind, another."

The Great Khan considered his options. "Plan for the worst," he decreed. "But let us act as if we had no such plans at all. We, too, may lie."

Trebizond

Michael Magheretti, the podesta of the Venetian community of Trebizond, had moved his life into a well-practiced nonroutine since the fleet had left. Tasks had to be done, and work dealt with...but according to no preordained pattern. Trebizond was still in the grip of mayhem and fear. The sultan himself had survived an attempt on his life. Michael...three.

The city had degenerated into a series of cantons, with barricades and armed men with crossbows at the windows, watching them. Still, somehow, life went on even with the honest—or at least, the more-or-less honest and honorable—confined to their houses and their work places constantly under guard, de facto prisoners, while the murderers and thugs roamed free. The wrong people behind bars...

One got used to it, thought Michael glumly. And the Venetians had at least been able to draw together. It had not been good for their cohesion with the local Greek-speaking inhabitants, and even less so for the newer settlers from the hinterland. Once this had been one of the melting pots of East and West. Now they were separating out, with agony for many of the mixed families.

He settled himself at his somewhat dimly lit desk—away from the barred window—where his eyes would struggle but at least he would not be visible. He looked at the pile of paper. At one of his bodyguards picking his teeth with his dagger. "What is that noise?"

One bodyguard moved to the window, obliquely. The other came closer to the desk, hand on his sword. "Cavalry," said the window-peerer with some satisfaction. "The Ilkhan's troops, by the looks of it."

Technically, Trebizond was an independent state. But they paid tribute to the Ilkhan. It looked like the illusion of independence might be being suspended. Right now that seemed like a good idea, if it got rid of the Baitini.

But it was still not a good idea to go to his window to look, because a watcher could, all too easily, take that opportunity to shoot him. Was a prisoner less free because the guards were changed?

At least the prisoner might get more reliable meals. Privileges perhaps. And would not have to fear the guards would be suborned.

Constantinople

Since her worshipper had left the city that now stood at the tear the Earth-Shaker had made in her gates, Hekate had walked there with her dogs more often than just at full moon. More than merely walking, she paid attention to the city around her, to the people, to their doings, even though they seemed at times incomprehensible. She was a goddess; she had no limitations except those she chose to impose on herself. Eventually, she would comprehend.

She also began to roam across the fringes of the lands of her people, the parts that had survived the deluge, the ones that still might contain some of the bloodlines of those that had sought shelter there. The world had changed a great deal, but some things not at all. Robbers and murderers still watched the crossroads. She'd been aware of Antimo's libation, and watched and given him guidance. She had welcomed the fact that his action had caused another to copy him, and had graciously allowed the second man to share in her protection. Already... she felt just a little stronger.

And then one night, to her surprise, she found she had another human pouring a stoup of wine out at the crossroads, asking for her guidance. She heard his desperate question clearly, as she turned her feet towards him. In the way of a goddess, she was beside him before he had completed it.

"Do I go on to my mother or back to Eleni?"

She recognized him. It was the young farmer who had been on his way to market on the same road as Antimo, the one she had extended her hand to because he had copied Antimo. Thrace had once been hers, and although he spoke Greek, well, worship was worship. And this was clearly worship; he understood what he was doing.

"Eleni is your wife?" she asked, from out of the shadows.

He started. "I didn't see you there, Kyria. Yes, my wife. Our baby is near. I... I just wondered whether to go home or go on to my mother. Either way, I will make one of them unhappy, and this is not a time to make either unhappy."

"Go this way," she said, pointing. She walked with

him a little way too, with her dogs. He too could see her. That was interesting. He had deliberately invoked her. That was even more interesting.

She inspected his thoughts, gravely. His mind was troubled not so much with the path to choose, but with one of her other aspects, that of birthing. So much so that he confided in a total stranger, chance met, or so he thought, at a crossroads. "Eleni and my mother... they don't see eye-to-eye. And she lost her own mother when she was young. So I can't turn to her mother. But we're far out. Old Zathos farmed the land next to us, but he died last year and his boys have yet to come back from the sea. Before her time comes I must get her closer to the midwife in Thasaski. If she would stay with my mother..."

He was troubled by a problem that he could see no answer to. "But she will not. There is only my cousin. And how do I know when to take her to Thasaski? If she stays in the house of my cousin, there will be no space for me. And the animals on the farm?" He spoke of the small concerns of peasant farmer. Who would milk the goats? See to the hens?

Hekate had not been the goddess of warriors and great kings. She'd been the confidant of just these sorts of people. Small farmers, hunters, herdsmen. She'd been the goddess of their concerns; no one had ever called on her for victory in war, but rather, for victory over a threatened harvest. It was something of a shock to find the same kinds of people were still here, even if the gate had failed and flooded the lowlands that had been the center of her worship. Yet here they still were, though the people of the city seemed opaque to her, and so much else had changed.

She bent her mind to his problems. The peasant's wife's time was not supposedly that near, but Hekate had her ways of seeing, and...

It was a good thing he had invoked her.

She went with him to the cottage. It was a humble little place with the mountain behind it, and the stream close by for water, laughing across the rocks. Nature had put a hard sill of rock there, so a rich little pocket of good earth was retained, while most of the mountainside was stony and not productive. It was a beautiful spot, if lonely. They ran the last part of the journey to the cottage, because they could hear in the distance that his wife was calling, desperately.

They arrived to find a very young woman on the verge of tears. Her waters had broken, and having been too proud and in too much conflict with her mother-in-law to ask for help before, now she wanted, with a terrible desperation, to go to the village, to the midwife. She was too inexperienced to know it was far too late for such a journey. But she was also afraid, too afraid to want to know or to care just what her husband had been doing on the mountainside with a tall woman with two red-eared dogs.

Hekate looked at her with her wise, old eyes. Read the signs as others might a book, for this too had been a part of her purview, in the days before the gate broke and the waters came. "It is too late for the village. The babe is on his way." She gestured imperiously towards the hut. "Come."

The wife looked at her with relief and disbelief. "You... you are midwife? Spiro brought home a midwife? He is—"

A pain silenced her and she gasped instead of speaking.

Hekate had been an actual midwife too, as well as the goddess of childbirth, and it was just as well that she was here and had experience to draw on, and her magics too. The baby was coming early. It was a first child, and it was not going to be an easy birth. In fact, without She who opens, it would have also been a last birth, with mother and babe going to Aidoneus' shadowy land.

But that would not happen today. All because a young farmer had poured a libation.

"Be calm," she said. "Now come inside."

The woman grasped her belly in both hands and stooped to enter the house, obedient, and glad to be so.

Hekate pointed at the peasant. "Go and bring me yarrow, and the root of the valerian plant. Be off with you." She needed neither herb, but she wanted to examine the mother properly, and the spells she needed were not aided by male presence.

It was apparent that both of them needed to be told what to do. "I . . . I am not very good with herbs," he said, wringing his hands. "Eleni does that kind of thing."

Hekate shook her head. What was the world coming to? "You must learn better in the future. Who will gather herbs for healing if your Eleni is herself ill? But do not fear."

She called one of the dogs. "Here, Ravener. Take him and show him," Hekate said to the dog. She turned back to the farmer. "He will point with his nose. You will gather the whole plant, root and all, that he points to; I will separate what I need. Now go." She turned back to the dog. "And bring me some Lad's Love too. There are fleas."

So he went, following the dog, and left Hekate to her delicate task.

When he came back she set him to boiling water to make an infusion of the yarrow, and to chopping up the Lad's Love and scattering it on the floor. He needed to be kept busy and out of the way. It was always thus with young fathers; older ones, seasoned ones, might actually be useful, but young ones? Good only for fretting if you did not keep them busy.

Hekate worked her magic loosening cartilage, and easing muscle, dilating, and helping the young woman to breathe and to push. Still, this was going to be hard. Hekate knew she was going to be here well into the night.

In the midnight hour the child was born. And with that first cry Hekate bound herself again to the mortals she had left behind.

It hurt of course, bringing back memories of her own children, prisoner of her faithless lover. But that was hardly this grateful peasant girl's fault, as she stared lovingly at the babe being put to her breast.

So, there it was. She had a people again. And two—maybe three—worshippers. There might be more. She had taken up her ancient responsibilities. And though it hurt...perhaps it was a hurt like birthing, that would bring something good into the world.

But there were practical things to deal with now. Hekate had already taken steps to deal with the bleeding and possible infection, and the baby's first attempts at suckling would help. Once the placenta was out, the babe was warm and asleep, and the exhausted young mother close to joining her in sleep, Hekate's work was done.

She called the husband, who was pacing outside, watched by the dogs. "Now, your question is answered; now you can go back to where we met, and choose the other path, and go to your mother. Tell her she has a grandson. He is well and strong and has fine lungs. Tell her to come at once, and that your wife called for her. I think that will do much to reconcile the two of them. Your mother needs grandchildren, and your wife needs help."

He bowed respectfully. "Yes, Kyria." He paused a moment. "Kyria...who are you?"

"I am Hekate, She of the Crossroads and Gateways. Childbirth, the Hunt, and the Darkness were mine once." She swept the night around her and left by the third way, as the astonished young farmer scrambled for a drop of wine to pour when he reached that crossroads again.

The dogs seemed happier, somehow.

Chapter 24

Corfu

Benito and the Old Fox had engineered everything quite carefully, with information gathered from the tritons. Getting the Venetian fleet to sail east in the teeth of winter was still plausible. The Venetian sailors trusted Benito Valdosta; they assumed that he had at least a personal audience with the powers of nature. Besides, what storm would dare to stop the man? If he said they should leave Corfu in the middle of a tempest, they'd be there, manning the oars. But the fleets of Genoa and Aragon were a different matter entirely. Benito knew once they got snug at anchor or hauled up on the spit outside the little Arsenal, they'd be hell to shift. Once they had sailed together, perhaps. And Canea, while safe as an anchorage, would be the least welcoming port in the entire Mediterranean to a Genovese fleet without a Venetian guard, after Admiral Mosco's failed and bloody attack on the port. Thus, they had to meet the fleet at sea, before they had begun to head for Corfu. This had meant a dogleg over to the Italian coast, as the Genovese were planning to cling to it after coming through the straits of Messina.

To meet a fleet at sea was always a dangerous and awkward thing. Any sensible admiral would avoid it if the wind would allow them to do so. You could see mastheads and sails a great distance off, well before one could see the identity of the same. And the Venetian fleet was plainly large. So, being informed by the tritons as to where they were and what heading the combined fleet of Aragon and Genoa were on, a small galliot with the Winged Lion emblazoned on its sails was sent ahead to convey polite messages that the Venetian fleet was bearing towards them.

It was still a very stiff meeting, on board the flagship. The admirals of the Genovese and Aragonese vessels were the most unhappy guests one could imagine, and the atmosphere in the crowded captain's cabin was decidedly frigid.

"We were given to understand," said Admiral Borana, not quite refusing a glass of fine Veneto red, "that we would overwinter in Corfu." If his tone had been any stiffer Benito could have planed the splinters out of it and used it for deck planking. Though it was daylight, the shutters were all closed against a bitter wind, and the ship's lantern above the table they had gathered about swung with just enough energy to serve as a warning, making the shadows on their faces shift with every swing. Forbidding old faces, most clean-shaven, though the Aragonese had a little beard.

Benito nodded. "Yes. So was everyone. We have been reliably informed that the emperor Alexius is preparing himself to meet us then. So we thought we'd arrive early. When he wasn't expecting us."

The Aragonese admiral looked like he was about to explode. Benito smiled in what he hoped was a soothing fashion.

It obviously wasn't.

"You deceived us! Your allies! We cannot work with such deception."

"The news only reached us when you were already at sea. And you may ask Admiral Dourso. It was as much of a surprise to us as it is to you," said Duke Enrico Dell'este, smoothly, soothingly.

"We'll have to sail back to Naples," said Borana. "It's not safe to have vessels out at sea in midwinter."

Benito cleared his throat. "Then you and your crews will surely die, M'lord Borana. There is a very large storm front to the west. We are making haste for Canea."

Borana looked at him as if he were mad. Not that Benito blamed him. "Storm? How can you know that?"

"We have certain magical warnings and methods," said Benito, apologetically. "Nothing of witchery! This has the blessing of the Hypatians on it. That was how we knew where to find you. As your allies we wished to protect you. If you join us we can at least attempt to keep you safe. We may divert to Cerigo."

Venice had safe ports on various Greek islands. The Genovese had lesser advantages. And ships flying the Genovese flag would not be permitted to enter those ports.

A fleet might pretend to sail under the Genovese admiral...but here, in practice, and certainly in Canea, they would sail under Venetian orders. The sooner they became accustomed to the idea the better, Benito thought wryly. He wasn't about to fight this battle in their manner. He needed to win and get home to his wife and daughter, in as little time as possible. These fools would drag this war out for years.

Hades

In Aidoneus' shadowy halls beneath her flowering almond tree Maria looked into the shadow-warp and weave, looking out as if through rain-streaked windows onto the hills and sunshine in the distance. The loom of the Fates allowed her to see what she wished to see, and that was one of the things that Aidoneus had granted to her, to keep her less restive, more content. She had—as one did in this shadowy place where her purpose was to give life—time to gaze as she pleased. And anyway, she'd have made time for this. She needed, as any mother does, to watch and see how her daughter did without her. If she'd not had this—well... But Aidoneus evidently knew this and gave it without being asked.

The answer shocked her a little, and then cheered her. 'Lessi was laughing and content. Maria watched as she ran as fast as her plump little legs would carry her down the long, Turkey-carpeted halls of the *Casa* Montescue. It made her smile to realize that the child, her child, the daughter of a poor canal-brat, was being fostered and tended to in the sort of place she used to look at without seeing, because she knew she could never, ever so much as tie up her boat at their mooring. To think that her daughter would be so at home and at ease there! It was a blessing, a real blessing. 'Lessi would never go hungry, never need to be tied to the boat to keep from falling in the water. She could run and play and be spoiled as much as Maria would spoil her, were she there now.

She watched as 'Lessi hugged Marco. How she teased Kat. How she played peek-a-boo with a woman that Maria had never seen before. And strangely, how she waved to her mother. *She knows I am here watching*, thought Maria, comforted and yet puzzled. She resolved to ask Aidoneus about it. She was curious about the new woman, too. There was something... odd about her.

Without her calling, the god was suddenly there, at her side, as if her thoughts had called him. Maybe they had. Gods could do that sort of thing. He gazed at the shadow-threads of the loom and nodded his handsome head.

"She has lost a child," Aidoneus explained. "You do not see the colors fully yet. But there is an aura. Deep unhappiness. Betrayal. And your daughter... I do not know why she can see you. The very young see things which older minds shut out. But so long as she can do this, you need not be afraid she will forget you, for she will see you every day."

Resolutely, Maria did not look at Benito. She did take a broad peek at the entire fleet. But she had a bargain to honor. For this four months she was the bride of the Lord of the Underworld, queen and life of his bleak kingdom. She'd made her bargains and she lived by them, even among the dead. So she looked instead at Corfu, at the empty shipyard and then again at Venice. Marco was studying a book of some heathen script with Alessia on his knee, and a lithe, balding man with a well-used sword instructing him. Maria looked very carefully at the stranger. Listened in too, as she could. He had something of the look of Caesare about him, of the professional mercenary. But he did know a great deal about medicine.

Out of curiosity, when her daughter was asleep she turned her gaze through the shadows to the great city Benito was heading for. *There could be nothing wrong in that, surely?* she thought, faintly guilty. He wasn't there yet. It was a great place girded with walls and towers, and the sea on two sides. But the image was harder to resolve. Instead she kept finding herself staring at a tall woman with tears running down her cheeks. She wore a type of dress that Maria had never seen the like of, and clasped around her throat a complex neckpiece of jet and gold. At her right and left hand, like a pair of guardians, was a pair of dogs with red ears and bright eyes. The dogs saw her; she could tell by the intensity of their gaze. But they did not alert their mistress.

She tried to look past the woman, and failed. Who was she? And why did she stand between Maria and her view of the city?

"Hekate," said Aidoneus. "Her mark on the weave of fates there is very strong. She was a powerful goddess once."

Maria looked up at him. "Hekate? I thought she was the queen of witchcraft or something."

Aidoneus shook his head. "She is a goddess, and very old. She is associated with powerful magics, but those were merely the attributes of one of her aspects. She was once the guardian of gateways and crossroads, lady of the night, of the hunt, and of childbirth. Very powerful and much loved among her own people. But when the Earth-Shaker came, she could not defend them. He broke down the natural wall that kept the sea from them, and flooded them. Most died. She still weeps for them, and for her lost child and her murdered son. I have felt her stirring lately, after long eons. She walks the crossroads again. She may even take up her guardianship of the gateways of the dead. Had she been watching, your earthly lover would have had to pass her guardians on the lake called Acheroussia." He looked thoughtful. "I wonder why? It would take something quite powerful to make her cease her mourning and turn her eyes to the mortal world again."

It was on the tip of her tongue to say that it would take more than a weeping woman to stop Benito, but Maria held her tongue. She was the bride of Aidoneus for these four months. And he was a kindly if cold lover.

"I have seen enough for now," she said instead, and put her hand in his, and let him lead her away.

Chapter 25

Milan

Carlo Sforza paced, ten paces up the hard stone floor of the room he had taken for his command post, ten paces back, feeling somewhat like he should be renamed the Caged Wolf of the North. From time to time he looked out the window. The view hadn't changed. Nor did his mood.

The duke of Milan had gradually but steadily distanced himself from Sforza, who had once been one of his deepest confidantes. Filippo Maria was a conniver and plotter to his very core, and that had not changed. But since Venice had defeated the forces of Milan under Sforza, he had withdrawn from talking to Carlo. He could not, Carlo knew, afford to easily dismiss him. That would weaken Milan further, and could easily turn Sforza and his forces against the duke. So, instead, he was eroding Sforza's reputation: A mercenary commander's troops followed for money and loot. Sforza's men had been unusual in that they followed him because he won. But money and loot had been factors.

And now he was being allowed to nibble at little towns. Barely worth looting as far as the mercenaries were concerned. They were *in* one of those little towns. He was in the best house in it. There had been so little to loot that he'd simply taken the entire place over, using it as a bivouac for his men. At least they had shelter that wasn't tents; a little less for them to grumble about.

Filippo Maria was planning something. It could only involve Venice. The duke had always handled intrigue, plotting and murder himself. Sforza had been the military might. But in years before he'd at least listened to Carlo Sforza. And right now they could probably sweep southwest and take Pisa and Tuscany. Both were in political and military disarray. Instead Filippo Maria wanted Venice, which had its strongest and most astute leader in decades, and whose finances were in far better shape than Milan's.

Whatever Filippo Maria Visconti planned this time, Sforza hoped the consequences of it were not going to be dire, at least not for him or his soldiery. He had a handful of men in Venice, reporting back. Men who could take decisive action if need be.

He hated the uncertain waiting.

He hated *not knowing* even more.

And he hated this town.

Vilna

The Black Brain was well pleased, right now. He'd turned his gaze on the lands of the Ilkhan Mongol, and seen how his stolen minions worked for him. Died too, but that was unimportant. The important thing was that the maneuver had worked just as planned. It had taken a great deal of heat off the Byzantine Empire's borders. That fool emperor could recall ten thousand troops from the provinces in Asia Minor and by spring, hold the Hellespont, let alone Constantinople, secure and safe from any attack. And that would give the grand duke's proxies in the Lands of Golden Horde time to assemble and march south, and his fleets time to finally be ready to sally out and take the soft underbelly of Europe.

There were some untied ends in the Lands of Golden Horde, but soon those too could be dealt with.

Milan

Filippo Maria Visconti, the duke of Milan, sat in council with his new favorite, Count Augustino Di Lamis. He had found a good co-conspirator there. And it amused him, still, that the count was sometimes taken for Carlo Sforza. Of course, the difference was clear enough to anyone who knew the men. Count Augustino Di Lamis was the master of sartorial elegance with brightly slashed clothes, and Sforza was conservative in dress. Manners, too.

The count displayed those manners, and that deference, to perfection, as he stood in an attentive posture before the duke—a posture that said without words, *whatever you require of me shall be performed* without looking even remotely servile. The tilt of the head, the slight rounding of the shoulders . . . art. It was art.

Even the way he had placed himself so as not to stand between the duke and the welcome sunlight from the nearest window was artful.

"It appears," said Count Di Lamis, "that we have found the chink in Petro Dorma's personal armor. As you ordered, his habits have been studied. His food is, of course, carefully tasted, and the staff of the Doge's palace are carefully vetted and selected. But he is inordinately fond of fish. And not just any fish. He has a weakness for his namesake fish, pesce San Petro. They are not always abundant. The Doge's agent has an arrangement with several fishermen. And we, in turn have one of them in our pocket."

Filippo Maria nodded. "And we can put a slow poison in all of the catch. It could work."

The count smiled a thin-lipped smile. "Ah, but it does not end there. I have uncovered yet another habit that will ensure your desired conclusion without alerting anyone to how it was done. Petro Dorma is something of an epicure, Your Grace. He likes the fish broiled in wine, whole. And he loves to pick out the little nugget of flesh from behind the pectoral."

"It does have the finest flavor," said Filippo Maria, who lived in fear of poison himself, and who resolved to give up on enjoying this particular morsel thenceforth.

The count nodded deferentially. "And we can insert several slivers of poison into it. They will not poison the whole dish, just he who eats that part."

Filippo Maria forgot himself enough to pat his count on the shoulder. "Well done. There will be considerable rewards for you for this." The count would have to die, of course. But he would enjoy the rewards of his success, briefly. After all, it was almost criminal to have to take such an artist out of the world. "And of course steps must be taken to see that the fish-seller dies, without any link pointing to us."

"But of course, Your Grace," said the count. "His hours are numbered."

And so are yours, Count Augustino Di Lamis, thought Filippo Maria Visconti. But all he said was: "And how goes the other affair?"

The count sighed, and the corner of his mouth dropped a little. "I believe they have an agent close to the target. That is all the information I have at this time. It is difficult working with outsiders."

Filippo Maria drummed his fingers on the arm of his chair a moment. "Hmm. I think we will proceed with our plan to deal with Petro Dorma first."

The count gave a hint of a bow. "Arsenic can be—"

Filippo Maria shook his head, interrupting. "The Council of Ten have employees with keen noses. Arsenic can be smelled, especially when heated. No, I have recently obtained some gum of oleander from the Barbary lands. It should serve, and is less well known."

The count gave a real bow. "As you say, Your Grace. All will be as you require."

Of course, Filippo Maria thought sardonically. *Because anyone who fails me dies.*

Venice

In Venice, Poulo received a package from one of his regular couriers. The black lotos was coming from Barbary, but it was coming in through Trieste, and thence to Milan. And then overland, to the Villa Parvitto where his couriers fetched it. The Council of Ten's agents were intensifying their searches of all the vessels coming in, trying to stem the tide.

The courier handed it over to him with some trepidation. "Here. They even searched some people on the ferry today."

Poulo smiled, a horrible sight on his damaged face, a smile that never spread to his eyes. "They never search a priest, do they? And they know you go to minister there."

The priest shook his head. Probably, beneath his robes, far more was shaking. "I want out of this."

Poulo laughed cruelly. "I know your wants. I've seen them served in the past. They won't go away. So you will do as I order you. And I'll see you get... what you need."

His courier licked his thick lips. He was nervous, scared, but still driven by his desires. And for now, his desires overcame his fears. "I got the snatcher in place for you. Isn't that worth something?"

"When she has done her job," said Poulo. "When she has done her job, then you get a reward. Until then... well, do what you're told and you'll get a taste. Fail, and you're someone I can replace."

Chapter 26

The island of Cerigo

After running before the storm for a week, the fleet had had to take shelter at the Venetian-possessed island of Cerigo for ten days, barely beating their way into a sheltered anchorage at Kapsali on the southern end of the island. It was a slightly battered and tired fleet that waited out the sheeting autumnal rain, in the safety of the half-moon bay, under the Venetian fortress high up the hill. The sailors had to make do with what entertainments the small huddle of houses on the isthmus between the two bays offered. They put some security measures in place with the local captain-general, as Benito had a feeling there might be more fleas than wine or women there, but it seemed, right now, that making landfall was good enough, especially for the crews of the great galleys. It was cold wet work on them. Benito, Enrico Dell'este, Count Alfons and Admiral Dourso... and at the request of Admiral Dourso, prompted by Dell'este, the Genovese admiral Borana, and several osenior officers, and also Count Alfons of Aragon were offered lodging in the fortress. It was a far smaller and less important Venetian possession, and Benito had the misfortune—as far as he was concerned—of being obliged to ride up there. But it did let him meet and get to know the Aragonese and Genovese commanders. The Old Fox told him this was an advantage.

Benito was less sure. Count Alfons of Valderobes was the model of a tall, slim aristocratic gentleman. He had poise, distinction, charm and an a la modality of dress. He also had not the vaguest idea of just how a ship sailed, let alone of how to run a naval operation. His idea of strategy was a frontal charge. And he was, in Benito's assessment, the better of the two. Admiral Borana alternated between being submissive and aggressive. It was hard to tell just how he might respond next.

It became apparent that was at least partially due to the fact that his dignity was affronted, and that he was, at the same time, very afraid. Some of the reasons started to come out during dinner; while Count Alfons was busy examining his reflection in the little mirror facets in the Murano glass goblets, Borana had drunk enough out of them to start talking. It came out in a frothy rancor. "I am supposed to be admiral of this fleet. Supposed to lead. To decide."

"Admiral," said Enrico Dell'este. "Indeed you are supposed to lead. The fleet flies your flag as well as their own. We sit here as guests of the Venetian governor. Did you not hear yourself announced as we came in?"

It had been, indeed, an impressive recitation of titles and honors. The admiral's chest swelled a bit, and he sat slightly straighter. "But...but..."

"Your contribution to the leadership is vital to our cause," said Benito, responding to his grandfather's kick.

"Precisely!" said the Old Fox. "You show that you understand the greater and wider view. It shows the wisdom of your duke in choosing you to lead Genoa's fleet."

No one could believe that, thought Benito. But it was plain that Borana did. He stuck out his pigeon chest still further. Yet the injured dignity refused to give up. "But, you did not even consult me about sailing eastward. It's contrary to my instructions. And, well, the common sailors on my vessels are saying that you have magical means. That we only survived the storm because of you. That this...you, Milor' Valdosta. The braggartry among the Venetian sailors about you is just insufferable. They're affecting my discipline."

In other words they're looking to some unknown young Venetian for a spot of leadership and not you, you old blowhard, thought Benito. *And somehow that's all our fault.*

The Old Fox looked grave. "We'll have to do something to affirm your status. Only...There is a problem."

"And what is that?"

"Canea. If your vessels with your flag led the fleet into Canea, well, they'd probably bombard us. Genoa really doesn't enjoy a good reputation there."

"Which is exactly why we must return to Corfu. Or remain here!"

"I'm afraid return is not an option, M'lord Admiral," said Benito, humbly. "Weather. And I promise you, the weather knowledge I have is completely sound. If you wish to risk your ships of course, I can't stop them, and I certainly would not dare to contradict your orders. But as we've displayed, we have ... information. It would be unwise. This little garrison doesn't have the food for us to spend the winter here. And it's not a good anchorage in the face of wind from the south, which will be coming, and very soon. Too shallow and not sheltered enough." Benito hoped saying this confidently would work. He really had no idea.

What he had said was certainly true about the food, and even the admiral could see that.

"Of course," said the Old Fox, as if the idea had just come to him, "We could push on for other Venetian possessions. Say ... the Cyclades. Maybe Negroponte. If you gave that instruction as opposed to going to overwinter in Crete, where you'd have to pretend to be vassals. And stay on your vessels because the local resentment runs high ..." The Old Fox sighed. "It is irksome to see someone of your dignity being forced to play such games, but as you well know ... politics." He shrugged. "It's a pity that the Duchy of Genoa has arrangements with Byzantium about port facilities, or we could use your possessions."

"That would be seen as an astute piece of leadership by all our crews," said Benito, staring pointedly at the fish-mouthed Admiral Dourso—who knew where they planned to go next, which was not Canea. Not for the first time, Benito wished they could have had Admiral Lemnossa instead. But Venice had elected to keep the old man home. He claimed to be too old, but Benito had reason to suspect that certain parties had worked very hard to keep him as a last reserve if La Serenissima needed it. He couldn't blame them. If he himself needed a wily old shark for a last-ditch defense, Lemnossa would have been his first choice.

Admiral Borana nodded.

Enrico smiled and patted him on the shoulder.
"That'll show them who is in charge!"

"Yes. Real leadership," said Admiral Dourso, catching
on at last. "Even the common sailors will recognize it."

Benito did his best to scowl and look irritated.
"But . . . I have told people we are going to Canea."
That was not strictly a lie, but the only people he'd
told that to were listening to him at that moment.

Admiral Borana beamed. "I'm afraid you'll have to
tell them you now have fresh sailing orders from me.
Let's have some more of this fine wine."

Count Alfons, having examined his countenance from
every angle, leaned in and said to Benito thoughtfully,
"What I want to know is . . . was it really true about
the bridge? And where did you find such a woman?"

And so Benito was obliged to tell tales that did
nothing to convince Borana that he was a sober and
responsible fellow these days.

However the evening did have its positive points.
There was a Genovese captain in the admiral's entourage who had headed the fleet that had returned from
Theodosia, and had, after a run-in with the "pirates"
of the Black Sea, been lucky enough to encounter the
Venetian Eastern Fleet and Admiral Lemnossa. Benito
questioned him on the finer points of the engagement,
while the Old Fox alternately flattered and coached
Borana. He was plainly disappointed that the Doge
and the Council of Ten had not sent Lemnossa out
again. "He was a gentleman, and a great strategist.
I . . . I had assumed Venice would send him."

"I'd have preferred it myself," admitted Benito.
"Politics, I am afraid. That and fear, I think."

The captain nodded. "Which is why we have Admiral Borana." He looked uneasy. "Forget I said that. I am a little puzzled, though. My men said you had no intention of going to Canea for the winter and were planning on kicking Emperor Alexius's door in before he closed it."

There really were no secrets in any military force, Benito reflected. *And this was an officer who listened to his men.* "It seemed a good idea to let the admiral believe it was his idea," he said with a shrug. "I would like to talk more about those pirates..."

The captain nodded. "But perhaps not now. The admiral is looking at us, and he still considers Venice the enemy."

Benito laughed, as if he thought the captain had told a joke, and the admiral looked back to the Old Fox. "Tomorrow morning? My grandfather likes to get up early to ride. I would like any excuse to avoid it."

There was a small snort of laughter, carefully bottled. "I'd heard. I am going to turn away looking angry, as if I had taken offense at that laugh of yours. I will see you tomorrow...after Matins?"

Benito groaned. "Not another early riser."

"The admiral is not," said the captain, turning away, and stalking off as if enraged.

The Genovese admiral was, however, a night-bird. He was still drinking when Benito quietly left, having been given a wine-keg's worth of bitter maundering already. Admiral Borana had enemies and disloyal underlings. Benito started to appreciate Admiral Dourso more by the moment.

The storm they had run before to take shelter here had not spent itself by morning. The wind still howled around the battlements and sneaked in chilly gusts into the stone chapel.

Every church seemed to provide little but shelter from actual rain and snow in winter... and they all were chilly even in summer. The church had to believe that being cold was good for the soul or something, thought Benito sourly. And the Genovese captain had not shown up...

But Benito's patience, what little there was of it, was rewarded after all. The captain was waiting outside when Benito came out of the chapel, looking even colder than Benito felt. "Just been down checking on the vessels. Nasty wind blowing. It looks like the *Santa Bellina* has dragged her anchors a bit. If this blow continues I'll have to get them to row another out."

"It should start to blow itself out today. But there is another just behind it," said Benito without thinking.

The Genovese captain looked at him, curiously. "So you do have knowledge of the future. Demonic, the admiral calls it."

"That's why I've got frozen knees and I'm just leaving the chapel," said Benito wryly.

The Genovese captain laughed. "My name is Carlos Di Tharra, M'lord Valdosta. We never got introduced yesterday. Why don't we go and find a fire for your knees, and my hands and face."

"Call me Benito. Everyone does. If we find that fire in the kitchens, we'll be likely to get some hot bread. They were baking when I came down."

"The idea of raiding the kitchen in person had not occurred to me," said Carlos, blinking. "It is a good one, now that I smell the bread."

"That's the key to good strategy," said Benito,

pushing open the door to the castle kitchens, full of warmth and food smells.

"Thinking of something different?"

Benito grinned. "Maybe putting off thinking until the distractions of an empty stomach and frozen knees are dealt with."

The chief cook was somewhat taken aback by the invasion into his warm noisy domain by two gentlemen, but he did provide them with a loaf so hot they had to juggle it, a bowl of olive oil, and a jug of small beer and a couple of wooden goblets. Pity there was no butter or cheese, but such things were hard to come by in winter, and likely were being hoarded by the locals and not to be had at any price here. They retreated from the bedlam of the morning kitchen to a fireplace in one of the lesser salons, and huddled on a pair of little benches at the hearth. Carlos kicked the smoldering logs into a sullen flame. "The kitchen was warmer."

"But noisier." Benito broke off a piece of bread and handed it to the Genovese. He dipped his bread in the warm, fragrant oil. "I think we need to see the crews get some fresh bread, too."

The captain smiled. "I can see why they'll follow you."

Benito shrugged. "It takes more than hot bread."

"But it shows that you know they are cold and uncomfortable, and they believe it matters to you," said Captain di Tharra. A chill draft tickled Benito's neck, underscoring his words.

The bread was excellent, the olive oil quite good. Benito found himself liking this man more with every word. "I suppose it does. I have been cold and uncomfortable myself, and they know that, too. But I

wanted to ask about your experiences with the Black
Sea pirates, not talk about bread."

"They're not pirates," said the captain, with an
uneasy glance. "I'd say that they're a navy—not very
experienced, but numerous. I wouldn't sail into the
Black Sea without a fleet at my back now. And I'd
prefer it to be commanded by a clever admiral—the
great Duke Doria, or maybe your Admiral Lemnossa.
I developed respect for the man."

Benito had already heard about it from Lemnossa's
point of view, and that of several of the sailors from
that journey. But Di Tharra had survived one more
encounter with them. And as he continued his nar-
rative, Benito found him intelligent and methodical.
He was, Benito found, a methodical thinker, given to
counting things—the number of men, the number of
sails, the number of cannon. "My admiral says I sound
like a shopkeeper," he said, a little embarrassed.

Benito snorted with thinly disguised contempt. "I
will avoid telling you what your admiral sounds like.
But I can say that your habit would make me very
wary about attacking Genovese vessels."

Di Tharra looked a little taken aback, and pleased.
"It makes organizing much easier."

"I will refrain from mentioning this habit to the
Council of Ten. They like Venetians to have a monopoly
on these habits and I have decided I like you," said
Benito. "I need to know these ships. It makes planning possible, and even successful sometimes. So I
am grateful."

"I will tell you what I can. I make notes in my
diary." Di Tharra tugged at his beard. He tilted his
head to one side, took a bite of bread and added

tentatively, "In exchange I need to know how you can foretell the weather."

Benito laughed, and tossed another chunk of wood on the fire at their feet. The flames rose up to bite into it. "Here's the truth. I can't. But I have reached—with the full blessing of the church," added Benito, knowing the superstitions about nonhumans, but feeling he needed this man's trust, "an agreement with the tritons. They can speak across great distances of sea. And thus they can tell me what weather is coming."

To his surprise Di Tharra looked delighted and not, as he'd feared, horrified. "Tritons! Ah, that makes perfect sense! I know that the Hypatians are given to speech with all manner of creatures; I presume that is how you managed to work this little arrangement. They are the bearers of my family coat of arms! All my life I have wished to see one of them. Many people think they are mythical...but I have seen the remains of one. And also spoken to many sailors about them. Too many stories, and too alike."

"I'll have to see if I can arrange a meeting some day," said Benito, rubbing the spot where he'd pricked his thumb to make a drop of blood fall on the water to call Androcles.

The captain looked as if he had almost forgotten the cold, he was so grateful. "Please! I would be forever in your debt. It is...rather why I adopted a maritime career. My father was much opposed."

"What did he want you to do instead?" asked Benito, curious as ever.

The Genovese captain smiled sourly. "Stay home and run the estate. Chase wild boar. We are landholders in

Sardinia. I think our lands had some coastal villages once. But what is left is far inland now."

They talked for a while about his home, and the problems a "colonial" had in the navy of Genoa. He was very touchy about the "colonial" word apparently, just by the way he said it. He was not the complaining kind, and Benito had to draw it out of him. But it was clear that talent was being stifled here, and that he had far more to be dissatisfied with than the politically and socially well-connected Borana. Di Tharra was, however, enthusiastic about the new duke of Genoa, who was an ex-naval man himself after all. "Things are changing under Doria. Not fast, because the old order has strong roots, but he is a great man. Sharp enough and experienced enough to cut them clear."

Benito wondered if the Holy Roman Empire knew just what they were doing when the emperor had lent his weight to the election of Admiral Doria to that role. Venice didn't need a stronger Genoa, especially in the light of the concessions they'd made for Genovese help in this endeavor. Talk came back around to the current mission. "So given the weather cooperating, you wish to lay siege to Constantinople for the winter?"

"A winter of siege sitting outside the walls of Constantinople would probably have half our men dead of flux and the other half with the malaria. And I don't fancy laying siege to a great city all on my own," said Benito, easily, stretching out, taking the goblet of small beer. "Let's put it this way, Captain Di Tharra. What the men believe . . . is right some of the time. But we will have to play it by ear at Naxos."

Di Tharra smiled and shrugged. "I shouldn't have asked. But when the admiral wants to stick to the island of Naxos like a limpet, I will say that I had heard that was exactly as you had planned it."

That was quite a valuable prize, Benito thought. "And I will see if I can persuade Androcles to come and speak to you with me one night. No promises, though. They're wary. It was really only because of my brother that I got to meet them at all."

"Your brother is less well known than . . . shall we say your exploits, in Genoa. But I have heard of him. He is a healer, is he not? Anyway, it would be the wish of my heart," said Di Tharra, "just to actually see a triton, one day. To speak with one . . . call for me if this can ever happen. Borana can complain about my treachery for that."

He said that last with a smile. "I would rather he did not know that we met, otherwise. I will send a sailor I trust to collect my diaries, and let you have a summary at church tomorrow. But otherwise, like the rest of the admiral's staff, I will keep my distance. Much politics there, you understand. But we have good captains and good crews."

Benito left, well pleased with his early rising. It had been worth cold knees, and that was better than the bruising he would have had from riding out with the Old Fox that morning.

But of course, the first thing he would have to do would be to explain his absence. He doubted the Old Fox would mind once he heard what Benito had to say.

Enrico Dell'este was back in his chambers, peering at maps again, when he got there. But there was the unmistakable scent of horse around, as well as a much warmer fire than the one he had just left. The Old Fox's chamber was smaller, and tighter, than that drafty reception room. It was as cozy and comfortable as a visitor could expect here.

"I have a sore head, as I was left to keep that buffoon company last night," said the duke grumpily. "I doubt if Venice, or the Empire or Christendom appreciate what I have done for the sake of this alliance. And I wonder if it is worth it, considering the leadership they have."

Benito grinned a little. Fishing for information already? "It's worth it, Grandfather. They've got some good vessels, and at least one exceptional captain. You would hire him as a spy. He has Bartelozzi's habit of putting figures to everything."

Dell'este looked up sharply. "Di Tharra? I saw you speak to him last night. I wondered what you'd done to offend him. He's in some disgrace back in Genoa for cooperating with Venice, and for parting with some of their cargo. And for losing some vessels."

"I didn't offend him; it was his way to keep from getting pulled into a reprimand for speaking to me at all. The Genoese admiral doesn't want his folk being friendly with us, and he himself is under a cloud for saving the fleet after their defeat. Is Genoa populated by idiots, or is it the entire world?" asked Benito, shaking his head.

"Oh, some of the grandees that lost money were all for making an example of him. But all the other captains spoke for him—putting themselves at risk. That says a great deal about the respect his fellows hold for him. Also, he was not in charge of the fleet when they put out from Theodosia. He merely took control when their flagship was lost, and it was borne out to the nobility of Genoa that he stopped the losses from becoming a total disaster by doing so. And when word got out . . . the crews threatened mutiny, and the refugees from Constantinople got very vocal—some of them are well connected, too." The Old Fox waggled his eyebrows knowingly. "Duke Doria knows well enough that he did exceptionally well, and saved far more than could have been expected. But that does not stop the stay-at-home warriors from winning wars with their mouths, and fat purses. So he came on this mission to try to retrieve his honor. I gather Admiral Borana does not like being saddled with a second-class colonial noble like that."

"I see," said Benito, now realizing just how the captain had understated his problems. Not a complainer, then; that boded well, so far as Benito was concerned. He pulled up a stool without being invited. "Well, despite that, he's disposed to like and help us."

"Good. Because Borana is not. It's to be hoped that we can pull the same trick in Naxos. With anyone more intelligent, or less fond of wine, I would say, impossible. But the admiral is a good example of breeding and money making for a poor choice of leader."

And indeed, they were able to do something very like that at Naxos. That included convincing Admiral Borana that the status of Genoa meant that sailing up the Hellespont under his flag would be something the Byzantines would treat with respect, given all their treaties and historic links to Genoa. Once convinced, it was child's play to lead him to think that this was all his idea, and that the Venetians had immediately seen his brilliance and fallen in with the plan.

Borana readied his part of the fleet in a happy,

slightly alcoholic haze of self-congratulation. *His* brilliant diplomacy would succeed where the Venetians had failed. *He* would personally repair all the damage that had been done. After all, the fleet arriving in Constantinople beneath the Genoese flag would naturally restore the balance of the emperor Alexius's mind, and they could overwinter there before their mission against the pirates in the springtime.

Fortunately, his captains were not so sanguine, and on seeing the preparations the Venetians were making, copied them. Of course, the little hints that Benito had dropped to Di Tharra might have helped....

Naxos Island

One other thing happened at Naxos. Something that might—or might not—have consequences in the future. Good consequences, but...consequences, nonetheless.

Benito had had a conversation with Androcles—in his usual fashion, leaning over the bow, strictly alone. The crews respected his desire to think and commune with the water. Whatever he was doing, it had the blessing of the Church, and he was somehow able to read the weather. That was only a little short of a miracle. Maybe it was witchery, but it was sanctioned witchery. He kept them safe. If he had wanted to hang upside down from the bowsprit and talk to the waves, that would have been fine by them, too.

In fact, he was communing with something *in* the water. Riding the curving bow-wave, Androcles swam along easily. He was the color of seawater himself, with his long fishtail and human torso with broad barnacle-crusted shoulders, and spume and spray colored hair.

"And now, Benito Valdosta? What do you want this time? The lost conch of the waves? The route to my grandmother's palace?"

Benito blinked. He'd never heard of either of these things. "Um. Not at the moment, thanks. Maybe later."

Androcles chuckled. "Now is your chance. It's down there somewhere in these waters. But it's only fair to warn you that we've looked for it already."

Benito blinked again, feeling no less baffled than before. As the spume sprinkled his face with icy droplets, he allowed himself to be distracted for a moment from his actual intention. "What? This conch, or your granny's palace?"

"Well, both, though the way to my grandmother's hall is probably a bit more interesting to you, given your other adventures." Androcles grinned, looking entirely too much like a shark at that moment. "Except in truth she's a little further back than my grandmother. The story goes that she came from here. She had a fight with Poseidon about another woman, and the Earth-Shaker—the father of all tritons— shook the place down. So the place was buried along with Triton's horn, which is the conch I mentioned, because he dared defend his mother. We've found a fair number of wrecked ships but no sign of a palace. But besides triton myth, what do want of me, Benito Valdosta? The weather continues good for this time of year. There are no Byzantine naval vessels about. There are a few fishing boats. There is little else I can tell you."

Benito pursed his lips; he had to phrase this carefully. "I want you—no, that's not right. I am requesting, asking you, to please greet another human. As a favor."

"No." Androcles shook his head. "We're not some rare-beast show for you to display to some drunken captain." He turned to go.

Benito called out quickly. "His coat of arms has two tritons as supporters. And he is a captain in the Genovese fleet, from Sardinia. He says his family has old tales of friendship with tritons, but he has never met one, and wishes to more than anything. He is a good man, in a crucial position, and I need his help, Androcles. Please."

Androcles paused in the very act of diving, but Benito had the feeling that his "please" had very little to do with the triton's hesitation. Androcles' next words confirmed that. "Sardinia. Hmm."

"Even letting him see you would be appreciated," said Benito, in his most wheedling tone.

Androcles laughed at that. "Tell him to fall overboard, then."

"To see a triton?" Benito smiled wryly. "You know, judging by his reaction when he knew I had seen you, I think he might just do it. Even in these seas and this cold."

Androcles plainly had thought it over while Benito was speaking and it appeared that the Sardinian's eagerness was the last thing he needed to make up his mind. "We have ancient ties with Sardinia. Very well. I will see this captain of yours."

"Thank you. This will be something he has wanted for all his life. I think it will make a bond between us, and you are doing me a tremendous favor." Benito tried to sound as grateful as he felt. He was remembering everything that Marco had said about showing these creatures that aside from the bargain, you valued them for themselves. "I'll take him for a stroll along the sea-wall at Naxos. It would have to be late in the night or early morning."

Androcles grinned, showing his exceedingly sharp teeth again. "You love the early morning. So that would be good for me. Before Aurora's red fingers scratch away the night."

"What?" Benito asked, startled. Red fingers scratching? The image that came to *his* mind was someone clawing at... something... till their fingers bled.

Androcles shook his head sadly. "Just before dawn. You have no poetry in your soul, Benito Valdosta. Even the Romans had more poetry than you. You should spend more time with the ancient poets and less with bladesmen." He dived.

Benito went off to ask his grandfather just what "Aurora's red fingers" meant. It sounded murderous, not poetic.

"Who's Aurora?" he asked without preamble, as he entered his grandfather's cabin.

The Old Fox didn't even look up from the papers he was studying. "Latin. Goddess of the dawn."

"Ah." He pondered that. "She has red fingers?"

"According to Homer, yes." Now the old man looked up at him. "Well, 'rosy' would be a more poetic translation. 'Rosy-fingered dawn.'" The old man looked nostalgic. "It used to be the vogue to address one's mistress that way when you woke."

Benito decided not to ask who or what Homer was, and resigned himself to early rising. "And Poseidon?"

The Old Fox blinked, then frowned. "Your education is severely lacking, Benito. He was an ancient Greek god of the sea. And earthquakes, if I remember it rightly."

Earthquakes. The sea, Benito thought he had... well, not control, but at least a kind of understanding with. But earthquakes? "Hopefully he'll stay away. Or level the walls of Constantinople for us."

His grandfather shook his head. "Earthquakes we just hope stay away. You weren't born yet, but I was traveling to Rome for a pilgrimage... well, on Ferrara's business really, when there was a small tremor. Well, they told me it was 'small' but I tell you, it was large enough for me. It destroyed the town I had overnighted in, and made my gut feel like water. I would rather face a score of wild boars. Such things are too powerful for any man."

Benito decided to take his word for it. And about Aurora too. "Rosy-fingered dawn"... he had an idea just how Maria would respond to being saluted that way. First she'd take him literally and look with dismay to see if her hands were stained with something. Then she'd tell him he was insane.

On to more important matters.

Benito sent a message to Captain Di Tharra, who—as everyone knew—always personally checked on the fleet when he woke, which was always early.

Someone had to like daybreak.

They met on the sea-wall as the sky began to pale, Benito yawning fit to crack his jaw in half. "You said that it was necessary that we meet?" said the Genovese officer, a little warily.

"I said I would try to arrange a meeting for you, rather," said Benito, yawning again. "If it was me wanting to meet I would have chosen a better time and a warmer place."

Di Tharra peered intently at him. "You mean the—"

"Triton. Yes. There he is." Benito didn't point, but he did nod down into the ocean at their feet.

Di Tharra stood, transfixed, staring, agape.

"Is he a statue?" said Androcles sardonically. "I'd have carved him with the mouth closed myself."

"You, you speak?" said Di Tharra, his voice quavering.

Androcles snorted, but he didn't seem displeased. "Several human languages. So, Valdosta says you are from the colony."

Di Tharra stiffened slightly and drew back. "The Genoese refer to us as colonials," he said as if he were not in fact captaining a vessel of Genoese fleet. "But my family has been in Sardinia for many generations."

"Oh, long before for the sailors from Liguria," said the triton, showing his sharp teeth. "Long, long before that. But you humans have probably forgotten. The Shardana, the Sea People, the people of the rootless tree, eventually settled there, a good many thousand years back. They were colonists then. We were once allies of theirs. Of yours. I recognize your blood. Thinned, but unmistakable."

Di Tharra stared as if he were receiving revelations. Perhaps he was. "My family coat of arms is the uprooted tree of Aboria, and the greatsword, supported by tritons!" he exclaimed.

"A fish-tongue sword," said the triton with some satisfaction.

"What?" Di Tharra was beginning to sound like Benito had. Benito was secretly pleased that he wasn't the only one to be baffled by the triton.

"The hilt is shaped like a fish," Androcles explained patiently. "With the mouth wide, and the blade protruding. The Shardana used them. Take a closer look sometime, you'll see."

"It does have a rather odd hilt," Di Tharra said slowly, then with growing pleasure.

"And the crest?" asked Benito, curious.

"It's not a real crest," Di Tharra said, then amended, "Well, not what the Genoese would call a 'real crest.' It's a conch-shell."

Benito looked at the triton, and then at the captain from Sardinia. "Well, I hope you don't mind my saying, but I'm pleased to have been the one to reintroduce your families. However, I think our time is running short. Dawn will be along soon, and people will start stirring."

Di Tharra took a deep breath. He bowed to the triton as if to the duke of Genoa himself. Actually, he probably bowed to the triton with more respect than he would to the duke. "I am honored to have met you, Milord Triton. Our families had an ancient alliance, you say. Well, I'll hold to that. Call on me if I can be of any aid in any way. I would love to talk further of the history, someday."

"Like the Shardana still," said Androcles with a smile. "Not like you, Valdosta. You hear that? True Shardana, asking what can they do for *us*, not just to bargain."

"Firm friends forever," said Benito wryly. "Now, I see a sailor walking down the quay. I don't think the captain and I should be seen together, or even seen, so I suggest we go our different ways."

"Until next time," said Androcles, vanishing in the swirl of a long, scaled fishy tail.

Di Tharra stood looking into the water, beaming

as only a man who has just had his heart's desire can beam.

Benito slapped him on the back. "I'll leave you to stare at the sea. I am going to go somewhere warm."

Di Tharra finally looked up from the waves, with a suspicion of moisture in his eyes. "I am in your debt, Signor Valdosta. Deeply."

Benito shrugged. "I'd take to sitting on the bow alone, in the early morning or late evenings, if I were you. Androcles is not usually this forthcoming, and it's plain he has more to say to you, but you'll need a more private space, or at least, one where he can't be seen so easily."

Di Tharra smiled. "That explains the rumors of you 'reading the ocean.'"

"Not so much 'reading' as 'listening.'" Benito laughed. "But yes. And now you can start the same rumors about you."

And with that, he left Di Tharra and headed for fire and food.

PART IV
December, 1540 A.D.

Chapter 27

The Aegean Sea

They sailed from Naxos to Lesbos, one of the few
Genoese possessions in the eastern Mediterranean.
Benito thought winkling Borana out of there would
take a crowbar. But fortunately the Archon Gattalusi
was even keener to see the back of the admiral than
Benito was to move on. He assured the admiral that
there was no reason that the fleet should not sail to
Constantinople and overwinter there. There was no
conflict between the Byzantine Empire and Genoa.
And he had no spare food for a fleet. They'd had a
drought, and there was no spare food to be had for
any amount of money. Nor wine.

It was probably that last that was the final item
needed to convince Borana that it was time to leave.

Under slate skies they proceeded toward the Hellespont, and—unbeknownst to most of the fleet—with
a small number of fast galliots, to the western side
of the Callipolis peninsula.

There were a number of castles and fortifications
along the Hellespont. The fleet would have to pass
under their guns.

The ships from Genoa led the fleet in towards the Hellespont, approaching Cape Hellas, their flag proud. They probably weren't even aware that some three hundred men from Venice—all veterans of the Corfu guerilla campaign—were missing, along with their vessels.

Benito and his grandfather sat in the Mediterranean scrub on a small hill just west of the castle on the southern point of Morto bay. The early morning sun shone on the fleet sailing toward the Byzantine castle on the point. Hidden in the scrub a hundred Venetians waited.

It had been a long, long night already. They'd timed it as well as possible with the tritons signaling the fleet's progress and Admiral Dourso with strict instructions that somehow, no matter what it took, the fleet was to approach the Hellespont in the early morning. In the dusk the shallow-draft galliots had sailed closer to the western shore.

"I hate this, Benito. Sailing inshore without local knowledge in the dark. It's madness," said Captain Splenta.

"I'd ordered the stars out for us to follow. They don't seem to have got the message," said Benito sardonically. "We've got to get in, Captain. And we have to keep this heading. With luck everyone will be in bed on this miserable night."

"At least Spiro has a village's lights for guidance."

"And we have that," said Benito, relieved, pointing. They'd landed seven men in a small fishing smack a few days before. Poachers. Veterans of Corfu. Greek speakers. And, traveling as tinkers to a little-populated corner of Byzantium, sleeping rough, and making two fires with a little of the bracket fungus that burned with a green flame. As long as they had got themselves to the right spot, the galliots had something to aim for. The Byzantines would have been amazed at how much the Venetians knew of the geography of the Callipolis peninsula.

"What is it?"

"Our path to a safe landing I hope. Get a man to grab that green lantern with the bracket on. Run it up the masthead."

So they did. And the fires flared slightly. The lantern came down, and under cautious oars the galliots eased their way forward. The beach at the mouth of the small ravine wasn't wide enough to let them land, so the men climbed down into stomach-deep water. Most of them, veterans of getting wet at night, abandoned dignity and stripped off, holding their clothing and weapons above their heads, then pulling in a small raft with Dell'este and quite a lot of black powder on it.

It began to rain softly again.

"Keep that powder dry or you'll be chewing down the portcullis, damn you," snarled one of Benito's lieutenants at the slightly overeager poacher-scouts, as they unloaded. The galliots—lighter now, and very undermanned, began pushing out into the relative safety of the night. They'd hopefully anchor within signaling range.

Benito, shivering, dressed himself. His grandfather, who had barely wet his boots, chuckled. "You've done away with the bright trumpets for this charge of yours, but your teeth are doing good castanets."

"Next time I will show you less deference and let you wade with the rest of us, Grandfather. How ready are we, Captian Gamba?"

"Ready when you are, m'lord. Shall I have the men issued that grappa now?"

"One measure. We've a few miles to march tonight. And then a long fireless wait for morning."

So they'd moved out, with some quiet stumbling and cursing, led by the scouts to the relatively easy rutted track that ran down to the coast from the village to the castle. It supposedly had a mounted patrol, but they were—like much of the Byzantine army—underpaid, demoralized and in bed on this chilly night. What wasn't abed was a drunken farmer, singing his way cheerfully and tunelessly homeward.

"Avoid killing him. We don't need the local peasantry against us."

Soon they had a Greek peasant thoroughly gagged and bound with eyes as wide as a full moon brought to Benito. "Listen to me, my friend," said Benito, in Greek. "If you behave, tomorrow you will go home with a few bits of silver to make your wife smile. You can tell her the truth then—do it right away and she'll cry and thank the Virgin you came home safe to her, instead of throwing a pot at your head for being out so late drunk. We've no quarrel with you. But try to escape or betray us and we'll cut your throat like a hog. Understand?"

The wide-eyed peasant, a lot more sober than he had been, nodded. They took him with them and went on. Soon they could see the dark bulk of Cape Hellas Castle. "Not much of a castle."

"It will have guards."

"Antimo had one on either tower. The ditch helps us though." The castle had no moat but there was a deep ditch running along its landward edge. Benito and his sappers were able to crawl along it and place their charges at the very gate of the castle.

And now, though night would have been a good time for the attack, they waited for the cold dawn—which was not far off by the time they'd finished. They watched a shepherd boy chase his goats up into the rough grazing. Being nuzzled by a goat had not been part of the plan either. But fortunately the shepherd boy sat down to make himself a fire and then try to kill birds with his slingshot, unaware that he and the castle and the channel beyond were being watched.

From here they also had a good view of the Genovese ships trying to make it past the Byzantine forts. It was almost like watching some strange mobile artwork. A rather cruel one. The smoke from the cannons on the forts, and the panicky sail-work and the desperate tacking. So much for Constantinople's special relationship with Genoa.

"The only thing I regret is that I can't be there to listen to Admiral Borana swearing, and demanding that we assault the forts," said Benito to his grandfather.

"I'll do it for you," said Enrico Dell'este. "Otherwise you might make me walk up here again. And it is too cold for me to want to do it twice."

"I'll consider it done," said Benito, cheerfully. "Secrecy and a lack of opposition would make it worthwhile. There'll be Byzantine patrols going out soon to stop any landings, so I think we shall go in now, while they're still cheering."

The castle could have been quite secure, and hard to take, had it not been for the fact that Benito and his sappers had been busy long before dawn, and that the Byzantines decided to send a messenger to the garrison at Callipolis. They raised the portcullis and he rode out. There was a stopper squad not three hundred yards away, and the men on portcullis and gate duty were in no great hurry to close up.

The shrill horn call soon changed that. The small cannon carried so laboriously off the raft was very well positioned, and the sudden boom shattered the unprotected gate. The charges set carefully into the stones at the base of the gate-towers exploded too. Merely intended to shift some of the rock the ditch-boards lay across, they did their job. The portcullis crashed down—but it no longer reached the ground. Men scrabbled through the gap, as the Byzantines, who had been standing on the outer wall jeering, cheering and laughing, tried to run to defend the inner wall.

The Byzantine soldiery in the castle were probably very nearly as surprised to have the gate and portcullis blown as the Genovese admiral had been to have his flag fired on.

It was an almost bloodless affair, by virtue of its suddenness and the fact that most of the Byzantines had assumed that the enemy was far away, at sea, and fleeing.

Almost bloodless. There was one spectacularly blooded prisoner.

"What's wrong with him?" Benito asked, staring at the captured Byzantine commander with a gore-covered shirt. He looked as if he had been fighting off the entire invading force single-handed. Except that he had no visible wounds.

"I punched him, sir," said the brawny sailor standing guard over the officer. "His nose bled a bit. He called me a Genoese whoreson."

Benito laughed. "Inexcusable! Doesn't he know the difference between a Genoese accent and Venetian one? Let him explain his ignorance to the Genovese admiral."

Benito could only hope that the attack on the fort opposite the guns of Dardanellia had gone as well, and as easily. His information via Antimo still appeared to have been accurate so far. That was the true danger point of this strait, where the channel was not quite a mile wide. They had to take that other fort. Unfortunately, according to the spymaster, the fort's garrison was the most disciplined and best run of the defenses on this side of the Hellespont, even if it was more than two miles to its opposite number. Obviously the fortifications at the narrows opposite the city of Dardanellia should have got the best guns and best men, but it was one of many fortifications that had been intermittently being constructed for the last fifty years. The castle at Dardanellia suffered from being in the rebellious Opiskon faction—one which with any luck and a little push from Venetian gold was in a foment right now.

On the positive side, Alexius was an idiot. One who wavered between wanting to protect his city and being afraid that if the castles were *too* well manned, someone might realize that what could defend could also bottle up, and revolt—leaving his city with no way to the seas.

"Well, Grandfather. I will leave you to the explanations. I want to see if my men succeeded at the narrows. If they haven't, we have problems. And if they have we need to press on for Callipolis as fast as the galliots can carry us. I'll leave a bare handful of men in the fortifications—you'll have to get relief to them fairly quickly, in case of trouble."

"Why you didn't have them bring you a good horse, is the part that I don't understand," said the Old Fox, "That, and why do I get to explain all this to Admiral Borana?"

Benito patted him on the shoulder. "You get to explain it, because they still expect it from you. The Venetians and the Corfiotes will accept it from me. The Genovese and the Aragonese will become upset, but coming from you, they will nod and say, *ah yes, the Old Fox is up to his old tricks*. And horses are the best reason I ever had for maritime warfare. The galliots up the west coast and a forced march across should get me there nearly as fast as a good rider, and faster than I could have ridden seven leagues."

Enrico Dell'este smiled. That had been happening more and more often. He sometimes wondered of late if people thought that the duke of Ferrara was becoming senile or something. Behaving like a perfectly ordinary doting grandfather every time that rascal *Benito* did something clever, instead of the Dell'este. Still . . . The fact that the boy was not much of a rider was a small price to pay for such a grandson.

And, all being well, for the cost of defending a narrow strip of land north of Callipolis town, they could hold the Hellespont. Even if they failed on Constantinople, this too would do. It was not as easy to control as the Bosphorus, but they could make it very difficult for Jagiellon's fleet to reach the Mediterranean. It had been one of the first objectives discussed in the secret conclaves of the Council of Ten. To have made their arrival less than a deadly secret would have meant there would be a garrison of thousands waiting. Instead there was a mere eight hundred cuirassiers garrisoned at Callipolis; in theory available to defend and patrol the lands beyond the walls of the forts, but in practice, staying warm and dry and utterly unaware that they were about to be attacked.

To land and take the peninsula in face of a determined enemy would have been suicidal and expensive of men. To take it some months before they were expected, and by surprise, on a fairly miserable winter night, graced with rain and a little sleet, had been unpleasant, but not hard.

If the Council of Ten's agents—warned by Benito's Spiro—had done their work properly, most of the Byzantine cuirassiers would be stuck in their barracks right now...or close to their privies. Buckbean in the issue wine wasn't going to kill them. But it would loosen their bowels to the extent that many of them might wish they were dead.

Some might cavail at such ploys and say they were without honor. Not Dell'este. Oh no. *The young cub got the Old Fox's cleverness,* the duke thought, with another contented smile. Perilous though this enterprise was—well, it was good to know there were two sets of sharp wits to attack it.

Chapter 28

Trebizond

One could not move the Ilkhan himself from the great palace at Baghdad without considerable upheaval. A great deal of movement of troops. And tents and equipment. Of course certain preparations had to be made. An upsurge in security and a few summary executions were to be expected.

And in various satrapies and vassal states, of course, they were glad that Ilkhan Hotai the Ineffable had heard their pleas and sent some of his troops.

Trebizond breathed easier. Michael Magheretti did not. The young podesta's breathing was one of the things that worried the Siblings caring for him most, as he lay somewhere between life and death.

Barricades were being gradually taken down. And as the fear diminished, so the anger rose.

"Here is where he stood," Signor Gambi pointed. "There is only one place that the bolt could have come from, signors. There."

He pointed to the minaret of the place of worship of followers of Mohammed. The new religion had come with settlers from the hinterland but it was not widely embraced here. The city was still principally Greek speaking and was mostly Nestorian, despite the sultan and his men being followers of Islam. The city and the coastal plain had been part of Byzantium once, before the Seljuk conquest. Old memories and old hatreds, because there had been a great deal of persecution before the Ilkhan had come to their borderlands, and resentment of the Dhimmi tax surfaced. After all, under the Ilkhan, tax or tribute was rendered by all non-Mongols, regardless of religion.

That had been mere hours ago. One man pointing, and a loose tongue to say what he pointed to. Old hatreds and new. Fear of the assassins turning to rage. Little enough, in the greater scheme of things. How it turned from unrest, to a baying mob with burning brands heading for the mosque no one was quite sure. Local Greeks and Venetians all united, wanting someone or something visible to punish for their misery of the last few months? Something more than that? It didn't matter. The mob was loose now, and a mob is an animal with many tongues, many teeth, and no head. Those many tongues were howling now. "Burn them! Burn the heathen bastards!"

But somehow word had got to the mosque before them.

Two dozen of the sultan's Seljuk foot soldiers stood there, nervously holding their swords, facing a mob of at least a thousand angry men and women.

"Go back! Go back on the order of the sultan," said the guard commander, nervously. Clearly he was in no mood for a fight, even if his men had not been outnumbered.

One of Venetian merchants pushed forward. "They've shot our podesta from that tower. They've been hiding those Baitini bastards. Get out of the way. We've no fight with the sultan, but we won't let you stop us burning their rats-nest to the ground."

And into this mess walked two men in their Hypatian robes: the abbot and Brother Ambrose, the sibling who had given communion the day the Baitini had tried to commit murder in the church. They were cheered—until they turned around just short of the guards and the elderly abbot addressed them. He was old, but his voice carried. "I cannot let you do this, my children."

The mob suddenly ceased to be a mindless animal—but it was still made of men and women determined to have rough justice. The merchant spoke for them, sternly. "Stand aside, Father! We're doing God's work here."

The abbot was just as stern—and had respect, age and notoriety that the merchant did not. And also, perhaps, the aura of one under the hand of the divine. Certainly at that moment a beam of sunlight touched him, turning his white hair to a kind of halo. "How can you be sure? Was it not Saint Hypatia herself who said the understanding of God by any man is flawed, because God is beyond all human understanding? I cannot stand by and let you burn this place. So Ambrose and I will go inside. If you burn it, you will burn us."

"Those Baitini murderers will kill you, Father."

"Then we will have died an honorable death in the service of God," said the abbot calmly, turning and pushing past the handful of Seljuk guards.

❀   ❀   ❀

Abdullah looked incredulously down from his hideout behind one of the fretted windows just beneath the dome. There was a sill there about three cubits wide, and thanks to the respect the mosque was held in, this place had never been thoroughly searched. The imam, who was now angrily berating the two foreigners who had walked into the holy place shod, was one of the brethren. "Malkis. Look. It's the old infidel priest!" He began reaching for his crossbow. This could not have been better. God smiled upon them, putting their enemy into their very hands. It was surely intended. They were meant to destroy this blasphemer, and strike fear into the hearts of the infidels.

He was unaware that his companion, who had only recently recovered from the beating in the Chapel when they'd attacked the Hypatians at their morning devotions, was staring in horror at the sibling next to the old abbot. Instead he took careful aim and fired . . . just as the furious imam grabbed the abbot, and shoved, intending to send him out the door.

He was also unaware that Malkis, one of the hidden hands of the blade, had drawn his stiletto. A moment after the crossbow-bolt struck home, he drove the thin point into the crossbow-man's brain.

The bolt hit the imam as he grabbed the abbot. The other three senior members of the mosque council, who had been trying to restrain him from this insanity, screamed in unison. Several of the Seljuk soldiers ran inside.

The mob outside, which had been subsiding and starting to trickle away began to rumble and turn.

The Seljuk guard commander stared at his dead

imam, a crossbow bolt protruding from his chest. "Who killed . . ."

In answer one of the mosque's senior counselors pointed to a man sliding down a rope from an opening in the open ornamental fretwork high up the wall, just beneath the dome.

There were yells from outside. "I think I will go and speak to them," said the abbot calmly, as if the chain-mail vest had not helped the bolt to ricochet and left him with bruising that would last a month.

The Seljuk nodded hastily. "Please, Father."

So he did. A little later he came back, with two of the Venetian merchants and a local Greek ship chandler. "It is easier to show them." The three Seljuks were surrounding the man who had lowered himself down—warily and at a safe distance. The Baitini still had a fearsome reputation.

He, however, paid them no mind. "Brother. Holy man," he called to the slight Sibling Ambrose.

Ambrose looked at him. "You were one of those who came to the church and killed Sister Eugenia."

The Baitini assassin nodded. "Yes. You said then that . . . we could repent and accept grace."

"Christ will always accept those who do that," said the sibling, even if his tone indicated that right now, he would rather that it was otherwise.

The Baitini knelt. "I want to do this."

One of the Seljuks, who had been stalking forward behind the assassin, raised his sword. "Hold!" said the abbot. "Let us hear what he has to say."

"They will kill him for his treachery. They always do. Their own are more afraid of their enforcers than anything else," said the Venetian merchant who listened to the confession, along with the rest of the people now crowded into the mosque—to the shock of the council—but at least they were not considering burning it, and all of those in it. In fact, there were murmurs of miracles. Well . . . there was no reason why this could not be a miracle. The abbot was more inclined to believe in God turning the hearts of men than he was in angels deflecting crossbow bolts.

The abbot looked at the still kneeling Baitini assassin, still holding the cross Brother Ambrose had given to him with both hands. "He knows that. He knows that perfectly well. I think he has accepted it."

"What do we do about it? He's a murderer."

"Yes. I think eventually, if he lives long enough, he may come to understand that, too. I think if he lives long enough he could also become a saint," said the abbot.

"So what do we do about it, Father?"

"See that he lives long enough, if we can."

Chapter 29

Off the coast of Callipolis peninsula

"It's not right," said Admiral Borana angrily.

Enrico Dell'este looked coldly at him. "What should we have done, sirrah? Sent messengers to tell them of our actions? Earlier you were demanding that we cannonade the fort, and storm it, for its arrant insolence. You have heard its commander tell you that they had orders to fire on any fleet of vessels regardless of flag. You also heard the man say that we were not expected until early spring. Our ruse on Corfu worked."

"But, but, but..." the man spluttered. "We were not at war! And now the Venetian vessels sail past us. *We* are supposed to lead the fleet."

The Old Fox kept his expression schooled. It was not the first time that he had been forced to deal with a well-born booby, one who was more concerned with appearances than results. "I give you my solemn word. Had the men in that fort allowed you to sail past without firing on you, we would not have captured their fort. We would have sailed on peacefully. We only took action after they had fired you."

Now the booby veered into another complaint. "But they might have sunk us. The ball took away my foremast."

Enrico searched for patience. He did not find much. "The choice was yours. To accept the honor of leading the fleet or not. And had we attacked before they fired on your vessels...we could have started a war that we want no part of."

The admiral was not about to let logic deprive him of a good fury. "But the Venetian vessels do not follow my lead! Several of the great galleys are rowing along the Hellespont as if their lives depended on it. And you gave that order. Not *me*."

"My grandson and two hundred and fifty men have gone to hold eight hundred in their barracks at Callipolis. Would you like them to die while you fuss about precedence?" Enrico stared unblinkingly. "The men of Venice, yes, and Ferrara, and belike your own common sailors by now, would hang you on your own yardarm if you'd caused them to fail those men and Benito Valdosta. And I would cheer them. We need to sail and we need to sail now. No one will know or care which vessel reaches them first, so long as *any* vessel does. There will be ample opportunity for you to go first into the cannons, when we reach Constantinople and beyond. In the meantime we need to take and hold Callipolis."

"Hold?" demanded the admiral suspiciously. Genoa did not want any more strategic territory lost to its rival.

"Until the matter of the fleet in the Black Sea is sorted out. Genoa can remain with the garrison here, if you have no stomach for the fight," said Enrico, with the edge of disdain in his voice.

The Genovese admiral was shocked at the implication. "We will lead it!" he said, proud and, as was his wont, arrogant.

Enrico shrugged. "Well then. Let us see you do so."

"But they're ahead of us!"

"Catch up."

"This is a ship, not a horse," spluttered the admiral. But he called to his captain to tell the men to damned well cut the cables and make all possible sail.

Enrico Dell'este decided to forego telling him that they would not be stopping in Callipolis. A horse-messenger would carry the news to Constantinople fast enough, but there were still many preparations that could be made before a city was ready to face siege. Expensive preparations. Alexius, being the spendthrift wastrel that he was, would not have done those any earlier than he had to.

If they pushed hard and fast, they'd get there just after a panicked city closed its gates. Not later, once the city had had time to order its affairs and be ready for the siege.

Right now they had to keep close to the Callipolis peninsula side, as far as possible from Dardanellia on the Asia Minor shore. There was one narrow point, just over a mile wide, but that was still better than sailing within five hundred yards of the guns.

Strangely enough, the guns were silent. Then Enrico figured it out and had to sit down, after laughing himself into a coughing fit. They were close to the guns on the Callipolis side. Which were silent. No one knew that Benito's goal had been taken, at least not yet. So some clever officer had decided, plainly, that the fleet had somehow got permission to sail through. The military mind's rigidity and assumption that things ran to order was the one advantage that a cunning strategist had.

Callipolis Peninsula

Actually, he was only half right, as he later found out. The opposing fort on the Callipolis side of the Hellespont had been taken entirely by surprise. The Venetians had not even had to blow the gate. On Benito's instructions they had done some investigation about communication with the other fort. One of Benito's men had "persuaded" the officer in charge of the fort at the narrows that he could choose between a fall over the battlements or making a signal to the fort across the water, that word had come from Constantinople that the fleet was to pass, unmolested.

They had some four leagues to row, and little help from the wind. This section of the peninsula was forested and steep, but even so, it was going to be impossible to get to Callipolis before a horseman, or even a runner did. On the other hand, Benito had the advantage of the westerly, and should get to landfall on the western shore long before them. Speed was of the essence as most likely the element of surprise had been lost.

On the west coast, the galliots were making good speed. Part of that was due to the wind. Part of that was probably due to the snoring. Benito would have loved to have a fresh set of legs, and a fresh set of men for this venture. Men lay, or leaned against each other in the cramped space the fast little galleys had to spare. The larger vessel they were supposed to rendezvous with, which would have food, and more men, and even some twenty light cavalry... had not been sighted. So Benito had his leftovers from the Cape Hellas campaign, and two squads of Swiss pikemen—his grandfather's elite footmen that Enrico had insisted come along. They at least were well rested, but that was all Benito had. Callipolis town was relatively small and poorly defended. There was a small village on the bay on the western side of the isthmus that would provide an anchorage of sorts for the round ships and men if they needed to lay siege to Callipolis town. That had to be secured—and would allow them to set up check-points along the main track along the peninsula from the mainland to the town, as they were farther north. In the short term that would mean that they could stop the garrison sending for immediate help, too. It had been his plan to leave the men from the Cape Hellas raid there. Now there was no help for it but to stretch themselves even thinner.

When they landed, they found the village had been recently deserted. Nets were still hanging with net-needles swinging and fires and cookpots were untended. That was hardly surprising. Even if the locals had taken them for Byzantine vessels, which was unlikely since they were fishermen, a group of warships was unwelcome in a little undefended harbor. Not that there was much to steal besides their wives, thought Benito, looking at poverty that made the Libri d'Oro look like the kindest of masters. He'd heard Byzantium was falling apart from the inside: here, he thought, was one of the reasons for that.

"Right. Lieutenant Barassa. You and your three squads will be staying here. You're to hold the town, and interdict the road. Rest some men—you'll need to find horses or runners to keep in touch with us. Keep the men from looting—not that there is anything much to take. And you know how we dealt with rape on Corfu. Tell them the gelding knife is ready for them. We do not need the peasants against us. If you are attacked by a massive force, retreat under arquebus and cannon on the ship, but we won't be able to get back here—so we'll run along towards the forts we hold farther up the peninsula. "The *Cuttlefish*"—he pointed to one of the galliots—"and a skeleton crew will be staying here with you. That means you have a bow-chaser cannon, and something to flee on if need be. The other two vessels will be out there looking for that . . . captain, and the round ship with our reinforcements, and my light cavalry scouts. If they get here, send them on to Callipolis."

He pointed to a steep bluff above the village. The peninsula was barely three miles wide here. From up there they would probably be able to see all the way to the Hellespont. "And put someone on that hill up there to keep a look-out."

The serious-faced young Corfiote-Italian nodded. He knew his skill as a Greek-speaker made him valuable, and he also realized that this was a good opportunity to show that value. "I'll have the men move the cookpots off the fires."

"Good idea. And ready a really big signal bonfire to let us know if there are more than a handful of Byzantine soldiery coming."

"M'lord. I have Henri, who is good with a trumpet. I'll have him sound it too."

"He makes enough noise with it," said Benito wryly. It was true enough. Venetian generals had begun using the brass instruments for maneuvers and Benito had been thinking about it himself. The sound carried well.

And with that Benito had to leave, leading his scanty supply of tired troops on the seven mile march to Callipolis.

It was already well after noon when they began the march, and nightfall would come too soon. But they had little choice, just as they had little choice about their route. There were only two possible roads, if the paths involved could be dignified with the term. Of the two, furthermore, one was a great deal shorter than the other, which would have involved two miles of cross-country and farmland before it was even reached.

Reluctantly, Benito decided they had no choice but to take the shorter of the two routes.

It didn't take long for his reluctance to be justified. The problem with taking the most obvious route to any wartime objective is that the enemy also has a brain, usually knows how to use it, and can come to the same conclusion. They hadn't been on the march for more than an hour and a half before they began encountering Byzantine cavalry units.

Benito knew perfectly well that battle plans seldom survive encounter with the enemy. But this plan, he thought sourly, looked to be coming apart before the first shots were even fired.

He'd learned a lot about war by now, partly from listening to advice—especially that coming from his grandfather—and partly from his own experience. So, sensibly, he'd had his own scouts ahead of the main force precisely for the purpose of warning him if the enemy approached.

The problem was that Benito's "scout unit" was even less qualified for the term than the "road" they were following. The unit should have consisted of light cavalry—and a fairly strong force of cavalry, at that. Strong enough to be able to delay the enemy's advance while sending couriers to the rear bearing the warning.

What Benito had instead was simply a squad of half a dozen men—infantrymen, not cavalry—selected for their physical fitness and carrying nothing beyond their personal weapons. Their gear had been divided among their mates in the units from which they'd been selected.

So, when the scouts encountered the forward units of Byzantine cavalry coming from Calliopolis, they could do nothing more than sound the alarm by blowing their horns—and then racing aside after firing a few (and ineffective) shots. If they'd tried to put up a serious resistance and slow down the oncoming enemy they'd simply have been crushed and run over.

Still, the horns and the fired shots carried far enough to give Benito a warning.

There were forty of Enrico Dell'este's Swiss mercenaries and their long pikes, and Benito deployed them in the road. Had this been a normal battlefield he would have moved his Corfiote irregulars forward of the pike line so they'd have a clear line of fire at the oncoming enemy. The Corfiotes had a mixture of hand-cannon and arquebuses, and a *spada da lato* each. Such weapons were good for a first hard blow at cavalry, but were slow to reload. Once the firearms were discharged, the men would be slaughtered by the cavalry unless they could find shelter behind the pikemen.

The road was too rough and narrow for that sort of standard maneuver, though. The arquebusiers would just get tangled up with the pikemen as they tried to retreat through their lines, which would disorganize the entire force and place all of them at the mercy of the Byzantines.

And Benito thought he had a good alternative. The fields on either side of the road were filled with rows of dead pease drying on their stems—which in turn were twined around and through the lattices that supported them. The lattices consisted of nothing more sturdy than dead branches thrust into the ground, but the end result were fields consisting of what people often called pea brush.

The enemy could drive their horses through the stuff, but they'd be slowed down and their ranks would get disorganized. That might let his Corfiotes inflict enough casualties on the Byzantines to drive them off.

If worst came to worst, he could always set fire to the pease fields. He wanted to avoid that if at all possible, though, since it would make his own route impassable for hours. But he might very well have to do it. They were pretty heavily outnumbered.

The pike-wall held, forcing most of the Byzantines into the pease fields, which slowed their momentum. The arquebusiers fired into the mass; fired again; and yet again.

There came a horn call and the Byzantines broke off. The enemy's commander realized his men had gotten too disorganized—too flustered, also—and wanted to bring order and steadiness back into their ranks. Benito was almost sure he'd order a charge into the pease on one side or the other of the road. If the charge was driven home smartly and forcefully his own forces would have no choice but to retreat onto the other side of the road. They'd probably lose the road itself, after which his own forces would start getting disorganized.

Still, the battle was far from hopeless. Then he heard the sound of a trumpet in the rear. Was this another Byzantine force? If so, they'd be caught between two foes and their situation would be desperate.

But just as dismay became to take hold of the small Venetian band, they heard the sound of the battle hymn of the Knights of the Holy Trinity on the same trumpet. Fear had driven away the tiredness and Benito's mind was sharp enough to work out what was happening. He'd heard the trumpeter Henri practice that tune.

"*Hurrah!*" he yelled. "A rescue! The Knights! The Knights are coming! Hold hard, men!"

He yelled it in Greek, which might have given his men pause. "Cheer, damn you," he said quietly to the men on his right.

They did and, like a ragged volley, the cheering spread. In the distance, the trumpet sounded the brave tune again.

"Hear that!" yelled another man, again in Greek—which was the first language of a fair number of the Corfiotes anyway.

"They're coming!" yelled another.

"Can't be more than a mile away!" shouted one the sergeants.

The Byzantine cavalrymen—reforming in good order just moments before—began milling. A few milled right back down the road toward Calliopolis.

Using every last bit of volume he could muster in his lungs, Benito yelled: *"Prepare to advance!"*

If anyone among the Byzantine cavalry wondered why he was giving orders in Greek, obviously the thought never crystallized. A single rider advanced towards them... waving a white rag.

Benito yelled. "If you lay down your weapons, we will protect you. No one will get hurt." *Except possibly the trumpeter, with the amount of wine the boys will pour into him,* he thought to himself. *Or if the real Knights of the Holy Trinity get to hear of it! That Henri will go far. I really have to look into using trumpets as signals.*

Some of the Byzantines fled. But Benito wound up with nearly two hundred prisoners. It was only a little later that he discovered that a vast fleet had been sighted, news had come that the Cape Hellas fortifications had been captured, and the troop had been in the act of retreating from their indefensible and plainly diseased barracks. Running away, in other words, when the fleeing priest from the village told them there was a small force of Venetians ahead of them.

In the meanwhile Benito sent a man back on one of the captured horses to find out just what was happening behind them.

The horse came back with Lieutenant Barassa instead. "I was on the bluff where you told us to station a lookout. I saw the cavalry coming from Calliopolis—I had to run back down to call Henri... And we didn't have a signal for 'they're in front of you.' So I had him play the Battle Hymn. I... hope I did the right thing, m'lord."

"You did indeed . . . Captain Barassa," said Benito slapping him on the back. "I'll see the Council ratifies that promotion. You have earned it several times over with that bit of quick thinking."

"Thank you, m'lord. And also we've sighted a round ship with the two galliots out in the bay."

"They'd have been in time to bury us. Right. Get back there and tell them to move along. You can take two squads of my men—anyone who can ride, to escort these fellows to the village. The city of Calliopolis knows we're coming now. Let's see if we can make it look like a lot of us are coming."

They set to cutting some of the scrub from a patch of forest land a little farther on. Bunches of branches were tied behind the horses, and in a very noisy company to the sound of horns and whatever the men could find to beat on—from shields to pots—they marched toward Calliopolis, with the men from the round ship and the little group of scouts. Even after the rain, the dust they raised was substantial.

The town came into view soon enough. It was less than five miles from their battle, and, as they came closer they found a fair number of dropped and scattered bundles on the road—people fleeing the town who had heard or seen them coming. They were in reality a pitiful force, but in the dusk that wouldn't have been obvious to the burgers or the merchants.

The troops generously picked up the bundles. Fair enough loot, Benito figured. Besides how would he stop the troops from appropriating it? In the town would be a different matter—the last thing he needed was a drunken sack when he had so few men. The reality was there'd be some trouble. That was the nature of

war, but, as his grandfather said—who was good at
lecturing on these subjects, and because of who he
was, worth listening to—more than one city had been
lost in the counterattack while the conquerors were
in no state to fight back.

The gates were not open, but white flags flew
above them. The emperor Alexius was not going to
be pleased when he heard about that. Neither were
the townsmen when they discovered that the conquering army was less than half of the size of the town's
supposed defenders. True, they could probably not
have stood off a long assault by the fleet, but that
would have taken time, and bypassing Calliopolis
would have meant leaving a festering trouble spot for
the fleet's return. The Council of Ten and the Doge
had decided: the passage to the Black Sea must no
longer remain under Byzantine control. That meant
taking and holding the Calliopolis peninsula. Having
looked at the maps Benito could see the practical
possibilities of keeping control of the peninsula. At
sea the Venetians were a more potent force than the
Byzantines, and already held various islands. This was
a matter of holding a narrow strip of land whose garrison could be supplied by sea, well out of reach of
the Byzantines and their allies.

The local governor was plainly a man of nerve, as
he came to the gate to greet the invaders. Alone. "I
would like to discuss terms for surrender," he said,
with scarce a tremor to his voice.

Worth keeping on, thought Benito. "We will agree
to reasonable terms," he said, calmly. "Provided there
is complete surrender. No violence against ourselves
or the fleet. Most of our troops are remaining outside

the city. I'll bring a couple of hundred trusted men to police things. Of course, food and a limited amount of wine must be provided, along with defensible quarters. And the Winged Lion of Venice flies above the city."

"Er...how many men?"

"As many as we see fit," said Benito, grimly, beginning to revise his initial impression.

"Just for catering m'lord," said the man hastily. "There are stocks in the military barracks, and I will order some sheep fetched. But it appears you have a vast host."

"We'll pass on their wine. I will, however, *buy* wine. Say three casks of mavrodaphne. I have a very good idea of costs," added Benito, "so tell the taverner that, and that he'll get to drink a healthy measure in my presence before the troops get any. And we'll have a few hostages to good behavior."

Benito set about organizing a roster of watches and frightening his men out of rapine and obvious looting. Some would still happen, probably. He also let the men know that they'd be doing well out of the town's revenue for the next year. "So keep it in one piece so it can earn for us. And don't, whatever you do, drink the wine from the Byzantine barracks unless you want to believe your innards have melted."

The first vessels of the fleet, looking as if they were racing and not proceeding in an orderly and dignified manner, came into sight in the twilight. Benito had a bonfire lit in front of the flagpole on the harbor-wall tower, so that the Winged Lion of Saint Mark and, just above it, the red cross of Genoa, and just below, the flag of the Kingdom of Aragon could be seen. That might make Borana a little less upset, Benito hoped.

He could hope for the rain showers to turn into gold flakes too.

By nightfall the next day the fleet—less those who had stayed to hold the Callipolis peninsula—had sailed out into the Propontis, despite complaints from Admiral Borana about how dangerous it was to sail at night. They had a strong following wind, moonlight, and merpeople to keep them well clear of any shoals or islands.

Benito wondered if Captain Di Tharra from Sardinia was making pre-dawn visits to the bow, alone. He'd bet on it being likely.

Chapter 30

Venice

Venice, the Serenissima, settled toward winter, with high tides and strong winds and some flooding. A slowly sinking city built on lagoon mud and with water-streets was prone to problems at this time of year. So were her people. This was when cold kept the smell down and mixed with the damp to bring out the chest complaints instead. It became the city of fogs and coughs, and Marco found himself very busy treating the latter and wishing the fogs would go away. Also, for the first time, he was suddenly very worried about transporting some of these illnesses from the poor to the *Casa* Montescue, and his brother's daughter. Kat—well, he had never worried about Kat, she was an adult, had grown up on the canals, and was as healthy as he. But children were so fragile. He'd seen for himself how a cough became a fever, and the fever raged through the little bodies and carried them off. Benito and Maria trusted him, and he loved the child. He would not risk her.

So as soon as he came through the door, even though he knew Francisco was waiting, he went through the careful ritual of washing and changing his garments that

Francisco had said to be the normal way with physicians among the Barbary, where he'd apparently been enslaved and begun learning most of his medical skills. The garments themselves went off to be fumigated with pungent herbs. The origins of the ritual might be religious, but Marco was willing to take a chance on pleasing some unknown god if it would keep Alessia safe.

His Arabic teacher was waiting in the library, with what he called life's essentials: a mug of beer and a book. There was also a fire burning in the grate, and the place was warm—which after the damp foggy chill outside Marco found welcome. He doubted that Francisco had asked for the fire himself. He'd concluded after visiting Francisco's chambers that if the man had beer and a book he wouldn't notice the temperature. This must have been Kat's doing, bless her. He had to clear his throat before Francisco even noticed he'd come in.

His tutor looked up with no sign of annoyance that he'd been kept waiting. "Ah, m'lord. How does the reading progress?"

Marco sighed and sat down on another comfortable chair and put his feet up to the fire. "Slowly. This part of that Sina treatise appears to be entirely composed of lists—most of which are items I have no translations for."

"It's essential that you build up your vocabulary somehow," said Francisco, smiling crookedly, "or you'll never cope with the Qanun. He was methodical, you have to grant that."

Marco nodded. "Oh yes. It's all quite logical. And fascinating. I am still learning a great deal about new treatments, and some of the ideas make sense."

"And some don't. Still, it's better than a lot of what passes for medicine in the Empire."

The door burst open and, with a shriek of delight, a small toddler hurtled in and flung herself on Marco Valdosta.

Marissa came hurrying after. "I'm sorry, m'lord. I don't know how she knew you were here."

Marco cuddled her; she giggled. Why did little children always smell so good? The clean ones, anyway. "She always does, somehow. I'll come and read to you later, 'Lessi. Go with Marissa."

She smiled and clung to him. "Come too."

"Later, my love. Just now, Uncle Marco has schoolwork to do." Marco kissed the curls and handed her back to Marissa. Alessi made a token protest as she was carried out, but no more than that. "Now, let me just find those notes I made."

But this was not going to be the peaceful, studious afternoon he had wished. Running footsteps in the hall heralded another interruption, and the door burst open a second time. "M'lord!" the footman in the door way said urgently. "M'lord, the Doge is calling for you. He wants you immediately."

Marco sighed. "Francisco. Another day. Perhaps Tuesday?"

"Tuesday is fine, M'lord Valdosta."

"The Schiopettieri are waiting with a gondola, m'lord," said the footman. "The capitano said it was very urgent. And to bring your medical things."

"I'd better run then. Goodbye, Francisco. Please finish your beer!"

He left at a run. Francisco drained his beer and stood up. So... someone important, possibly even the Doge himself, needed medical attention. Well, they

were wise to call young Marco. That information must
be sent along.

In the passage he saw the child again, and her...
nursemaid? The woman seemed a little more than
that; there was something about her that called to
mind the gently-reared. Francisco looked at her face,
trying to think where he'd seen her before. Ah. That
was it. In much poorer clothes, and at a secondhand
shop down in Cannaregio. With the fellow, Poulo,
who had said that if he had any problems he should
go to the Villa Parvitto. Odd...

It wasn't a gondola waiting, but one of the Schiopettieri's fast little skiffs with six oars to the side.
And the men rowed as hard as they could. Plainly this
wasn't just that the Doge needed him for something,
but that it was a disaster, and whatever the disaster
was, it was urgent. Marco wanted to ask, but knew
better than to do so. The rowers might well—by the
way the Council of Ten and Petro worked—not have
been told. Rumor could affect the safety of Venice
and the value of trade, all too easily.

They cut through the cold, greasy water and the
drifting fog as fast as a shark; other boats cleared
out of their way. Marco didn't even have time to get
chilled, they were moving so fast.

They went to the side entry of the Palazzo Ducale,
to the water-door. Marco was greeted by a waiting
captain of the Swiss guard, and rushed upstairs to
Petro's chambers, his apprehension growing with every
step. The palace was *too* quiet. He sensed hysteria
under the quiet, waiting to break out at any time.

The moment he got inside the door of the Doge's

bedchamber, Marco could see why he'd been called. Petro Dorma was as pale as his bed-linen.

"Marco," he said weakly. "Stop these idiots from bleeding me. My heart. Like my father..."

His hand, when Marco took it to take his pulse, was cold and trembling slightly. The pulse was racing.

Within Marco Valdosta, the Lion stirred. Was this an attack by magic? It had no feeling of that. Yet the Lion was aroused. "When did this start?" he asked.

"About twenty minutes back, m'lord," said the Swiss guard captain, pointing to one of the late Doge Foscari's ornate time pieces.

And that would have made it perhaps three quarters of an hour from lunch. The Lion was roused, and the Doge had been healthy before lunch. This was no ailing heart. Marco grabbed the silver bleeding bowl, opened his bag and hauled out a bottle. "You are going to drink this, and you are going to vomit." He had read of symptoms like this in one of the Arab texts, and he was sure he was right.

"What is it?" said Petro weakly, pushing it away. "I feel sick already and my mouth is full of saliva."

"Salt-water and mustard-water, together. Drink it now. You have been poisoned and we need to get it out of you while there is still time."

There was a gasp of horror from those there, but Petro let Marco help him to drink the mixture. And then he was sick as Marco held his head.

Marco turned to the captain. "I need one Francisco of Genoa. He may be found at his chambers above the *Sotoportego* Marciano in San Polo. And tell him to bring his Ibn Sina. And keep this bowl. See no one touches it."

"Aben Sinner?" the captain puzzled out.

"He'll know. It's a medical book. As fast as possible." He gestured abruptly. "Go, man!" The captain ran for the water-door.

Marco looked about at those filling the Doge's chamber. With a man as important as Petro Dorma, not even illness was private. He was not surprised to see two of the Council of Ten there, sans masks. He knew full well who they were, even though officially he was not supposed to. "We will need to check, with speed, on the taster, and the cooks and anyone else who could have handled his food and drink."

Lord Calmi nodded. "How bad is it, Marco Valdosta?"

Marco looked at the Doge, pale, lying back exhausted on his pillows. "I don't know," he admitted. "I think . . . get Patriarch Michael too."

"Am I dying?" asked Petro weakly.

"I'm going to do my best to stop that from happening," said Marco, taking his pulse. It was slightly improved, he thought.

"Then why are you calling a priest?" He must be getting better. He sounded irritated.

"Because you can always use a few prayers," Marco told him. "And you are the Doge. He is the Patriarch of Venice. He needs to know what has happened to you, and if possible, how. You were poisoned despite all your precautions. That is *not* a good thing."

The Doge nodded weakly. "Do your best, Marco. I'm not really ready to die yet."

Marco did his best to look competent, confident, and reassuring, though he was not himself certain of any of the three. "I will, Petro Dorma."

"If we bleed him we could drain off the toxic

humors," said the physician whose bowl Marco had used, waving his cupping-tools.

Toxic humors indeed! "OUT—NOW!" Marco roared. It was a true roar, and it was unmistakable. Someone threatened the peace of the Lion's lagoon, and the Lion was in a mood to tear into something. The physicians fled. The Council stayed.

Very soon after that Marco had to roar at the rest of the Council of Ten. "The Doge is still very much alive. I intend to keep him that way. Go and find out who did this."

"We have the cooks, baker, servitors, taster," said Lord Calmi, not moving. "Schiopettieri have gone to the fish-market, and to the vegetable sellers. But three people dined with him—I was one of them. We had some antipasto, bread, Saint Peter's fish, peas, and preserved artichokes, and a simple mascarpone cream. Nothing exotic. I am not ill and neither is anyone else. Are you sure, Marco Valdosta?"

"Have your rat-catcher catch some rats," said Francisco, who had entered with the Swiss guard captain. "Feed them on the vomitus—split as much as you can into components. Rats will eat anything. If any die—you will know it was poison. And if they don't die, it wasn't."

Lord Calmi blinked. "That makes sense . . . who are you?"

"I called him to advise me on this poison," said Marco. "As you've just said, Francisco speaks sense."

Francisco cleared his throat. "And, I am afraid, m'lord, you'll have to get at least two other *Case Vecchie* to oversee the test. You see, those of you who ate with the Doge are suspects, too."

Lord Calmi turned red, then white, then red again. "What? How dare..."

"He's quite right," said Petro, his voice still weak, but his tone firm. "You must remove all suspicion, Niccolo my friend. And if you order it so, it does reduce it. Now please. Leave me in peace." And finally the room cleared. Marcos turned to his tutor.

"Francisco," said Marco, "it looks like that 'Vobulis' I read of in that list of toxins in the Sina treatise. The racing and irregular heartbeat, the tremors, the excessive saliva. I don't recall... is there an antidote? I made him vomit."

Francisco pulled at his lower lip. "Oleander. It could be, m'lord. I've seen men poisoned with it before. Accidentally, but still. They died. No, there is no antidote, but getting it out of him was a good idea. With luck he hasn't gotten a fatal dose. Well, luck and sending for you right away, instead of going with those quacks. And now we need to absorb any that is still there, if we can."

"You're not bleeding me. I feel faint enough," protested Petro.

"I've never seen any good effects from bleeding," said Francisco. "No, I would say that the best I could recommend would be to eat a handful of coarse crushed charcoal or burned bread. Al Fafis found it effective in countering certain poisons. It's harmless at best and may help. Al Fafis experimented on slaves and condemned men. He used the rats, too."

"Get me some charcoal," said Marco. "I have a mortar and pestle in my bag."

"Make it burned bread," said Petro. "It's easier to swallow."

It was a long evening, and Marco watched anxiously as Petro's heart rate raced and then slowed and then raced again. But it did show signs of moderating. And then Lord Calmi came back with the entire Council of Ten. "It was something in the fish, Marco," he said grimly. "The rat that ate the fish has died and two of the other rats are dying as well. We have found the fish-merchant dead—murdered. Probably a falling out among thieves. We searched the fish-merchant's premises and found far too much gold."

Marco frowned, puzzled. "Somehow they poisoned the fish—yet you ate the fish, and you are fine. Francisco says that unlike other poisons, you cannot build up a tolerance to this one. You all ate the same thing, but for some reason it only affected him."

Calmi peered at him, anxiously. "Will the Doge live, Marco? Rumor runs around Venice already."

Marco shrugged, helplessly. "We've done all we can. He's somewhere between coma and sleep right now. And we don't know. He may recover."

"I'm awake," said a frail voice. "And I can tell you how they did it. I always eat the bit of meat between the gill and that little fin. It tasted a bit odd today. No one else had that piece, because my guests were courteous enough to let me have it."

Marco hurried to the bedside. Dorma looked a little better. Still pale, weak, but no longer cold, and his heartbeat seemed stronger. "Your Grace! Are you feeling better?"

Dorma made a face. "No. But I no longer have my mouth flooded with saliva. Now please leave me in peace. Go and find out who paid the fish-merchant."

❁   ❁   ❁

The Black Brain of Vilna had no magical entry into Venice. But the news of the success of the poisoning carried to Milan, to Duke Filippo Maria, and thence to Vilna. Filippo Maria was delighted. The Grand Duke of Lithuania, merely pleased. Word would reach the Venetian fleet eventually, and that would have a demoralizing effect.

The news came slightly sooner to Carlo Sforza—and he was a great deal closer to Venice than Milan. Well. This would probably mean war, and Enrico Dell'este and his son were not in Venice to defend it.

He began preparations.

It was late, but the *Casa* Montescue had been in a foment with Marco being called to the Doge. Poulo would be pleased to know that. He might reward her. The craving overrode every other thought in her head. She hugged Alessia . . . with that brief flood of terrible torment of memories of her own babe . . . and what had happened and what she'd done, warring in her breast. But soon. Soon she would have some more. More with the happiness and heartsease it brought.

Marissa made her way to Cannaregio, past the now deserted hulk of the *Casa* Dandelo. She did not look at it, but she still knew it was there.

Chapter 31

Constantinople

Constantinople, great Constantinople, the golden city, crowned in the evening light, the immense dome of the Hagia Sophia almost glowing, surrounded by walls and towers. It looked as if it would stop the sea itself, let alone the forces that the expedition had at its disposal.

"It's the weakest it has been for centuries," said Enrico Dell'este, obviously reading Benito's thoughts, as they stood at the brow of the hill on the Island of Antigoni, one of the so-called Princes' Islands, barely a league from the city. The islands had been a soft and easy target, and gave them a relatively secure place to store materiel and allow troops to rest and regroup. They'd barely been defended. "There are perhaps fifty thousand souls inside the walls, whereas once there would have been half a million."

Benito shook his head. "That's still a lot more force than we can bring to bear—nor can we afford to leave it behind us."

The Old Fox nodded agreement. "Not with two

leagues of the Bosphorus to make targets of us on our return."

"And we really need somewhere to lay up for the worst of the winter." To some extent the islands' little harbors would do. But that would leave the fleet scattered and less able to defend itself. And, besides, they needed the momentum. Right now, every man in the fleet, from Admiral Borana to the lowest oarsman on a Venetian galliot, was boiling with anger. The fleet had split to launch as near simultaneous attacks on the islands as possible. It was likely some fisherman or merchant vessel would get wind of the fleet and run to Constantinople, but the city had probably been alerted to the loss of Callipolis anyway.

Admiral Borana had been assigned the capture of Plati—on the grounds that it had a church manned by the order of Saint Pelion, from Genoa, on it. It was also very small and had, as a place of exile, no more than a handful of residents.

Only when they arrived to capture it, they discovered that it didn't have a "few." It had a lot. In chains. Emperor Alexius had decided to purge his capital of possible trouble, and had rounded up all the Latins his troops could find. Those that had not been killed had been confined on Plati, to be sold.

"We were lucky I suppose," said one grim Venetian merchant. "My family, all but my eldest son, went with the Eastern Fleet. But the bastards killed my boy. I don't know how I will explain this to my Liza. But it was just as well we got so many out. Some people did escape the city as the troops rounded us up, but they killed any man that so much as looked as if he might resist, and raped women in the street. Those of us left alive were herded onto cattle boats and brought here against the summer slave-trade. And we got off lightly compared to the Genovese. They weren't as frightened when things started to get bad, they relied on their treaty, and there were more of them, and more of their families stayed. The Jews were treated even worse. Alexius had them tortured to find hidden monies. He was neck deep in debt to their bankers. Of course the bankers had mostly left."

The enslaved Latins wanted Greek blood, and the head of Alexius on a pike, and the sooner the better. The problem now was not so much getting the fleet to proceed on to Constantinople, as stopping a precipitous and unplanned attack. That took all Benito's influence and skill, and Enrico Dell'este's flat veto of any headlong rush.

"Tomorrow afternoon, we sail in formation, keeping almost a mile away from the walls," Benito announced. "The bombards will be charged now by the specialists we've brought along. They will fire sequentially, not all at once. And don't even think about any crazy ideas like putting anything else into them. Don't even think about it. You'll kill yourselves and you'll sink your ships. At the signal from the flagship, the vessels will turn and repeat the maneuver."

"We want those Greek bastards' blood! And we're willing to die to get it," said one of the enslaved and now freed Genovese, waving a sword around with grave danger to his cheering comrades.

Enrico Dell'este stared at them coldly until the cheering subsided. "You all know who I am. Let me explain this clearly: We're here not to die, but to see that they do the dying. You won't be pleasing your families or your state by spilling Greek blood only to have yours spilled immediately afterwards. Revenge is only satisfying when you survive to enjoy it. I do not make sails, or row galleys. I would not do those as well as the men who are fitted to those tasks and experienced at them. But I win wars against the odds. And the odds are against us. Do you want to win or die?"

"Win, Old Fox," said one of the sailors, daring to use the duke's nick-name.

"Then you will do as you are instructed to do. Now, prepare yourselves. Benito—" There was a cheer from the Venetians, and a good few of the rest. His reputation and following had spread, it seemed. When the cheering died down, Dell'este continued. "Benito and I go to talk to the cavalry in the horse-transports, and to the marines."

"More dare-devilry I bet," said one of the big Venetian bo'suns, grinning. "Well, mates, I'll personally clout the head off the shoulders of any man who spoils the young Fox's tricks."

"He's not just a fox," said another. "He's a good half lion that one! But I am with Barto. To work, lads. We do precisely what the schemers want us to do. They'll have us fight soon enough, if I know them. And I served on Corfu with the young Valdosta. I could tell you a tale or two."

"You already have," said a third man, but there was no more talk of storming the walls.

The cavalry, such as they were, and the marines were going to make two landings, one to the southwest of the city walls and the other on the northern side of the Golden Horn. That was across the harbor from the City, beyond the citadel of Pera, or Galata as it was sometimes called. The great chain that prevented vessels entering the shelter of the Golden Horn was spanned from the Galata tower to the tower at St. Dimitrios in the City.

Both landings would hopefully establish a beachhead. Both would attract a response from the defenders of the city—but with luck more attention would focus on the bombardment from the sea.

Up on the hilltop of Antigoni, a large bonfire burned. They could see that in the city and wonder. They could see it in Galata, too.

Antimo Bartelozzi could see it as well.

Antimo had returned to city of Constantinople, against a tide of fleeing refugees. The Greek countryside was not a very hospitable place either for Latins—Venetians, Pisans, and Genovese and others from across Italy and farther afield, fleeing the city. But there was a chance outside the city, if you had money and luck, of getting away. For those who stayed, it appeared that the emperor Alexius had other ideas.

On the positive side, Antimo was now in the guise of Dimitris Maskaritios, and spoke Greek like a trader from northern Thrace. Coming into the city attracted far less predatory attention than fleeing it, right now.

Anyway, he did not plan to stay long. Just long enough to verify certain things—and long enough to see if he could find a woman with long dark tresses of soft curls, and slightly reddened eyes. And her two dogs.

Antimo Bartelozzi was good at ferreting things out.

He was also afraid for her, when he saw how social order was breaking down in the city. Rape of foreign women was now proclaimed a public service by some of the louder thugs.

He was, by force of necessity a good artist. The picture of her face was recognizable. But asking questions in the area he'd seen her in...no one did recognize her, except a couple of drunks.

One shuddered. "Her an' her dogs. I seen them, yeah. Early morning. Not the kind of face you forget."

The drunk was vague as to when, but it had been recently. "I thought she was going to open the gateway to hell for me. What do you want to find her for, mister? Now, you got the price of a drink about you?"

Antimo gave him some coppers, enough for the sort of wine he was drinking. So why *did* he want to find her? And just who was she?

Antimo knew magic existed. He knew that there were forces above and beyond the natural. He had just spent his life avoiding thinking about them. Part of his mind knew already what he was dealing with, he just wasn't quite ready to actually acknowledge what it was. So he went on looking for a mundane and prosaic answer to the conundrum that was the tall woman and her red-eared dogs in the night-time city.

Hekate watched. She watched the happenings of the city. She watched some of the wider world, now, more aware of it than she had been in millennia.

She, naturally, saw her believers. They were few, it was true, but the old strength began to flow in her. She saw Antimo searching for her. So: he had come back.

The disturbing thing for the goddess of the cross-roads was that he did not seek her as a devotee. He searched for her as man might for a woman.

She was Hekate. Goddess of the Crossroads, Opener of Gateways, Lady of the Night, Mistress of the Hunt, She who watched over birthing of children. She was the guardian of passages, whether it was of children as they passed from one world into this one, or as the one who opened the way below as mortals passed again through the gates between life and death.

She had also once been a woman. She had loved as a woman—and she had been a woman hurt and betrayed by her lover. He had taken their children as hostages, killed one and destroyed her gate.

He'd never wanted anything but conquest, she now understood. She would not go down that road again.

But she watched Antimo Bartelozzi. Now that she was regaining some of her old power, that was not hard.

If she'd watched the Earth-Shaker like that, instead of like a besotted fool, she would have known how false he was to her, and to Amphitre. And what he did to Caeneus.

Her dogs, however, wanted to talk to Antimo. She was a goddess, and a goddess forgets her dignity and what is due her at her peril.

Eventually, he followed the fitting forms. A libation spilled out at the crossroads. She could hardly not answer that. But he did not ask for guidance, as her dogs rubbed up against him and he petted them. Instead, he looked directly into her eyes and spoke, earnestly, as if to an equal, not a goddess.

"I had almost given up on finding you. Hekate, you must get out of here."

She stiffened. No one told her that she must do anything. She was a goddess! Who was this mortal man to order her about as if she was some mortal wench with no sense of her own safety, or her own power?

"I think not."

His face showed his distress, and his words came in tones of entreaty. "They're already attacking women because they look 'foreign.' And when the city falls, they'll attack them because they look Greek. You have to leave. I can arrange it."

"I need no protection."

"Soon you won't be able to leave," he said, pleading, even desperate.

"I go where and when I will. If I choose to leave, none will hinder my passing."

And to prove her point, she drew the cloak of night around her, and called her dogs and walked away.

Antimo Bartelozzi looked around in the darkness for a while; wondering, not for the first time, what had got into him and why he should care about her—and just who, exactly, he was dealing with. Eventually he gave up and began preparing for his move to Pera. He hoped that he had not wasted too much time here in Constantinople. He didn't want to be inside the city when the fleet got here.

He found a ferryman to row him over the Golden Horn in the morning. "They say that Callipolis has fallen!" said the oarsman. "You're lucky to get me. I'm taking my boat upriver and going to visit my cousin Thanni later this week."

Antimo made no comment. That was best. But he wondered if the man had a week. Enrico Dell'este took his method of battle from working iron. Strike fast and repeatedly while the metal is yet hot. Constantinople was going to be a dangerous place again today. There was going to be more trouble for the remaining Latins. They'd been rounding them up again yesterday, and not even money was saving them.

He still worried about Hekate, even if logic said that she had refused every attempt he made to help, and that she plainly wielded some very powerful magic.

By afternoon he was quietly making his way north, away from Pera and heading for a village some five miles away.

He could see the Princes' islands from here, and a column of smoke rising. The metal was hot. The blows would fall.

Chapter 32

Constantinople

The galliots and horse transports sailed past the slowly forming-up fleet, heading on toward the mouth of the Bosphorus. Another group was heading southwest to make and hold a landing there.

"Right. Have we all got this clear?"

"Are you sure you wouldn't rather ride?" said Captain Terraso, grinning. It was the time for nervous jokes. None of this group of veterans had any delusions about Benito choosing to ride anything. It was afternoon already, with the lowering sun casting long shadows on the water.

"Do you want to swim that badly?" growled Benito. "Otherwise you can help with the palisade sections. Or I'll make you carry hay."

That was a dire threat. The hay bales were oil-soaked and stank.

They were out of effective cannon range when they made the landing. That did not stop the cannon on the walls of Pera fortress from being fired. They could hear the distant boom and whistle of the stone balls and see the billows of smoke—at least until a far louder boom echoed across the water from the lead great galley in the Venetian fleet. The Genovese and Aragonese fired their ship-cannon too, ineffectually and without anything like the sort of vast flash and smoke that came from the Venetian galley.

By the time the fifth great galley fired its forty-eight-pound bombard, a fifth of Constantinople's citizenry were standing on the walls. Benito could hear their jeering from a couple of miles off. And with each shot that had absolutely no effect but to wreath the vessels in smoke and provide a noisy show of pyro-technics, their mocking got louder. Even on the walls of Pera, and of the Galata tower, there was limited attention paid to a possible landing to the north. To the southwest, the same was happening, but with Aragonese knights and Genovese marines.

At the beach, which had been so carefully sounded by Antimo in the guise of fishing off a local dingy, the vessels swung sharply for the shore, the rowers giving their all. The horse transports—basically little more than flat barges with oarsmen—led, and struck the sand.

"Charge!"

The horse transports allowed the handful of knights and light cavalry to sortie through the shallows and up onto the beach. The Byzantine knights who had been riding along keeping watch on the vessels were still trying to get down to the beach, when the weight of the charge got to them.

For once the battle plan did not go horribly wrong. Byzantine cavalry was no match for the heavier Italian knights. They sounded their horns calling for support.

Which of course came sortie-ing out of Pera. A troop of Dacian mercenaries—light cavalry, but outnumbering the Venetian horsemen.

In the meanwhile, out in the bay before the walls of Constantinople, the pyrotechnic display had now turned and was sailing south.

The specialists Benito had hired had done their work well. When the traveling firework maker from far off Hind had found his way to Corfu, Benito had thought that there might be war-purpose in his flashy rockets. Unfortunately they were very inaccurate.

But a delight to watch.

The marines waited behind the hastily set up pre-built sections of palisade pushed onto the beach, not watching the light and smoke show from the Venetian fleet. As the sortie chased the knights and their light cavalry outriders back toward the palisade, they lit the hay bales and used the small trebuchet to toss them about the area. It was smoky and chaotic looking. The knights reached the palisade gate, which was opened. In they charged, and straight back into the water and onto their transports. The Dacian mercenaries and the few remaining Byzantines charged the half closed gate...which opened.

There was lots of smoke and dust and shots fired.

From his observation post on the hill Antimo could see dust and smoke. And then galliots and horse transports pulling away from the shore, and the palisade burning as the mounted troops retreated from it.

Out in the bay, the light-show continued.

The Dacians had obviously taken some captives. They had hauled a cart from the palisade, and they were herding prisoners onto it, and heading back, cheering and blackened, toward the gates of Pera.

Lying in the cart, bumping along with the two small cannon and the other "loot," Benito wondered if maybe they should have saved a little hay. Or if maybe he should learn to ride properly. Force of circumstances had made him better at it. But Marco had merely to take a few lessons to ride like a gentleman born. Benito still looked like a peasant on a stolen pony. He wouldn't fool anyone.

Dacians were not popular. The eastern postern gate opened for them all the same, but all the duty officer wanted to know was where Captain Nelbaskortious and his cuirassiers were.

"They took off after some of the Venetian knights who didn't make it back to their boats," answered the leader of the Dacians, in heavily accented Greek.

"Well, get back to your barracks. You have prisoners?"

"Our prisoners. Our slaves. No officers. Half dead anyway." The leader of the Dacians had a fierce look on his face.

The duty officer wasn't looking for a fight. "They'll be wanted for questioning," he said placatingly.

"We drink first. Then I send to Commander Haberdegiou."

"I can have some of my men take them."

"Nu! Our captives. Our honor."

The duty officer sighed. He'd swear he'd never seen this particular hairy barbarian before. "Go on. See you have them at the Galata tower in the next hour."

The tired-looking grimy mercenaries got little further notice for their efforts, which was just how they wanted it. They proceeded to ride on toward their supposed barracks.

At least as far as the first corner.

There they turned a sharp right and headed toward the inner wall and the Galata tower.

The guard commander on the inner gate was a mere sergeant and mercenary too. Half the Byzantine force were mercenaries, Slavs and Bulgars, Armenians and tribesmen from Asia minor. Byzantium offered citizens the chance to pay someone to serve for them.

The problem with that system is that while mercenaries don't mind being paid to serve, they're not at all keen on being paid to die. And if someone were willing to pay them more...

A cavalry captain for instance could earn twenty thousand ducats by changing sides. It was the common practice to hire a captain and his company, and not to recruit individual mercenaries. So if a captain changed sides, he took his men with him.

"Where are you going?" demanded the sergeant.

"Orders from fool captain on the gate," said Captain Terraso, peering out from under the rim of his Dacian helmet. The original owner of the helmet was now at sea on a Venetian galley. "Take the prisoners to Commander Haberdegiou."

"Not all of you!" said the guard sergeant.

"All!" insisted Terraso. "All need honor. We beat up Venetians!"

"Where are you from? You don't sound like a Dacian."

Which might not have been a clever thing to say as a number of the mercenaries had edged closer and were now surrounding him and his four men.

He died without getting an answer. One of the others did scream, briefly.

The new gate guard of the inner gate was a lot more numerous. Still, subduing them didn't take long at all. The survivors were left in the care of the men who'd been slightly wounded in the fight. The rest of Benito's marines headed onward and upward toward the Galata tower.

The tower was at the highest and the strongest point of Pera on the wall away from the sea. It was intended to be a crucial defensive point against any land-based attack, and a deterrent and a point of fire to prevent a repeat of the Rus attack of 870 on Byzantium where they'd avoided the great chain by portage.

It had an outer gate. A well-guarded double outer gate with two gate towers and a second inner gate.

The tower also had a back entrance, with a somewhat less effective door and a portcullis, giving access to the citadel.

They didn't try to take that en masse—although the two cannon were ready, back in the shadows, as was the charge. Instead, Benito and three of his best knife-men were led up to the door by a mere half dozen "Dacian" mercenaries.

"Venetian captives for Commander Haberdegiou!" sang out Terraso, proudly.

The Byzantine guard looked out of his peephole at the small, scruffy group standing in the flare of the brand at the door. "I'll send someone to see if the Tourmarches Haberdegiou will see you." His snotty tone suggested they should have washed and polished their armor first.

Nonetheless, the door was opened shortly, by a squad of far smarter looking foot soldiers ready to accompany them. Their sergeant decided that he wanted to spit in Benito's face.

Matters got very ugly, briefly.

Fortunately, the screams were a long way below the battlements where the commander and most of his officers were enjoying the show out in the bay. The very loud and spectacular show.

The rest of the "Dacians" filed hastily, but without any unseemly running, into the tower, and then closed the door and dropped the portcullis.

Out in absolute darkness on the crowded vessels the cream of Ferrara and Aragon's knights and a lot of anxious seamen edged their way toward the beach that the Venetians had "retreated" from earlier. There were a good hundred men on the beach already, and they had been hard at work, constructing leading bonfires. But they hadn't lit them.

Everything had to wait on cannon fire from inside Pera.

The nervous wait nearly ended badly. The clatter of riders brought weapons to the ready. "It's us, you fools," said someone in Frankish. "The Valdosta says to light the fires. We didn't even have to use the cannons. We hold the gates and the access to the walls."

Soon troops were pouring onto the beach, heading for Pera in a solid, dark mass, with the duke of Ferrara at their head.

Unopposed, the column marched in through the military sally port of the Galata tower. Benito had had his men strip off their Byzantine gear by then.

They hadn't needed the cannon. There were nearly two thousand invaders inside the city of Pera before more fighting even occurred. And that was with a badly outnumbered patrol, intended to keep the peace in a military citadel, not deal with an invasion.

Falkenberg had once told Benito that more castles fell by treachery than by siege, and Benito had never forgotten it. And anyway, it had been the first thing his grandfather had suggested.

The morning saw a very surprised Constantinople wake to the sight of the flags of Genoa, Venice and Aragon flying over their fortress, and the chain no longer protecting the far less well-built city wall along the Golden Horn.

But their surprise was less than that of the Megas Droungarios, the grand admiral of the Byzantine central fleet, as the Venetians and Genovese vessels attacked his fleet. The Greek admiral had thought his ships safely at anchor in the Golden Horn, protected by the great chain and the cannon on the walls of Constantinople and the citadel of Pera.

The great bombards they'd laughed at yesterday were being set up today on the horse transports behind wicker gabions filled with earth. Horse transports were, after all, little more than big barges, quite large and stable enough to sustain the effects of being firing platforms, and anchored in shallow water, where, if they sank, they could be hauled out, to continue to fulfill their true purpose—blasting holes in the smaller walls facing onto the Golden Horn.

And that too was merely one of the plans the Old Fox, Venice, and Benito had engineered.

PART V
January, 1541 A.D.

Chapter 33

Vilna

The roving eye of Chernobog slid across the strange landscapes of other planes of existence, whose geography bore but tenuous links to that of the world where Jagiellon was on the throne of the Grand Duchy of Lithuania. Great distances became small and some small distances, great.

She was watching him. No longer weeping—and not so weak. An old goddess, just as he was an old daemon. She drew on worship for power. He drew on other things, not least the life-force of his host. He slipped past and upward into his host-spy, one of the beardless ones of Constantinople's civic administration.

What he discovered did not please him at all.

Cannon fire did not worry Chernobog. The sound of it, and the smoke, were quite pleasing to him.

But it had no place here and now. It did not fit in with his plans, not with the fleet he was building icebound in the Dnieper, and the Golden Horde not coming south in a conquering wave, but fighting a civil war. A civil war that in winter consisted of sitting in their gers.

He walked the eunuch, jerkily, toward the windows of the palace of Mangana. His eyes saw precisely what he should not see, over to the north of the city of all places—The Lion of Saint Mark, and other emblems, flying above the fortress to the north.

The fleet he had not expected here until, at the earliest, spring-time. He knew just what the Lion of Saint Mark had deployed against him. He could no more believe this was mere human work any more than he could accept that the Lion was willing to be confined to the ancient marshes of Etruria.

He was interrupted in his staring through inadequate human eyes by a tall dark-haired woman, accompanied by two red-eared dogs. She clutched the old bone harpoon, and raised it.

Chernobog fled. She was there in more than just spirit. She could certainly hurt, if not destroy him. And now he recognized the weeping woman of his dreams. She looked different in the between-worlds.

Constantinople

Vestarch Kasares lay on the floor. He did not recall how he had come to be in such an undignified position. Worse than that, there were dogs on either side of him. Dogs! And not proper little housedogs, but huge things better suited to hunting. What were they doing in here? They should have been in the kennels. The two great hounds sniffed at him, teeth bared. A strange woman in a dress of a style he had never seen before—but made from remarkably fine linen—stared down at him. "Get up," she said coldly.

She seemed to have no idea of rank and station! But

there was a king's ransom worth of gold and jet that she wore at her throat and in her ears. Some foreign princess perhaps? But why did he not recognize her? He would have known about her, surely, been advised as to how she should be quartered, arranged for her household? Why did he not remember?

"Who are you, lady?" He sat up. He wondered, again, what he was doing on the floor.

Her eyes made him shiver. Those were not eyes that belonged in a human face. "I am Hekate. Now take that binding off."

Binding? Had he been a prisoner? "What?"

"Around your wrist." she pointed and he looked.

There was a ragged thong of parchmentlike skin around his arm. Not something that he would ever have dreamed of wearing! He was always an elegant and well-perfumed official. Except by the smell of himself and the look of his robe, he wasn't right now. What had been happening to him? How had he gotten in this state? And why, in God's name, did he not remember?

He pulled at the disgusting object, at first gingerly, and then urgently. It did not break.

Next thing he knew, the woman had thrust a long sharp bone spear under it. He yelped at the nearness of the sharp object, but she paid him no attention. The binding split and fell to the floor. Kasares felt a weight lift from him, and a fog lift from his mind. The woman was blurred, as insubstantial as smoke. He crossed himself.

Her voice came to him from a great distance. "You were almost among the dead, taken there by evil binding you. This too was my place once. I will not tolerate the thing of northern darkness here."

Kasares had a fine classical education, as befitted one of the eunuch vestarches of Byzantium's administration, no matter how low that status itself had fallen. And now that he could think again, he *knew* who and what it was that faced him, that had freed him. The sudden urge came upon him to throw himself to the floor again, this time to prostrate himself.

He knew who Hekate was, and of her dogs. And he knew what gateways and crossroads of life and death she guarded. He knew, believed, and was very afraid.

Men should not have to face gods in this life. Or goddesses. Her eyes bore into him, and he knew that she knew all that he knew. He remembered now getting the order to put that ... disgusting thing on his wrist, from the emperor himself.

An honor, he had been told.

To be possessed? It was not an "honor" he cared to be given a second time. And for some reason, unfathomable, Hekate had saved him from this thing.

He shivered. First he was going to get clean. Then he was going to dress and go to the Hagia Sofia itself and pray. He'd been, well, less than religious before.

And on the way he would offer a libation and some ancient Greek respects at a crossroads. He was deathly afraid of Hekate, but he certainly respected her now. She had saved Byzantion once, myth said. That was why her crescent and the star she had used showed on the old coins.

But before he did any of that, he gave in to his urge and went down on his face before her. "Lady of the Crossroads, Lady of the Hunt," he mumbled into the paving-stones. "I do not know why you saved me

from that darkness, but I thank you and I will give
you all honor for as long as I live. I am not worthy."

"True. And it was not for your sake," she said,
blunt, as a goddess was like to be. "It was because I
will not tolerate that filth in my domain. But...the
honor is good. That is as it should be." She sounded
faintly pleased. "I shall accept your worship."

He made a private vow that the libation he poured
would be the finest money could buy. And he did
not look up from his prone position until a certain
absence told him that the goddess was, in fact, now
walking other paths.

Vilna

The Black Brain roiled not only with the contact, but
also with fury that some of its complex plans were
going awry. Chernobog had ambitions, for reasons of
its own, for extension of power over certain areas of
human geography. If Venice was here, so fast, that
could only mean that the human who had thwarted
his design on Corfu—a cunning trap he'd been lucky
to escape, true—must have contrived it so. His spy
in Venice had told him who headed the expedition
for the Venetians, under the convenient fiction of the
commander of the marine forces.

He knew too just what Poulo had been setting in
place with the connivance of his ex-slaver contacts
from the *Casa* Dandelo. They were involved now with
the trafficking of black lotos and children. He knew
of the arrangements with Milan and Filippo Maria, of
course. He had eyes and ears in Milan. He selected
a messenger—a minor sprite and a slave. Now was

the moment and now was the time. The sprite would die in contact with the Lion, belike. But that would be all the Lion knew.

Humans had an irrational attachment to their young. It would be possible for this Valdosta to be drawn from the siege, along with his forces by such a hostage.

Once the Earth-Shaker had used that against the Goddess of the Gates, after all. He'd lied to her, but by the time she'd realized that, it was too late.

Valdosta would abandon the siege and by the time he returned, it would also be too late.

Venice

In some shadow-world of the ancient marshes of Etruria, the heart of which became the Venetian lagoon, the Lion roared. The echoes of that roar were felt even in Marco's Venice. Marco had been at Petro Dorma's side, as he had for most of the last three days. The Doge had slipped for a while into a shallow coma, from which he had awoken occasionally. His heart had raced and then slowed and slowed more, until Marco had been forced to intervene with a stimulant, and then later with small quantities of the leaves of the bloody-finger plant. That too was a poison and the last thing he wanted to add to Petro's system. But it had worked. The patient's heart rate had settled and had been approaching normality. Now he was wide awake and so was the exhausted Marco.

"What was that!" asked Petro Dorma, fearfully.

Marco had gone very still, as he heeded the thoughts of the creature that half-inhabited him. "The Lion of Saint Mark. Some sending of Chernobog made an entry here." Petro knew of the magical connection between the Valdosta family and that ancient power, of course.

"In this room?" asked Petro, warily.

Marco shook his head. "No. Venice. The Lion destroyed it. But not before it made some entry into the city. Cannaregio. We've felt dark magics there before."

Petro leaned back against his pillows. He was pale—but he had been pale for days now.

Marco paced. "You're doing a bit better," he said, abruptly. "I—we—aren't easy about this. We have a foreboding. I had better go and have a look. Have another talk with the *stregheria*. This threatens them as much as the rest of Venice. I'll be back soon."

Petro put a hand on his sleeve, halting him before he could leave. "You will need some rest, too. I am not unaware of what you have done, my boy. How many days has it been?"

Marco reckoned it up in his head. Nine meals. Three dawns. "Three."

Petro grimaced. "It felt longer. You've not had any rest in that time."

"Not much. I dozed for a bit while Francisco kept watch. Just after Katerina brought me food. She refuses to trust anything from your kitchen." Marco smiled, thinking of how she had tended to him without fussing over him and without rebuking him. She knew this was something he had to do; if he did not spend himself like this to save this man who was so important to them, to Venice, he would not be the Marco she had married.

"Francisco?" Petro asked, a little sharply. "This is not someone I know. Who is he?"

"Francisco?" Marco scratched his head. How to sum up such a complicated man in a few sentences? "My Arabic teacher. He was a slave once, he tells me, in their hands. A very knowledgeable man. He knows a great deal about medicine and other matters. I think he was also once a mercenary."

"We must look to a suitable reward and place for him. It sounds like he could help these fools who want to bleed me," said Petro, relaxing a little again.

Marco gave a tired crack of laughter. "He would 'help' them all right. He very nearly 'helped' them into the canal with his boot to their fundaments. Anyway, I must go. I will give strict instructions that no one is to bleed you."

Marco set out—to be met in the hall by Patriarch Michael and his retinue, and several of the Council of Ten. The old Patriarch took Marco by the arms. "Tell us the worst. Is our Doge dead?"

"No. In fact he is showing some signs of recovering," said Marco.

"But, I...we felt some great spiritual roaring..."

So, it seemed that he and the Doge were not the only ones sensitive to the Lion now. Interesting. "Yes. Venice has had, and seen off, some form of magical attack. I am trying to go and investigate. Why don't you all make a brief, and I mean brief, visit to the Doge's chambers? I have left instructions with the guards that they are to evict any visitors after three minutes, regardless of who they are. Try not to get him excited or upset. That means not suggesting bleeding him."

Marco went out, with a small escort of Schiopettieri and agents of the Council of Ten, to Cannaregio. All along the way, people called out to him. Marco got very tired of yelling back that the Doge was doing a little better.

They take heart from that, you know, said a leonine voice from within him. Well, of course they did. But couldn't they at least pass along word and not have to hear it directly from him? But he already knew the answer. Of course they did. They knew that he would not lie to them.

So he resolved not to be irritated by it. "Good. Now where are we going?"

Somewhere on the Rio di San Alvise. Close to the Campo Ghetto.

It was a poor quarter, that. An area of secondhand shops and crowded tenements. Marco tried to think of who he knew around there. Several of Maria's cousins, caulkers and boatmen. The priest who had brought Marissa to him. Quite a few of the *stregheria. Being there in body may help me to narrow it down.* the great Lion informed him.

"I'm barely here in body myself."

You need sleep. I will watch. I always do.

"First we'll have a look around Cannaregio. Then I'll check on Petro again. Then, if possible, I will sleep."

But the prowl around Rio di San Alvise yielded nothing. Just as the searches for the source of the black lotos coming into the city had yielded nothing.

That too had roots somewhere in the area.

So Marco went back to the Palazzo Ducale and looked in on his patient. "You are looking worse than I feel," said Petro. "Go and sleep. Your wife is here. I think in all the rooms here you might possibly find a bed. One without an occupant, even."

Marco smiled. "Your sarcasm is returning. Good."

Petro managed a genuine smile in return, though he was so flat to the pillows that he looked as if he had been sculpted there. "Yes, but you need rest. Stay here. Tell Katerina it is my order that she does, too. Lodovico can hold the fort at the *Casa* Montescue without you."

"There is also Benito and Maria's daughter," said Marco, thinking of the innocent havoc the little thing could wreak if she thought Marco and Kat were avoiding her. She would insist on a personal examination of every room, including looking under furniture and turning out closets and wardrobes.

"She has nursemaids, surely?" asked Petro. "My stomach says it is nearly midday. They must be at work at such an hour."

That was a very good sign. "If your stomach is speaking to you again, Doge Dorma, then I can rest a little. It is only mid-morning. But I must make sure of what you eat."

"More burned bread?" asked the Doge, plaintively.

Marco laughed. "It may have been what worked. But I think we can allow something a little more to your taste now."

The look of gratitude on Petro Dorma's face made Marco smile again. But he wondered just how grateful Petro would be to discover that he would be dining on broth and barley for a while yet.

Chapter 34

Venice

Francisco Turner made his way to the *Casa* Montescue, walking along the Fondamenta, rather than taking a gondola. He needed to get to the mainland again, and take himself for a decent run. Few people were about. It was a rainy, wet morning. He passed one woman so wrapped up in a large shawl that he almost didn't recognize her. She was the nursemaid from the *Casa* Montescue.

That was odd. Perhaps his pupil was back and Marco had given her a bit of time off. In Francisco's opinion, sooner or later everyone needed a respite from a child, and with that lively little girl, probably more often than most.

That would mean that Marco Valdosta was home and awake. Francisco wouldn't mind getting first-hand news of the Doge's present condition. To think that he had been instrumental in advising the physician who kept Petro Dorma alive! Francisco didn't know if his master would be too amused by that. His master's master certainly wouldn't. The assassination attempt had had all the hallmarks of the duke of Milan's operations.

He was greeted respectfully at the *Casa* Montescue. "Come in, m'lord. M'lord Marco is still up at the palazzo. So is M'lady Katerina."

"What is the point in my coming in then?" asked Francisco, amused.

"M'lord Marco gave very strict instructions that if you came you were to be given a mug of our best ale and taken to the library. With a fire. And I think M'lord Lodovico wishes to speak with you."

Francisco had briefly been introduced and spoken to the redoubtable Lodovico Montescue. It was not something he sought to pursue. Lodovico was a lot more worldly-wise than his grandson-in-law. But it was raining harder now, and the idea of the fire and the ale sounded worthwhile. He hoped that that nursemaid of theirs had got home before the downpour started.

The ale and the fire were both marvelous. And, somewhat to his bemusement, so was the company. Lodovico was pleased to see him, and not inclined to ask the sort of probing questions that Francisco would rather avoid. "I saw Marco this morning. He asked if you had been in. He had some good words to say about your advice, sir."

Francisco felt oddly flattered. "He is an exceptional physician, that young man."

"Indeed!" said Lodovico, eagerly. Marco, it seemed, despite the heir that the boy worried about, was still a prime favorite of the head of the *Casa* Montescue. "I think his skill goes even beyond the natural and is a God-given thing. He's worked miracles on my hands. And I truly thought our Doge was a dead man. And

I hear he's back to cursing anyone who threatens to bleed him. I'm a great believer in bleeding myself. But Petro has always disliked it, and Marco positively refuses to use it except in the rarest of cases."

"I do not believe in it myself."

They talked for some time about the merits of bleeding. Francisco held back from telling the old gentleman that he thought it was probably more a case of the bled patient believing it would help. He'd seen belief work often enough. But somehow a mention was made of Rome and Florence. And very soon the two of them were locked into an amicable argument about the architecture of the rival beauties. Francisco could understand now why Carlo had always said that old Montescue could have been the Doge had he not been so wrapped up in the vendetta against the Valdosta. He was exerting himself to be a pleasant host, possibly because he felt Venice and his grandson-in-law owed this particular mercenary a debt. He had a charisma about him, that would draw men and hold their loyalty.

They were laughing when a servant knocked at the door. She came in without waiting, wringing her hands. "M'lord. M'lord, have you seen little Alessia? I can't find her, nor Marissa, and it's time for the poppet's bath."

Unease stirred in Francisco. "I saw the nursemaid—Marissa, isn't it?—on my way here earlier. Near St. Marcoulo's."

The nursemaid shook her head violently. "Oh, no, sir. She's not due to go off until it is time for Vespers. She can be so dreamy, but she's good with the tot."

Lodovico got to his feet. "We will organize a search,

Maria. My friend, sit. It cannot take long to find a child even in this house."

The initial unease Francisco had felt when the nursemaid came asking for the child escalated into full-fledged alarm. But he wasn't going to show it. Lodovico would want to know how he knew what he knew and that...could be bad. "Thank you, m'lord. But I had better go. Convey my respects to Marco Valdosta."

Francisco left while the household was searching for Alessia. He flagged down a passing gondola. "Cannaregio. The Campo Ghetto. And as quickly as you can, man."

He could run across from there to the Fondamenta del Riformati the rest of the way; it would be faster than going by water. He checked his blade and his *main gauche*. If he was right, it could be ugly. He was one man and they would not be. He took a deep breath and made a decision. Marco was popular among the *populi minuta* of Venice. He took out a piece of parchment and wrote with a stick of charcoal he kept in a little bag in his pouch for just such emergencies. He didn't have much time, or much space on the parchment.

"When you drop me, I need you take this note to the Palazzo Ducale," he said to the gondolier. "They won't let you in, but tell the guard to tell M'lord Marco Valdosta you have an urgent message from Francisco. That may work. Otherwise can you take it to the *Casa* Montescue. And here is gold ducat for the task. It is important."

"For Marco Valdosta," said the gondolier, nodding. "Ah. I know you. You're the foreigner who has been teaching him. I hope your teaching is better than I heard your doctoring was. You could learn something from Valdosta. He's a good man."

Under other circumstances, Francisco would have been amused. Now he was only cursing himself for not noticing that the nursemaid had been carrying something under that shawl. "He is. Will you promise me that you will see this note to his hand, and to his hand only, and tell him that it is from me, and that he should hurry."

The gondolier nodded. "I'll do my best. But he is seeing to our Doge, you know. They say he was poisoned."

Rumors. He forced himself to take the time to counter this one. "Yes, but he is getting better."

The gondolier looked skeptical as he poled. "That's what they always say. Here you are. Campo Ghetto."

Francisco paid him and left, briskly.

But when he got to the secondhand junk shop, it was shuttered and closed. He ran back to the Rio della Senta, and found another gondolier. He had to get out of Venice before it closed like a rat-trap. He had to get to his master very very quickly.

There'd be blood to pay for this.

He just prayed it wouldn't be innocent blood.

Hades

Maria, back in Aidoneus' shadowy kingdom, looking to see how her daughter was doing, actually saw it happen. She watched the woman carry a sleeping Alessia out of the small water-door. There was a ramp along the side of the *Casa* that allowed her to walk—she didn't seem to mind getting her feet wet—to the Fondamenta. The woman swathed Alessia in a shawl and was walking away from the *Casa* Montescue with her.

This could not be right!

She called Aidoneus. He came, as always, as soon as he was called. She suspected that he was actually everywhere in this place.

"I need you to stop her! She's taking my daughter!"

Aidoneus shook his head. "It lies outside of my realm. I cannot affect things within the world of the living. I can only lend my strength to the Mother. And she too has little influence there. It is the realm of an ancient power. And we cannot reach him." Aidoneus shrugged. "In truth he dwells somewhere in the past."

His apparent indifference threw her into a frantic rage. "Damn you! That's my daughter!" she yelled furiously. "*Do* something—or else I will. You can't just ignore her."

"I cannot help," said Aidoneus, as if to a child. "It is beyond my powers. It is surprising to me that you can even see events within the ancient marshes of Etruria."

He seemed so final about it, that it cooled her fury. "Then let me go out and deal with it myself. I give you my word that I'll come straight back."

"I would, if it were possible. But I find the hell-dogs guard the portals again. I cannot leave, and neither can you. This matter lies beyond our ability to do anything about," he said with a grim finality.

Fury gave way to fierce determination. "Then I'll go and ask someone who will at least try!"

Aidoneus plainly knew exactly who she was speaking of. "You may try, of course. But you cannot, from my realm, easily speak to the living. And anyway, what do you think that a mortal outside the walls of Constantinople can do about something in the city of Venice?"

"He might not succeed, but that never would stop Benito trying his best." She turned away, ignoring the god, and quested through the tangle of shadows.

The magic of this loom seemed to grow stronger the more she used it—or perhaps it was she who was growing stronger. She could see many strange things here that were not visible to the mortal eye. Her gaze slipped across the city of Constantinople, seeking Benito.

And there was Hekate, suddenly interposed between Maria and the city. The woman with her two dogs was no longer weeping, but she could plainly see Maria just as well as Maria could see her. And she did not look pleased. "What do you want here?" she demanded.

"Nothing. I mean, nothing that will disturb you. I'm just looking for the father of my child. She has been kidnapped." Maria's voice was fearful and desperate. "I watched her taken."

Hekate looked startled. "Kidnapped? By this man?" It sounded as if she was sympathetic. Except for the part where she said "man."

"No, no, no!" Maria replied quickly. "It was some enemy—I don't know who, but they bribed the nursemaid to take her. I cannot leave this place, and I'm looking to Benito to rescue her."

"And what do you do within the realms of the cold one?"

Maria stamped her foot. She knew impatience would serve her badly but she was nearly beside herself with fear and worry. And yet, she had finally learned enough caution to be patient. This *was* a goddess after all, and one who was even keeping Aidoneus pent within his own realm. "Look, I'll tell you all about it, but not now. I need Benito. I need him now. Our daughter needs him; I don't know *what* they plan for her, but even if they don't intend to hurt her, she'll be alone and terrified."

Hekate considered her for a moment, then nodded. "Very well. I grant you my permission to speak to him. Speak and no more. The guardianship of the gates is mine. And I give you fair warning, mortals will seldom listen to that which they fear, and do not wish to hear. Most will not hear you."

"He'll listen all right," said Maria, grimly. "Or I will give him such an earful his head will ring!"

That seemed to meet with Hekate's approval. Maria scanned the threads of the men beyond the veil, and by chance, saw another she recognized, and one who was a welcome sight. Ah! He would know. That would save her some searching.

Hekate seemed to be watching over her shoulder, and recognized the man at the same time that she did. "Him? He is the father of your child?" There was something of an edge to Hekate's querying tone.

If she had not been so desperate, she would have snorted. *Leaping to conclusions, Hekate? And why should you care?* Because she obviously did. That sounded like jealousy.

"Saints alive, no," she replied, with enough indifference that Hekate was immediately mollified. "He's just the most likely person in all of that city to know where Benito is."

And he had damned well better be able to see and hear me too.

Pera

Antimo Bartelozzi had assumed that Maria—still officially
Verrier, as the law would not call her Valdosta—was safe
in Venice. He knew exactly who she was, and what she
looked like, of course. He'd even gone so far as to tell
Duke Enrico Dell'este that in his opinion, she was the
right choice for his grandson, even if she was a commoner. Dell'este's reply, "If he settles on any woman and
sticks to her it'll be a good choice," he remembered also.

He did not expect to see her wavering ghostly form
here in Pera, and his first panicked thought was to wonder how she had died and why she was haunting *him*. He
would have possibly been even more terrified if Hekate
had not been standing behind her. So, she had got out
of Constantinople in time. The dogs, of course, came
to greet him, and that was enough to steady his nerves.

He bowed. "Lady Hekate..." He looked at the ghostly
Maria, wondering if he should run. "Maria."

"I am looking for Benito," she said. Her voice seemed
to come from very far away. There was an echoing
quality to it. "I need to find him, and I need to find
him *now.*"

He swallowed. His mouth seemed terribly dry. "Are
you...dead?" he asked carefully.

"No, but you will wish you were unless I get some
answers instead of a lot of stupid questions!"

Her sharp tone had the effect of making him relax.
No false phantom this! No ghost would speak in that
way nor in that tone of voice. Magic then. Why did
a prosaic man like himself have to deal with that?

"He's gone across to the Princes' Islands." He
pointed. "Out there."

An odd expression came across Hekate's face. "I cannot come with you there, my dear. I agreed. He betrayed me. Broke the gate with his earth-shaking, without leaving the island. But he had our son as a hostage, and I swore I would not go there."

Antimo wondered if she knew that the prisoners from Constantinople had been freed. Ah...so she had a son. And presumably a husband.

"Who?" asked Maria. "Who betrayed you?"

"The Earth-Shaker. Poseidon, they called him later. He swore to be my true and only lover, when he was merely one of my consorts. But he was one of those men who are serial philanderers. And we all believed him. Amphitre—his wife—tried to tell me, and to help me. He sank her palace."

Antimo had had a good education, for his station. He'd been destined to be a clerk before life had entrapped him into attempting assassination, and then into spying. He'd been unsure who Hekate was. But he had heard of Poseidon. Of course that was stuff of legends, long gone—but names were reused often enough. If her ex-lover had stolen her son...

He was one of the best agents and spies in Italy, which along with Aquitane might mean in the world. "I will try to help you get him back," he said, as the image of Maria wavered and vanished.

Hekate looked at him, wide-eyed. "You are a very unusual man, Antimo Bartelozzi." And then, like a curtain drawn across a statue, she too vanished.

The islands, lying a few miles off from the city in the sea of Marmara, were not as confused and stained with history as Constantinople had been. Except for one. A spike of an islet. Something drew Maria there, although she could not imagine what it could be. It was always confusing to look out through the shadows, through the warp and woof of the loom. But at first there seemed nothing much here: some ruins, and a small contingent of Venetians on watch—if "watch" meant cooking a thrush over an olive wood fire, at least.

But the ruins on the south side were more extensive than they'd seemed at first, and were very old. She began to feel annoyed as well as desperate; she was looking for Benito. Why was she looking at ruins? She must have said it aloud, because Aidoneus answered. "Because Hekate wishes you to. She is a goddess. And it is her will that allows you to speak to the living. There is something there she wishes you to see."

On the one hand—damn it all, she was looking for Benito! On the other—Hekate *was* a goddess, and maybe there was something here (other than Benito) that could help. The gods, Maria had found, were not always good at explaining things. Aidoneus was better than most, but he was still inclined to ramble and completely miss things she would have found important.

"I'd better have a quick closer look then," she said.

Aidoneus nodded. "It is an old place, deep in magics. Those are Roman temple ruins, but Greek and then older ones lie beneath them. Gods occupy more than one realm. Here and elsewhere, sometimes at the same time."

Which explained why sometimes you could walk through an ordinary cave to get here, and sometimes you couldn't. "Like your kingdom."

"Yes. But my kingdom has always been principally below," replied Aidoneus.

It sounded as if he was getting ready for one of his long-winded explanations again. "Why can't she just *show* me? We're wasting time! Alessia—"

Aidoneus waved his hand. "Time passes in my kingdom at the speed I wish. Day after dreary day can take eons. I cannot help you out there in the world, but I have slowed the passage of time here for you. So you can look for as long as it takes and be no worse off. What takes you an hour will be the passage of two breaths in the mortal world."

"That's a help," she said gruffly. "Thank you."

"Look deeper. There is something hidden there that may help more. But I warn you, the outcome of all this may displease Hekate. And even now she remains a power to be feared."

"What is it?"

"You must find it, I cannot tell you what it is. But there is a something long forgotten there, that may help your daughter's father to traverse the vast distances he will have to. Hekate wants you to find it. She knows it will help you, but she does not realize that things may not go as she wishes once it is found."

Maria stifled a scream of impatience, because Aidoneus was, at least, not wasting time—or to be more accurate, he was not wasting Alessia's time. So Maria searched through the ruins, and the reflections of the ruins, and the magical places that the ruins hid. And was startled when at last she uncovered the thing that Hekate wanted her to find.

"It's still alive?"

"Time passes very differently for it, too."

Maria was almost beside herself with worry about Alessia. But she still could not help laughing. "Oh, dear. Poor Benito!" And then she asked. "And why is Hekate going to be upset?"

"Because he is her son. And once he is freed, he may very well do what *he* wishes, and not what Hekate would choose for him."

Maria's mouth fell open. "But...but...he's a *horse*. Well, a horse with wings, but still, a horse!" For the life of her, she could not imagine it—Hekate looked human...and this was her son? Giving birth to a normal little human girl-baby had been bad enough. But...

"So was the Earth-Shaker, when he chose to be," said Aidoneus. "Such disparate forms were common among his offspring. You should have seen his siblings."

Benito had gone to Plati where, with their chains struck off and access to food and drink, the survivors of the Latin enslavement who were not fit for combat were recuperating—the wounded and the few women who had survived rapine and murder, and the elderly. Benito was picking brains, as usual, trying to find weak points that he did not already know of in Constantinople. She caught him alone as he brooded over another little fire, trying to get fingers warm while he thought. He jumped to his feet as soon as she appeared.

He did not think Maria was a ghost as the spymaster had. He tried instead to embrace her. His arms went straight through her.

"Isn't he feeding you properly?" he demanded, smiling so widely it endangered his ears, and breaking her heart in the process.

"I'm only a sending, Benito. Something terrible has happened. Someone has kidnapped Alessia. I...

I can't talk to them in Venice, I don't know why. Not even Marco can see me. I saw it all happen, I know where she is, but I can only reach you. I can go almost anywhere, and see everything but I can't *do* anything."

Benito drew a deep breath and swore. Long and colorfully enough to get him an extra year in purgatory. He slapped a very meaty fist into his palm, and then drew himself together. "Can Aidoneus help us?"

"No, and not because he isn't willing but because... I can't explain it very well, but there are things he can and can't do, and helping us is one of the ones he can't. But he has helped me call you and watch Alessia. And on the next island there is a way you can get to her quite fast."

He was already thinking, frantically. "I can't think of any boat that would be fast enough. Given the season it will have to be overland. And it will take a long time, Maria. I need to start now, and I need to tell the Old Fox. Fortunately we'd planned on a siege phase; maybe I can get there and back before..."

She interrupted him. "Getting there will take you a lot less time than you think; you'll hate it, but it will be really fast. Benito! They have put our baby into a padded cell under a house in Cannaregio. She is awake, screaming and scared." Her voice broke on a sob.

"Lead me to it," said Benito, grimly. "Someone is going to get very badly hurt. They're going to wish they were dead when I am through with them." As an afterthought he said: "My brother and Kat. Are they all right?"

"They're frantic and they search for her. But I can't talk to them. I have tried. They can't see me." She bit her lip. "I think you could tell Duke Dell'este. It will take some hours at least for you to get there and back again... I am not very good with distances, outside of the canals."

Benito looked at her as if she was mad. "It must be a hundred and twenty leagues, even as the crow flies, Maria. Days, not hours."

She looked rather guilty. "No... hours, I think. But... better make sure you are dressed as warmly as you can."

Chapter 35

Venice

Francisco's gondolier-messenger was kept waiting at the Palazzo Ducale. Eventually he nabbled a servant, and enquired with impatience about the physician.

"Marco Valdosta?" The servant shook his head. "No, he left in a great hurry—oh, perhaps half an hour back. Some family disaster."

So off he went to the *Casa* Montescue. At the *Casa* Montescue, the gondolier found himself pushing through a mass of Schiopettieri getting orders from M'lord Lodovico. He was a determined man, so he pushed on through until he found another servant.

"M'lord Marco Valdosta? He's just gone to the Palazzo," said the servant. "To call on some of the Council of Ten. Blood in his eye. Never seen him so angry! Someone has kidnapped Benito's daughter. M'lady Katerina put her pistol in her belt, put on her canal gear, and went off to the Caulkers guild."

The messenger swore. "Hell's teeth. I have a message for him. It must be about this. From someone who called himself Francisco. I took him to the Campo Ghetto. He paid me handsomely to deliver it."

The servant nodded in recognition. "Ah! Francisco. He is a teacher to M'lord Marco. I can give the note to M'lord Lodovico for him." He held out his hand for it.

"He said to M'lord Marco's hand only . . ." The gondolier hesitated a moment, took in the scene, the information he just garnered and joined his own pieces into the puzzle. "Take me to M'lord Lodovico. Now. I think it may be important."

The gondolier's conscience was assuaged by the return of Marco, in a Schiopettieri boat. The crew were stroking for all they were worth. It looked like Marco would still leap off the bow and run over the water any minute. He jumped onto the Fondamenta before the vessel touched and the crowd parted in front of him. "Get to it, Grandfather. The Lion will fly over Venice in the next few minutes."

"M'lord Valdosta! I have an important message from M'lord Francisco!" said the gondolier, determinedly into the sudden silence.

"Francisco!" Lodovico Montescue slapped his head. "He *said* he'd seen the bitch on his way to see you. I forgot. Damned fool that I am."

The gondolier passed the roll of parchment to Marco's hand.

Marco peered at it, frowning. "Saints! It's in charcoal and half smudged."

"He wrote it in a hurry, m'lord. I took him to Campo Ghetto. He crossed over the bridge there heading toward Sant' Alvise."

"What's it say, Marco?" demanded Lodovico.

"Child. Poulo Borgo. The *Sotoportego* Galpa . . . I think."

"Galaparto," inserted the gondolier. "Bad part of town, m'lord. Secondhand dealers and cutthroats up there. It was good area in my great-grandfather's time—"

Marco cut him off, looking rather like his brother Benito in a cold rage. The gondolier was passing familiar with the young physician, as were many of the canalers, and he could not recall ever seeing Marco like this. "I need thirty of these men, Lodovico. Fresh arms on the oars, and something to break down doors. Now. That priest came from San Galatha. Near there! Send the rest to block the quays. No vessels leave until we find her. I told the Council of Ten, and they can deal with any problems. And I don't care who anyone is or what their cargo is, they don't sail!"

By the time Marco and the Schiopettieri had got halfway to the Campo Ghetto, they were joined by Kat and at least a hundred gondoliers and trade boats. And there was fury in every face.

Marco Valdosta, the poor of the city loved. And Benito . . . he was their scapegrace. Their hero. And Maria was one of them. News spread at yelling-speed through the city.

In the leading boat, Marco, his father-in-law, and his wife were like a trio of leashed hounds with the scent of blood in their nostrils. Only Lodovico seemed marginally calm. And not by much. His face was fixed in an expression so cold that people turned away from him, shivering. "If we find this woman, you'll have to stop them tearing her apart. At least until we know who they are, and how they did this. Then they have her as far as I am concerned."

"Only when I have finished with her," hissed Katerina.

"Let's find 'Lessi first," said Marco. In his mind to the listening Lion he said *Alive and unhurt. Please.*

The Schiopettieri knew where they were going. "We've searched a few places in that area for black lotos. It's coming out of there, we think. But those enslaved to the stuff are petrified of being caught without it. When it became hard to get after the last time, they learned. They don't talk. Losing the drug frightens them more than the Doge's torture chambers do."

They arrived at Poulo Borgo's shop—which was shuttered and closed despite the other shops being open. The Schiopettieri had brought a brass-headed ram. Ten of them swung it at the door.

It did not break. They tried a second time.

"Enough!" snapped Marco. "Stand away. Keep people away. And I will want your squad to keep the people back when we go in, Sergeant."

The rammers looked puzzled. "Get out of the way, men," said Lodovico.

Marco walked forward and struck the door with his hand, and all the force of a vast golden paw, "*UNBIND!*" he roared, calling the very fabric of the lagoon to do his bidding.

The door fell in. So did half the wall. Marco pushed into the junk-filled interior, walking over smashed cassones and piles of worn clothes. There seemed to be no one here, but, swords out, the Schiopettieri fanned into the place.

They found nothing but signs of filthy living. Kat looked ready to set the place afire. Marco...no one could meet his eyes. The Lion stared from them, and the Lion was roused to fury.

Lodovico stepped into this chaos. "Sergeant Amrosio. You and these gentlemen from the Council of Ten will remain here. Search the place thoroughly. Look for trapdoors and hideouts. Come, Marco. We will try that priest."

They walked to the priest's parish house. "I was uncomfortable last time I was here," said Kat, taking her wheel-lock pistol from her sash, where she had stuck it like a pirate. "Something wasn't at all right here, that priest...I wish I had said something!"

This door fell in to a well-directed kick. Inside...

Was blood. The priest was lying in a puddle of it. At least most of it must have come from him. He'd bled out slowly, trying to reach the door, after he'd been stabbed in the back. Kat rushed past the body, as Marco paused.

"He's dead," said Marco, kneeling, next to him.

There was a scream from Kat in the second room. "Got her!"

Marco, his heart full of desperate hope, was up and through that doorway like a lion pouncing. Which was just as well, because Kat was on top of Marissa, slapping her hard enough to break bones. "Where is she!? Where is 'Lessi?"

Empty eyes looked up at her. And rolled away, unseeing. She muttered something.

"Is she dead?" asked Kat, shocked now.

"Drugged to the gills," said Marco, looking at the dilated pupils. He felt for a pulse. "But she'll be dead soon enough. I need this poison out of her. Search this place! You, bring me my medical case from the boat."

He set about emptying the stomach of Alessia's kidnapper. What came out of her mouth was black.

"Black lotos," he said bleakly. "A lot of it. Kat, find me the bottle in my case marked 'Belladonna.' It might kill her, but this certainly will. And I want answers before she dies."

There was the sound of running feet and a Schiopettieri officer came panting in. "We found a hidden passage, m'lord. And a cellar!"

"Alessia!?"

"No, m'lord. But we found a lot of black lotos in sealed bottles." He held out a small flask that one might use for expensive perfume. He paused. "And... m'lord, a sort of padded cage. It wouldn't take an adult easily."

The sergeant who had been rifling through the priest's drawers coughed and held up a small girl's dress. "M'lord. Were these...the little girl's things?"

Marco felt for a moment if his heart might stop. But no. The dress would fit a larger child, not a toddler. And it was good fabric, but Alessia's linen had been of the finest. Kat had had great pleasure in getting more new clothes for her.

"What...what are those stains?" asked Kat.

Old and brown, on the child's white dress. For a moment, Marco's mind would not accept what his physician's eyes were telling them. But the Lion knew, and the Lion growled deep in his mind. And the Lion would not allow him to see less than the truth.

And there were two more dresses, in different sizes in the back of the drawer.

As the sergeant held one up, ornamented with little faded rosebuds, the ex-nursemaid's head came up. "That's my Bettina's dress. Have you seen her?" and she began to sob.

Kat slapped her again. "*Where is Alessia, you puttana?*"

"I stopped him. He wanted to have her, like Bettina. I stabbed him. I stabbed him. The woman-ghost told me to, she wouldn't let me alone until I stabbed him. And then Poulo came. Oh, Bettina..."

Marco and Lodovico exchanged a look. "Poulo. That's the secondhand dealer. Francisco was right!"

Marco looked at Marissa. "You want the black lotos, don't you?"

She nodded, seemingly unaware of her racing heart or her torn and vomit-stained clothes. "Give me. Please. I will do anything. Anything. It makes me forget."

"Tell me where Alessia is. I have lots of the black. You can have it all."

"Don't believe you."

"Lieutenant. Give it to me." Marco held out his hand for the perfume flask. He broke open the top and poured the black seeds out. She reached for them, grabbed at them.

Marco held him out of reach—not hard, given that she was in no condition to move. "Not until you tell me where to find Alessia."

Her hands crooked into needy claws, reaching for the flask. "Poulo took her. He was a runner for the Dandelos. He takes children. He took my Bettina."

Marco stood up. "I think you have told us enough. Take her away. Keep her alive if you can. She's rope-ripe."

The woman made a frantic grab at the lotos jar and a few seeds spilled as the Schiopettieri seized her. She managed to snatch a seed off the floor, and cram it into her mouth.

"Hell bound," said Lodovico heavily. "If I am understanding it right, she sold herself, and then her daughter for that stuff. My God! Selling a child... your own child!"

"And then used it to find refuge from her guilt," said Marco, quietly. "All the time becoming more bound. I said she was rope-ripe, but I think she is already in hell. Come, let us search that secondhand dealer's pit for more clues. I wish we'd got Francisco's message earlier. I wonder how he knew?"

Lodovico looked uneasy. "I don't know. He was with me after she went. He seems a solid enough fellow, but he is hiding something. I am sure of it. He's careful in his speech, but he's used to giving orders. Not what one thinks typical of a poor wandering teacher."

"The Doge wants to reward him. I think we should send a runner for him." Marco sucked at his teeth. "Perhaps a squad. He was with you...but...he knew too much. How did he know of this Poulo?"

"There may be a good explanation," said Lodovico, doubtfully.

"Then he can give it and I will be happy. But there is a child's life involved. More than one, by the looks of the evidence. But right now, it's Benito's little girl we must save, and I will not rest until we have her back with us."

Lodovico sighed. "The one good thing about this, is that she has a lot of value as a hostage. Those other victims did not have that."

"And dead or abused she could be a casus belli," said Marco grimly. "There is value in that, too. Come on! We are wasting time."

❅ ❅ ❅

A little later, while they were still picking through the cellar of the secondhand shop, the Schiopettieri lieutenant they'd sent to find Francisco reported back. "M'lord. He's left the city. He left just after the noon-bell. He was overheard offering a fisherman a great deal of money to take him to *Casa* Giare."

"We need to get patrols to the mainland. I want this man alive," said Lodovico. Marco had said not a word, but he walked away.

"The Lion of Saint Mark will fly over the city soon," said Katerina to her father, quietly. "Heading for that little marsh town. In the meanwhile Marco is going to the water-chapel at St. Raphaella. He wants to solicit the help of the lagoon undines. And then he will get the *stregheria* to try magical scrying."

"We'd better back him up with soldiery, too," said Lodovico grimly. "It's time we mobilized our forces anyway. This is more than just a kidnapping. This is part of a larger plot. Someone is looking for war. First our Doge, and now this."

"By water, or by mirror?" asked the wild-haired child-woman that Marco knew only as "Trillium." He was fairly certain that was not her real name, but he was also fairly certain he would never know it. The Strega were secretive, and rightly so. Even with him, whom they trusted.

"The mirror is clearer, but water is more trust-worthy," croaked an old man Marco had never seen before. "Water carries the energies most truly." He looked at Marco. "And the waters here belong to the Lion. And are blessed."

There were only four people here besides Marco.

He hadn't been short of magicians willing and even eager to help him. But everyone had agreed—and the magic-workers of Venice rarely agreed on *anything*—that more than five would muddle things. These four, with Marco, were the most powerful magicians in the city.

The nameless old man. The fey little child-woman out of the marsh. The midwife Bella Santini. And a Hypatian Sibling, Sister Serenity.

Marco looked to Sister Serenity, who nodded. "Water will be best," she said, in a voice so calm it even soothed him a little.

She looked around her at the others. She was a plain-faced, soft-voiced middle-aged woman in the loose, linen robes of her calling, who looked as if she should be growing herbs or baking bread, not getting ready to engage in what might prove to be a dangerous magic attempt. "Does anyone mind if I provide the vessel?"

No one objected, so she removed a black glass bowl that was unmistakable as the work of the island of Murano, filled it with water from the little inlet at their feet, and set it on the altar. Then she passed out colored tapers to everyone but Marco.

They've worked together before, the Lion in his mind observed.

Clearly, they had. Each of them invoked the protection of a Guardian, one of them for each of the compass directions, and set a candle into the chest-high holder there intended for that purpose. The old man uttered his invocation in Greek, the midwife in good plain Venetian Italian, the woman-child in a language that Marco didn't even recognize, and the sibling in Latin. As each of them completed his or her incantation, the plain white candle suddenly ignited and flared with the color of its direction, turning into a little pillar of flame. The Lion—and perforce, Marco—sensed the *presence* there. The Lion rumbled approval. Then, as the last flared into life, there was a pause, as if the universe took a single, deep breath. Then light erupted from all four at once, and when it had died down again, there was a faintly glowing dome over all of them, just contained within the chapel.

The four of them turned back to the altar and joined Marco. "Foulness out there," said the wild girl abruptly. "Can't be too careful."

"She means we all sensed the incursion that alerted the Lion," the midwife elaborated. "It isn't that we don't trust the Lion to protect us, because we do, but there's no harm in having more protection than you need." She glanced at the wild girl. "I don't know what her people call this, but my grandsire called it 'the Shield of the Light.'"

"The 'Dome of the Saints,'" offered the sibling.

"*Tutaminis Obviam Malum,*'" the old man put in.

The girl just shrugged, then said, "'Lady's Hand.'"

I approve, said the Lion.

"Now, for the scrying, have—"

"Here." Marcus had done scrying before, and he knew that the results were always better when you had something connected with what you were looking for; the more intimate, the better. He laid a few strands of hair from 'Lessi's comb on the altar, and the old man grunted with satisfaction.

But the girl made an abrupt gesture before he could say anything. "Wait." She carefully teased one of the fine threads from the rest, wrapped it around and around her heart-finger like a ring, and indicated to the others that they should do the same.

They joined hands, and Marco immediately felt the power rising. He stared into the bowl. From this angle there were no reflections from the bottom, and it was unnervingly like staring into a bottomless well.

Then there was a misting of the surface. As Marcus stared into the water, it clouded over, and it seemed to him that there were faint tracks, like lightning in miniature, arcing through those clouds. He felt the power building, and as the sibling, the old man, and the girl muttered or chanted under their breaths, he concentrated as hard as he could on the child. The little band of hair around his finger grew warm, then hot. And just when he thought he couldn't bear it anymore—

The bowl cleared. And there was Alessia.

She was in some sort of imprisoning small chamber or large box. She was asleep at the moment, but from the dark circles under her eyes, the raw, red state of her cheeks and nose, and the tearstains on her little dress, she'd cried herself into complete exhaustion.

But she was alive. And as far as he could tell, she was unhurt except for fright and grief. Not that fear and grief couldn't hurt you . . . but he had hope that if they could rescue her quickly enough, the terror and loss would fade into a shadow she could forget.

He tried to move the vision in the scrying bowl outward, away from her, to see where she was.

And it was as if he hit a literal wall. There was nothing. No point of reference. There were no openings in her containment to see out of, and he could not move the point of view away. It was as if something had anticipated that they might try to do this, and had laid a trap, ensuring that while they might *see* her, they could not actually *find* her. He strove with it until he could feel the power bleeding from him, until even the Lion within said *enough.* The others tried, but they could not even see Alessia, probably because they didn't know her.

But they, like he, refused to give up.

Until the wild girl looked at him across the bowl, and fainted dead away, breaking the circle.

"Enough," he said, hoarsely, as the girl came to almost immediately and tried to get to her feet. "I won't let you kill yourselves over this. We know she's all right and alive." Before any of them could protest, he turned and thanked and dismissed the Guardian of the West himself. The powerful shield came down, and the other three candles shrank down to merely half-burned-out candles.

The old man nodded, slowly, then dismissed the North. The midwife and the sibling dismissed the East and South.

"Come," he said to them. "Let me offer you the hospitality of my House. We'll rest and eat, and think. Maybe we'll come up with another idea. But right now, none of us are good for anything."

Only the girl looked as if she was going to protest, but when she swayed on her feet even she was persuaded into a gondola and off to *Casa* Montescue.

Marco himself nearly fell into the boat, he was so exhausted. As he closed his eyes against the pain that the weak sunlight was causing to erupt in his head, he heard the Lion say, *I will search for her. I will not stop. I do not tire.*

For now, that would have to be enough.

Up to the point where the stupid woman had brought the child and the priest had sent him word, things had gone more-or-less according to Poulo's plan. She was late, but that hadn't made much difference. That was typical of them once they were far gone into addiction, but in this case, maybe she'd had to wait her chance to make the snatch. He hadn't been there, and he didn't really care, anyway. The child was lightly drugged, and had woken in the priest's house. That shouldn't have been of any matter either; where she'd been put, no one would hear her.

And then the fool had let his desires lead him. With this child of all children! And that was where things started to go wrong. The woman had stabbed him, possibly the best thing she could have done, despite being as full of her reward as to barely be in this world. He still wasn't sure how she'd managed it. He hadn't known what was happening, of course. If he had, he'd have slit the fool's throat himself.

When he'd come on the scene, the priest was bleeding to death, and the woman clutching the child. A mess, and complications he didn't need. He'd had to go and fetch more lotos to get the brat away from her, unhurt, and that had taken time. But that amount of lotos would see her dead soon, which at least saved him killing both of them. There was nothing to link him to her. Or him to the priest. Those who knew had their own reasons for fear and wouldn't talk. It was a mess, but a manageable mess.

Still, his clients had reasons to have well-hidden places of incarceration. And it was best to be far from here when the bodies were found, which they would be, and likely soon. Valdosta would have the canals roused, and canalers had their noses in everyone's business. Someone would remember seeing her come here.

He bundled up the brat and made a swift—but not hasty—escape.

The *Case Vecchie* house of Lord Paletto in the Doursoduro quarter of Venice, facing onto the grand canal, had every fashionable accouterment for the delight of the visiting Venetian *haut monde* who came to appreciate his lordship's soirees and fine wines. A few selected ones came to enjoy his other interest, too, the ones that Poulo and his predecessor had supplied for the padded and hidden room up in the attics.

Poulo pushed the delicately built aristocrat into his own house, in a most unrespectful way. There was a little unobtrusive side door to which these deliveries had been made and it was here they'd met.

"I told you never to come here in daylight!" hissed Paletto, using his anger to mask his fear.

"Shut up. I need that little dungeon of yours," said Poulo Borgo.

His lordship pouted and scowled. "But I don't like them that little—"

Poulo slapped him. "Even touch this one and I will cut your stomach out and shove it down your throat. She's not for you. I will have her shipped out early tomorrow morning. In the meanwhile we need to hide."

"Hide? You? I mean, this . . ." The spoiled nobleman was horrified by the idea, though Poulo likely thought the horror was because he would be hiding a piece of low-life canal scum in his precious den, rather than any other reason.

Poulo backed him into the wall and hissed into

his face. "If I am caught, I know far too much about you and your friends, and be sure, I will tell it all. Now shut up and take me and this child up to your hidey-hole."

Alternately seething and cringing, his lordship led the way to the attic and the currently empty, curiously luxurious room where he indulged the vices that would get him hung, noble or not. That seemed secure enough. Now all Poulo had to do was wait for dawn, drug the brat, get her out, be on his way.

But several hours later his involuntary host came back, gibbering with real fear. "You didn't tell me that was Benito Valdosta's child! You're insane! You've got to let her go, Borgo. Quickly. Somewhere on the street far from here. They've tracked down some of your associates. The crowd ripped one of them apart. The Schiopettieri have taken the others to . . . to face further questions. They tore your shop apart, found the lotos. It's ugly out there. They won't just kill us if they find us! And if she's hurt . . . Get out! Out, out of my house. If you don't go, I will go to the Council of Ten myself. I know Lord Calmi, I think—"

That was as far as he got, because Poulo stabbed him. Idiot. If you are going to betray someone, it's not smart to babble about doing so in front of him. Poulo made sure to kill him immediately. The last thing he wanted was to have to listen to the bastard whine while he died.

Probably not the best thing he could have done, but it shut the bastard up, anyway. He had made things more difficult for himself; well that was the result of giving in to his temper. It would be awkward because he'd planned to use one of Paletto's enclosed gondolas to take the brat down to the warehouse, and then across to Guidecca, and away. The servants were hardly going to obey *him*. But there was a paved walkway, and it was barely two hundred yards. If he went at dawn, and he moved quickly...if he bundled the brat on his back, like a pack, instead of carrying her, he might escape notice. No one would be looking for her in this part of town, anyway. Why would they? The only people who had known of Paletto's vices were those who shared them.

Chapter 36

Okseia Island

One of the many things that Maria appreciated about Benito was that he wasted no time once he started to move. And he could organize. Well, people jumped to do his bidding. That might or might not be the same thing, but at the moment she didn't care.

He had to get several oarsmen to row him across to Okseia. The little island was about a mile distant, and Maria had seen him row. He'd also written a long letter for Enrico Dell'este, and scrounged a pack of soldier's rations, and a wineskin, and a blanket.

The rowers wanted to wait for some word from the fleet. What could their commander want on that little island? What could possibly be there that would keep him for very long? And why was he so agitated?

Benito put his foot down. "No. No waiting. Get across to Antigoni, and see that message gets to Duke Dell'este as fast as possible. With the first galliots you can commandeer, Mario. I can't tell you what I'm going to do, or why. Dell'este must know first. I'll be away awhile. But I'll be back. Trust me. Have I let you down before?"

Maria realized suddenly, by the acceptance written on their faces, just how much these men trusted and relied on her man. She sometimes still had trouble accepting him as anything but a trouble-seeking boy, and a wild one at that. They didn't. They saw him as a man, as the proper heir to the Old Fox, as the Young Fox. Saw him as someone they could count on.

He had grown.

She'd been there for much of it, realized how he'd grown in their relationship, but not in his standing with, and attitude to, the rest of the world.

It was a side of him she had been too close to see clearly. Or maybe it was because she hadn't let her notions of him change even though he himself had changed.

She led him to the ruins. A broken column. Some cracked marble steps. Stone balanced precariously on stone. And a rotting arch. She led him through it. Benito said nothing. She wondered if he could see what she could see. *She* saw it for what it was, another gateway, a place where one world faded into another. But this wasn't a gateway Hekate commanded. She might know about it, but it wasn't *her* place to open or shut. It was as well that no one had stumbled into it, because it was wide open, and anyone could cross it. But then again, why would they? There was nothing here that anyone would want. At least, not that they knew of.

But Benito went on, deeper into that other world, and into what was, by now, to her, a colonnaded courtyard with stables at its far end. And that was where they met with an obstruction.

He was old, and his beard was long and matted with salt. His face was aged and careworn.

And he could see both of them. He looked from Benito to Maria and back again, leaning on a trident. It looked more like it was something to keep him upright than a potential weapon.

"What do you want here?" he demanded incredulously, as if he couldn't believe there was a mortal and a spirit standing before him. Maria could see that certain . . . shimmer . . . about him, the same shimmer that Aidoneus had very strongly, and Hekate had in a lesser measure. But his was scarcely visible. This was a god, but a god fallen on very hard times with few or no worshippers.

Benito stiffened up a little, and transformed again—taking on a look of authority and confidence. "I come here on a mission. My daughter has been kidnapped. I intend to have her back. Now."

The old man managed to look furtive. "It wasn't me."

Benito shook his head. "No, you mistake me. We know *you* didn't take her. We need to rescue her. We . . . I need transport." His tone made it a demand, one equal to another. Maria held her breath. How would a god, even one as weak as this one, take such a demand?

With amusement, apparently. "You mortal warriors! Still the same! Ulysses, Perseus, Heracles . . ." The old man cackled. "Well, you've done me no harm, have not blasphemed me. The children like you. I can see it on you." He laughed harder and wiped his rheumy eyes. "Why not? Go by sea. Hee hee hee. I can still raise a storm. I'll blow you there."

"A storm? A breeze maybe," said Benito with something that might have been disdain if it had had more effort put into it. "Any magician can do that much." His eyes narrowed in challenge.

Maria looked sideways at him, saw just how he stood, and realized he was baiting the old man. She didn't know who the old god was, and she didn't recognize any of the names he'd told off—and likely, neither did Benito. The two of them had fallen into this realm of gods and ancient magics by accident, and had no idea what they were dealing with. But maybe that wasn't a bad thing. Aidoneus had said, once, that many of the gods had taken on the characteristics that their worshippers insisted on giving them. *Gods made in man's image,* he'd said. So Benito, rather than being cowed in the presence of a god, was using the skills he'd been learning from the Old Fox, in the manipulation of men. And an old, half-senile, but powerful man *could* be manipulated and tricked.

The old god pushed himself a little straighter. "I'm the Earth-Shaker, mortal. Storm raiser. Lord of Aigai, God of Korinthos, Thebai and Pulos."

"I don't think I have heard of any of them." Benito shrugged. "Sorry."

The old man sat down on the step, heavily. "Not heard of them? Has it been so long, out there in the mortal world, that you have forgotten?" Before Benito could say anything, the old man answered his own question. "Of course it has. My followers have died. My power ebbs. My children turned against me..."

He looked up at Benito, and scowled. "But I am still the Storm-raiser. I have the conch somewhere. Took it away from the children."

"Prove it. Make a storm then. Not with a conch but with your own power. I'd believe you then. Better than that, I'll believe *in* you," said Benito. "But not here in the Propontus. Anyone could do that. Say the gates of Hercules. Or the Black Sea. I bet you couldn't raise a Storm in the Black Sea, not even in winter."

The old god snorted. "Ha. Even she couldn't stop me. Anyway... can't find the conch. I must have put it somewhere." He waved the trident vaguely and appeared to draw down into himself, staring into the distance. Maria could see small lightnings about his head. "Never mind. I'll do it the old way. Like in the old days."

"Let's go," whispered Benito.

They walked past the old man, and up the steps and into the stable. Maria glanced back, then whispered "What did you do? I mean, I know you were tricking him, but why trick him into making a storm?"

"Marco once told me weather magic is one of the hardest, and needs huge amounts of power. And I think it was one of *stregheria* who said that the old gods drew their strength from belief. This old man obviously was once someone that was believed in." Benito glanced back himself. "But look at him! He's lost most of his worshipers now. So I offered him bait—my belief—and lured him into performing a magic that will take his all. And might even do us a favor. Meanwhile, he's not watching us, and we can get what we came for—whatever that is—"

Just inside the door was a tack room. "Aidoneus says what you need should be a golden bridle. It must be here somewhere," Maria said, thinking aloud. The tack room was remarkably empty. And very dusty.

But there was a golden bridle on a peg beside the other door. Benito scowled at it, and then at her. "I had a feeling this might involve horses."

Maria scowled right back at him. "It involves rescuing our daughter."

With a heavy sigh, Benito took down the bridle from the peg, and they walked through into a vast empty stable, with nothing in it but a horse-statue. A very large golden-colored horse, perhaps one and half times the size of a warhorse. Bronze? Why put a bronze statue of a horse in a stable, where no one would see it?

With huge wings to match. The statue of a winged horse. What had Aidoneus been thinking? Was it magic? When you put the bridle on it, would it come to life? But then what?

Maria was about to explode with rage when it twitched its wings.

It stepped forward towards them, turning its head slightly to look at them with the other eye, too.

"I suppose," said Benito faintly, "that a saddle is out of the question?"

The great winged horse reared up, pawing air. "Come any closer with that bridle and I will kick you to death," said a voice with a distinct whinny to it.

Benito shook his head, but did not advance a single step. "Horses don't talk. Their mouths are the wrong shape," he said. "So you can come out, whoever you are, and stop playing games."

The wing-swat knocked him back against the wall. "They don't fly either, they're too heavy," said the horse. And it was definitely the horse, Benito decided, with the sort of decision-making skill that comes when there are flared nostrils blowing horse-breath into one's face.

"Are you magic?" he asked weakly.

The horse stamped a hoof. "I am Pegasus. Magic is my birthright. Gifted by my mother. But she has left me here, Trapped." The horse shook his head and looked both angry and aggrieved.

This was going to require another sort of manipulation than he'd used with the old god. Benito took a step closer. Another. "I need to rescue my daughter. I'll free you if you will take me to her."

The horse—Pegasus—drooped his head, flattening his ears. "Poseidon the Earth-Shaker guards this place. He has been robbed once, and now he watches. He watches carefully. You can never free me."

Benito smirked. Just a little. "He's busy right now. And we'll lead you out of here, but only if you'll carry me to my daughter."

The horse's ears came up, then flattened again. "How do I know you speak the truth? I would do it if I knew. I would give anything to be free again. My mother tried to free me, and failed. How could you—"

Benito used the moment to slip the golden bridle over the great winged horse's head. "You don't. But I have given you my word. I'm Venetian. We make bargains with everyone. We couldn't do that if we had a reputation for not honoring them."

"You tricked me!" There was rage in that voice, but the horse stood still.

It seemed that bridle was some sort of magical thing that would control the creature. So he wasn't going to get pounded into paste, which was a good thing. And this beast was just a bit simpleminded.

Then again, it might be magic, but it was still a horse. "No. I just stopped you wasting time. You agreed, but did not trust me. Well, I'm no fallen old god, full of treachery and deception. I give you my word, I will let you go free the minute you take me to Alessia."

The winged horse's skin shivered as if pestered by some passing fly. "Mount, then."

"Will you carry me there?" asked Benito, not liking the height of the horse's back, but not letting that stop him.

Pegasus mouthed the bit with distaste. "You hold the bridle. I cannot refuse."

Best to put a better face on this. "I didn't know that, when I asked you to carry me, and a bargain is still a bargain. My word is still my bond. Let us lead you out of here, and when we're out, you carry me to my daughter, and I will set you free."

The horse peered at Benito with one eye, then the other. "You are the strangest mortal I have ever seen."

"So they tell me," Benito said, dryly. "But strange in what way?"

"You say you are willing to let something go once you have it in your possession, and control it. That is very odd." The horse's ears flicked forward.

Benito glanced at Maria. "Let's just say I have had a lot of practice in learning that when you try to hold something too tightly, you're apt to lose it faster than if you opened your hand. Now, let's get you out of here. The sooner we get to my baby, the faster you'll be free."

So Benito took the bridle-rein and led the winged horse out. Poseidon was so wreathed in effort—and cloud—that he didn't even see them go. Out again into the places between and then out of that and into the ruins.

Benito used a fallen pillar capital to mount. Being out in the open air seemed to excite Pegasus. He tripled briefly and then broke into a gallop across the stony hillside—a good place to break knees. Benito thought that might be what had happened as they suddenly lurched, at full gallop, as he clung to the mane. But they lurched upward—not toward the ground. Up, up in bucking sweeps of Pegasus's wings. Up into the sky.

With nothing but his legs to cling on with, Benito spent the first ten minutes of that ride frightened out of his wits. No human was intended to be this high. And there was no natural way that even such vast wings could support them. There was magic at work. Would it suddenly stop? Then an eagle suddenly sheered off, with a squawk, like a startled pigeon, and Benito's sense of humor came to his rescue. He was certainly going up in the world. Higher and higher. And now it seemed, around in circles, over the land below. Upward, upward into the clouds. And then, when the air itself seemed to grow thin, downwards gliding northwest far faster than a man could run, or a horse could gallop or even a ship could move before the gale.

It was in a way far easier than riding a horse had ever been. And he was so high that height itself lost its perspective. It was like looking down on a map. What he needed was Antimo Bartelozzi here to carefully draw it all, precisely and to scale.

It was still a vast distance to cross. After a time, Benito started doing some calculations in his head. If they were doing seven leagues an hour...an unimaginable speed, but looking at the land below, perhaps a good estimate...It would still take even this magical creature eighteen hours to fly to Venice. That was a far cry from the six weeks it might have taken by sea, but it was still a long time for his daughter.

He began to worry about her all over again.

Chapter 37

Venice

Venice was an angry city, precipitously close to mob violence. Anyone who had ever had any linkage with Poulo the secondhand dealer, or the priest, or the woman, was in hiding. If they weren't hiding and had any common sense, they were with the crowd outside the Piombi calling for the woman and the other two of Poulo's gang who had been caught to be released—so the mob could kill them.

They were only quieted by the chief justice—coming out onto the roof with two masked executioners next to him. The crowd stilled, expecting to hear of their death.

"We do not just want these three. We want all of them. And that means that they need to be questioned very closely until we have all the answers. We cannot question dead people. Believe me, they will answer us and when we do . . . you, the people, will likely be asked to join the hunters."

There was a rumble of agreement. Angry agreement, but agreement still. The chief justice nodded.

"Now go away. You are disturbing the Doge and he is still not well."

Marco, having flown with the Lion over the lagoon and to the small village of Giare had found that his erstwhile teacher had hired a horse—a bag of bones, the hostler disdainfully called it, and set off along the trail to Adria. But Marco, flying overhead, could find no sign of any riders. It must have been a feint. He returned to Venice to see what, if any, progress had been made there, and, rather guiltily, to check on the Doge.

The news there was both good and bad. Good in that Petro had not suffered any form of relapse. Bad in that, in Marco's judgment, Petro was going to take several weeks if not months before he was fit to take on the full weight of governance again. And here it looked like Venice was plunging toward war.

Matters were not helped by Lord Calmi, who waylaid him on his way out of Petro's chambers. "I have not seen fit to disturb Doge Dorma about this, and I realize you have quite a lot of worries of your own right now," said the man who Marco believed controlled most of Venice's spies. He was, Marco noted, a little more deferent and . . . wary than he'd been in the past.

"What is it?" said Marco politely.

"The poisoning. You were quite correct about it, or rather that fellow Francisco you had assisting you was. Um. What more did you know of the man?"

"Not much, except I am looking for him. I think he was a soldier once. I thought that I liked and trusted him."

"We did an investigation on his background when he came into contact with you. We do that as a matter of course," said the man hastily. "Anyway, it appears that we were misled. There was another itinerant teacher, a man of blameless background, that we were led to believe was this man. We were mistaken. Well, deceived. He was vouched for, that is our normal practice, by two independent men from Padua who were trusted, which was where he claimed to be from last. I had my men do a second check...once he had come close to the Doge, you understand...and it appears a similar man does still teach there."

"So: who is this Francisco?"

Lord Calmi bit his lip. "We have found his real family name. And we know who he is now, m'lord. He is one of Carlo Sforza's most trusted lieutenants. Sforza played a part in gaining him his freedom, it appears."

"Do you think he poisoned Petro? He could have killed him while I slept."

"No. We know he had no direct role in the poisoning. We have established who arranged and paid for that. It did come from Milan, from one of the duke of Milan's closest confidantes. Count Augustino Di Lamis. But...that is not the same as Sforza, m'lord. You probably don't know, but Carlo Sforza has been in secret negotiation with Florence and Pisa. He and Duke Filippo Maria Visconti are said to be distant these days. So...this Francisco was a spy. Perhaps had a part in this kidnapping. But I cannot say he was part of the poisoning."

Somehow that felt better, even if it did still leave his friend, or former friend, as the agent of the man who had possibly had his mother killed.

Marco had tried to put all of that behind him. All the hatred and all the vendettas. It appeared though that they had not put him behind them. That left a bitter taste in his mouth.

He went back to the *Casa* Montescue in the winter dark, hurt, angry, tired and desperately worried. He was not going to get much more of the rest he needed so badly, until, somehow, Alessia was found.

And there was Kat, folding him in her arms, and holding him tightly. Saying things that could not be said with words. He was still worried, desperate; they both were. But now that he was with her—he was also very, very grateful.

Verona

Francisco Turner knew he had more than six leagues of hard riding ahead. He'd have to change horses, which would be a relief as this one was not much good. He pushed it into as much of canter as it could manage, and was grateful when he arrived in the little town of Vigonovo in the last of the afternoon light and was able to get some food and a good horse. Food, he told himself, was common sense. So was the beer. Beer was always common sense, except when you had too much of it, and when you had to stop to relieve yourself. He was glad to know which road he had to follow, and that the clouds seemed to be clinging to the coast this evening, giving him at least the benefit of moonlight. It was still a long hard ride, although he did manage to get a fresh horse along the way. One thing you could say about Carlo Sforza: he did his staff work well. He made a great deal of money at his trade, but he spent sensibly on things like friendly farmers with exceptionally good horses for his agents.

That didn't help the poor beast a few miles out of Carlo Sforza's current base of operations. Verona was in some disarray because of the way it had been dismembered. And anywhere near Carlo Sforza was almost bound to be patrolled. The crossroads just beyond Borgo San Marco village was.

In the small hours of the morning a solitary horseman was going to be challenged. And very probably shot and robbed.

Francisco didn't wait. He put his spurs to the horse and kept his head as low as possible. The result was him somersaulting out of the saddle and somehow getting to his feet and running into the vines. Ducking and crawling between them, and then running head low, and thankful for the scudding clouds, Francisco fled. Cross-country running was something the little patrol after him gave up on quite soon.

Francisco didn't have that option, though his shoulder hurt like hell. He ran on. Fortunately it was flat farming country, and he soon found another lane. He had more than two miles to run through the darkness to the walls of the Palazzo Bevilaqua. He ran into one of his condottiere's mounted patrols before that, but his ability to recognize them and swear at them prevented them from shooting at him.

Ten minutes later he was before Carlo Sforza. Carlo looked his physician up and down. "Get him some beer," he said, sharp eyes alert despite the hour. He rubbed a hand through his still-curly dark hair. "What brings you here at this time of morning, Francisco?"

Francisco wasted no time. "Filippo Maria Visconti's

new Venetian agent has kidnapped Benito Valdosta's daughter."

"*What?*" Sforza was on his feet, staring into Francisco's face. "When?"

"Yesterday morning, I am fairly sure. And I am sure this means war. Marco Valdosta is less soft than some assessments make him."

Carlo Sforza's eyes narrowed. "She is also *my* granddaughter, Francisco. That's why you were there. What more do you know?"

"I think I may know where they plan to meet. Borgo—that's the Visconti bully-boy—said he'd met you there before. I think however he may have meant he met Count Augustino Di Lamis."

"Filippo Maria's current favorite. Where is this place?"

"Casale di Scodosia, or rather a villa just outside it."

"Hell's teeth. That's in my back orchard, virtually. It's over in Veneto though. An act of war against the state of Venice." He sucked in through his teeth. "Alto! *Alto!* I'll want a troop ready and in the saddle in twenty minutes. And I'll want another two thousand men moving before dawn. Get Captain Melino, and Di Galdi."

"I have, I hope, a precise address. The fool thought he was buttering me up, as your emissary." Tiredly, Francisco drained his beer. "Or rather, as Di Lamis's emissary. Villa Parvitto."

"There is always someone from anywhere in a mercenary company. Alto! Find me someone from Casale di Scodosia."

He patted Francisco on the shoulder. "Ouch. That's... very painful," said his physician.

"Physician heal thyself. What can I do for you,

Francisco? I was going to ask you to come with me, but..."

"Nothing. I'll get someone to clean it up. And yes, I'll ride, m'lord. I owe this much to Marco Valdosta. Of course, they may have caught up with the kidnappers already. In which case, m'lord, they're probably blaming you."

Carlo Sforza pulled a face. "I once made a mistake about my child. My son. I will not risk making another. Ah. Captain Di Galdi. Go now, Francisco. Get that shoulder looked at, and get some fresh clothes. If you're fit to ride..."

"I'll be there."

Chapter 38

Venice

Marco had told Kat about Francisco, about the vetting process the Council of Ten's spies had used, and how they'd been misled. And then he'd fallen asleep in her arms on the seat in the salon they'd sat down in.

In the small hours he'd been in a deep sleep when Katerina shook him awake. "Marco. Marco. Wake up. I've thought of something."

He blinked at her owlishly. At the branch of candles, the blanket, and the tray of now cold food. He wanted that food now, cold or not! He reached, she forestalled him and fed him little bits as she talked.

"Marco, how did the Council of Ten find out where to ask for someone to provide a background on Francisco?"

He chewed, and thought. "I imagine they asked him. Not directly, but someone would have fished for his background."

Kat nodded. "Surely if they do that for anyone who comes into contact with you, they'd have done it for Marissa, too? I would think they do that for anyone in this household. Francisco fed them lies that were hard to verify because they were from outside Venice. But she is local, and she must have given them a local contact."

"Maybe the priest," said Marco, helping himself to a piece of proscuitto.

She nodded again. "And someone else. There must have been someone else. It's the Council of Ten, and they never do things halfway. They must have asked more than one person. And I don't think the word of that secondhand dealer would have counted for anything, except against her, so . . . it had to be more than one."

Marco sat up. "You're right, love. Saints, I am stiff."

"You should try my shoulder," said Katerina, pulling him to his feet. "Come. We need M'lord Calmi."

And they got him. He was not actually asleep. He nodded when Marco explained Kat's idea to him. "It would have been done. Wait. I will get someone to find out."

It took a few more hours, but they had names. "The priest said she came of a good family. And the references bear that out. We got them from him," explained the yawning agent. "Lord Paletto, and the trading family Di Faravelli. They're *curti*, but rich. And clean."

"Get me the Signori di Notte," said Calmi. "We are going to ask some hard questions of these gentlemen. Of course, it could prove that she is exactly who she claimed to be. But once the black lotos gets a deep grip on someone . . ."

Lord Paletto was closest, so Kat, and Marco and Lord Calmi went to visit him. His majordomo said that his lordship was at home. He started to say something about not disturbing his master, but then changed his mind. Or had it changed for him. Sooner or later Katerina was going to accidentally kill someone with that wheel-lock pistol of hers, thought Marco.

But it would not be Lord Paletto. He was absent from his bed—yet so far as anyone knew he not left the house. But there was a side door, and...the major-domo was becoming very nervous and more talkative.

It seemed that his lordship was a little odd at times...

"Did he like young girls?" asked Kat dangerously. The majordomo went ghost-white.

"Search this place," said Calmi. "Search it from cellar to roof."

The haughty majordomo stuck a finger in his collar. "There is a place in the attics he might be."

He was. He was also already cold.

And there was a silver button.

Alessia's little dress had had silver buttons.

The Di Farvelli clan did not get the benefit of a knock on their door after that. Marco smashed it in and went in hard—full with the Lion now—and Kat came close behind him.

She finally got to use those pistols. Some people got hurt and Signor Di Farvalli, who had a warehouse on the quayside, sang quite loudly. His role, it turned out, had been smuggling cargos for Poulo the secondhand dealer. He had never had any idea what it was, he swore on his mother's grave.

Someone else might have believed it, but Marco doubted Venice's judges would. The fact that the house was being packed for imminent departure would not help his hopes of being taken for a mere smuggler.

"We're about five hours behind them, and this Casale di Scodosia is beyond the marshes of old Etruria," said Marco. "I think, Lord Calmi . . . I need some soldiery and fast horses."

Calmi sucked his teeth. "There is one thing you need to know, Marco Valdosta. You know I mentioned Carlo Sforza? Well, he's based at the moment at the Palazzo Bevilacqua. That's very close to this place. I will grant you an order for two hundred of the Swiss guard and I will convene the Council. This could be some kind of trap. And this does point to his guilt in this matter."

"Sooner or later, if he is involved, we'll deal with him," said Marco.

"He had better hope that it is me that catches up with him, and not Benito."

Calmi looked at him. "I had thought you were a quiet, loving and forgiving healer, M'lord Valdosta. I am . . . I have reassessed my ideas."

Marco paused a moment, and passed his hand wearily over his face. "I am. But I am also the Lion. And it is not wise to arouse the Lion."

"I believe you, Marco Valdosta," said the spymaster. "But there is more. I wonder if Carlo Sforza knows."

Marco closed his eyes as old, old memories flooded through him. "I remember him, you know. I don't think Benito does much. He and my mother . . . Lord and saints. The fights. He was always ice-cool away from her. Good to me and Benito, to be honest. But my mother seemed to get to him, somehow. I always hated those fights."

Maria watched, helpless and angry and fearful, as her baby girl was transported to the hidden room in Lord

Paletto's palazzo. And then how the sleeping child was smuggled onto the vessel heading for the coast. Benito was still so far off. True, he was making dizzying speed, but it was a great distance. And it was not natural that Alessia should sleep like that! She must be drugged. One yell from her near to water and the undines would have come looking. But the one positive thing she had seen was that there was every sign that the kidnapper had no intention of killing 'Lessi—or at least, would not while he thought he could use her for whatever reason he'd taken her. And while she was alive, Marco and Kat and Benito would not stop.

Benito had not even let Hades stop him for her. And she'd not put it past him to go further for his daughter. She hugged herself, and that thought, very tightly.

Poulo Borgo was not one for thinking deeply or questioning why he did things. Or for any sort of morality—and that had been before Chernobog had twisted his mind. The Dandelos' normal trade had been enough to make sure that kind of human was largely excluded. The trade required people who, at the very least, were free of any form of empathy; a fair number of them derived active pleasure from the work.

Yet, simply from the business point of view, the *Casa* Dandelo had not wanted merchandise damaged. He did his work for money. The Di Farvelli were of a similar ilk, and as far as Poulo's now twisted rationality was concerned, that made them better to work with than the likes of Paletto.

Fortunately, he had a lot of money. The trade in lotos and suitable slaves was very lucrative. It made money, more than he had ever dreamed of once.

That had become unimportant to him, though. Just doing as he had been instructed was all that mattered. Right now, it seemed that it was as well he had arranged to have seven of his men waiting for him at the warehouse.

"Don't come back," Emilio Di Farvelli had said, with finality. "Do you hear me, Borgo? Nothing you can do will get us to transport anything for you again. Venice will be too hot for you anyway; it's too hot now for anyone who might be remotely connected with you. Get out. We're moving out while we can. Tomorrow, there'll be nothing left here."

He'd heard all of that once before. It was like a pus-riddled wound. Unless you scrubbed it out and poured raw grappa into it, the infection would start up again from the fragments that were left. But they could be useful, so he held his tongue.

From the warehouse to the low night boat with its flattened profile and muffled oars, to a landing in the marshes on the southern end of the lagoon-swamps, and then to the enclosed carriage, with outriders in case of trouble, down back-lane ways. And then to the Villa Parvitto.

The Patriza Parvitto's once sumptuous and very private walled villa half a mile outside the little town had been converted into a mixture between a manufactory and a headquarters. They were accustomed to early morning visits here. "The Milanese messengers. Send them," said Poulo, yawning. "He can tell Sforza we have the merchandise. It needs an escort. Hell. I am tired. See the brat into the cells, and get me some food."

His second in command, who ran this side of the entire business, and gave the Patriza her daily ration of black lotos, nodded. "Sforza is just across the border now. But I don't think these are his men. They spoke of Mantova and a garrison there."

"Whatever. They know where they have to go to. I think we might be wise to move ourselves over the border for a while."

The Milanese messengers rode off. Verona was not safe these days, so there were three of them. They had a lot farther to go than Bevilacqua castle—a thirty mile ride to Mantova. They were a little better informed on the roads and the whereabouts of military detachments than Francisco Turner had been, and avoided any delays or conflicts. Still, there was almost no way the escort could be back before Terce.

Pegasus flew on. The great winged horse made use of air currents, and, obviously, magic. Benito, with an interest in strategy, and thus maps and geography, had no idea where they were. But plainly the great horse did. What had begun as one of the most comfortable riding experiences he had ever had gradually became less comfortable, then uncomfortable, then excruciating. He was not used to staying in one relative position for so long, the cold ate into his bones, and he had to piss so badly it hurt.

Eventually they set down near a stream. Benito dismounted, stiffly stretched a little, relieved himself, drank, ate and stretched himself some more, while Pegasus did the same. It was cold and there were little drifts of snow next to the yellowing grass.

"Grass." Pegasus filled up greedily on the poor fodder. "I think I have had nothing but hay for the last century."

"I think it's been longer than that," said Benito. His grasp of ancient history was poor, but he was still sure that ruins took longer than a mere hundred years to get that ruined. "But I think you were sort of outside of ordinary time."

"Gods are," said Pegasus, shaking his mane. "I know you were in pain. You will be in pain again, but it cannot be helped. Now, you must mount again."

That, along with the galloping takeoff and running landing were the worst aspects of this means of travel. That and the cold and the muscle cramps. This time he had made certain not to drink too much. He was grateful for the blanket and the hood of the cloak and its fur—and the warmth of the flying horse. "You are not too tired?" he asked when he had managed to scramble up.

"I have drunk from the fountains of youth and strength. And I am the child of a god and a goddess. I do not know weariess." Pegasus tossed his head high and snorted. "You have said there is urgency. I know what it is to be a captive child. We must free yours. We will fly across the night, and by morning we will be where your leman has shown me you need to go. And then, I too will be free."

"If you're up for it, so am I." Benito thought that the horse was being less than accurate about being tired or when they would get there, but he had no choice.

They flew across the dusk and onward in the cloud-sharded moonlight, towards northern Italy and the dawn.

In the shadowy halls beyond, a worried, angry, frustrated woman tried to keep her temper and her patience. She watched as her confused, unhappy, imprisoned child swung an angry little fist at the man who had brought her food. "Don't *want* that. Don't want *you*. I want—"

He slapped her. She was too shocked for a moment even to cry. And then the tear trickled down her face. But she remained defiant. "You're mean! You're bad! Bad man! My daddy will *hurt* you."

Her guard threw the bread down on the pallet that formed her bed and set the bowl of whatever passed for soup they had on the floor. "Shut up, brat. Your daddy is a long way off. Now eat your food. Or don't. I don't care. Starve."

He walked out and locked the room behind him.

Maria seethed. If she could have reached into his chest, she would have torn his heart out. The only good thing was that Benito was not that far off and he was moving towards this place very rapidly. So rapidly it was hard for her to even watch him, let alone talk to him.

But something had drawn her elsewhere in her searching to see what Benito and Marco were doing, to strangers who had spoken Benito's name. There, she'd overheard the orders being given and messengers being sent to Carlo Sforza. It was not hard to find his thread and follow it. And to see just how close he was.

Maria wondered if Benito would get there in time. Or just what the man who was called the Wolf of the North wanted with her daughter? He had an army there. Asleep, true. But there were thousands of them. Too many for Benito unaided.

Would Venice go to war for her daughter?

Chapter 39

The Veneto coast

Benito would have given his life for a drink of hot brandy. Or, indeed, anything hot. Even one of Marco's herbal things.

From on high Benito could see the coming morning light, outlining the mountains to the east, and the faint glimmer of the waters of the Adriatic and the lagoons of the coast in the arms of the dark land.

He was freezing cold, stiff, aching in every joint, cramping, and knew that whatever else was coming he'd have to be ready to fight not just for his life, but his daughter's. It was very beautiful up here, and he appreciated that, but he concentrated on massaging his arms and legs as best he could.

They began spiraling inward.

"This is the place your woman directed me to. You must honor your promise when I land there, and free me," said Pegasus.

"Then, in order that you don't get shot, or get me shot, I suggest we land a few hundred yards from the place," said Benito, practically. After all, he'd landed with Pegasus earlier. It involved a lot of noise, running and some distance. "You might be the son of gods, but I don't think you're arrow-proof."

"You will let me go then?" demanded the winged horse.

He laughed a little. The poor thing had been a captive for so long that it still expected treachery. "I gave you my word. Actually, not only did I give you mine, but Maria gave you hers, and that's even more important to me. Set me down safe and sound and the world is yours to explore."

"Very well. There is a road, and no one is near it. We will land there." The horse began a steep descent towards the slash in the landscape that was the road he had spotted.

Benito finished his flying experience by falling off. Fortunately, falling well was something Erik had taught him, and Pegasus had nearly come to a standstill when it happened. The bank was mercifully free of stones or tree stumps. What was a bit of mud, when you came right down to it?

He got up and walked to Pegasus who was coming toward him to see if his passenger was in one piece.

"Thank you," said Benito. Pegasus lowered his great head and Benito took off the golden bridle. "Enjoy your freedom. You more than earned it. Go find yourself some sweet grass and a sweeter mare."

The horse shook itself and bowed its head. "You dealt fairly. I expected less. May you have success, too."

And then at a canter he took off down the road, spreading his wings, rising to greet the dawn.

In the next moment, Maria was there with him—or rather, that shadow of her was. She looked so strained he thought she would fly apart at any moment.

She also looked as if she wanted to throw her arms around him and cry. "Thank the great Mother. They haven't moved her yet, Benito. But they have sent for an escort for her. There's a guard on the gate, and another two patrolling inside the wall."

He nodded with appreciation. That was his Maria! She might be beside herself, but she kept the presence of mind to scout for him. "You tell me where they are, and I'll see if I can get over that wall before it gets any lighter."

She wrung her hands. He'd never actually seen anyone do that before. "One of them hit her. She's your child, Benito. She said her daddy would hurt them. I hope you do." Maria's tone made clear they would be lucky if it was Benito who did the punishing and not her.

"I plan to," he promised grimly. "I plan to hurt them a lot. But first I need to get her out of there. How many of them are there?"

Now she looked uncertain. "Maybe... fifty. Some are asleep."

Benito gave a crack of laughter. "Well, so long as it isn't more than fifty. Lead me to it, girl. Let's see if we can do this without waking any of them."

Some miles away, on the very fringe of what had once been the marshlands of ancient Etruria, the Lion stirred in Marco Valdosta. *A nonhuman, a creature of magic, has just flown over the corner of my realm. A winged horse. I was unaware that any survived.*

First the poisoning, then the kidnapping—was this the third try? "Is it coming to attack Venice?"

It would rather appear to be going the same way as you are.

That did not comfort him. "A sending of Chernobog, maybe? Come to fetch 'Lessi."

It did not feel foul.

"He can use things," Marco turned to the troop captain. "Can we go any faster?"

"No, m'lord," said the captain. "We have a good twenty-five miles to go, and if we press our mounts too hard, they'll founder."

Marco sighed worriedly. "I wish this horse could fly too."

The Veneto

Carlo Sforza had left the castle with two hundred men. They'd been given very strict instructions about not shooting, and an explanation that if the child was killed their own lives would be forfeit. Behind him, the encampment and billeted officers were stirring men to action. In two hours there'd be two thousand men heading this way, and by terce the better part of seven thousand up and ready to move—all the men at his disposal right now. They had none of the supplies and logistics arranged, but Carlo knew that sometimes hard, fast and brutal succeeded when planning could not. He wanted his options open.

They advanced methodically. Scouting, blocking all the possible flight routes with stopper-groups—circling the target to make sure it was enclosed.

"We should be there just after dawn. I hope, Francisco, that this is not a false alarm and that they have long since recovered the child."

The tired physician smiled wryly. "I just hope we're not too late, or that I am not wrong about the place.

I hope, instead, that I am wrong, and that Marco Valdosta has the little one back. She looks like you, you know. She loves Marco dearly."

"He was a soft boy." Sforza shook his head. "Forgiving, I never really understood him."

"There is that about him still. But there is steel, too." Francisco pursed his lips. "More steel than you know. I think you might mistake softness for foolishness, and there is nothing that could be called foolish in him. Sometimes I find it is the weak who cannot forgive, and the strong who can, and by that measure, Marco may be the strongest man I know. He's very different from what I have heard of Benito, though."

Sforza brooded for a long moment, staring at a point between his horse's ears. "Benito sent me back my pilgrim medal. At first I wondered if he'd stolen it from me. Been that close to me that he could have cut my throat. Later I heard he'd taken it from the thief." He sighed. "I've never been a believer in regrets, but I should not have let her take the children. She was no good to them. It is nothing short of a miracle that they survived, much less turned out as they have."

"Those are the walls of the villa, m'lord," said their local guide, pointing to buildings barely visible in the pre-dawn, maybe a little less than half a mile distant.

"Down!" shouted someone.

The great wings beat at the sky. Troopers tried to calm their panicked mounts. Some of them tried to catch the horses they'd fallen off. The thing passed overhead, arrow-swift, and out of sight. It looked like it was landing somewhere ahead.

"What in the name of all the saints was that?" demanded Sforza.

Francisco shook his head. "Either I landed on my head and not my shoulder, or it was a flying horse."

"I think we will approach this building quite cautiously," said Carlo Sforza. "And if it wasn't for the fact that my granddaughter might just be in there, I would be going back to Bevilacqua as fast as I could ride."

"Could be Marco Valdosta. He traffics with magic," said Francisco, rubbing his forehead. "Remember what I said about strength, my lord."

Sforza grunted. "And . . . surprises."

Benito Valdosta, who had up to now seriously avoided trafficking with magic, and had no skills in that regard, wished right now that he did have.

Roof-climbing had got him this far. But he'd never mastered more than the rudiments of lock-picking. And that was all that was between him and his daughter.

"We need the key. Or a big pry-bar. I can't take a chance shooting the lock out. It might hit 'Lessi and doesn't always work anyway. It would make noise, too, which we can't afford."

"And I can't even tell her you are here," said Maria, sadly. "I don't know what Hekate did, but it seems I can speak to you but to no one else."

Benito's mouth twisted into something between a snarl and a grimace. "I want to hug my girl . . . but it's best if she keeps quiet. Can you look around?"

"I will try. It's not easy, Benito. I follow people more easily than looking at places, unless there are . . . memories of people there. This is a sad, horrible place. But I will try."

A few moments later she returned, as Benito levered at the door with his *main gauche* to no avail. It was a door intended to keep desperate people confined. "There is someone sleeping in the next room. Perhaps he has the key?"

"I have to start somewhere," said Benito, and left the door to itself for a moment.

The sleeper awoke to a knife at his throat and a very strong hand over his mouth. "If you want to live longer than the next few heartbeats," hissed Benito into his ear, "I need the keys for the room the child is locked in. And I really, really would like to kill you. That's my daughter in there, and if it weren't that I need to know how to get her out, your life would not be worth a rusty pin. Now I am going to take my hand away from your mouth. Your door is closed and no one else is awake here. I'll push this blade into your brain if you speak above a whisper. You won't even manage a whole scream."

He took his hand away slowly, knife-point in the man's ear.

The wide-eyed man was absolutely rigid as Benito removed his hand, and in a strangled rasp said: "Alberto keeps them. He's...he's upstairs at the end of the corridor. With his woman. Please don't kill me."

Benito hit him instead, with the back of the pommel of his *main gauche*, hard, on the back of the head. Something cracked. The man groaned and slumped. Benito scowled slightly. He might just have killed the man. He wasn't sure—and, truth to tell, he didn't care that much. Right now he was of the opinion that if he got the chance, he'd kill every one of these bastards and let God sort the innocent from the guilty. If there were any innocent.

He turned to the shadow of Maria. "Upstairs?"

She gestured upwards. "There are several people awake up there now. The kitchen is getting going. But there is a door into the kitchen garden and stable-yard along the passage from here. You were looking for a tool. There is a pickax there."

"That'll have to do."

It was next to the manure pile, along with a wooden shovel, and, hanging on the wall, some old rope. Somewhere in the distance a lark began to trill. The sky was perceptibly lighter than it had been when he'd gone over the wall. Morning was breaking. Benito crept towards the gate—with the shovel and the rope.

"Where are you going?" hissed Maria.

"I'm going to quietly lift that bar across the gate. And then I'm going to tie this rope across the path from the stables. And then I am going to jam this shovel under the guard-room door like a wedge. Half of winning is having a good escape. Breaking her out is going to make a noise, and we'll need to run. I want a clear run. There's a copse about sixty yards from the gate and that stream I crossed is in it. If I can get there with 'Lessi the water-sprites will help her and hide her."

A few moments later, with the chisel edge of the pick forced into the narrow gap between it the jamb, the door was also, like morning, broken.

Noisily.

Wood and then the lock cracked and then broke out.

Benito hit the door with his shoulder and fell into the room. His daughter was standing there on a filthy pallet, thumb in her mouth, hair disheveled, face tear-stained.

She pulled her thumb out of her mouth and screamed "Daddy!" at the top of her lung capacity. Benito scooped her up. "On my back, little one. Hold tight. We're going to have to run."

He desperately wished he'd kept a winged horse on standby. This had not been part of his plan at all. In quietly and out quietly, had been what he'd had in mind.

But he'd also not considered that there was going to be noise. Or a garrison of fifty. This was the best he could do, considering, and he had to hope it would be good enough to get her out.

He'd also considered nobbling the stable door in some way, to prevent them following—but had rejected it. Horses were as good watchmen as dogs, and stable boys tended to sleep there.

Still, the main gate was effectively open and the stables were close. He could have taken a horse if he were a rider of Erik's capacity. He ran back down the passage, with 'Lessi clinging to his back.

Only to meet someone coming down the stairs to investigate the noise. A hairy half-dressed someone, with a hand-cannon in his hand. Benito didn't wait for anything, shot or challenge, but threw his knife, hitting the man just in the vee below his Adam's apple.

It certainly killed him, but reflex must have squeezed that trigger. The hand-cannon boomed, sending its load ricocheting around, as Benito ran forward with one hand still supporting his daughter, his rapier already out.

The shot inside was heard outside the walls, too. The small ram had been made ready while two of the scouts checked the walled compound. It had a gate to keep the house secure against bandits or a handful of raiders—not professional soldiery who had made something of a specialty of destroying small fortifications.

Carlo pointed at the gate. "Take it down!"

The ram—a brass-headed pole, slung on chains between eight riders—spurred at a gallop at the gate. The gate simply crashed open, almost knocking the men off their horses on the back-swing. The charge spilled into the enclosed villa's yard.

Inside, in the corridor he'd sneaked up to fetch the pick, Benito Valdosta was aware of none of this. He just knew he had a passage to traverse to the yard, which had access behind him and in front of him—and that a number of men seemed set on stopping him from both directions.

"Don't shoot! You'll hit the merchandise!" yelled someone.

Well, someone was shooting outside all right. And Benito wasn't going to give these bastards the time to think about the alternatives in a narrow passage.

He had been trained by various very fine swordsmen, and there were none better than Giuliano Lozza on Corfu. These men were not of the same rank, not even close, and the passage confined them. Even carrying a child in one arm, he cut them down. And he had Maria to cry warning of someone behind.

Still, as more men piled into the passage, he felt the exhaustion of the long and frantic ride pile on him. This not a winnable situation; somehow, he needed to change the odds.

There was a solid knot of three in front of him. "'Lessi darling. I'm going to need two hands. Walk behind Daddy."

He put her down and charged forward—and suddenly heard Maria shrieking "Alessia!" behind him.

A brief glance and he saw that someone had come up from behind and had grabbed her.

Fury lent him extra strength and reach. He slashed hard across the two remaining faces, and turned to plunge after Alessia and her new captor.

And now, another foe. The tall man who was *behind* the scar-faced fellow with Alessia in his arms...

Blocked the passage.

Before Benito could decide which of them was the greater danger to 'Lessi, the newcomer ran the scar-faced man holding Alessia through. He caught the toddler before she could fall, and stepped back.

Benito, running into the fray with his sword ready, was desperately afraid he might cut her, as he leaped over the fallen scar-faced man. He already knew he was in trouble, deep trouble.

That was a master-swordsman who had just performed that brutal but clinical thrust. He could feel strength running out of him like water from a broken barrel. He stopped, trying to assess the situation.

And out of all expectation, like a miracle, the stranger lowered his blade. "I think she is yours," he said calmly, setting Alessia down. "Go to your daddy, girl. It's all right now."

Out of surprise, Benito froze. On plump little legs his daughter charged over to him. Benito shook himself out of his shock and picked her up, still watchful, still wary. "My thanks. I owe you more than I can say for helping her."

The stranger's face changed to alarm. *"Ware behind you!"*

Benito turned. The scar-faced man he'd seen so efficiently run through was getting up, sword in hand.

Benito was in a poor position for a thrust, but settled for a slash across the attacker's throat, and stepped back as quickly as he could without stumbling.

The scar-faced man staggered briefly . . . and the wound began to knit—and he came at them again.

"Saints! I killed him!" said the stranger who had rescued Alessia. And proceeded to do so again, very clinically.

To much the same effect. Only faster, this time. The stranger cursed, feelingly.

He and Benito retreated back up the passage Benito had fought down, fending off the ever healing monster-man. "Hell's teeth. Can we cut it to pieces?" asked the stranger.

"I cut a finger off. Look, it regrows," said Benito slashing at the arm-tendons. There was blood and then glutinous stuff oozing out of the wound, as the sword it was carrying fell. They both thrust into the undying body . . . and it fell, more blood and more ooze . . . and got up again, healing, with the sword. And where it had been cut once and healed, the flesh was almost impossible to cut again, short of a thrust.

"If I call my men, they'll not stop running this side of the Alps," said Benito's stranger-companion, fencing with the undying creature, trying to force it back. But it did not care if it was cut, and simply pressed forward. At this rate they'd find themselves trapped in Alessia's cell.

"Francisco! *Francisco!*" the stranger bellowed at the top of his lungs.

"M'lord?" called someone from up the stairs.

"Down here. We have a problem for you."

A tall fellow with dark, thinning hair came in from behind the scar-faced undying man. "Ah. Poulo Borgo." He thrust his sword neatly up from behind under the ribs and into the heart.

And tried to pull the sword out, and failed. "God's teeth!" the newcomer said, aghast. "He's healing around my blade!"

He turned and ran.

Benito's companion cursed. "So much for that. Look, boy. I'll bring it down, and you try and get past with the child."

"He's back!" said Benito.

Francisco had returned—with a sack. "Cut him!" Francisco called. "Cut it as much as you can! And pray to God this works!"

They slashed at the scar-faced monster, and Francisco threw handfuls of salt out of the sack.

The blood still flowed but the clear ooze did not like the salt. It pulled away, the wounds gaped. "More salt!" cried out Benito's savior. "Again! I think we're getting ahead of it!"

They slashed and slashed and Francisco threw salt. Among all of their efforts, a wound was opened into the monster's chest. Francisco poured salt into that.

Poulo fell over. Several more men had come down and helped to slash. "Kitchen! Find more salt. Even salt fish!" said Francisco.

Benito had another idea. He stepped back into the cell, slid his sword into its scabbard, and retrieved the pickax, then said to Alessia's rescuer: "Hold my girl for a moment, will you?"

The swordsman, a man of perhaps fifty summers,

with a round, hard, muscular face and curly black hair with just a trace of gray at the temples, looked nonplussed, as he had not by being attacked by an undying monster. "Here, Alessia," he said. Tentatively, he held out a hand.

'Lessi looked at her father, and then leaned toward the stranger-swordsman. He looked oddly familiar, Benito thought, as he swung the pickax at the salt-covered writhing man's scarred head.

Unprotected heads are not intended to take a blow from the point of a pickax. And as Francisco poured salt into that gaping wound, it did not heal. The thing did not much resemble a man anymore, but a runny puddle of body parts. Horribly, some of them were still moving, but more men were coming with more salt, and the one called Francisco was grimly casting it over the grisly object by the handfuls.

"I think we can get past, and out of here now," said the oddly familiar stranger.

"I'd like my daughter back," said Benito.

The man nodded, kissed the top of her head, and handed her back. "Let us get out of here, Benito Valdosta."

They stepped past the remains of Poulo. The man knew his name. How did the man know his name? "You have the advantage of me, Sir. I am in your debt. Who are you?"

"Ah. I think we will leave the situation just like that," said the older man, plainly amused. "On a different day you might have killed me instead. Let's just say that someone wanted me blamed for this, and probably wanted you, in particular, thirsting for my blood. And, well, I will admit that I have kept something of a watch over her. I must tell you one of my first concerns for this little one, was that Venice is an unhealthy pest-hole, according to my experience and to Francisco. It's him you owe this rescue to, really."

So the fellow was good for more than thinking quickly and coming up with monster-poison. Good God. Benito wondered just how many nightmares 'Lessi was going to have over this. He hugged her tightly. She had her arms around his neck and her face pressed into his shoulder. "He has just to name his reward. If I can do so, I will give it to him."

"I'll tell him that." They had walked out into the courtyard, where men—obviously soldiers, but not ones Benito recognized—were rounding up prisoners, pushing them into the gate watchtower. There were a fair number of dead men lying around, too. "Just one question," said the older man. "I had been informed that you were on your way to Byzantium and expected to overwinter in Corfu. I didn't believe that, but I expected you to be besieging Constantinople. You definitely were not in Venice yesterday. And if you came in yesterday, there'd be a lot more Venetians here right now."

How did this man know all this? Did he have more spies than the entire Council of Ten? "I flew in on a winged horse," Benito said, before he even thought about it. Ah, he was tired, to blurt out such things. Dead tired, and now that it was all over, all he wanted was to sit down. The man would probably think him insane for blabbering about a winged horse. But there was just a germ of a worry that this might actually be worse trouble than he'd escaped from.

"It *was* a winged horse. That is explained."

A rider came galloping in the gateway. "M'lord! There's a large party of horsemen approaching from Saletto!"

"Ah. Venice I think." He turned to one of his men. "Sound the retreat, Alto." He reached out and tousled Alessia's hair. "To avoid any misunderstandings, we'll leave you to greet them. I'd take one of their horses and get moved from here a little, just in case my fellows missed anyone."

Benito struggled to process it all. His brain was no longer working. He wasn't thinking, he was just... experiencing. He didn't even have the strength to react now. "Who are you?" he asked again.

"Not exactly a friend of Venice," said the stranger, swinging himself up into the saddle of a magnificent warhorse. A horse worth a duke's ransom, Benito guessed, although he was no judge of horseflesh. "Goodbye, boy. Take care of her."

Francisco stood behind him with a horse, already saddled and bridled. "Hello, 'Cisco," said Alessia.

"Hello, poppet." He held out his hands for the tot. "Here, Benito Valdosta. Let me pass her to you, once you're in the saddle. And give my regards and apologies to your brother. Tell him I have taught him as much as he needs to begin with, anyway."

"What?" said Benito, letting himself be helped into the saddle. He then took his daughter and settled her before him. He was tired, and more confused by the moment. But no one seemed to be threatening either him or Alessia.

"He'll understand." Francisco gave the horse a slap on the rump, which started it toward the gate. Benito almost fell off.

The soldiers—and they were plainly that—were either mounting up or already riding off, northward, toward Scaliger domains—or what was left of the Scaliger domains.

So, blinking a little in the sunlight, with one arm around his daughter, Benito headed south towards the stream on the edge of the copse. Whatever happened, he could get help from the water-spirits for his daughter.

"Well, Maria, we did it," he said quietly.

But there was no reply.

Chapter 40

The Veneto

Marco Valdosta had felt the sudden terrible, horrible, outpouring of dark magics just a few minutes after dawn. They had changed horses and Marco had been assured they were getting close.

His head went up, and his voice was the Lion's growl. "We need to gallop. Now."

The captain demurred. "We've still got a few miles, M'lord Valdosta."

Marco whirled to glare at him, and even in the dim pre-dawn light, whatever the fellow saw in Marco's face, it made him shrink back. "If we don't gallop now," Marco hissed, "we will be too late."

With that *look* to spur them on, they did. But it was simply too far, the horses began to tire and balk, so they had to slow up again.

Marco could barely contain his anxiety. If only...

There was a distant horn-call.

He put spurs to his tired horse, which lurched back into a gallop. The captain called out in alarm. "M'lord...it could be trouble. You'd be a rich prize. We should hold back, scout."

"And my niece's life may be at stake!" he shouted over his shoulder. "Ride, Captain, ride. And let's have our banners and pennants out. If any attack us let them know that they attack Venice. We can't have more than a mile to go. I just hope that is not them fleeing with Alessia."

Benito saw the Winged Lion flag on the brow of the hill, before he saw the horsemen. The final relief was such that he almost fell out of the saddle.

Or it could have been his daughter deciding to stand up, and dance, and yell: "Marco, Marco!"

Marco heard her little voice and then saw, of all mirages, his brother, with Alessia in front of him, on a horse riding towards them.

He rubbed his eyes. It had to be an illusion. Benito was an improbable sight. Benito sitting on a horse, more so.

It was only when the horse shied and Benito nearly fell off that he was sure that it was real. Benito, muddy, bloody and grinning, with his daughter yelling "Marco, Marco!"

"Am I ever glad to see you, big brother," said Benito.

Marco urged his tired horse to Benito's side and steadied him in the saddle. "What in the name of all the Saints are you doing here?"

"It's a long story. But you'd better send your men to that villa up there. There are some prisoners in the gate-tower we wouldn't want getting loose." He reached over, and squeezed his brother's arm. "And I cannot tell you how glad I am to see you. Even dressed up for war!"

Marco didn't know whether to weep with relief or cheer. "I can't tell you how glad I am to see you too, 'Nito. And how glad I am to see 'Lessi."

Benito passed her over to Marco, since she was trying to jump to him anyway. She was babbling something. Benito laughed—an exhausted laugh, but a laugh—and translated. "She says she needs breakfast, and I could eat an ox. It looks like you have three hundred or so men. Let's keep half and send the rest on to clean up."

Marco nodded, and hugged his niece, who continued to babble in his ear. "I'll definitely send a hundred and fifty back towards Venice with you. But I must go on. I felt some very black magic..."

Benito nodded. "Ah. That. The monster. A fellow named Francisco dealt with it with a few bags of salt. He seemed to know you very well. I think it is dead, but we'd better check, I suppose."

Marco gaped at him. "Francisco?"

Benito nodded, and Marco noted that his words were slurring a little, probably from fatigue. "Yes, he was with the small army that rescued me. He said to give you his regards and apologies, and that he'd taught you enough to begin with. They left. Said they didn't want misunderstandings."

Marco blinked. "He's Carlo Sforza's personal physician."

Benito was silent for a moment. "Well. Huh. That explains the other fellow. The one that looked... familiar. Hell of a swordsman. He said on another day I might have killed him." Benito slowly blinked his eyes. "So that was Sforza. I think I knew. I just wasn't ready to accept it." He shook himself and reached for 'Lessi, who was quite ready to go back to him. "Come on. Let's deal with the mess in that Villa, make sure the monster is dead, and then we can ride back together. I rather fancy having several hundred men around us."

Marco was still trying to put all the pieces together. If Sforza had helped to rescue 'Lessi, then who had kidnapped her? "Sforza is supposed to have about seven thousand with him."

Benito nodded, and yawned fit to crack his jaw. "I'd believe it. Let's get on with it. I'm nearly asleep in the saddle, and for me . . . that's saying something."

Well there was one thing for sure. Marco needed to let it be known that whoever their enemy was, it wasn't the Wolf. At least, not this time. "Yes. Let us just send some messages back to Venice, posthaste. I think avoiding misunderstandings is a good idea."

Riding northward Carlo Sforza, the Wolf of the North, was in an unusually pensive mood. He'd *thought* the boy might have learned some strategy and cunning from Benito's maternal grandfather; now he was sure of it. Carlo knew that Enrico Dell'este hated him—for Lorendana—with a passion, but he had some respect for the Old Fox. And it appeared that the Old Fox was doing right by the boys, which gave him even more respect for Dell'este.

Which was more than he had for Duke Filippo Maria Visconti right now. He had been considering a dangerous and potentially expensive break for some time now. Feelers had been put out, feelers that would have Visconti out to kill him if he'd found out. Well, maybe he had; maybe that explained what Visconti had been doing with him for a while. Nothing was ever truly secret in Italian politics.

A rider came galloping toward him. "M'lord. The San Salvaro stopper-group . . . they report sighting a large party of cavalry. M'lord, they are wearing Biscione on their livery."

The Biscione . . . the Serpent swallowing a child . . . the heraldic charge of the House of Visconti. The symbol of Duke Filippo Maria. It seemed dangerously appropriate right now. "How many of them?"

"It looks like about seventy or eighty, m'lord."

"Right, Vichonta. We're going to intercept some of the duke of Milan's men," said Carlo Sforza, his face setting into very hard lines. "And then there will be some questions asked. And then . . . it will depend on the answers."

Venice

By the time they got back to the waiting fusta at Mestre, Benito had learned a great deal about the tribulations of Venice in his absence. And the worries about its stability with Doge Dorma unwell, and Sforza rather closer than was comfortable. It had rather woken him up, given him a sort of third wind. Funny, that. It had been Marco advising him; now it was him advising Marco.

"You need to dig out Admiral Lemnossa. Lodovico knows him. Put him in charge of the military side, and you and Katerina deal with the crowds," said Benito bluntly. "You can't do military, Brother. But you can do being loved. And now that I have got off that damned horse, I am going to lie down and sleep. You can play with your niece. God's Love, I don't know where she gets all that energy."

And so he ate and drank and slept in the fusta like a corpse, only waking when they reached the city.

In Venice however, Benito found that the city was just as pleased to see him and his daughter, riding high on his shoulders, as they were to see Marco—or he was to see Venice. They became something of a parade, and he decided that he had found a second wind somewhere.

"Change of plans; we leave the little one to be fussed over at *Casa* Montescue, and I need to get moving as quickly as may be," he said, over the cheers and greetings. "We go to see Petro, and the Council and then I am off south—if I can find a vessel to carry me at this time of year. I need to get back to Constantinople. Grandfather will be having fits."

Guiltily, Marco realised that he'd spent most of the horseback part of the trip back telling Benito about his problems, about Petro, about the poisoning, about Francisco. He'd found his little brother had matured—a lot with his experience on Corfu, and also with this campaign. He actually knew a lot more about the wider world than Marco did, these days. And he had more practical experience of governance. "Yes. I should have thought of that. How is it all going?"

"About as well as can be expected," said Benito, as they got into a gondola and the gondolier sent it off without being prompted towards *Casa* Montescue. "And yes, I have learned a few things. The value of pikemen. Not being outnumbered. The danger of treachery. But I think Petro will be pleased enough.

Come and listen, and then I won't have to tell it twice. I'll prevail on the Council of Ten to let you sit in."

Lodovico was overjoyed to see them all, if dreadfully puzzled by Benito's presence. Kat accepted it all in her stride and carried off 'Lessi to be fed and washed and fussed over and put to bed with trusted ancestral servants watching her.

Then it was off to *Casa* Dorma. Petro was relieved. And amazed to see Benito. But he ordered food and wine to be brought to his bedside for all of them, before starting on the questioning. "I thought I gave you orders to deal with a fleet in the Black Sea?"

"We've got as far as Constantinople. Took the Calliopolis peninsula, and Pera. But shall we say, I came back by magical means, which I have no desire or ability to ever repeat, in one day," said Benito, between bites and swigs. He looked at the Doge, lying pale and weak in his great bed. "And, Petro Dorma, you have for years told me what to do. Looking at you now, I am going to tell you what to do, if you want to go on living and recover. For the good of Venice, and yourself you had better not resume your duties until my brother says you are fit to do so."

Petro demurred. "The city needs me, Benito."

But Benito snorted. "All it needs to see is that you're alive. For his last few years, what else did they see with Doge Foscari? What else can not be dealt with by the Council of Ten?"

"It does not make for a strong Venice," said Petro, tiredly. Benito was shocked to see a small tear on his cheek.

"Bah," he replied, with a bit of grin. "Neither will

prolonging your illness. Marco says you will recover fully. In the meanwhile—I think Venice will stand."

"I would once not have valued your opinion," said Petro, showing just a hint of his old spark. "Except about acrobatic dancers. But I think you know a little more now. Very well. I'll abrogate control to the Council. For as long as your brother decrees—*and* as long as he sits in on their meetings. He can tell me the worst, gently."

"He will surprise you, I think." Benito raised an eyebrow, and Marco echoed the gesture.

"Amaze me, perhaps. Nothing you two do will surprise me anymore. But if you find a way of getting from Constantinople to Venice in one day as a regular thing . . . it could be very profitable."

Benito laughed. "You're showing signs of recovery. Now, let me tell you just who decided to abduct my baby—and I think you will be even more surprised at who turned out to be my ally."

The Serenissima, Venice the serene city, was anything but serene. It was a dangerous, angry city. Rumor swirled like winter fog. Rumor had Carlo Sforza massing an army at the borders. Rumor had Doge Petro either slowly dying or dead already.

What was certain was that Benito and Maria's daughter had been returned to the city. She'd been seen riding on his shoulders by enough people, coming in to the Rio di San Nicolo.

And then it had rained. It was winter, after all. So they'd returned to the *Casa* Montescue huddling under cloaks and oilskins, hard for any watchers to make out details.

Lodovico was in a state. "I lost my Alfredo, my grandson, to one traitor in my household. And then we let another in! That child will never go out of my sight again. And what are you doing here, Benito?"

"She's a lot more guarded than the Doge, Lodovico. That's why I am here. I'll bet her mother is watching her right this moment, for a start."

"I've never really understood that, my boy," said Lodovico, putting a heavy hand on his shoulder. "But I felt I'd let our houses down. And we have failed each other enough."

Benito embraced the old man, who looked at first surprised, and then gratified. "Lodovico, I'd not have left her here if I didn't trust you with something more precious than my life. Now, stop fretting and offer me some wine. I'll have to soon cope with Petro Dorma."

Lodovico gave a crack of laughter. "Good luck. I was summonsed to see him this morning."

"How is he?" asked Benito.

"Hmm. Peevish I think is the best description. He's mending, but tired. Behaving like an old woman."

"So are you," said Benito cheerfully. "Now where is that wine?"

The next day, which dawned bright and cold instead of raining, things started to come to a head with the people gathering on Piazza San Marco. More and more. Nobody orchestrated it, word just spread.

And spread.

"They sound like angry bees out there," complained Petro. "It's time I addressed them, Marco."

"Can you keep it brief?" asked Marco.

"Can you keep from fussing over me like a mother

hen?" He took in the look in Marco's eye. "I will.
But if they see me it will be better than if they see
anyone else."

"Very well. But I will arrange a litter to carry you
there."

"I'm not dead yet," said the Doge irritably.

"You will be if you don't listen to your physician,"
growled something from Marco's throat. Petro felt an
odd...chill. Something very old and very powerful
looked at him out of Marco's eyes for a moment. The
look was admonishing.

Petro Dorma decided it was best not to provoke
the Lion further.

So Petro Dorma was carried up to the balcony
overlooking the Piazza. He insisted on standing there,
holding onto Marco's shoulder and the rail.

That got a cheer from the crowd. And more cheers
and more cheers. Marco felt the tremors in Petro's
grip. "Enough," he said. When that produced no result,
the Lion came into his voice. *"ENOUGH!"*

The crowd hushed. Petro spoke, his normally robust
voice reedy. "I am better than I was two days ago." He
managed a wave with the hand he had been clutching
the balcony with. "Our fleet triumphs in Greece. And
now I am going back to bed."

Marco led him to the litter. The Doge looked drawn,
but he waved Marco away. "Talk to them, Marco."

So Marco did. He talked of the need for vigi-
lance and unity. He told them of great success in
Byzantium. He talked of the greatness of Venice,
and of the greatness of the hearts of her people,
and how he and Katerina appreciated their help in
looking for Benito's daughter. In between cheering,

the crowd lapped it up. And then he helped Petro up again and the Doge waved to the crowd, and he had him back to bed.

"That'll hold them until they get home and start thinking," said Petro, tiredly.

Marco blinked. "I thought it was all fixed?"

"They know Carlo Sforza is just over the border. And they know I was poisoned, Marco. Soon some people will start joining up the points. And then they'll be demanding that the lists go up in the Piazza San Marco."

"My brother said you should get Admiral Lemnossa to see to the defense of the city."

"He did, did he?" said Petro. "Lemnossa's an old Doge Foscari appointee. Good with naval matters and trade but no general. I was asked to retain him here in case of a major naval attack. The Senate has these moments."

"Venice is a little like a ship at anchor right now. My brother has moments of being right. He could hardly be worse than General Lorenzo."

"That's true enough. And he's popular with some of the old-school members of the Senate. Very well."

Pera

Duke Enrico Dell'este stared at the letter again and shook his head. "Antimo, just what am I to make of this? Has the boy gone mad? His wife is back in Venice."

"I don't think he has gone mad—unless I have too," said Antimo Bartelozzi.

The Old Fox stared at him. "What?"

"I saw her too, Your Grace." He did not mention Hekate. "There is magic involved. I would guess at Marco Valdosta myself," he added, diplomatically.

Dell'este shook his head, his brows creased with worry. "It could have been a trap. Magical traps are one of the specialties of that thing at Vilna. Why didn't you warn me, Antimo? I could have taken steps to stop him."

Antimo Bartelozzi steeled himself. His employer had specifically asked him, repeatedly, to speak the truth and to say what he thought, and not merely say what he thought Enrico wanted to hear. "My Lord Duke, do you honestly think anything can stop that young man when he has decided on a course? All you would have done is lost someone you wanted very badly to find."

Enrico glared fiercely at him. Antimo thought that this time he might just have gone too far. But the glare subsided to a smolder. "Find him for me, Antimo. I have come to love him far too much."

"I will try, Your Grace. But ... I think any trap that tries to take Benito Valdosta had better have very strong jaws. And ..." He paused.

The silence went on long enough for the Old Fox to say, sharply, "And what, Antimo?"

Antimo grimaced. "M'lord. I saw her too. It was no false sending, that. She acted in ways that Benito recognized. I do not think it would be easy to fool him with an illusion. They ... Venetians, I mean, use magic in ways we do not. In the attack on Venice— she had powerful magical elements defending her. You know that Benito deals with the tritons. You told me so yourself."

More silence. Two men who preferred magic to remain the provenance of tale-tellers and Hypatians and not a part of their lives struggled with having its unpredictable power insert itself into the heart of their world.

"What am I to do, Antimo?" said Enrico Dell'este at length; sounding, probably for the first time in his life, like a plaintive old man.

Antimo had to shrug. He had no answer for a question like that. "What you always do, Your Grace."

The Old Fox growled. "I need to find a forge, and beat some hot iron."

Antimo fully sympathized. He very much wished he had some sort of similar outlet. Dell'este had accustomed himself to caring for nothing but Ferrara and himself. It had been a comfortable, if lonely, sort of life—because it meant his only worries were for Ferrara. Now he had Lorendana's boys, and one of them in particular had become very dear to him.

"He's as tough as old boot-leather, Duke Enrico," said Antimo. "Steel tempered by fire. Both of those boys. You can be proud of them."

"Caring too much is a mistake for a noble house, Antimo. I have Ferrara to think of. But...I have let that boy get to my heart. Just as I let Lorendana get to my heart. And look where it led." Bitter words... and Antimo decided that he was *not* going to allow that bitterness to bite in and take hold.

"It led down a hard path to two fine boys and more wealth and security than Ferrara has enjoyed for centuries," he said, firmly, and with complete conviction. "I believe that, even as I believe that the best steel must be forged, hammered, and tempered. The forging was painful, but the result is worth the pain. Now. I will begin searching, Your Grace."

Privately, Antimo was fairly certain Benito was in Venice.

He was wrong, though. Benito was already in the lagoon, on a vessel with the leads-man measuring the depths in the channel past the Lido, about to head south. And thinking about what he might do to speed his way back to his grandfather's side.

Chapter 41

Pera

So Duke Enrico Dell'este did exactly what he had always done. Coped. At this stage, with winter closing in around them, much of the siege process consisted of practical arrangements to keep the men healthy, fed, warm and reasonably dry—and with supplies of clean water. Having taken Pera helped a great deal with all of that. More than one siege had failed because half the men were down with flux and the other half had malaria. Of course, he also sent out scouts and spies—the last thing they needed was to suddenly become the biter bit. There were, after all, several small Byzantine armies out there.

The Byzantine *Themata* system meant those tended to have local command and association, and all of Enrico's information said the empire was in grave danger of falling apart, because Alexius had been an exceptionally weak emperor. The forces in Greece itself were rather taken up with winter, and the traditional raiding season from the north. And in Asia Minor, the border-fighting kept them busy. That was a long war of attrition on both sides. The Seljuk principalities to the east and the Armenian kingdom of Cilicia to the south both fought Byzantium and as well as each other.

Only, if reports were to be believed the Cilician-Seljuk border war had slowed. The Opiskon and Thracesion *themes* were both governed by men with some hunger for independence and personal power. They'd find excuses to avoid sending much support to Alexius.

But both would snatch at any chance of the throne itself. And between them they could field an army—and a lot more cavalry—of comparable size to the combined force of Aragon, Genoa, and Venice.

So Enrico snarled, dug into the expedition's treasury and sent a gift to King Gabriel of Cilicia, and promises of more aid with a letter signed by the Doge of Venice. Enrico could do little to get the Seljuks to restart their campaigns. But if the Armenians at least kept Opiskon and Thracesion busy, then that was one less worry. Then all he had to deal with was ill-discipline and the flux among the besiegers.

Antioch

The reason for the Seljuk Principalities of Rūm and Germiyan not harassing Byzantium was simple. They were riven from within. Assassination and mayhem had broken loose. Along with the sultan of Trebizond they had been calling for help from the Mongols, to whom they rendered tribute.

But the Ilkhanate, it seemed, had troubles of its own.

This was not the Great Khan's throne room, but it would do. He was, after all, on Progress. Certain amenities could be overlooked. Especially in light of the fact that his spies were ever so much more efficient with him close at hand.

The Great Khan sipped tea, and waited to hear the latest intelligence.

"Great Khan," Grand Vizier Orason bowed respectfully. "I have, I think, come to the center of this plague. As we said it is not Alamut. The center of their power is Damascus. It appears that after your great-uncle broke the power of Alamut, the Baitini moved many of their people to Damascus. They have a madrassa near the Al-Faradis gate."

"I assume, Orason, that you mean that they used to," said the Ilkhan. One eyebrow rose, ever so slightly.

The grand vizier bowed lower. "You are most astute, Ilkhan."

The Great Khan put aside his tea, and leaned forward, slightly. "But you wouldn't be telling me this, if something had not gone wrong. My generals would simply bring me baskets of heads."

"Once again, O Ilkhan, you are correct." Orason looked pained. "They had somehow got word, and many of the masters, as they call themselves, had fled through tunnels under the walls. But we captured some, and also much correspondence."

He paused, and then rushed the last hurdle. "Quite a lot with Bashar Ambien of Jerusalem. It appears that he sent one of their assassins as a tarkhan to the Golden Horde, with instructions to kill or thwart the election of Kildai of the Hawk Clan to the khanship— in direct contradiction of the orders you had issued."

Hotai the Ineffable sat, absolutely motionless, not even appearing to breathe. Eventually his breath hissed out. "I want the bashar of Jerusalem brought to me. And we will need a new envoy to the Golden Horde. I assume the purpose of this was to engender war with our northern kin. There will be a suitable reward for the man who kills this tarkhan, especially if they manage to thwart him. Have the documents drawn up at once, stripping him of all authority and setting a price on his head. A generous one."

Orason approved. This Progress was doing Hotai the Ineffable a great deal of good. He had become somewhat quicker of thought, and definitely more decisive in action. But . . . "It will be done immediately, Ilkhan."

The eyebrow rose again, higher. "I read in your tone that all of this is not quite as easily done as said."

Orason clasped his hands together under his sleeves. Tightly. There was a great deal more bad news to deliver. "There is the issue of getting the envoy and the message through to the Golden Horde, Ilkhan. And the issue of the original tarkhan's escort."

Both eyebrows rose. A good sign, or a bad one? "Explain."

"The bashar of Jerusalem made use of the good offices of certain pilgrims to Jerusalem. Pilgrims of high rank in the Holy Roman Empire." How tangled his web of deception was! Orason felt his scalp prickle with sweat. "There was . . . an aspect of diplomacy and politics in their pilgrimage. They were glad to oblige, therefore, in dealing with the Venetians who do a great deal of trade in the Black Sea, and have vessels capable of taking envoys and messages to the Golden Horde. Our relationship with the Republic of Venice is a little tense over certain issues. It made sense to use the Franks as an intermediary."

A frown. A very bad sign. "Thereby tarnishing our reputation among the Franks. Who were these 'pilgrims,' Orason?"

The worst news of all. "The highest among them was Prince Manfred of Brittany, who is the nephew of the Holy Roman Emperor."

The Ilkhan sighed. "It is to be hoped that this Baitini scum does not try to kill him, too. Better relations with the Holy Roman Empire...I am not sure that this is in our interests, anyway. But that sort of tarnish on the reputation of our Khanate and our diplomats, we cannot tolerate. We will have to be prepared to make certain gestures. And we had better see if we can reach some accommodation with the Venetians or the Genovese about transporting our new tarkhan, and sufficient escort to see our will done."

Orason stifled a sigh of relief. The ax would fall on other necks this day. The Ilkhan was usually temperate even in the face of dreadful news, but it was never an easy thing to step into the den of the dragon and tell it that its pearl had gone missing. "It shall be as you order, Ilkhan. In the meanwhile, there has been something of a contagion with the fleeing masters of Damascus's Baitini. I have taken the liberty of sending word to the commanders of the military units."

"They like to work in darkness. Let's give them some curfews and military patrols to deal with," said the Ilkhan irritably.

Trebizond

The streets of Trebizond had been one of the early beneficiaries of the steps taken by the Ilkhan. And now,

with the Baitini humbled by the Hypatian humility, the
streets began to edge back toward normal—arguments
and chaffering—and people quietly marveling how close
they had come to the brink. The Hypatian chapel was
rather fuller than usual. And the podesta Michael was
still breathing. Not conscious, but breathing.

Chernobog, in those other realms, passed through
this place. She saw him, and she no longer wept, with
her dogs at her side. But her attention was taken by
something to the west. She was stronger now.

Hades

Maria occupied herself in the quiet life of the netherworld. It was hard, here, to stir passions. She understood why Aidoneus needed a human bride to bring
some life to his kingdom. She'd felt terrible just leaving
Benito once Carlo Sforza had plainly rescued him, but
although that had scarcely been fair to Benito, it was
the letter of her bargain and her word. She'd asked
to be allowed to rescue her daughter. That was done
now, and she was back to being the queen of the gray
realms. Alessia was safe, and seemed none the worse
for the horrors she had seen and the trauma she had
weathered. Maria was pent in the netherworld again,
able only to look, and not touch, and not speak, with
those above. It would probably take Hekate's help to
be able to do so anyway.

And now, belatedly, Maria wondered *why* Hekate
had taken a hand.

The subject was raised by Aidoneus, as they walked
among the asphodels. "Hekate's intervention is strange.

She has begun to reassert her traditional roles. She has taken up her guardianship of my gates again, and her dogs watch to make sure the living do not accidentally enter. Nothing passes the gates that she does not permit. Do we see the old gods being reborn, I wonder?"

"That old man with the winged horse . . . was he a god? If so, I hope not," said Maria. "I didn't like him. Even though he seemed half mad with age, there was something very nasty about him. Crafty, in a low and mean way."

Aidoneus nodded. "Poseidon, the Earth-Shaker, ruler of the oceans. He was once one of the great ones. He fades, though. He was once a seducer and a ravisher of note, my dear wife. I would have kept you away from him." He said the last with a slight smile, but Maria knew him well enough by now to tell that he was actually dead serious. There was plainly no love lost there.

Maria sniffed. "He was as charming as a flea. And Hekate, it seems, hates him with a passion."

"He seduced her once, too," Aidoneus replied, and stooped to pick her a flower. He handed it to her, and she took it, still studying his face. "He was both cunning and charming at times. He was also powerful and some women are attracted to that, and ignore the rest, but not in her case, I think. He tricked and deceived her and then sent the sea in through her gate to flood her people."

"I thought nothing went through her gates?"

"Gates in the world above. Gates of earth that kept the sea from the land where her people dwelled. Very real barriers against the sea. He broke them with an earthquake and the water from the Mediterranean did the rest. A great many souls came to the gray lands that day. She lost her people, and still he did not keep his promise and free her child. He killed the other child. Slandered and lied about her, called her a monster, and broke his word and kept the child."

A pang went through her, an echo of the pain she had felt when her own baby was taken. "Should I get Benito to free her child? I . . . we owe her. And I'm a canaler. We pay our debts."

Now Aidoneus actually laughed, something that came seldom to him. "Benito did. I told you, Pegasus is her child. When Benito was finished with the wind-lord, he turned the winged one loose, gave him freedom. But Pegasus has not gone back to his mother."

"So she doesn't know he's free?" Maria bit her lip. "Perhaps . . ."

But she didn't finish that sentence. Sometimes it was better for gods *not* to know things that mortals were contemplating.

Chapter 42

Illyria

Benito had ample time to regret not bargaining for a return-trip from Pegasus. Five hundred miles by sea, with little more to do than endure the rain and read a book on classical Greek mythology, and a further five hundred overland. It took just under three weeks to get as far as Corfu, and then Benito had to go and beg for help from Iskander Beg. It was winter now, too, and the snow lay on Illyria. Benito had resigned himself already to crossing large parts of Byzantium incognito. That was a risky business, especially in winter when merchants were not often on the roads, and local soldiery and bandits were around, and were hungry. The difference, Benito had been told, was not always easy to establish.

Benito had no trouble getting taken to see the King of the Mountains. Iskander Beg was at Xarrë—which was nearly as low as he could go and not be at sea-level. The village was set in the midst of fertile flat-lands with the old port of Bouthroton on the estuary to the north west.

There was tea, of course—there was always tea—and little sweet pastries, and sitting on flat cushions on the carpet. "Very agricultural and flat for a King of the Mountains," said Benito, grinning at the vast moustache of the legendary lord of the fractious tribes of southern Illyria.

"Ah, Benito Valdosta, I have missed your sharp wit!" Iskander Beg motioned to a servant to refill Benito's tiny glass. "How comes it that my information puts you in Crete?"

Benito sipped, and shrugged. "I get about, kinsman, I get about. Why, three weeks ago I was just outside Constantinople. I need to get back there. But sieges are so boring I thought I'd take some time off."

The white teeth were showing through his moustache now. "I don't think I want a Venetian empire on my southern border, Benito."

Benito waved a disparaging hand. "I don't think you're going to get one. Petro Dorma regards holding vast amounts of territory—especially hostile territory—as an expensive waste of effort. He'd rather have trading bases and suck the money out of the territory without having to look after it. He's said as much to the Council of Ten. I was there. I heard him. And they agreed. Such things would take an army, which Venice does not have, and would have to pay for. No Venetian likes to pay for anything as hungry and greedy as an army."

The grin widened. "How very Venetian."

Benito laughed. "It works for us. Any word from our last joint venture, by the way?"

"The Knights of the Holy Trinity and the Mongol? No. I still have a messenger waiting in the village nearest the border. I learned a great deal from them."

"Oh, such as?" asked Benito.

"I have learned that they are not King Emeric's Magyar cavalry. And the Mongols are not the Croats. I do not think we want any part in fighting against either." He proceeded to tell Benito about the ambush and how the Knights and the Mongols had given the hopeful "bandits" of Peshtanc a very pointed lesson. "This is Illyria. Someone will always try it out."

"I shouldn't think they'd try it twice. Or anyone else will be in a hurry to try it a second time."

Iskander chuckled. "No. You were lucky to find me here, by the way. I go east tomorrow. There are raids to conduct, kinsman, and work to be done."

Benito nodded with satisfaction. "That's convenient. I need to go east as fast as possible. I'll even put up with riding to do so."

"I had forgotten your legendary skill in the saddle," said the King of the Mountains. "It's a good thing we are taking sleighs full of equipment then. Snow in the mountains makes moving easier, not worse, as long as it is hard-packed and not too deep. We have a few little cannon we plan to reduce some fortresses with. And I must talk to various chieftains in Macedon about the news you bring. I think this may be a good time for some territorial expansion."

It would keep the thematic *armies of Thrace and Thessally busy*, thought Benito. "Our mutual profit then."

"Yes, it'll keep them off your back," said Iskander, to whom this had plainly occurred too.

Not for the first time, Benito realized that they were rather alike in their thought processes. "It'll make for a bloody summer."

Iskander nodded. "But we might as well take what advantage we can."

The next few weeks were cold, and interesting. Benito got to know the enigmatic Iskander a great deal better, and to realize just what a task he had dealing with the various mountain tribes and clans—and their many feuds and raids. The Derrones would sooner kill their neighbors the Agriones than fight Byzantines, and would only combine to fight Byzantium if a third party—Iskander, whom they both respected and gave fealty to—acted as intermediary. They were tough people, but fiercely independent. If they'd been a little less inclined to fight each other, Byzantium would long ago have fallen.

Then in Macedonia, Benito struck out on his own, heading south with a guide Iskander provided to Aenus, a small Genovese colony and trading city at the mouth of the Maritsa river.

From there it was a mere day's boat-ride to the Callipolis peninsula, where he nearly gave the guards stationed there conniptions by turning up at their post.

"M'lord," said an unobtrusive, sandy-haired man, as Benito walked into Callipolis-town. "M'lord, Duke Dell'este has been . . . inquiring after you."

The man had all the hallmarks Benito had come to associate with *successful spy*—that is, he was very ordinary. "Is he incandescently angry or anxious?"

The spy bit his lip. "I really couldn't say, m'lord. Both I think. Can I send him word that you are here, safe?"

Benito was sure his permission would not count for much. "I'm going there, as fast as possible."

"There is a galleass from the Genovese fleet in port."

That was the best news he'd had in weeks. "Good. Let us go and talk to the captain. I'm sure he can be persuaded to give both of us a lift to Pera."

Pera

Enrico Dell'este looked up from his maps at the knock at the door. Antimo. He knew that knock.

"Enter," he said, using a magnifying glass to peer at the print and not looking up. "You can tell me just what you wrote here, Bartelozzi. I don't imagine you have any news of that grandson of mine?" There was just a hint of anxiety in the old duke's voice.

"I do have news," said Antimo.

"What? What news? Tell me quickly, man."

"He's walking up the hill," said Antimo, smiling. "I got here faster because I don't have men cheering and holding me up."

"Where the Hades did he come from?" Enrico demanded, unable to hide his relief.

"According to my man, he just came from Callipolis on a Genovese vessel."

"Then that letter was some kind of forgery. Has he been a prisoner? Was there treachery?"

"You can ask him yourself, m'lord. By the sounds of it he is entering the tower now. You can hear the cheering."

"I think, Antimo, that I will not go to meet him. I will sit down."

"As you wish, Your Grace," said Antimo. "I shall leave you."

"Stay, Antimo. I . . . I have reasons. Observe him closely."

So Antimo Bartelozzi was in the room when Benito strode in, beaming. "I thought, at the very least, Grandfather, you would have reduced the wall a bit more by now."

"Where the hell have you been?"

Benito paused. "I assume you did not get my letter?"

"I did."

"Ah. Well, I have several more for you." Benito dug in his pouch. "From Doge Dorma. He is not too well. He was poisoned by Visconti agents, but is recovering."

Benito put the letter, bearing the seal of the Doge of Venice, on the table. "And these two were waiting in Venice for a vessel to carry them. They are from Baron De Terassa."

De Terassa was acting as regent in Ferrara in the duke's absence. Enrico looked at the letters without touching them. The seals had not been broken.

"I spoke with M'lord Calmi about them," said Benito. "I thought if there was a problem in Ferrara I'd best know what it was before I left. He seemed to know. Said it was a tempest in a wineglass."

"De Terassa is an old woman," said Enrico Dell'este, still not taking either letter. "Now tell me exactly where you have been, and why you could not tell me before you left, boy?"

"I have been to a villa just north of Venice, on the edge of Veronese territory, and rescued my daughter," said Benito evenly. "And I came back, as fast as I could, by way of Venice, Corfu, and Illyria, where Iskander Beg is now moving to attack Thessaly and Thrace."

"And without the fairy tales?" asked the duke Dell'este, frostily. And then, startled, he turned his head to stare at new arrivals. "Who the hell are you? Get out!"

That was perhaps a natural reaction to the intrusion into the room of two large dogs and an imperious and angry-looking tall woman with a queen's ransom in gold and jet jewelry.

He had not seen her arrive there, and the door was still closed.

Chapter 43

The Veneto

Carlo Sforza was not a man who had spent much of his life musing on might-have-beens or regrets. He was a man renowned for finding the weak point of an enemy's defenses and applying overwhelming force. Brutal efficiency was his strength, not sensitivity.

Right now he was indulging in some strange feelings, and some regrets. That boy . . . and the child. What would have happened, had he taken the boys, raised that one himself, had him by his side? What would Benito Valdosta have become?

Well, he could not undo the past. But he could look to the future.

He rode forward to meet Count Di Lamis. The count was suffering from a bad mixture of terror and attempted hauteur. In an era when most Italian noblemen had had to face combat, Di Lamis had been singly good at avoiding it. His enemies died or were imprisoned or betrayed. Lances at his throat were a novelty to him, and not one he was enjoying, by the look of it.

"Sforza! These men of yours have no respect for rank," he blustered.

Sforza wasted no time on niceties. "Explain what you're doing here, Augustino."

Di Lamis was sweating, but he drew himself up and looked down his nose at Sforza. "I am about Duke Visconti's business. Get your troops out of our way. They killed several of my men. You're going have to explain that to the duke."

Francisco smiled at him from next to his master. They'd done this before. No one believed Carlo Sforza could be gentle or sympathetic. "Count Di Lamis, this is a dangerous and lawless country. Can we escort you?" he asked silkily. "Perhaps assist, if we can. It is, after all, our task to help the duke's men if possible."

Di Lamis faltered just a moment. Did he suspect that they knew? Surely not. "I am on an important mission . . . I cannot tell you of it."

"Then we can't help you. Or trust you. There is treachery about, and accidents happen out here, and no one will know just who killed you," said Sforza. There was no threat there. Just promise.

Di Lamis plainly knew how Duke Visconti viewed his mercenary general. "I am ordered to . . . to fetch a valuable hostage. Nothing to do with your campaign, I swear."

"Where from? There is fighting south of here," said Francisco. "Venetians."

Di Lamis began sweating again. "How close? We may indeed need an escort. To the Villa Parvitto, close to Casale di Scodosia."

And that was all the Wolf needed. Carlo Sforza pointed to two of his sergeants. "Take him to Bevilacqua and toss him in the deepest dungeon there, under heavy guard. I will forgo the pleasure of beheading him myself, immediately. That may come his way later."

Count Augustino Di Lamis went white as they grabbed him, and hauled him off his horse. "Unhand me! *You dare not.* Duke Visconti will see you die slowly and painfully for this. I am a personal friend of his, you cretins!"

Francisco looked at the count. The sergeants were paying no attention at all to his ranting.

"M'lord. I think we should strip him. Filippo Maria used Di Lamis's appearance against you. And the two of you look quite similar."

"I think I'll have to grow a beard," said Carlo Sforza, with utter disgust. "I do not wish to be taken for a poisoner and child-kidnapper. Strip him, boys."

"But I'll die of cold!" squalled Di Lamis.

Sforza grinned the grin that had given him the nickname of the Wolf of the North. "I think that would be the best you could hope for."

A little later, they rode north, with a set of elegant slashed breeches and a doublet, showing crimson silks—with a great deal of gold embroidery, and a cloak lined with Vinland timber-wolf fur.

"What are you going to do with him, my lord?" asked Francisco.

"A poisoner and a schemer? I have a use for him. Or I'll take his head off if we fail," said Sforza.

Behind them, the mobilization of Sforza's mercenary forces proceeded at a rapid pace. The winter was generally a slow time. A time to recover from the campaigns of the rest of the year. But if the Wolf wanted them to march or ride, they would. This was no orderly move, this was typical Sforza: strike hard and with overwhelming force. No one questioned it or wasted time. He commanded a great deal of personal loyalty, still.

So by mid-morning, they were moving northward toward Mantova, with almost nine thousand men in his force. The duke had considerably reduced his funding and men since the lost battle at the Piave. But even excluding the soldiery left to hold secure Bevilaqua and Moldanro, Sforza's nine thousand had the edge on Milan's other condottiere, Di Valmi, and his larger army. But those troops were dispersed in Matova, Pavia, Cremona, and Milan. Bressica had a small garrison of Sforza's men, too, and messengers rode ahead to their captain.

Carlo would have preferred to ride directly to Milan, but such a mass of soldiery does not move fast. The cavalry—a mere three thousand, would be there. The rest would come as fast as weather allowed. And his guns . . . Well, if he needed them Carlo knew he would have failed.

They rode from Bressica to Milan on the third day. Mantova had made no real resistance, the captains of the garrison assuming that Sforza acted on the orders of the duke, and that these were reinforcements against impending attack. At Bressica, his men held the gate, and the city suffered for trying to resist. But looting would wait.

Milan would not.

Sforza donned the cockscomb clothes of Augustino di Lamis, and rode ahead with a mere three hundred men, all with the Biscione charge on their livery. Some of the clothes had bloodstains too, if anyone had looked closely.

But no one did.

Milan

They rode into the city unopposed. Plainly the gate guards were instructed to admit Count Di Lamis. Captains Melino and Di Galdi split off, with a hundred and fifty men. Their task was quite simple: take and hold the gates until the cavalry arrived and keep any of Di Valmi's men out.

Carlo Sforza and his handpicked men rode on. Sforza had no intention of trying to deal with Duke Filippo Maria Visconti's Swiss mercenaries, until his own men arrived. Instead they siezed control of key places in the city. The armory, the central barracks, the Duomo. They could not keep the usurpation of power secret for long, but his cavalry entering en masse made that unnecessary.

Sforza believed in applied force—and that meant cannon. But those he did not have to bring along; they were in the city armory already.

The Palazzo Reale gates were not built for cannon fire. Nor did the five hundred mercenaries guarding it wish to die for their wages—and that was the only choice they were offered.

To give him credit, Duke Filippo Maria Visconti had not tried to flee. He was sitting on the ducal throne, very much alone, when Sforza and his men burst in.

"For a moment I almost thought you were Count Di Lamis," said the duke.

"He's sitting in a dungeon in Bevilacqua. He told me entirely too much to allow you to live, Duke Visconti." Sforza walked forward a few yards, but did not approach the duke too closely.

Filippo Maria sneered. "The noble houses of Europe—and I am related to all of them—will never accept a usurper ruling Milan, Sforza. Come and kill me if you dare."

"You will never know what they do or don't accept," said Carlo Sforza, taking a wheel-lock pistol from his belt. Standing exactly where he was, he shot Duke Filippo Maria Visconti dead.

The great chandelier in the roof came shrieking and rattling down on its chains to crash and shatter onto the marble. It was a marvel that the emperor Carl Fredrik himself had admired: a heavy structure of wood, iron, gold leaf and Venetian glass, with great chains and pulleys to raise and lower it so that the fat candles could be replaced. If Sforza had answered that challenge with a sword, it would have crashed down on him.

"I am entirely too familiar with your treachery, Filippo Maria," said Carlo Sforza, tuning away.

Milan was in for a very hard day. Sforza had protected certain valuable assets, but his was a mercenary army and they had just taken a very rich prize indeed. Once the looting and rapine were over, it would be a matter of holding what they had taken. But it would take days for more than the petty opportunists to start to tear at the edges of the corpse of the principality. It would take weeks for the news to spread, and months for an organised campaign to oust him. By then, Carlo Sforza would be ready. He would send emissaries out and see if he could divide his enemies. He knew that they would be attacking him on his territory, and he had attacked enough others to realize what an advantage for him that could be, and how to use it. But first he would let Milan suffer, and then he would rescue it and restore order. The citizens would be grateful. Sforza had taken enough cities and towns to know this was not just the reward of conquerors, it was a rite of passage.

Venice

Matters did proceed as Petro had predicted, with calls for the militia to defend Venice, something Admiral Lemnossa seemed cheerful about. "It keeps them busy, makes them feel constructive. And they can be used to put out fires. There is little enough real work at this time of year anyway."

And then came the first of the rumors from the north. Confused and scared rumors. Rumors not of invasion, but of insurrection in Milanese territory.

Two days later a Venetian spy came down in person to brief the Council of Ten. Or maybe he decided that Milan was a good place to flee from for a while. Marco was allowed to sit in, behind a screen. The Doge did not attend, simply because Lord Calmi didn't tell him about the meeting. Marco knew he would have insisted otherwise. But Petro was recovering, liverish and somewhat sorry for himself, principally because he enjoyed rich good food, not the simple slops he was being allowed.

"M'lords. Filippo Maria Visconti is dead. I saw his head on a pole myself. Milan is in a state of anarchy right now. They're looting and raping... the very men paid to guard her."

❈   ❈   ❈

"I wonder," said Petro Dorma, later, "how long it will be before the various claimants to the Duchy of Milan come beating their way to our door, looking for our support."

"It might be worthwhile," said Lord Calmi. "A compliant and suitably weakened ruler controlling access to the Holy Roman Empire and Aquitaine—"

"Marco says I am not supposed to get over-excited," said Petro dryly. "Otherwise I might point out just who those mercenaries belong to."

"Sforza? But they're out of control..." Calmi's words trickled away into silence.

"Because he will let them be that. He'll call them to heel by the end of the week, mark my words. I would guess that the armies under Di Valmi, possibly with Pisa or Florence in support, will attack soon."

"It would be a good time to try to flank him," said Calmi.

"With what? General Lorenzo?"

"You have a point, Doge Dorma," said the spymaster.

Later, when Marco came to check on his patient again, the subject came up. "But...you think Carlo Sforza will try to make himself duke? He's...he's a commoner isn't he? I mean he is very rich..."

"I suspect this argument will be used again and again. He'll probably marry suitably. And let's be honest here, Marco, how deep could you cut the noble houses of Europe and not find a rich commoner? We may use this as a fiction to make war on Sforza, but it won't be the real reason. That will be because of the opportunity a weakened Milan presents."

Lord Calmi coughed. "If I may intrude? Doge

Dorma, we have just received a gift—or so it was labeled—from Carlo Sforza."

"What? Overtures?" aske Petro Dorma, suspiciously.

"Of a sort, yes. He sent us Count Augustino Di Lamis, in chains, with a message."

"Ah. One of the Late Filippo Maria Visconti's cronies, one, if I recall, implicated in my having to eat burned bread and not goose liver. And what was the message?"

"'I suggest you ask him about kidnapping and poisoned fish. Force majeure is how *I* deal with enemies.' And it is simply signed, *Sforza*."

Petro was silent for a while. Then he sighed. "The decision will of course have to be made by the entire Council of Ten, but I would suggest we thank him for the gift and say we look forward to the news of his nuptials."

"What?"

"To *whom*, you mean, Calmi. I would guess to one of the impoverished Visconti relations in Pisa," said Petro.

"Are we then to expect peace from Carlo Sforza?" asked Marco, hopefully.

"Hardly. But I would forgo expecting any clever assassination ideas in dealing with Carlo Sforza." Petro pondered a moment. "And...who knows? Perhaps the Wolf has finally found enough to occupy him without going to war anymore. Even a wolf gets old, and the warm den and a complacent mate look better than another round of teeth and claws."

PART VI
February, 1541 A.D.

Chapter 44

Pera

Antimo recognized the woman at once, even before she announced herself.

"I am Hekate," she said imperiously, showing not the slightest sign of deference to Enrico Dell'este. Nor any sign that she intended to obey him and leave. How had she gotten into the room in the first place?

The red-eared dogs, large plume-tails waving, advanced on Antimo, obviously pantingly pleased to see him. "Er, Hekate," said the agent. "Perhaps not..."

"You know this woman?" Enrico Dell'este's tone was so cold that it would have been at home in the north of Norseland.

Antimo tried not to wince visibly. "Yes, m'lord. Hekate..."

Dell'este was livid. "Take her *out*, Antimo. And find out just who let her in. I have words to say to Benito."

The woman turned her dark gaze on the Lord of Ferrara, and frowned slightly. "You are impertinent, mortal. You will be quiet."

Enrico opened his mouth, a vein on his forehead throbbing, eyes narrowed. But no sound came. His mouth moved but no sound emerged.

Benito looked at his grandfather and then at the woman, and put several pieces of the puzzle in place. He'd had nothing to do on that voyage across from Venice but read for several days, and had only had one book of ancient Greek myths as his supply of reading matter. And given that he seemed to have fallen into the middle of them, well, he deemed it to be a very good notion to commit them to memory.

He bowed respectfully. "Hekate. Goddess of the Night. Queen of Magic. We beg your pardon that we did not treat you with due deference and respect. My grandfather is in some distress." Benito, as politely as possible, gestured at the duke who was mouthing frantically and looking as if he might just give himself apoplexy. He'd plainly worked himself into a state of anxiety and anger.

"He is an old man and spoke without understanding who he addressed. Please release him. I am afraid for his health and well-being."

Hekate looked at him with some suspicion. "I am She of the Night, but magic is merely one of my attributes. Who is this man, Antimo Bartelozzi?" she asked, pointing at Benito Valdosta.

"Um."

Another piece of the puzzle fell into place in Benito's head. "This is Hekate who you asked us to protect, Antimo?" *She needs protection like I need Admiral Burana's brains,* thought Benito.

Antimo nodded, then turned to the annoyed goddess. "This is M'lord Benito Valdosta, Lady Hekate.

And my master, the duke of Ferrara. I must also ask that you . . . let him speak. Please."

She ignored that part. "Benito Valdosta. The man that the woman from Aidoneus' halls sought."

"Maria," said Benito, nodding. "Yes, Lady of the Night. She's my wife. She came to tell me our daughter had been kidnapped. I went and got her back."

Hekate's brows furrowed. "And what have you done with my child?" she demanded.

"Alessia?" Benito blinked. "She's back with Kat and my brother Marco. Probably the most closely watched girl in all Italy right now. I think I owe you much for letting Maria speak to me."

The goddess rapped the butt of her bone harpoon on the floor. "Not your daughter! *My* child. My child that Poseidon tricked me away from and stole away. Pegasus. *What have you done with him?*"

It was Benito's turn to gawp like a landed fish, his mouth moving. No words came out, but not because she'd put a spell on him. "Uh. I got him to carry me to Veneto. And then, as we'd agreed, I let him go."

"You returned him to captivity with Poseidon!" She began to raise her old bone harpoon.

Benito frantically waved his hands in negation. "No! I let him go, I told you. He said he wanted to be free. I let him go. Go on his own way, free as a bird. That was our bargain and I honored it. I took the golden bridle off him and I told him to go where he wanted. Eat grass, fly, whatever. I wished I hadn't, later, because it would have made it a lot easier to get back, but I did set him free right then."

"I believe him, Lady Hekate," said Antimo, quietly but firmly—and stepping in front of Benito.

There was fire in her eyes. "Bargain? You must have made a bargain with Poseidon to betray my son, or he would never have let him go."

Benito laughed. It took a great deal of courage to do so because he had no delusions that he was better, faster or smarter than this woman. "Poseidon? You mean the old fool with a beard and three-pronged spear? He could hardly stand up, let alone stop anyone. I tricked *him*. He was weak, maybe from lack of worshippers, and he was easy to fool."

That caused her to pause. Benito dug back in his mind, a long way back, to the duellist-and-murderer-for-hire, Ceasare, and the lessons he had taught them. *Keep them talking. While they talk they don't do.* "I am sorry," he said. "I didn't know he was your son. Pegasus, I mean. I didn't know why Poseidon had him imprisoned there. I thought he was . . . Gorgon's child. He's a great flier."

She scowled. Was the room darker? "The lies that Poseidon put about!"

"Look. I swear I let him go," said Benito, earnestly. "I will happily go with you to Okseia island, and you can have a look for yourself. He's gone. The last I saw, Poseidon was sitting on a step trying to raise a storm all by himself. I tricked him into trying to call one up, told him I didn't believe he could. He couldn't resist the challenge."

Hekate's brows relaxed a little, and the room lightened. She looked faintly troubled. "I cannot. I can never go there."

That didn't seem like such a huge barrier to Benito. "Well . . . can't you send someone you trust? I will stay here as your hostage."

"If you will trust me, I will go," said Antimo. "I am very good at such matters, Hekate. I did offer before."

There was a perceptible change in her hostile expression. "Yes. You did. But he is a god, and you are a mortal magic-worker."

"I'm not a mage," said Antimo. "Just a good agent and spy. But I will try, if you will tell me where you need me to go."

If Hekate had not been a Goddess, Benito would have said that there was despair in her eyes. "I have no idea where Poseidon hides his stables."

"There is a Roman ruin on the south side of the island...there's some sort of passage through it. But it looks like any other ruin, Hekate," said Benito. Then something occurred to him. "Maria led me there. So, can you ask her? You could ask her about Pegasus, too. You know she'll tell you the truth."

Slowly, Hekate nodded. "I watch the portals to Aidoneus' lands. I will ask."

She did not go anywhere, but Benito had the distinct impression that she was not exactly there with them. And then two more people were. Gray and ghostly people, shadows—shadows of a sort that Benito was very familiar with. Benito took one look at Enrico and stepped over and sat him down. Squeezed his shoulder. He got an agonized look from the silenced old man. He very carefully did not say anything. He tried not to look at his wife, standing hand-in-hand with Aidoneus.

"Goddess of the Crossroads, Opener of Gateways, Lady of the Night, Mistress of the Hunt," said Aidoneus, formally, bowing slightly. You could tell this was a meeting of equals or near-equals—at least in Aidoneus' mind.

"Lord of the Cold Halls, Custodian of the Dead, Winter-king," she replied with equal formality. A slight tilt of her regal head toward Maria questioned her identity.

"My consort and bride, the Lady Maria, priestess to the great Mother."

"A mortal, a living one, in the cold halls?"

"For four months of the year," said Maria, chin up. "And I must thank you, Hekate, for your help in freeing my daughter from those who had kept her prisoner."

Hekate was glowering again. "For which you have repaid me with the captivity of my son," she accused.

Maria shook her head. "Oh, no. Pegasus is free. The last I saw of him, he flew off southwest. Benito and I promised him freedom if he took Benito to where our baby was held. Once they landed in Veneto, Benito took the bridle off and tossed it into the bushes."

Hekate made a rude sound. "It is made of golden threads. No mortal would throw it away."

"What is gold compared to the life of your child? He had no interest in anything but in getting to our little girl." She looked at Aidoneus. "He is a good man, Hekate."

"He does honor both the letter and the spirit of the agreements he makes," said Aidoneus. "Even as regards my bride."

"It's not easy," sighed Benito. "But see? Even Aidoneus vouches for my word. And I have more proof for you. Look, Hekate. My brother Marco is bound to the Lion of Saint Mark."

"The ancient Lion of Etruria, Hekate," said Aidoneus. "He was there even in our earliest years. One of the great neutral powers, bound to the marshes and a part of them. His power in his realm is not diminished."

Hekate nodded slowly. "I remember the Lion."

"Well, my brother says the Lion was aware of a winged horse flying over a corner of the lagoons." Benito shrugged. "It could have been me flying in. It could have been Pegasus flying out, alone. Marco was talking a blue streak, and I was very tired."

Now Hekate looked...not exactly doubtful, but as if many things she had thought were true had been shaken. "I shall enquire of the Lion of Etruria. We faced dangers together once. And distances are great here, but different elsewhere."

Then Hekate was gone. Benito looked at his grandfather, then sat down beside him. "Can you speak again?" he asked worriedly.

The duke shook his head. He pulled a piece of parchment and a quill toward himself and wrote: *Sorry*.

"It's nothing. Hard to grasp what I blundered into, Grandfather."

The old man squeezed his hand. He still beat iron rather often and had a grip like a blacksmith—which he closed still tighter, moments later, because the room was rather too full of lion. A lion with vast wings. Hekate was there as well, but she seemed as insubstantial as a shadow beside the Lion. Benito was just glad he was sitting down already. Antimo looked as if he wished he was.

"I do not leave my marshes easily or happily, Hekate," said a voice which reverberated inside their skulls. "As your dogs are to you, the marshes are to me. My lifeblood. My reason."

Hekate's eyes flashed, but not with anger. "I need to know what has happened to my child."

"He is now within my demesnes. Grazing and eyeing some wild horses in the water meadows near Chioggia."

Hekate rapped the butt of her harpoon on the floor again. It reverberated. "I need him to come home!"

The Lion shook his mane. "I will neither constrain nor bind him, Hekate. I can tell him, but not make him."

"May I say something?" asked Benito cautiously, trying to display the tact he was not famous for. They all looked at him. Having all those unhuman gazes on him was enough to turn the knees and bowels to water, but he went bravely on. "I spent quite a lot of hours with Pegasus. And, um, I haven't left behind being a young colt myself, entirely."

Leonine laughter filled the room.

Hekate looked at him, nodded. "I was mistaken. But you should have brought him back to me."

"Then you would have lost him forever, Lady Hekate," Benito said, earnestly, not-quite-pleading. "I know this is very, very hard for a mother to hear. He's been a prisoner for a long time. I know you would cherish and love him. I can see that with your hounds. But he's a colt, really. Young, a little wild. He needs to feel unconstrained for a little bit. Sow some wild oats maybe. It's...a phase a lot of us go through before settling down," he said above the echoes of more Lion-roar laughter.

"He should know," said the Lion. "And now, Hekate, open your gates. I must go back. If you take young Valdosta's advice, you'll let me tell Pegasus that you miss him and would love to see him again, but that he must enjoy his liberty. And while he remains in my realms, I shall watch over him. But I will not tell him he must return, nor will I try to constrain him."

Hekate took a deep breath. "Will you do that? Tell him I would like to visit, briefly. Will you permit me to visit your marshes, great one?"

The Lion folded his wings. "A bargain. I have learned from my people. They are great bargainers. The human to whom I am bound and his mate are of a bloodline I need to continue. They are the last of their line. You had powers with childbirth..."

"With birth yes. I will assist in opening that gate." Hekate actually seemed...eager...when she said that.

But the Lion bent his head a little. "I think intervention is required...earlier."

"It is not within my ambit," Hekate said, with real regret.

"It is mine," said Maria. "I just didn't know. She, uh, Kat, didn't say. And I didn't want to ask."

"Very well. My need is served. Let me go. I shall deliver your message," said the Lion.

"My thanks," said Hekate. Benito briefly glimpsed an endless sea of shifting rushes, reeds and waterways and the scent of Jesolo and mud and marsh waters. The Lion vanished among them.

It might stink less than Venice. But the stench of Venice was also full of memories. Hekate turned back to those within the room, closing the way. "It appears you dealt fairly and spoke the truth," she said to Benito. "I owe you my apology."

Benito shrugged. "It's my face. Antimo told me last year. I have the kind of face that people believe the worst of. Sometimes they're right. And now, please, can you let my grandfather speak again?"

"He did treat me with a lack of respect," said Hekate, eyes slightly narrowed.

"I am sure he won't ever make that mistake again," said Benito, trying to keep a straight face. He had a feeling not many people had laughed at Hekate. "But as you must know, you have not walked openly in the world for a very long time. People have forgotten you, your power, and what your due is. You cannot blame him for not recognizing what he has never known."

She plainly did not quite know what to make of that. But a sense of justice won. She waved her harpoon at Enrico.

The duke stood up. Bowed very low. "Lady Hekate. I make my apology. My manners were those of a d—of a pig," he said, looking at the two dogs. "I beg your pardon. I need to beg Benito's pardon, too. I was an old man being angry and afraid. I didn't understand all this. I still don't, but I thought he might have been, well, had his mind seized. There are magics that can do that, I have been told. Marco and Benito are all the blood I have left. It is easy to forget all else when your own are endangered."

She nodded regally. "I wish to ask him about my son, and how he dealt with Poseidon." There was a bitterness in her voice, deep bitterness.

"May I suggest, Your Grace, that we offer our guests some of that excellent mavrodaphne," said Antimo.

"We two cannot remain here," interrupted Aidoneus.

Maria closed her eyes briefly, and nodded. Benito had seen that look before. Aidoneus was in for a fairly major explosion from Maria. She did not like being told what to do, even if, right now, she might be pretending to be a good little wife. He didn't like being a part-time husband but he had the satisfaction of knowing that he knew her moods and ways far better than the Lord of the Cold Halls.

Hekate nodded. "Although I wonder why you still choose mortal brides, Aidoneus."

"They may die, but they also bring life. It seems that it is their fragility that is important, Goddess." Aidoneus stepped through into a place of immense gray distances.

"Wine," said Antimo firmly, looking at his master. Enrico was definitely a little gray-faced himself. The duke shook himself. "Yes. In that cupboard, Antimo. There are good goblets of Murano glass too."

Spirits of wine might be a better choice after this, thought Benito. *Even Iskander's Slivovitz. At least after you'd drunk that, you'd expect to see supernatural beasts and ancient gods.* But he was glad to accept the glass of ruby-red wine anyway. Benito noticed that Antimo was being fixed with an expectant stare by a couple of dog-faces.

"Your Grace. Could I get someone to bring us a couple of mutton bones?" asked the agent.

I need to ask you just how you got to be friends with a goddess's dogs, thought Benito as the rather stunned duke nodded. *If we get through the next few minutes without her silencing us all forever. And I would guess that that is not the worst she could do.*

Hekate wanted to know about Pegasus. So he told her. But she was plainly still hurt by the idea that he had not come to see her. "I didn't understand how a parent feels about their children myself," Benito said, "Until I was one. I don't think you can. You worry. You would move heaven and earth for them. You would do anything, anything at all for them. But when you are the child, you don't always understand that means love. Sometimes, all you see is barriers, when what you want is to fly. It's—like holding an egg. If you want to keep it whole, you can't hold it too tightly."

"Antimo is correct. Your face belies you," she said, nodding, just a hint of a smile showing.

Benito shrugged. "It's useful sometimes. And Maria has got used to it."

"She is a very powerful woman," said Hekate.

Benito chuckled. "I know that. I don't think Aidoneus has figured it out yet. He's in for a few surprises, I think."

From there it was a short step to telling Hekate and his grandfather just how he'd ended up in the position that he was in with his wife. It was nice to finally tell someone—beside Erik and Manfred who'd been there, and Marco who had been left holding the baby, literally—what he'd done, and why, and how he would honor his word and his bargain even when he hated it.

For Hekate it was all a little like heady wine—as well as, of course, the heady wine they were drinking. But she had for so long been withdrawn from humanity that it was almost like binding herself into the world of humans again. She was still hurt and saddened by Pegasus and his desire to be self-centered and free. But, now that this Benito had pointed it out, it was behavior which she had seen in many young people over many generations. It was as sure as the sunrise, at a certain age.

Also, their belief made her stronger still. They knew and acknowledged her, and her power.

The dogs were content, warm and gnawing at bones at her feet. This after all was a dog's idea of paradise. To roam and hunt yes, but be with their person, warm and with food. It did not take much to make them happy. And, Hekate found, they were not entirely incorrect.

And then there was the pure satisfaction in knowing that Poseidon, who had thought that he would rule everything for always was a forgotten, fading old god. He was nearly powerless, senile, and now that he had lost his captive and only companion, utterly alone. There was no one who cared to be with him, who loved him as her dogs loved her. That, perhaps, was the most satisfying thing of all.

"Men, they make terrible war. That is their way," she said rather dismissively. As if it was a man thing and had very little to do with her. Benito, with the experience of Thalia on Corfu, knew all too well that when women made war, you really didn't want to get in their way. She'd been entirely pragmatic about killing their enemies. Besides Hekate wasn't a gentle goddess from what he'd read. The huntress, well, hunted with her dogs.

"Actually," said the Old Fox, who was becoming quite mellow and philosophical in the presence of wine, a beautiful aristocratic woman and his grandson back again, "while that is true, sometimes, we fight now merely so that we have a safe return through the Bosphorus. We've offered Alexius terms, although he's a treacherous little vole. But we're left with little choice but to reduce the wall and take the city, and hold it. Or hope he comes to his senses. We are

Venetian—well, Benito is. The Venetians don't like to make war. It's expensive. The Venetians like to make money."

She stiffened slightly. "Why do you wish to sail down the tear through the gate—the channel you call the Bosphorus?"

The Old Fox dipped his finger in the wine and began drawing pictures on the table. Hekate leaned over to look at them. The pictures somehow became more . . . real . . . as she bent her gaze on them. "Jagiellon of Lithuania is building a huge fleet up on the Dnieper River. He has been pouring gold into Alexius's coffers. We believe he plans to take control of Constantinople and attack us through the Mediterranean. It is said that he is merely the human form of some dark demon. The church calls it 'Chernobog.'"

"The Black God . . . the demon of the northlands. Cursed and feared," said Hekate darkly. "He has trespassed on my old demesnes in the last while. He has eyes that he uses."

Benito looked up at the goddess. "Watching us?"

"Not anymore," said Hekate with obvious satisfaction.

"Still. I think he saw too much. We had planned," said Antimo, speaking with an openness that his employer plainly was taken aback by, "to have a gate opened for us, so we could take the city without a siege. Sieges are hard. But the agreed signal was given, and there has been no response. I assume either someone found out, or he was moved. So we continue to pound the walls on the Golden Horn. They are weakest. That was our fall-back plan."

"Women always suffer worst in a siege," said Benito, meditatively. "Or so Maria said. And children. And babies." He patted one of her dogs. "Not much fun for the dogs either."

"At least you are not in there, Lady Hekate," said Antimo. "I . . . I did not understand. I still don't fully, but I am glad you and the dogs are not in the city."

Benito grinned. "I thought he'd gone finally mad when he asked my help in protecting you, when we take the city."

The Goddess of Gateways looked at first offended . . . and then, as she saw Antimo scratching the base of a dog's tail with his foot, a little flattered. "I cannot be confined. There is always another way."

Antimo hunched his shoulders a little. "I didn't understand. I didn't really want to accept . . . the way you appeared and vanished. It's magic. I'm a very unmagical man. I understand what is ordinary. I can manipulate it, calculate it. I can't . . . calculate magic. I'm quite ordinary, really."

"You are not," said Hekate. "But I think you are unaware of your skill at enchantment."

She stood up. "My people would wage wars and go a-raiding. That never was my domain. Many passed through the final gateway because of it, though. I can take you within that city, Antimo Bartelozzi, and bring you out again. You can walk under my cloak and even without your powers, none would see you, if you can arrange an end to this. You speak sooth. Women, children, horses and dogs suffer worst in wars."

Antimo blinked. "I . . . well, I might find out what is happening. Why the eunuch I had reached the agreement with—and paid the first installment to—has not fulfilled his part of the bargain."

"Then let us go." She reached out her hand. He

took it, and before Benito and Dell'este could blink, they were gone.

Antimo found the folding of light and darkness around him, and the sudden chiarascuro glimpses, as if through deeply shadowed gateways onto bright meadows and distant places, disconcerting but not frightening. The artist in him wanted to draw them, to capture their promise. And then they were in the alley where she'd met him in Constantinople.

"Where do you go from here?" she asked.

One does not tell a goddess, to whom a siege-tight fortress is an open door, that it is none of her business. For a moment the impact of what he was dealing with—what he had taken for granted—made him feel a little dizzy, a little weak, and very afraid. Then he got control of himself again. "The Hippodrome Palace kitchens. I have a contact there."

So they went along the back streets, cautiously because there were patrols and signs of social disintegration—burned houses. And the smell. There was much less of it.

Less to waste. The city had been ill-prepared for the siege.

It appeared that Hekate and her dogs planned to walk beside him through the streets of Constantinople, and, now that he was beginning to grasp what he dealt with, that was welcome. There were patrols and guards—and his contact in the kitchens was not there. So Hekate led him up into the palace and into the quarters of the beardless ones, the eunuchs who ran Byzantium's bureaucracy.

❁   ❁   ❁

Primikerios Melekaniodes had just finished a pleasant repast. He was not feeling the hunger that was already gripping the city. The last thing he expected, by the look on his face, was to encounter, here in his inner sanctum, a certain merchant he'd received a bribe from some months earlier.

"I thought we had reached an agreement, Melekaniodes," said the fellow, quite insolently, the primikerios thought.

"What are you doing here?" demanded the eunuch in charge of allocations. He had reason to wonder. He'd given as detailed a description to the guards and to Byzantium's spymaster as possible. They'd told him the man had fled the city, long before the attack. "Guard . . . urk."

The knife was pressed against his fat throat. "I had expected you to be dead. But plainly that is not the case. Yet."

Sweat started from the forehead of the Byzantine official. "I can't help you. I'll give you the money back, I'll . . ."

"In other words you went back on our bargain."

The "merchant" stepped away. Melekaniodes made a dash for the door.

He saw a door open before him.

Only it did not lead to freedom or even life.

Antimo looked at the fallen man across the threshold. He hadn't even thrown the knife yet.

"Treachery and betrayal are an affront to me," said Hekate grimly.

Antimo decided it was not the time to mention that those were major components of his trade. "A pity. I had hoped to force him to get us through the wall. We'd agreed on minimal destruction to the city and his promotion in the ranks of those who actually run it."

"I thought you wished its destruction," said Hekate.

Antimo shook his head. "You don't know the Old Fox—Duke Enrico. He avoids destruction where possible. That is probably why he does not rule northern Italy—but the cities he does rule, love him." Then he added, "And you heard him speak of the Venetians. They don't want corpses, they want customers. You only loot a city once; you can get money out of it indefinitely if you keep it alive."

Hekate stood a little taller. "Then under the same terms I will open the gate. I am a huntress, not a conqueror. And that would be some repayment for freeing my son."

Antimo looked at her for some time. And then slowly nodded. "I misunderstood who you were. I think you need to talk to the duke first though. I am loyal to him, but, Lady Hekate, you must deal carefully with him."

"He is not honest?" she asked, brows furrowing.

"Honest as steel, but also clever as a fox," Antimo replied. "He is one who will wring every advantage he can from a bargain. Not unlike a Venetian. He'll also be sure he cannot be held to something he knows he cannot promise."

"He can deal fairly or choose at the crossroads, as that man in the doorway did," said Hekate. "Life is full of crossroads. There are different ways, each with sure outcomes. But there is always another way and the choices are free."

That, decided Antimo, was a cryptic warning which, coming from Hekate, his master would be a fool to disregard.

But when they got back they found that the Old Fox was either before him in understanding her, or simply obdurate.

"Lady Hekate. First, we cannot expect no resistance to our attack. My first loyalty is to our own, and their lives cannot be expended to spare an enemy's life. And second, if we win, soldiery are not pawns on a chessboard. They can be ordered what to do and what not to do, but when cities fall, orders fail. And there is great bitterness at the massacre and enslavement of the Latins. Alexius must die. His treasures must go to pay for the lives of men and ships. And I will be hard-pressed to stop all of the other looting and rapine. I will give you my word that the orders will be issued. I can promise the headsman's axe to those who fail to obey, and the block and the knife for rapists. But it will happen. And they will hide it from my eyes, if not yours."

"I see what Antimo meant. That is a cleverer answer than a glib assurance." She looked thoughtful for a brief while. "I will guide your soldiery. But they must be blindfolded. As a measure of trust."

"Then Antimo and I will lead them," said the Old Fox calmly. "And you can tie our blindfolds on yourself."

"And me?" asked Benito.

"You'll be constructively engaged in an assault on the seawall a little earlier. So they'll be tired and happy at having beaten you off," said the Old Fox. "It's time someone else had a share of the derring-do."

Chapter 45

Constantinople

The assault on the seawall began just after dusk. As usual, the repair work on the walls after the day's cannonading was busily ongoing. The assault had no chance of being undetected, but it had more of a chance of success than it was supposed to have, simply because the assumption was made that if Benito was to lead it, it must be more than it seemed. There had been a number of other such probes, led by young officers who were willing to risk life and limb for the off chance of great glory, but this had to be different. Even if Benito told them the idea was to make a lot of noise and not get killed. It had been a mistake to include some of the evicted and enslaved Latins in the attack, Benito concluded. They were going to be a problem. They wanted vengeance, no matter what.

It would take all of Benito's authority and a few sharp blows to stop them getting either vengeance or death.

In the meanwhile Enrico Dell'este's men waited in the encampment outside the Blachernae Quarter.

In their armor, weapons ready...and blindfolds too. It had taken all of the Dell'este reputation to get them to do it, but at about midnight, they put on those blindfolds.

"It is time," said a sonorous, female voice that put atavistic chills up the backs of each and every one of them. "Do not look until I give you permission. The way is perilous for mortals."

"As we drilled it," said the Old Fox, "Be steadfast, men. I'll be first in the line. Now, link up. And forward."

And so, each with a hand on the man before them, they walked forward...away from the sortie-barricades and abatis of the camp, following blindly into the moonless darkness. It was a cloudy night and the dark, even without a blindfold, was thick and impenetrable. It was cold too, and there were...noises, in the distance. Then they walked on a solid floor of some kind. Some of them may have tried to see where they went, but it was dark and creaked. Once there had been a tunnel here. Perhaps there still was. Perhaps that was what they walked in. Nerves were on edge, as they passed onto a floor of solid stone. The air was damp, and smelled faintly of wet rock. From time to time, the Old Fox called back a word of encouragement; it echoed down the line, and they took heart from it.

And then, they stopped.

"You are inside the gate called Gryrolimne in Blachernae," said Hekate. "There have been many gates here. You may remove your blindfolds."

"Thank you, Lady Hekate," said Enrico with utmost politeness. The few soldiers he had with him were insufficient to take a city. But the district of Blachernae was in itself a small fortress. With that fallen, the men of Aragon, Genoa, Ferrara and Venice could march in. The men gathered themselves for a moment, and when they thought to look for that strange lady again, she was gone.

In the darkness, even with Antimo's excellent knowledge, it took some time to position the stopper groups, and await the changing of the guard. Oddly they met several patrols—who saluted politely to a larger force. Men always saw what they expected and wanted to see, unless you thrust their noses into it.

Enrico led them up the steps that gave access to the *chemin de ronde* on the inner wall. It was guarded, of course, but the guard expected relief just then.

He was quickly disabused—too quickly to issue any warning. From there it was a case of assaulting the tower door and they were inside the gatehouse of the Blachernae. The door was the usual crossed ply of oaken planks studded with iron. It was a solid door. Less so after a small V-shaped keg of gunpowder was placed against it and heavy sacks of earth laid over that. Enrico had kept his explosive experiments close to his chest. But this was an effective way of directing force. It also muffled the noise and flash.

Soon they were pouring into the tower. Half the defenders were still asleep. And none were going to get out. Enrico Dell'este made no attempt to restrain his men. His Latins wanted revenge against the Greeks, and revenge he gave them. Every one of defenders of the tower was butchered, many of them still groggy with sleep and unarmed.

Wiser or simply more callous with years than his grandson, the Old Fox knew that there would be no way to completely prevent the savagery. There had been too much hatred built up by the atrocities committed by the Greeks—which, by now, were known to the entire invading force, even if they hadn't experienced any of it themselves. Better to let the men vent their rage now, against other soldiers. Perhaps they'd be sated enough that they could be kept from inflicting that fury later, on women and children.

Three hours before the dawn the great gates swung open, while most of Constantinople slumbered, and Benito Valdosta and Count Alfons of Valderobes rode in. In the pale dawn the Lion, the Cross, and the flag of Aragon flew proud over Blachernae, and the dark mass of the invading troops marched in good order toward the Great Palace near the Hippodrome. More men marched onto the curtain walls. There was some fighting on the streets, mostly with the Prasinoi and Rousioi Deme-gangs and the Varangians, rather than Byzantine troops, who had mostly been garrisoned near the walls, and whose barracks were now under attack. The people of Constantinople woke to the banners of conquest flying from the top of the third hill and on the forum of Constantine. Only the Hippodrome area and the Great Palace resisted, and even that could not hold.

By late afternoon Enrico, Benito, Admiral Borana, Count Alfons and a dozen other officers filed past the guard to pray in the Hagia Sophia. Parts of the city burned. The invading troops were firefighting next to locals. But it had been a very minor battle compared to others that Constantinople had inflicted on itself. All in all, atrocities were few. Whether that was due to the grandfather's sagacity in letting his troops slaughter everyone in the initial fight, or his grandson's fierce discipline once the city was taken, could be debated. Dell'este's own opinion, based on his decades-long experience at war, was that the key factor had simply been the ease of the conquest itself. For one thing, men led to easy victories tended to obey the commanders who had led them there. For another, their own casualties had been very light, so new hot rage had not been piled onto anger that had grown a little cold with time.

And there was loot—always something that cheered up soldiers and improved their mood. True, Emperor Alexius had made his escape over the sea-wall in the dawn, taking much of the treasury with him. He was no Justinian, and obviously felt royal purple would not make a good shroud for himself.

But he left much of the treasury behind, too, due to the haste with which he fled and the small numbers of retainers who fled with him. And leaving that aside, the Great Palace had enough gold plate alone to pay for the entire campaign—with plenty more in the way of gems, jewelry, precious metalwork—all the hoarded baubles of Byzantium's centuries—to make every soldier a richer man than almost any of them had ever been in their lives.

Here, too, Benito's talent for organization played a part. A big part, in fact. He saw to it that special squads rounded up most of the loot, and did so in a reasonably disciplined manner, rather than just letting the men run wild. Then, also in an orderly manner, he distributed the booty evenly among all the soldiers. So there was no festering resentment on the part of men who felt they hadn't gotten their just due, and Benito came out of the process as popular as probably any commander in the history of Venice.

"Well," said Enrico, when it was all over. "This should get us a place in history anyway. How does it feel to have conquered the greatest city in Christendom, boy?"

Benito yawned. "The place only looks like Mainz because of the mosaics," he said.

Enrico cuffed him, gently, about the ear. "Humph. Mainz. You've never seen it boy. I have. And the Hagia Sophia is one of the marvels of the world."

"It is quite a building," admitted Benito.

"What's wrong, boy?" asked the Old Fox, a little worried.

"I miss my wife, and I miss my child, Grandfather. Not all the gold in the world can substitute for them."

Chapter 46

Anatolia

The hands were unaccustomed to life in the country. Winter was no time to be sleeping under the cold stars here in the Anatolian highlands. For the first time for many of them, food was scarce. But the cities had become too dangerous to survive.

All that was left of the group huddled together in the shelter of a rocky little valley, with only thorn trees for shelter. The sunlight was thin and did nothing to warm them. "I need you to go to Trebizond," said Kamil, Senior Master of the Blade.

"No," said the Senior Hand.

That was something that the master had never heard said to him. Not as a reply to a direct order! He gaped, silenced for a long moment. "Kill him," he said, angrily.

No one moved.

"I said 'kill him.' Do you know what happens to those who disobey?" The master was accustomed to schooling his emotions, but this mutiny had ignited a fire of fury in him.

"Who disobeys who? The Masters of Damascus or the Old Man of Alamut?" said the disrespectful hand. "You want us to stick our heads into the viper's nest again? No. I've heard that the Old Man is moving himself. You are dead meat walking."

The master was silenced again. The Order had made infiltration a major way to make up for their small numbers. Some of the masters had wondered if the Old Man—the Master of the Mountain in Alamut and their titular overlord—did the same, only...to them. He had few devotees in that mountain fastness with its walled garden. But they were trained not only in one of the disciplines of killing, but all. And a few extra.

The master took a deep breath. "Then I will go myself."

"Good riddance. I am going back to my village," said the hand.

"No, you are not, you disrespectful dog!" shouted Kamil, and launched himself at the hand.

He wasn't the only one to leap into the fray. The beast that was the Baitini turned on itself, biting at its own vitals.

From a nearby hilltop, the Old Man of Alamut watched with grim satisfaction. Rumor and fear were tools that needed to be wielded well. He had been remiss in not keeping a closer eye, and a surer hand on the masters. He'd thought their training would be enough. Bah. Fools who had been seduced by the peacock angel. They had to die. If any survived, let them go, either to crawl back to the villages they had come from and try to scatch out a living at work they no longer understood, or to play thugs to some tiny overlord—or to come back to him, where they would be purified, made stronger.

As for the ones who died here, he would make a gift of their heads to the Ilkhan. Alamut played a long slow game. The hidden hand and the one in plain sight. The Mongols would be much weaker when he finally struck. And now, that would have to wait a little longer. Perhaps two generations. Not so long as all that.

Aleppo

The Grand Tour had taken the Ilkhan as far as Aleppo. Aleppo was a comfortable city, with reasonable amenities. The Ilkhan settled into a palace. He was unsure whose it was, and in truth, did not really care, though he would reward the owner because he wished to be seen as generous. He waited for news to come to him.

And so it did, in the mouth of his grand vizier, who presented himself as was appropriate, the morning after the Progress had settled, as the Ilkhan was breaking his fast with almond rice and preserved fruit and tea.

The grand vizier bowed low. "Interesting news, Ilkhan. We have reports here from a Venetian trader at Latakia that the Hellespont has been captured by a fleet from Venice, Genoa, Aragon and a few other western powers. Constantinople is under siege."

The Ilkhan quirked an eyebrow. "Interesting, indeed. Did you succeed in getting them to carry a new envoy to the Golden Horde, Orason?"

The vizier bowed again. "Yes, as far as Constantinople. But I fear things become more complex, Great Khan. Do you remember the Franks I mentioned acting as intermediaries?"

"Prince Manfred of Brittany."

The vizier coughed. "It appears they may have accompanied the false tarkhan to the lands of the Golden Horde. Or so my informant inferred. They were supposed to go overland to Rome, and then onward. But my informant was in Venice for two months and they were not seen. He spoke to others from Rome. No word of the prince there."

The Ilkhan rubbed his forehead. This was not welcome news. "So are we at war with the Holy Roman Empire? We share no borders but..."

The vizier nodded and spoke the obvious. "But they could supply men and materiel to our enemies. I fear this may be true, in the worst case."

Still, it did not do to jump to conclusions. "Instruct our emissary to the Golden Horde to investigate this most thoroughly and report to us."

"It shall be done, Great Khan." The vizier bowed low. The Ilkhan gestured to a servant to renew his tea.

"In the meanwhile I have some further news from Anatolia," continued the vizier. "It appears that the Old Man of Alamut has played a role in dealing with the Baitini problem. Your generals are not alone in sending you heads."

Ilkhan Hotai pondered this. "The Old Man of Alamut... It is questionable just how far one can trust him, after our last experience with his acolytes."

The grand vizier appeared a little taken aback by this. It was the first time Hotai had ever seen him look even slightly put out by anything. But he answered correctly enough. "We continue to watch them, Great Khan."

Hotai said nothing. He resolved however to talk to General Malkis about his grand vizier. The Ilkhan might appear soft and civilized, but in his veins flowed the blood of the Great Khan, Genghis, who had been born into treachery and had it snapping at his heels for much of his life until he had the strength to crush it. Those who considered taking that road with him would do well not to forget that.

Hotai never did.

Chapter 47

Constantinople

Constantinople, great Constantinople, sitting astride the gateway between the West and the East. The key... and the bickering point.

Alexius was out there, somewhere in the hinterland of Greece. Perhaps gathering adherents, perhaps wasting what substance he had left. Some of the Latins—Italians from Pisa, Genoa, Naples, Venice, Apulia, who had been evicted and attacked and enslaved in Alexius's purge of the city—still wanted vengeance. Benito and Enrico were generally able to maintain discipline, and they prevented any large-scale atrocities from taking place. But there were constant little explosions of fury taking place, almost on a daily basis. Most of which, to make things worse, were being inflicted on people who were quite blameless in the matter. One of them had been a six-year-old boy, his skull crushed against a wall by a little group of Pisan soldiers who'd just come out of a nearby tavern. They'd been drunk, as much from the rage of retelling stories of Greek bestiality as from the wine they'd consumed. The poor child had just been in the wrong place at the wrong time.

The Prasinoi and Rousioi Deme-gangs still wielded huge influence and were infiltrated into every aspect of life in the city. Breaking them could take years. They were used to being a law unto themselves.

The eunuchs who ran the Byzantine Empire's civil affairs, and those of the city, had had most of their administration in the city. Right now, they were not doing any administrating. "They want their protocols and ranks recognized," said Di Tharra, who had been sent to negotiate with them. Even after two days the conquerors of Constantinople had realized that they needed a civic administration.

Or to burn the city to ash and start again—which admittedly had its attractions.

"And their old perks, of course," said Enrico sourly. "The big problem is just to whom do they answer?"

"You need a governor, rather than an oligarchy," said Antimo. "The Prasinoi have been making advances to Admiral Borana, the Rousioi to Count Alfons."

"And the various merchant houses to Borana and me," said Enrico. "For some reason they find me more appealing than Benito."

"They think he is too young and too flighty," said Antimo, smiling. "Besides, all the seamen like him. You can't associate with someone who is that popular with common seamen."

"My men think very highly of him," said Captain Di Tharra, who seemed largely immune to sarcasm or irony. "And that does mean that some of Admiral Borana's confidantes do treat Signor Valdosta with distrust."

"Which gets us no closer to running the city, and, after our agreement with Hekate, it does need running," said Benito.

"And besides, we need somewhere as a base for the winter," said Enrico.

Patrols now watched both sides of the Bosphorus, and the smaller cities and towns in nearby eastern Thrace had made their submissions, but the winter had bitten deep and hard. The sea was no place to be out on right now. Gray seas and whitecaps, wind, sleet, with interspersions of fog. They were stuck in Constantinople, with its restive population and fractious conquerors as the days dragged on. Benito found excuses to spend a fair amount of time in the dockyards hauling ships up, repairing and preparing and talking to Di Tharra, who also spent a fair amount of time overseeing the same. Fortunately, Admiral Borana was far too busy meddling in the affairs of Constantinople to notice what his underlings were doing.

"I have had many conversations with Androcles, since you introduced me to the tritons," Di Tharra informed him as they sat in a brief patch of weak sunlight.

Benito wondered what Di Tharra, who seemed to have failed to grasp the basic elements of sarcasm, had in common with the sharp-tongued triton.

"They are an ancient people, with long memories," said Di Tharra.

Ah. History. Or the triton seeing how much he could get Di Tharra to swallow, thought Benito, nodding.

"He says we are descended from an ancient people, the Shardana people of the drowned lands, near here. Our tribes survived as sea-rovers and warriors for hire, until they were broken by one of Pharaohs and fled west, settling on Sardinia. Before that...we fought with the gods and the sea itself, allied in those far off times to the tritons' forefathers that helped my people to withstand the sea's rages," said Di Tharra dreamily.

"Ah." Benito smiled. "So now you live in the middle of your island."

"Yes, but I have seen the stone Nuraghe. They are exactly as the triton described. Only the ones he has seen lie lost beneath the waters of the Black Sea! He could hardly have seen the ones in the highlands of Sardinia. I think it must have been the very Biblical flood itself!"

Or the triton is pulling your leg, thought Benito. "Well, my family go back to at least my father," he said, thinking of that father, who made no secret of the fact that his father had been a commoner, a minor landowner.

"But Valdosta is an ancient and honorable house!" protested Di Tharra, as quick to defend Benito from himself as anyone else. He was disarmingly loyal.

Was Di Tharra the only man in all Italy who didn't listen to gossip, or perhaps just didn't believe in it? "That's a...shall we say convenient fiction," he said, a bit tersely. "Valdosta was married to my mother before he was killed, and she ended up as Carlo Sforza's mistress. She ran off, and he ordered her killed."

"Oh. I didn't mean..."

Benito shrugged. "Most people know the story. It doesn't worry me anymore."

A panting sailor came running up, "*Milord!* Come quickly! The city is burning and the streets are full of riot!"

Captain Di Tharra leapt to his feet. Benito held up a hand. "Wait. Tell us a bit more," he said to the sailor. "We need to plan this, Di Tharra. This is their city and running into it like our tails were afire is probably exactly what someone wants. They must know more than half the men are out here, and our men man the walls."

The picture that emerged from the sailor showed that indeed someone must have planned this quite well. Most of the Latin forces had been scattered by the sounds of it. And this fellow had come curiously unchallenged out of the Neorian Gate to the harbor but had been pelted with rocks and chased when he had tried to cross the old Severian Wall to head for the Perama Gate and the Venetian Quarter.

"The Severian Wall—I'll bet they have some culverins up there. There were some not accounted for. They'd have a fine field of fire if we charge in via the Neorian Gate." Benito took a deep breath. "I'll take a thousand men via the Gate of the Drungaries. I am sure we hold that—I know the officer charged with it. And we'll send messages over to Pera, and have men shipped up to Blachernae, and I want you to take some of your good Genovese sailors in via the Kontoskalian harbor. We have enough men and enough crews to sail around there."

Marching his hastily marshaled men along the shore, Benito entered the gate of the Drungaries and they surged into the Venetian Quarter, picking up a growing following. At the Basilica of St. Nicolas they made their way up the hill, along the Makros Emblos to the Milion tetrapylon, and then, meeting with Di

Tharra's sailors there, went toward the ruins of the hippodrome. There they met with riot and burning buildings, but they were behind the rioters, and Benito was in no mood to be gentle. The Prasinoi and Rousioi Deme-gangs had expected the Latins to continue with the restraint they'd showed on capturing the city, but the Greeks soon discovered that they'd used up their ration of that gentleness.

The city had the blood-letting they'd avoided. And this time, Benito was in a much worse position to hold back the frightened and vindictive victims of the last pogroms. He did try to keep the violence aimed as much as possible against the remnants of the gangs, and succeeded to a considerable degree. But, inevitably, much of it spilled over onto the general populace, especially wherever gang members tried to hide among friends or relatives.

He'd dealt with angry goddesses before. He'd just have to do it again.

Chapter 48

Constantinople

The Black Brain studied the progress of his push to the south. The winter, of course was considerably harsher on the shipyards on the Dnieper than it was in Constantinople. Chernobog had always despised human frailty with cold, but the ice on the river thwarted the movement of barges from December through to March. It slowed the material aspects of shipbuilding. Still, the slaves were driven hard. The Venetian and Genovese fleet outside Constantinople was small by comparison, though they did have more skill and experience at sea.

The Black Brain turned his gaze southwards. And what he saw was not pleasing. The Golden Horde, divided and fighting still in their winter encampments, much gold spent and little gain made. And then, in a place which corresponded with the southern margins of the Black Sea...he was stopped.

She showed no signs of tears. Instead she looked angry. Depths of emotion were strange to the Black Brain. Chernobog understood and used pain and terror.

A desire for revenge had driven him on occasions. But anger was really something he had to draw on Jagiellon to understand at all.

"No further," she commanded. "I have destroyed your slave-eyes here, daemon, and these are my demesnes. Go, before I set my dogs on you."

Here, Chernobog saw her two companions as they really were: no mere red-eared hunting dogs but the hounds of the gates of Hades. Terrible vast beasts with eyes of flame and multiple heads and adamantine teeth. Even the likes of Chernobog did not want them tearing at him.

She had her origins within humanity, so Chernobog drew on his human, too. It was many years since Jagiellon had had to exercise diplomacy but he had once done so. He made his voice silky, strived to look conciliatory. "You look troubled, Hekate. What is it that frets you?"

She lost a little of her fury. At him, at least. He had managed to deflect her, and divide her anger. "They kill each other. They burn and violate. Even those who foreswore such violence for my aid. They lied to me. I am not easily lied to."

Chernobog made as if to sigh. "Humans. They are deceptive. Especially the ones from Venice."

Hekate grounded her harpoon, and her eyes smoldered. "I had thought this Valdosta was an honorable man. They are allied with the ancient Lion."

"Benito Valdosta. Ah yes." Chernobog nodded. "I know him. No wonder he could deceive you. He has magical help from another power. An old friend of yours. The Earth-Shaker and Master of the Sea."

"You lie, Chernobog. Go back to your northern

forest fastness." But there was doubt there, hidden under that attempt at certainty. He could sense it.

"Test him," said Chernobog. "See if he does not indeed have an alliance with the children of Poseidon, the tritons. It is not wise to trust mortals."

"I will do this. I will put him to the magics of truth. Even Poseidon cannot resist that. Now get away, before I loose the dogs and my spear," said Hekate, the anger rising in her again.

"If I speak truly, will you consider speech with me again? We have interests in common." Deception was less risky than open conflict. Chernobog was sure he could defeat this old goddess, but not easily and not without harm done to himself. In addition to her two monstrous companions, she had certain objects of power and still drew from deep wells in this, her once-homeland. And if he were wounded and weakened, there were other dark powers questing this plane. There was no honor among such powers, only endless striving: to devour, lest one be devoured.

"Yes. Now go," she said.

So he went, well pleased with his work.

"I think," said Benito to Antimo Bartelozzi, when more attention was finally being turned to putting out fires than dealing with the mobs, "that I need to talk to your girlfriend." He leaned against the wheel of an overturned cart, and regarded Antimo with a steady, if weary, gaze.

Antimo was a middle-aged man with a very ordinary face and a normally placid expression. He flushed and looked anything but placid. "She's above my touch, m'lord. You know as I do, now, what she is."

Benito nodded. "Which is why I need to talk to her. If life with Maria has taught me anything, it is that talking sooner is better than talking later, and it's much better if you go to her than waiting until she comes looking. How do you find her?"

Antimo coughed. "Usually, I don't. Usually, she finds me. She did say that I could call on her at crossroads, with a libation."

"That makes sense." Benito cast around him for a suitable crossroads. "That tetrapylon—the Milion— must be the biggest crossroads around here." The tall double arches and their dome were the meeting of the city's major roads and, while neglected and cracked, they were still one of the major landmarks. "I'll get some wine."

"I have a wineskin, m'lord. I will accompany you," said the duke of Ferrara's chief agent.

Benito could not resist a little teasing as he pushed himself up off the wheel and prepared to do a bit of walking. "As you said, Antimo, she's not exactly your girlfriend."

"I am content to worship from afar, m'lord," said Antimo, with an odd humility. "But I have a loyalty to you because of your family, and a loyalty to her. She saved my life, although I didn't realize it at the time."

Benito clapped him on the shoulder. "Well, let's go then. I'd guess at order being well enough restored for us not to need an escort."

So they went to the Milion, where beneath its decaying brickwork, after spilling a little wine, Benito found that he'd waited too long not to confront an incandescently angry Hekate. She pointed the bone harpoon at him before he could even address her properly, and then produced a small wooden beaker. "Drink this."

Benito was far too used to Maria to argue. He took it, and drank it. "What was it?" he asked, wiping his mouth with the back of his hand. It tasted like small beer laced with herbs... mint, and rosemary, and something else. It was actually quite pleasant for something he *had* to drink.

"Kykeon. The holy drink. You will see the unseen. And you will be constrained by the magics and virtues of holy plants to speak faithfully and only the truth. I am sick of the lies of men."

Well. At least it wasn't poison.

Whatever this kykeon *was*, it was certainly potent. Benito could see blurred lines around things—and strange shapes, and dark eyes, peering and leering at him from behind pillars that wavered and shadowy fountains that played. A procession of horses, ridden without saddles by swarthy men in mailed skirts rode transparently and triumphally through the arch. And there sitting under a distant flowering tree was Maria. His Maria looking at him... He began to walk to her. A tall woman, her flowing wavy dark tresses crowned with a diadem of finely wrought gold and jet took his hand in a grip of iron, as hard as winter. "Stop. First you will deal with me and my questions, and you will answer me truthfully."

He blinked at her. "I would do that anyway. Lies are best saved for when you really need them, and I know better than to lie to a goddess." He was a little distracted. Maria had stood up and walked now toward him, looking puzzled.

"You will need more than lies if I find you have

deceived me. Speak now. Have you some compact with the children of Poseidon?" She really was very angry, and he could not imagine why.

"Pegasus. I told you..." he began.

She slapped him, hard enough to rock his head back, and to clear it slightly. "Not my son. Poseidon's sea-soldiers. The tritons."

"Well, yes. They guide our ships," said Benito. Why should that matter?

"Ssssso!" she hissed. The dark waves of hair seemed to stand out in a nimbus around her head. "You lied." she began to raise the harpoon and the dogs snarled.

"I didn't!" protested Benito. "You never asked about the tritons! Why should that—"

"You said Poseidon was a helpless old man. Yet you truck with his offspring. You made a deal with him to destroy me. He *let* you take my Pegasus!"

The strange drink, and possibly the nearness of death and the nearing of Maria, made him interrupt her tirade. "He damned well didn't! I tricked him. Besides, he's a weak and helpless old man, and I'd never seen him in my life before that day."

"You lie!" she screamed. She was about to plunge the harpoon into him, and he could not think of how to stop her or dodge in time.

Maria grabbed her arm.

"How *dare* you? How dare you, mortal?" Hekate raged. They wrestled for the harpoon.

Maria still had canaler shoulders. She held Hekate's arms. "And you think I would let you stab Benito? Think again! Come to your senses, and act like a goddess and not a fishwife! You fool, he *can't* lie. You gave him that drink."

Benito saw that Aidoneus had appeared, too. "I cannot let you harm my lady, Goddess of the Crossroads, Opener of Gateways, Lady of the Night, Mistress of the Hunt. She only says what should be evident to you."

Hekate froze.

"My compact with the tritons is because they are guardians to my daughter," said Benito. "My brother helped me make the pact with them in exchange for a sanctuary, and maybe a little because they like me."

Benito was by no means pleased to see Aidoneus, let alone having to feel grateful to him for helping Maria, "You can ask the Lion, if you don't believe me. Anyway, from what they've said they have no love for Poseidon themselves. If I remember it right, Androcles told me that Poseidon took Triton's Conch in punishment because he dared to stand up to his father about his mother. I think maybe he might have killed Triton too, but I'm not sure. I can tell you this much, there wasn't so much as a hint or fin or triton scale anywhere near where Poseidon is. They've left him alone to rot."

Hekate lowered the harpoon; looking faintly guilty. "Amphitrite tried to warn me. I assumed she was just bitter. I . . . was at fault too, there."

Benito nodded. "Poseidon sank her palace in the quarrel, or that is what Androcles told me."

"And I was there when Benito was making his deal with the tritons," said Maria. "They wanted a piece of the Lagoon to themselves for their help. Nothing to do with that old god. Who did you hear that story from anyway?"

Hekate looked at her. Then she ground her teeth audibly before speaking in a low, dangerous voice.

"From the black demon of the northlands. The one you call Chernobog. Curse him! I see now what this was. He sought to deceive me. To make me kill you and destroy your people, as Poseidon destroyed mine. He has been meddling here, and to the east. Well, that is the end of it. He will cross my demesnes no more." She turned to Benito. "I have done you a great wrong. I almost did worse. I make my apology, to you and the lady of the Lord of the Cold Halls. And I am at your call to make amends and restitution."

This brew of hers had definitely affected his judgement. "For a start, you can stop calling Maria Aidoneus' Lady. She's Maria. And she's only his for four months of the year. The rest of the time she's mine. Or I'm hers. I'm hers all of the time."

Hekate turned her gaze on the Lord of the Dead and Maria. "Demeter's bargain. Have you learned nothing, Aidoneus?"

The god shrugged. "I need living mortals in my cold halls. They alone can bring life and warmth. They stir the ancient tree to life and seed. You know how important that is."

"I am the mistress of crossroads and gates. There are choices, and there is always another way." Hekate bit her lip. "I think I was too foolish to see that myself, sometimes, so I will not hold it against you, Lord of the Cold Halls. But you need to think anew. Build a new road. I am . . . coming to terms with that myself."

"Well," said Benito, as things started to fade. "Start by not listening to demons. They *always* lie."

Someone was slapping Benito's face. Benito opened his eyes and was bitterly disappointed to find that it was Antimo Bartelozzi, not Maria. "Stop that!" he said crossly.

"Lie still, m'lord. The physicians are coming. We'll have some men with a litter here in a minute."

Benito sat up. "I don't need physicians or litters. I'll tell you what you need, though."

"What, m'lord?" asked Antimo.

"You need to tell that girlfriend of yours to be a little less gullible, and to check her facts before she jumps to conclusions. She's all too prone to it." Benito stood up. "Ah. Just in time for a nice walk back in the rain. Well, that'll help with the fires anyway."

Antimo looked uncertain. "You appeared to be having some kind of fit. Speaking to no one."

"I was speaking to Hekate. Who was very angry, and is, if I am any judge of women who have got over it, and I should be, now very contrite. Ready to be nice to us. She's got a temper. But Maria at least mostly keeps hers for throwing crockery." Benito sighed. "I must be getting senile. I even miss that, you know."

Hekate could, should she so desire, move between crossroads. Right now she felt she stood at one herself. She recalled that the Lion of Etruria had given her his permission to enter his demense and, while she'd shied from it before, it was time to deal with her relationship with her son.

The Winged Lion of Etruria did not lightly tolerate other ancient powers in his realms, and knew she was there at the muddy crossroads in between the rushy water-meadows and the tall cypresses. He appeared beside her, looking at her meditatively. He must have approved of what he saw.

"Walk westward. He's grazing at the copse down near that mill," said the Lion.

So she did. And there he was, cropping the sparse green grass growing in the shelter of the trees. She stood, frozen. He had grown so! No longer was he the leggy colt, but had become a magnificent palomino stallion, coat gleaming, his flaxen mane and forelock long and flowing, with a broad chest with strong quarters... and enormous golden wings folded onto his back.

She stood like that, watching him until he raised his head and looked her with an ale-brown eye. He turned his head the other way to look at her with the second eye. "Mother?"

He sounded...wary.

"Pegasus. Son. Are you well?" she asked, not moving, voice gentle, her heart full.

"I am not going back, Mother," he said defiantly.

For a moment she was hurt. Then she remembered the advice she'd been given. "I have not come to take you back, Son. You are your own master now. I just...wanted to see you. To see that you were well and happy."

He turned his head again to look at her out of each eye. Picked his head up slightly. "Oh. I thought... Yes. I am well."

"You have grown so," she said, admiringly. "You're beautiful. I was worried; I was worried every moment that you were pent in that stable. I was afraid—afraid you were being starved, or stunted or—well, I was worried. Mothers worry."

He stamped a foot, but his head was held high now. "I'm handsome. Not beautiful."

She felt the smile grow on her face. "Handsome

and beautiful. Spread your wings. Let me see how fine they are."

He did, stretching the vast pinions out, each feather gleaming in the weak winter sunlight.

She held out her arms and smiled. "So very fine! Ready to fly you anywhere. I am so proud of you, boy. You are magnificent."

He bowed his head, and sounded . . . contrite. "I'm sorry that I didn't come to see you, Mother. I thought . . . I assumed you'd stable me, confine me. Look after me, and love yes. But keep me. I don't want to be kept. I have been kept for so very, very long!"

"I might have," said Hekate, honestly. "But I think I have learned now not to try. There will always be protection, shelter and food for you with me. And love, always love. But never confinement. You will always be free to come and go as you please." She paused. "Someone who is a great deal wiser than I had thought, told me that the only way you hold an egg safely is not to hold it tightly."

Pegasus turned his head again, very like any other horse, assessing. Reassessing. "I didn't realize you'd be upset or worried. I just wanted . . . space."

She nodded. "I understand. I've done a fair amount of accidental harm without thinking, too, and I had less excuse. Being a goddess, it was all too easy to do so. Too much power makes you behave like an adolescent, without the reason." She sighed. "We should be wiser than mortals. Sometimes it seems that they have managed to form us in their image, and that . . . well, that has mixed results."

Then he came up to her and nuzzled her. "I will come to visit you."

"That is all I will ever ask." she said feeling the warmth of his breath against her cheek. She paused. "The human that freed you. Did he treat you well?"

Pegasus whickered a chuckle. "He gave me an apple that gave me wind, but other than that, he kept his word. He was very worried about his child. Did he find her?"

"He did. And I very nearly killed him because I did not know he had been honest." She sighed. "I do not know what to make of what he said about the tritons. They were Poseidon's warriors, after all."

"They sided with their mother. Poseidon was very angry with them," said Pegasus. "He held that horn of theirs to ransom, making them work for him. Triton himself fought with Poseidon over the way he had treated Amphitrite. Poseidon killed him."

"Oh," said Hekate, faintly. "I had hoped . . . the mortal said as much, but I thought he could not possibly be right." She paused for a long moment, stroking Pegasus's long, warm neck. He leaned into the caress. "He is not so much a god as a monster. Only a monster would kill his own children." She paused again. "I would say that I was a besotted fool and nothing good could ever come of him, but *you* did. There is at least that much."

Pegasus nuzzled her as a slow tear dropped from her eye. "The children of Triton fought for him, forced by the horn until some human stole it. Then they were free." He snorted a little, and it had the sound of bitter triumph. "I was there when it happened. The humans crept right into Poseidon's palace and stole it. I smelled them, but I did not give warning. And now, I am more glad than ever. You are right,

Mother. He is a monster. If there were any justice, he would be as hideous as Cetus, to match the ugliness of his heart."

Mother and son walked together for a long while. And when they parted, both hearts were lighter.

It had taken insurrection, riot and burning part of the city to finally inject a measure of common sense into the various factions—the Genovese, the Argonese, the various "Latin" traders, and even a few of the Byzantine civic leaders. They held a meeting in the Grand Palace and decided that the answer was that Constantinople needed a single unitary ruler. A governor to keep it all together.

"If the Bosphorus was solid dung I'd rather burrow through it looking for diamonds," said Benito. "Gentlemen. I have a wife and a child to get back to. And they are tied to a small island in the Adriatic. I have no desire at all to rule this festering city. It may be the greatest city on earth as far as you are concerned, but I am not fond of it. And I don't think it is fond of me either."

That was true enough. The citizens of Constantinople had, it seemed, been prepared for siege and war. A proud and desperate defense. Not the shameful business of waking up to find that the guard had changed and their emperor—be he never such a wastrel and an ass—was gone. He was their wastrel and ass, and they did not like the Venetians or their attitude. They certainly wouldn't want Benito Valdosta—of all Venetians—to be their governor.

"But M'lord Valdosta. What will we do? You are the

only person with governance experience, other than
Duke Enrico, and he will not stay here."

It was all something of a quandary for the conquerors. No one had thought much beyond taking
Constantinople. No one had thought that while taking the city might be a feat, holding it might be far
harder. Normally, after a bitter fight, the conquered
were happy to just have a little respite. Now, instead,
with the city taken by stealth without much loss of
life and relatively little loss of property, the fleet commanders had a problem. The citizenry were restive.
And there were three factors at play here:

First, it was necessary, when they sailed in spring,
that their way home be secure. Second: there was
temptation and the future. The traders of Venice
and Genoa wanted to return, year after year, to the
caravan-heads in Trebizond and to the ports of the
Black Sea. And finally, this was a rich city. Trade
would keep it that way. Venice and Genoa and
Aragon all saw it as a plum to be seized. None of
the leaders involved showed much forethought about
the matter.

Benito Valdosta, it seemed, was the only person
who saw it as a poisoned chalice. More hard work
than reward. Which, naturally, was why they wanted
him to keep it running for them while they bickered
over the loot. Benito wanted to get into the Black Sea,
sink Jagiellon's fleet, and get back home. Before the
first day of spring, if possible, or as soon thereafter
as he could manage.

"Gentlemen," he said, "I don't care who you prop
on the throne here. Find someone. One of Alexius's
relations perhaps? Personally, I have orders from my

Doge to pursue and sink Jagiellon's fleet. That is what I will do. And that is all I will have to do with it."

Benito would come to regret that decision bitterly, later. But it seemed a reasonable idea at the time. He had enough to do, making sure that he still had crews when he sailed. All he needed was a break in the weather. And that was all they weren't getting. Winter had arrived with a vengeance.

He wanted away from here. At first the city had been more stunned and confused than anything else. But they had too few people to control a city of fifty thousand souls by brute force. And the countryside around the city was turning hostile too, a sign that someone was organizing for Alexius, somewhere.

People were amazingly stupid, Benito thought. The city had once supported nearly half a million people. It had been in a decline for a while, but had shrunk further under Alexius's misrule from seventy thousand to its present fifty. Public works were decaying. Sewage and garbage lay in the streets—and they wanted Alexius back?

But there were always those who had done well under the oppressor. He'd seen that in Venice, and again on Corfu. And there were always camp-followers and fools ready to deny their senses and follow them.

Chapter 49

Constantinople

The Mongol tarkhan Qishkai arrived in considerable state, with a small army of Mongol guards. There was no doubt whatsoever in Benito's mind that this man was a shrewd and skillful politician. He was also a man of immense affability and fondness for wine, for which, it appeared he had a hard head.

The banquet with which the tarkhan was greeted had taxed resources—finding delicacies, or even decent food, in a city that had been under siege, and then sacked, was no easy task. Benito had had an idea, though, and quietly put out the word that there was a bounty to be had—so-and-so much for a bottle of good wine, much more for a barrel, so much for a fat sheep, so much for a sack of fine flour, so much for eggs. And no questions asked. Provisions appeared at the palace kitchen doors, silver flowed out of it. The cooks were set to work. They didn't much care who the master was, so long as they were paid and had decent supplies to work with.

The banquet was a success. And the tarkhan got

great enjoyment from the wine; it did not appear that Mongols had the same prohibition against spirits that Moslems did. Benito was feeling half awash and had begun quietly limiting his input halfway through the banquet. Tarkhan Qishkai was large and plump and showed no signs of needing to do so. The Mongol was an expert at getting others to talk, and far from showing Mongol standoffishness he seemed to relish the company. He spoke impeccable Greek, and better Frankish than most Greeks. He was also very good at dredging information out of polite talk, Benito noticed.

"You mentioned," he said, signaling to the servitors to pour more wine into Benito's goblet, "that I had a very different manner to the last envoy you'd met. And where would that have been, my good young fellow? In Venice? I didn't think we'd sent a tarkhan that far in your lifetime, to be honest."

"This was on Corfu. A Tarkhan Borshar."

If the plump indolent-looking Mongol had suddenly been transformed into a rat-hunting terrier, and Benito's doublet had skittered and squeaked, he could scarcely have got more of a reaction. The tarkhan stared intently at his face. "You...will interest...the Ilkhan...extremely," he said pausing between each word. "Borshar is no tarkhan. The Ilkhan has set a price on his head."

Benito swallowed, his mouth suddenly dry. "What? But he was vouched for! He came from the bashar of Jerusalem! And he has gone overland with Prince Manfred to the lands of the Golden Horde!"

"You are certain of this?" asked the Mongol ambassador.

Benito wondered what hell he had sent Manfred walking into, all innocent and unwarned. "As certain as I am of sunrise tomorrow. I organized it. I was the acting governor of Corfu. I even know that they reached the lands of the Golden Horde and had made contact under the truce flag with what Iskander Beg said were members of the Raven clan."

The Mongol tarkhan hissed between his teeth. "We had heard rumors. Young man . . . I see I have made some mistakes because of your age. I am empowered to offer various inducements and considerable reward to reach the lands of the Golden Horde. Or, if you have the contacts to arrange this, the Ilkhan has offered a reward of one hundred thousand golden talents for the head of Borshar. He is not only no tarkhan but he is an outcast who has brought embarrassment to the Ilkhan Hotai."

Benito took a deep breath, trying to work out what his next move had to be. "Tarkhan, I need to discuss this with my grandfather, first. But we need to meet and discuss this, all of us together, and soon. Very, very soon. Manfred is the Holy Roman Emperor's nephew. He is second in line for the throne of the empire. If this Borshar has . . ."

Qishkai narrowed his eyes. He had not drunk from his goblet in all this time, which was probably a very bad sign. But, from his next words, *not* for Benito, the Venetians, or the Franks. "This too is the grave concern of the Ilkhan himself. It appears Borshar was tasked with fomenting war against the Ilkhan. He has abused our reputation and the integrity of our diplomats. All I can say is that the Ilkhan is deeply embarrassed by this and we will make what amends we can."

"I hope that that's good enough for Charles Fredrik. He's fond of Manfred...and he and Erik are good friends of mine," said Benito in a voice just above a whisper. "And I made it possible. They had a letter of safe-conduct from your Ilkhan." His mind was full of foreboding. He had not heard from, or about, his friends since they met with the Raven clan.

Qishkai nodded. "We know of this. It was the genuine article, and bore the seals of the Ilkhan. Surely no one would dare to override that. I believe...I hope that the Golden Horde would respect it, young Sir."

There was one thing he *could* do, and it would accomplish two things—first, impress the tarkhan that he was telling the truth; and two, maybe get some word as to what was happening. "If you'll pardon me, I'll need to get word sent to Iskander Beg as soon as possible. Tonight, actually, it is still possible. Antimo will have contacts. Excuse me."

So Benito left, hastily, to find Antimo Bartelozzi, who had been put to ferreting out the source of the riots and insurrection.

He found him at the Milion, looking forlornly about. He turned that forlorn gaze on Benito. "I have not been able to get her to speak to me again, Benito. Did you offend her? Drive her off?"

Benito didn't pretend not to know who the spymaster was talking about—and if Antimo was not a lovelorn man, then he didn't know what one looked like. "I'm sure not, Antimo. She said she was in my debt, as I remember it. Listen, I have a serious problem. The tarkhan has just told me that the fellow who went to the Golden Horde with Manfred was a fraud. An imposter and an assassin. The Mongols want him dead, badly. We'd better send word to Venice and to Iskander—if there is any chance of his getting a message to Manfred."

Antimo shook himself visibly. Maybe that was why Hekate liked him. He was rather doglike in some ways—a poacher's silent lurcher, rather than a lady's doe-eyed spaniel. "Iskander. I assume you set up contact points. It is snowing up there, Benito Valdosta. But we will do our best. Venice . . . we will need to make very sure that such a message goes as far as Venice, to Doge Dorma and not any farther. The last thing they want is the Holy Roman Emperor aware that they knew, and didn't tell him, but they also should wait with bad news until we are sure. And that is difficult."

Benito shrugged, helplessly. "We'll just have to do our best. In the meanwhile can you think of any way of getting this tarkhan and his half a regiment of escort to the Golden Horde?"

"Er. No."

Benito felt a weight descend on him. "Me neither."

Tarkhan Qishkai was also occupied in writing letters that evening, after leaving the banquet somewhat earlier than he had planned. Some traffic would, inevitably, go southward. He could if necessary, simply hire a vessel and put a messenger on it. But first he needed to formalize and refine his thoughts, and writing everything down was a good way of doing that.

He began the letter several times. How did he explain that the Ilkhan's worst fears about the impact of the traitor Ambien and his sending Borshar were likely to be correct . . . tactfully? Eventually he gave up on tact and settled for factual. No matter how he tried to put it, it wasn't going to be good news. At least the Venetians seemed just as keen to see him complete his mission as he was. He had also been actively considering the impact of the capture of Constantinople on the Asia Minor *Themes* of the Byzantine empire. At the moment it was an empire without an administration and an emperor on the run. But in reality for years now the *Themes* had run themselves and contributed to a parasitic empire for little benefit, rather than the empire running the *Themes*. It was a situation that suited the Ilkhan better than an aggressive and a successful Byzantium. It was in the Ilkhan's best interest to help Alexius back on the throne in Constantinople, and that would normally have been his advice. Funds were plainly wasted on the man, but Constantinople was relatively weak. The Ilkhan could provide troops, or have one of their proxies do so...

Only that could be awkward right now.

This...was a problem. And not a pretty one.

Chapter 50

Constantinople

Benito had time to weigh and analyze his conversations with the tarkhan and with Antimo and indeed, with Hekate. The winter sky decided they needed a deluge. It rained, and rained again, in between which they got some sleet. Benito thought. It was a choice, in this weather, of drink, womanize or keep one's mind occupied, and after Hekate's drink Benito found he was even less keen on losing control, and there was nothing like knowing your wife was able to watch you to take the interest out of banter. Besides, women, after Maria, always seemed like saltless food. So it was read and think. Constantinople was no Alexandria, but Alexius had had a large, old and neglected library. Benito spent some time looking things up and reading around subjects. There were pieces of an interlocking puzzle to put together as best he could.

Eventually he went looking for a crossroad with a small amount of wine, and a way of carefully avoiding Antimo Bartelozzi. That was taken care of by making sure Antimo was busy with his grandfather.

Antimo had mentioned that he'd tried to speak to Hekate several more times, asked her for guidance. Called to her dogs. She had not come.

The last thing Benito needed was Antimo Bartelozzi getting the wrong end of the stick. He knew, himself, that rationality sometimes flew out of the window in affairs of the heart. And unless he was very much mistaken, the spymaster was totally smitten. Maybe because he'd avoided it for so many years?

Well, the reason was of no matter.

Benito found his crossroad, suitably deserted. He poured the libation. "Queen of the Night, Lady of the Hunt, Guardian of the Crossroads," he said. "Um... I'd like a word, please?"

She answered his call, appearing suddenly at his side as if she had stepped through an invisible door.

She looked somewhat troubled. "I am here, as you request. And how can I repay my debts?"

"I'd be a liar if I said I'd never want help, but I am not sure about the debt," said Benito, a little doubtfully. "It really doesn't seem to me that you owe me anything."

"You freed my son."

"That was between him and me," Benito countered. "And if it hadn't been for his help, I never would have been in time to rescue my daughter."

Hekate shook her head. "I still maligned you. Did not trust you. Very nearly killed you."

"You'd be amazed how often that seems to happen. Antimo says it is my face." Benito noted the little twitch of expression when he mentioned the spymaster. *Ah. So sits the wind?* He thought to himself.

"Nonetheless, I have learned," said Hekate, refusing

to even smile. "As a goddess I had become distant and too confident of my infallibility. I acted before I thought. That is a great and terrible failing in one with power."

"That doesn't take being a goddess. But please, allow me to change the subject for a moment. I have a question to ask. A tribe called the Shardana..."

She nodded. "Some of my people. Long gone now. Lost in the great flooding."

"Are you sure?" He grinned. "I hate to question the infallibility of goddess, but I have it on good authority that a sea-people called the Shardana are the ancestors of one of our captains. He said something about buildings called Nurah—"

"Ah." Her eyes lightened a little with recognition. "Nuraghe. They were a warlike people and much given to raiding. But their lands were flooded."

Benito shook his head. "Might be something different, of course. My friend was positive these were buildings—sort of stone towers. And Di Tharra said something about a fish-mouth sword."

She put her hands behind her back, and intoned, very much like someone reciting: "With the black arrows, round shields and the fish-tongue sword, came the Shardana, down on our cross-plowed fields and our white oxen. Woe and blood came at the bite of the bronze fish-tongue," she grimaced. "It does not translate well, but it is the lament of the Lucca people. Like the Shardana, they were among those who gave me reverence. Their language is long gone, as are they."

"As I have reason to know," said Benito, thinking of the Mother Goddess, "the old that is strong is less than easily eradicated. I know this is a lot to ask but would you speak to Androcles the triton, if I arranged it?"

"I doubt if they would speak with me," said Hekate quietly. "It was because of me that Poseidon killed Amphitrite. She warned me. I . . . slighted her, and her warning. She challenged Poseidon over his infidelity and he sank her palace. I held back my harpoon from the place where he hid with my Pegasus, but I speared her son Triton's children as they rushed down the gulf to my flooded land after Poseidon cracked the gate." She sighed. "I do not know if they would ever forgive me that."

Benito made a face. "I've been reading, and it sounds to me, if your version of what happened is right, as if you might have been just the last straw. Poseidon seems to have fathered kids on nearly everything that breathed."

"Oh, he wasn't fussy about them breathing," said Hekate tartly, her tone and posture slightly more what he had come associate with her. A couple of years with Maria had made him a lot more aware of these cues than he once had been. Then she sighed. "At the very least I owe the tritons my contrition. Very well. If they will speak with me, call me. I watch. I watch over you . . . as I once watched my people."

"I'll do my best." He wondered if it was a good moment to mention Antimo but decided not. There'd be a suitable time. He'd bet watching involved keeping the spymaster under such observation as that expert at avoiding it had never experienced. He wasn't entirely sure just what her problem was, but he'd been around Marco long enough to guess it would be some form of idiotic self-sacrificing nobility.

❧　　❧　　❧

Later that day he chose a long, straight, well-lit passage to talk to Antimo Bartelozzi. "Have you seen Hekate yet?"

The spymaster looked like a mournful puppy. It would have been funny if Benito hadn't felt such sympathy for him. "No, m'lord. I go every morning and evening, and make a small libation at the Milion. It was probably sacred to her once."

"Hmm. I'd keep that up if I were you," said Benito.

He perked up a little. "Has she spoken with you?" Then he looked crestfallen again. "Have I offended her?"

"At a guess," said Benito carefully skirting the first question, "she feels that she has offended you. Or at least trespassed on an area that she should not have. Trust me on this. In most areas you're much more experienced than I am, but on this—"

He clapped Antimo on the shoulder. "In the area of women, consider me your wise, older brother. Women—well, men, too, maybe even more so—get these ideas. I'd consider taking...Oh, I don't know, a couple of mutton bones. Flowers are bit difficult at this time of year. And jewelry would be a mistake, I think. Perfume maybe. Women like perfume, but they like even more that you thought of bringing the perfume."

"It's not like that," said Antimo, stiffly. "I am content to worship."

"Of course. Respect and reverence are important. But a gesture to the dogs wouldn't go amiss, eh?" said Benito.

Antimo smiled as fondly as only a dog lover could. "Lovely animals."

Benito, who had seen Hekate's hounds in the form in which they guarded the gates to the underworld, nodded. He had a feeling Antimo would still describe the slavering hell-hounds as *soppy old things, really*.

"Just do it," he urged, "And see what happens."

"Talk with Hekate? The Goddess of the Crossroads, Opener of Gateways, Lady of the Night, Mistress of the Hunt?" Androcles looked quizzically at Benito, who was squeezing his thumb to stop the bleeding. "The Shardana asks endless questions already. What do we need with her?"

Benito considered that. "Well, for starters, she's woken up, she has worshippers again, and she's getting strong. I have a feeling if she took it into her head, she could close off the Black Sea. I think she has before, and this time Poseidon is not around to crack it open again. You said you had kin that lived there."

Androcles nodded. "You have a point. But she has a nasty temper on her, I've heard. And she's got no liking for tritons. Killed a lot in the early days. You want to treat her with respect, Benito Valdosta. She's no casual bit of fluff to take out on the water for a bit of rocking the boat."

"I only look stupid, Androcles," Benito chided. "Even if I were interested, which I am *not*, not under any circumstances..." He shuddered a little, and it was not an act. "...why would I think twice about it when my wife is the best thing that ever happened to me, *and* a part-time goddess herself? It'd make more sense to chop off my own toes."

"I'm glad you know that about your appearance," said the triton, grinning his sharp-toothed grin.

"If I didn't, enough people tell me about it. Now can I ask her to come here? Talk to you?" He tried to look as earnest and solemn as he could. "She's got no quarrel with you or your kind. Actually...look, the reason I am asking is because she said she wanted to apologize."

"What?" Androcles rocked back in the water with shock, and Benito didn't think it was feigned. "Benito, goddesses don't say sorry. There's more chance of Juliette telling me I'm right."

"This one seems to be indulging in some remorse. Probably a new experience for her, and she's not very good at it yet, but she is very determined. Humor me. It won't hurt us." Benito crossed his fingers behind his back. "There is a crossroad at the end of the pier. I'll be as long as it takes to pour out a bit of wine."

"Save some for me," said Androcles. "If you're right, I'll need it. And if you're wrong I'll need it more."

"You wish," said Benito, over his shoulder. But he did anyway.

Once again, Hekate appeared as if she had stepped through a door in the air, but she paid no attention to Benito. Her attention was on the triton in the water at the end of the pier.

Hekate approached the triton very warily. Bowed... Benito suspected it was not something she had much experience at. He tossed the wineskin to Androcles.

"Greetings, child of Triton," said Hekate.

"Greetings, Goddess of the Crossroads, Opener of Gateways, Lady of the Night, Mistress of the Hunt."

Hekate took a deep breath. "I wanted to apologize."

The triton looked thoughtful, and gave Benito a nod. "Long time back, Lady of Gateways. Our role wasn't exactly our idea. Or so my grandfather told me. And he had it from his grandfather. And we don't live the mayfly lives of these humans." He took a swig of the wineskin. "I think . . . maybe it is long enough ago, we can look at things differently."

"Time passes very differently in the otherworlds," Hekate said, slowly. "I, I was lost within myself. Grieving for Chrysaor. Grieving for my lost people. Fearful for my Pegasus."

"I heard about Chrysaor." Androcles blew out a breath, like a dolphin. "I'm sorry. It is hard to lose a child. Your people . . . well, some of them survived, lady. It was a vast area to flood. The crack in the gate isn't that large or deep. The Ekwesh, Teresh, Lucca, 'prw, and the Shardana were around afterward. Most of them are gone by now, I would guess, swallowed up by other lands and places."

"Benito has said . . . you have some trace still of the Shardana."

"They ended up as allies of ours. Story goes that they made a bargain to get back Triton's conch from Poseidon." He shrugged. "It's a pity they never succeeded, but they broke Poseidon's hold over us, and that was the point, really. No one likes to live a slave, and with the conch gone, or lost, there was nothing he could do to command us. What threat is a storm to us?"

Hekate's lips curved, verly slightly. "As little as a butterfly threatening an eagle," she said.

Androcles laughed. "Anyway, they were bold, daring and fairly stupid, lady. They attacked the Great Kingdom of Egypt, and lost. The survivors fled west, and we found them a refuge on an island now called

Sardinia. That was when we lost contact with them. But it is possible their descendants survive. You should talk to Captain Di Tharra. He's more interested in old history than I am. He's from Sardinia. Has a fish-tongue sword and an uprooted tree on his coat of arms."

"What is a coat of arms?" she asked.

"A display once shown on their shields, to say who they were, and whence they came from. And he tells me that they have Nuraghe towers, in ruins now, but there, on the island."

"The Shardana built those. So did the Ekwesh," said Hekate, plainly remembering, being hurt by the memory.

"I've seen them down in the dead zone in the Black Sea," said Androcles.

That didn't top the list of tactful statements the triton could have made. She glared at him, and then remembered she was being contrite. "The killing zone. Let us put that behind us, as you said."

"It wasn't exactly Triton's idea, lady, let alone ours," said Androcles. "But I mean the dead zone, when I say that, literally. The water down there is saltier, fish and other water-life cannot live down there. The buildings are as they were when the flooding came. We went to look. We do not go down there anymore."

She nodded, gravely. "It is fitting that it be left alone and remain as it once was."

"I'll pass that on," said Androcles. "Some of our kind live in the Black Sea. The fishing is good."

"It has been many years since I ate the fish from there. But it was. It was also a rich and fertile land." She sighed. "My thanks to you, and to your kind for what you did for the Shardana."

"They left us free of Poseidon's call. And now I go to drink this wine and to see when you can sail, Valdosta." With a flick of his tail, he was gone.

Hekate stared after him. "The sea...I never understood it. I think that was why Poseidon fascinated me so. Well, I wish you good fortune in your venture here, Benito Valdosta. I must find the Shardana, or their children."

"They don't exactly worship you these days, Lady Hekate," said Benito thoughtfully. "I'd guess that the blood of your people runs in the captain from Sardinia with the coat of arms that shows the old sword, and the uprooted tree. He's here with us, and he sails with us to deal with Jagiellon's fleet. But Di Tharra's a very conservative Pauline Christian, that I do know."

"It matters not who they worship now," said Hekate. "I was so busy grieving that I did not do my duty by their ancestors. I will not fail their children."

"Then you'd better watch over Di Tharra and the fleet."

"Show him to me. I will watch him," she declared.

As you watch Antimo, thought Benito but he merely nodded. He'd become quite familiar with perfumes and he recognized the one she was wearing. There was a small perfumier distilling his wares in the Venetian quarter. The man sold small beautiful and expensive bottles of his wares. Benito had bought one as a gift for Maria. He'd guess this was the same. An errant snippet of information from his brother's ardent reading of some foreign book said that the distillation of perfume was a relatively modern thing, and before that scented oils and fats had been made and used. Benito had said that it must have made for rather slippery lovers. Kat had tried to hit him, and said he was impossible.

Well, maybe he was. God and Saint Hypatia knew there was very little other explanation for his life.

Later that day, Benito found a chance to speak to Antimo. Again he chose his spot to do so carefully; this time, Antimo's own handsome room in the palace. There were hundreds of handsome rooms in this palace, and sometimes Benito wondered who on earth could have been in all of them. "Any word from the north?"

Antimo shook his head. "No, m'lord. Not much from anywhere. It's cold and wet and windy, and that makes for poor travel."

"I saw the triton today. He's going into the Black Sea to look for some of his kin. He'll bring us word when we can sail—and scout the Dnieper. We met Hekate together, by the way. We talked of various things, mostly history."

"That would be valuable information, m'lord," Then his self discipline failed. "Did she mention my name in among these various things?"

Benito shook his head, and helped himself to Antimo's mulled wine. Most of the alcohol had evaporated out of it, but it was warming and soothing. "No. It was mostly about one of the tribes who used to worship her. Some of their descendants ended up in Sardinia. Very interesting if you are fascinated by ancient history. Not thrilling otherwise."

"She is looking well?" asked the spymaster.

Benito almost rolled his eyes. "Yes. She has some nice new scent, I noticed. It was making the dogs sneeze."

Antimo was no fool. He colored slightly, but understood the message for what it was. "Thank you, m'lord."

"All right. We still need to find a way to get the tarkhan where he wants to go and as quickly as possible," Benito said. "In the meanwhile we need to work on the plan to defend the Bosphorus itself. Jagiellon has the manpower for a land-army to swamp ours, if he can get them here before we sink his transports."

"The people of Thrace could be quite hostile to him, m'lord. On either shore. And the channel is not so wide as to not to be well covered by the fortresses we have taken."

Benito grinned. He liked this side of Antimo very much. "Then let's figure out just how hostile we can get Thrace to be."

Chapter 51

Constantinople

Every morning, Benito went out to the pier and back. "Just for exercise," he claimed. He wasn't going to drop his blood in the water, but he hoped for a fin and a toss of seaweed hair, and some better news from the sea.

And one day, he got them. "Back, are you?" said Benito, as the triton flexed his sea-colored shoulders and tossed his hair.

Androcles shrugged. "We like to ride the storm-waves, but the seas on the other side of the Bosphorus are barely worth being out in now."

After two and a half months in Callipolis and Constantinople, Androcles' news could hardly have been more welcome to Benito. There had been a sequence of the nasty storms from the north that the Black Sea was known for. That had played havoc with any ideas he'd had about an early sailing date. Now, it seemed, the weather was settling. Benito knew that, inevitably, their foe knew about the fleet in Constantinople. He almost certainly knew what they planned to do. But it was a long way from Constantinople to the Gulf of Odessa.

Even more welcome—and surprising—news arrived that very day. A trader from Thessalonica arrived on a small coastal trading vessel that took advantage of local knowledge of the coast and weather to hop hastily from safe anchorage to safe anchorage and asked for an interview with Benito Valdosta. Normally, the man would have had as much chance as any of the other Greeks wanting to do this—which was to say none at all. But the trader parted with a suitable bribe, and asked that Benito be told that he had news from a kinsman in Illyria.

When that phrase arrived in Benito's ears, he had the fellow into his office with great rapidity. Soon he and the Old Fox were pouring over Manfred's letter and pondering over its contents and the implications of the news out of the lands of the Golden Horde.

"The most important news is that they're alive and reasonably safe," said Benito, exhaling. "I thought I might have sent them to their deaths."

"Not for want of trying, by the sounds of it," said Enrico, shaking his head.

"With Erik and Manfred? You do have to try very hard," said Benito, grinning all over his face. "It sounds as if they've stirred up a hornet's nest and a half. And swatted most of it to death." Oh, he wished he could be there...or that there were two of him. One for there, one for here.

"Whatever else they've done, they've reduced the threat to Constantinople," said Enrico, sounding as relieved as Benito, but for different reasons.

Benito bent his mind to their own strategy. Manfred

and Erik could handle themselves, and he no longer needed to worry that they were about to be bitten by a viper they didn't suspect. "Good. That means that I can take a lot more men with us. With Jagiellon forewarned, as is almost inevitable, it could be that we'll need them."

"By the looks of this, we should call for the Ilkhan's tarkhan," said Enrico, tapping the letter. "Just as soon as we have these other documents from this White Horde translated. One piece of treachery is enough. Let us make sure that they contain no second trap."

Benito nodded.

The fleet could sail. And soon. He went to give orders with a singing in his heart. That meant out of Constantinople, and hopefully home to his wife and daughter. Spring was coming . . . spring was coming. And in the meantime, he sent word to the tarkhan that there was word from the Golden Horde.

A little later he was called to a meeting with Tarkhan Qishkai. The tarkhan had taken for himself—Benito did not ask how—a little palace apart from the imperial palace. He and the Old Fox met the man in a room like a jewel box, ornamented with mosaics and warmed with a brazier. They gave him their news, and passed over copies of the pertinent parts of the letters as they sat on padded benches beside the brazier, which gave off faintly perfumed heat.

The man was a professional diplomat, but the relief was still visible in the set of his shoulders. "It appears that fortune has favored us. The attempt to cause a breach between the Ilkhan, the Golden Horde and the Holy Roman Empire has not succeeded. This is the best news you could have given me, short of telling me that you could transport me to the clans on a flying carpet."

"By my reading of the matter you may still have some fences to mend, especially with the Golden Horde," said Enrico dryly. "And it wasn't so much fortune as skill and force of arms that won the day, despite being surrounded by superior numbers. I just thought I might mention this. But at least you will not have the Knights of the Holy Trinity arrayed in battle against your forces."

The tarkhan smiled broadly. "Well, the Golden Horde are very traditional. They haven't really embraced modern weaponry. But it would appear that the reputation of the Knights is well-deserved." He clapped his hands, and a servant appeared with mulled wine.

Dell'este nodded sagely, taking a flagon. "I can find you a few foes of theirs that would agree with you. But anyway, at least your master the Ilkhan is relieved of that care."

"We are most grateful for this news, but," the tarkhan said, pausing, "if I may prevail on your goodwill a little further. It would be to our mutual benefit if we could reach the lands of the Golden Horde, so I may deal with this traitorous renegade. The Ilkhan has set a considerable price on his head."

Benito cocked his head to one side. "I'm not sure that would be possible. We sail to war, Tarkhan Qishkai. We've got a fleet to deal with, dockyards to destroy, and then we'll probably venture to the northwest coast, to see if contact can be made with Prince Manfred and his entourage. You'd be better advised to remain here until, or if, we succeed. Then trading vessels will venture out. We're not taking horse-transports with us. They, and some of the knights, remain here."

But the tarkhan waved that aside as a petty consideration. "Should we reach the lands of the Golden Horde horses will be the least of our worries, M'lord Valdosta. And I have a considerable escort. We are in conflict with your enemy too. You could use some extra men, if you are leaving some of your knights behind. And having us with you will make it easier to contact your Prince Manfred. No hand in the Golden Horde will be turned against us. The same would not be true of you, foreigners coming into their territory. They would attack first, and ask questions later."

Benito pursed his lips. The man was right. But . . . "You make a good argument. But it is not without risk, Tarkhan. We cannot guarantee your safety. We cannot guarantee our own."

The tarkhan's gaze was steady, and his voice firm. "To fulfill the Ilkhan's express order with all possible speed must be my first desire. And it would appear that this is the best way I could do so. The Bulgar remain our foes. A matter of an old slight—but they carry a feud, nearly as well as we do."

"Don't ever start a fight with the Illyrians then. They've got feuds that have gone on so long the original slight has been forgotten for centuries," said Enrico, with a little snort. "I am sure this can be organized, Tarkhan. We'll need to consult with our Genovese and Aragonese allies first, of course. And it may be necessary to split your men up onto a number of vessels."

The tarkhan smiled again. But Benito noted the steel behind the smile. He might be affable, he might be many things, but one thing he was not, and that was weak. "If necessary, that could be done. I shall compose a letter to my master now, and convey the good news, and the steps I am taking. I thank you once again for telling me this and conveying those documents to me. Your prince has fallen among very powerful people. They will protect him with their lives. Their honor is famous. So is their princess, both for her beauty and her wrestling skills."

"Sounds like Manfred will be right at home and Erik will be as uncomfortable as it is possible to be," said Benito, laughing at the thought. "I hope she throws our Icelander around a little."

"Oh, he can't afford to lose. She bets a hundred horses against her hand in marriage," explained the tarkhan.

"Ah. Well, he'd not want to win then," said Benito, laughing even harder. "Besides the fact I don't think he has a hundred horses. It's a pity."

The issue of getting the tarkhan's presence on the expedition around Admiral Borana and Count Alfons was more complex. Not that they minded—but they wanted to be the carriers. And of course, there was the thorny issue of who would stay and administer Constantinople. Benito surely didn't want to do so, Enrico Dell'este had more interest in his grandson than the possession—in whole or in part—of another city than Ferrara. Admiral Borana and Count Alfons both relished the idea. On the other hand—they needed someone capable of holding the city against their return.

"Look, why don't we split the roles. The civic administration is a corrupt mess anyway: we'll leave Borana to do that. *If* we can have a Venetian as military commander," said Benito. "Borana will huff and puff . . . and we'll give in, and agree to Augustino Leito of Ferrara as a compromise."

Another crossroads. Another libation. And another unnerving appearance of the Goddess of the Night out of nowhere. "You offered your help," said Benito to Hekate.

Hekate bowed slightly. It appeared that she had not forgotten anything over the last two months. Maybe the lessons were going to stick. "Yes. You said that you felt there was no debt, but I feel one exists."

"We're going after Jagiellon's fleet in the Black Sea—hopefully before it can reach full strength," said Benito. "And if you really feel you owe me a debt, I have a way for you to make everything even again."

Hekate frowned slightly. "I have little to do with war, Benito Valdosta. I am the guardian of gates and the chooser of ways."

"That's just it," he said eagerly. "We're trying to close a gate, lady. And to stop the creature you called the Black Demon of the north—it controls Grand Duke Jagiellon—from bringing an army and a fleet as a battering ram to force his way into our peaceful ocean." Benito pulled a face. "I'm talking to a goddess. Let's be accurate here, the Mediterranean is relatively peaceful. Most of it is under the influence of the Petrine church. It's a little after your time, but they have a doctrine of tolerance. That is all very well, but it needs a robust defense, sometimes. Something like Chernobog would destroy it."

Hekate looked inquisitorially at him, and Benito got the feeling that full declaration was always a good thing. "We're a nation of traders, Lady Hekate. The treasures of the east flow through Venice, and Genoa. It's our lifeblood and this would affect our trade and threaten our people. We'll go to war to protect them."

"You would make better guardians of the gate and the place between west and east than the black demon of the north or his minions," conceded Hekate.

"Guarding it is the last thing I desire," he said fervently. "I want to go and deal with this fleet, make all as safe as may be, and then go home to my wife and baby girl."

This actually drew a smile from Hekate. "Then what is it you want of me?" she asked.

He took a deep breath. "To make sure that this gate is still open, if and when we come back."

Her head came up a little, like one of her dogs scenting prey. "If and when?"

He was as honest as he had ever been. "It's war, Lady Hekate. People get killed. We might not win this. We might win the war, but still not make it back. I'm not the crazy young fool who thought himself immortal anymore. I haven't been for a while."

She was silent for a while. "Do some of your people remain behind?"

"Some of them, yes," he told her. "Some of the knights, the admiral of the Genovese fleet, who will be supposed to be administering the city. I don't trust him, and I don't think he is good for the city. But his ships are needed, and we're better without him, but with most of the ships. Enrico goes with me. His agent, Antimo, will be organizing in the countryside along the Bosphorus. This will be his base. I trust him, but he may not be able to deal with Borana's idiocy," said Benito, calmly. "And that is what I would like you to deal with, if it is in your power."

Hekate nodded slowly. That was plainly pleasing to her. Then she asked: "The descendant of the Shardana?"

"He sails with us. I could try to leave him here. But Borana doesn't like him." Benito sucked on his lower lip. "I'm not sure what would happen to him if I left him behind. At least if he's with me, I'll know that there is no one that's trying to use him as a scapegoat. And he's a damn good strategist."

"The Shardana always went raiding for grain and kine. It is their way. Has he a family?" she asked.

"I believe so. A wife and children back in Sardinia." This seemed to please her, too.

"I will do this," she said, with a little, firm nod. "I will guard the gate. And I will give you a gift, not without its price, that will hide you and your ships in need. Let me teach you the spell of the threefold way. At sea it will call the sea-mist to cloak you."

"That would be much appreciated," Benito said with a little surprise. "I will carry a lot of lives with me. I'd like to lose as few as possible."

"And this is why I will give it to you, Benito Valdosta," she said, her lips curving upwards, a little. "Because you will save as many as you can."

Chapter 52

Venice

The Doge plucked at the coverlet with an impatient hand. "I'm really much better," said Petro. "You can stop fussing like a hen over a single chick, Marco Valdosta."

"I'll stop fussing when you start listening," said Marco, secretly pleased that his patient was restive. "And that means eating food which is easier on your insides, Doge Dorma. Not the liver of fat goose potted with white truffles."

"I've had an unpleasant reminder that I may never get the opportunity to eat it again," said Petro, peevishly. "So I may as well enjoy it while I am still alive. While I have the chance."

Oh, this was a very good sign. Complaints, in Marco's experience, always meant the patient was ready to get back to his life. "Petro, most Doges die of old age. And now that Filippo Visconti is dead, assassination has become less fashionable. Give it a little time and you'll be getting back that avoirdupois you shed, by eating all your favorite foods again. In the meanwhile, moderation—and you need to get up more. Exercise a little."

Petro sighed. "I have not the strength for it these days. It's this diet of pap and pabulums."

Marco made a mock-sad face at the Doge. "And rationing your wine, no doubt. What happened to the Doge who was insisting on displaying himself from balconies, and attending all his meetings?"

"You slew him with barley gruel," Dorma said sourly.

A footman knocked at the door. "M'lord Valdosta? Sorry to disturb, but M'lord Calmi asked me to let you know that an emissary from the self-styled Protector of Milan has arrived."

Petro snorted. "Are you usurping my authority there too, Marco? The Council of Ten calls to you and not me?"

The footman shuffled, uncomfortable with being put in the middle of what seemed to him to be a dangerous almost-argument. "M'lord, he said to convey the information that he styles himself Cavaliere Francisco Turner."

Petro shut his mouth with a snap. And now it was Marco's turn to gape.

"I think," said Petro, "we will grant him a private interview. Well, somewhat private. Here. Inform Calmi. He will doubtless want his spies, or even himself listening in."

"And tell someone to find some beer and send it here," put in Marco with a faint smile. It was easy to smile, now that they all knew that Francisco had been a guardian, not an assassin and kidnapper, and that if it had not been for his quickness in getting back to his master, 'Lessi's fate might have been far different.

"Beer? Why beer?" asked Petro.

Marco shrugged. "Francisco seems to have a fondness for it."

Petro's eyebrow rose. "Well, can I have some, as you are rationing my wine?"

A little while later Francisco Turner was escorted to the private withdrawing room of the Doge, where Petro had graduated from a chaise longue to a Dantesca chair, and several extra satin cushions. Francisco was dressed far more elegantly than he had been as Marco's teacher, but there was still something military about his appearance.

He bowed first to the Doge, as was proper. "I am glad to see you in a more recovered state, Your Grace."

"Not as glad as I would be if Marco would loose the chains on diet," Dorma pulled a long, sad face. "Cavalier, he has taken your advice, I recall. Burned bread you prescribed last. What of a little goose liver now? Truffles? For God's sake, oysters, surely?"

Francisco remained solemn. "Poisons often affect the liver, Your Grace. And rich food and wine make one liverish. It is better not to put too much strain on one's insides, more particularly as I have not been able to find an account of anyone actually surviving that particular poison. I'm sad to say I support his position." But, as Dorma made unhappy eyes at him, he relented, a little. "A morsel at a meal might be acceptable. No more than will cover the blade of a knife. A table knife, Doge Dorma, not some giant barbarian hacking tool intended to cut down trees and heads equally."

"Well, a taste is better than none," said Petro Dorma. "And for that, I am grateful, as I am for my life." He left off his play-acting. "Marco says your skill and teaching helped, and your knowledge was what turned the trick."

"His skill, Your Grace. A little of my help with language, perhaps." The man smiled wryly. "I did wonder if my master would thank me for it, but it appears that he feels Doge Petro Dorma might be better for Milan and himself than your death would have been."

"That's not what Duke Filippo Visconti thought," said Petro Dorma, his face unreadable.

Francisco rose—slightly—to the bait. "Fortunately, that is no longer important, Your Grace."

A footman opened the doors and the butler, with an expression that could have curdled vinegar, arrived with two more footmen, carrying a silver tray, with a foaming flagon on it and three tankards.

A little tension eased from Francisco's face. "I was somewhat unsure of what sort of reception I'd get, Your Grace. Beer improves most meetings."

"I haven't drunk any for some years," said Petro. "But Marco has restricted my wine to watered slop."

"In this case, I can recommend it, Your Grace. Hops and other bitters are good for the liver and the digestion." Francisco smiled, and his smile deepened as he accepted a flagon, and took his first drink from it.

Conversation slipped into politenesses for a while before returning to business. "I make no pretense about Carlo Sforza, M'lord Valdosta," Francisco said, with some regret. "He is my commander and I think a friend, but he is neither good nor gentle. He told me himself that he would have killed your mother, had he had half the chance, when she fled to Venice. In open battle or as a matter of state, if Venice was in conflict with Milan, he would regard both you and your brother as foes to be dealt with as he deals with other foes: by force. But your brother exposed another side to him, when he returned his pilgrim medal. For some months, Carlo was under the impression that Benito had taken it, been close enough to kill him, and decided not to. To send the medal back as a warning. That was a dangerous message to send Carlo Sforza."

"That was never Benito's intention—" Marco began to protest.

Francisco nodded. "Exactly. And then he found out that he was wrong. That Benito had recovered a number of those medals from a fence, knew that one was his father's, and merely sent it back because he could. It's the first time I have seen him truly nonplussed. He did not know what to think."

Marco passed a hand over his face, and the Doge chuckled. "That is the reaction many of us have to things Benito does," said Petro.

"Even so. He began to take a great interest in Benito, and in the woman Maria Verrier." Francisco coughed. "He said to me that he was afraid that his son was too like him, and that Maria was . . . too like your mother." Francisco held up his hand. "He does not hold that opinion of her anymore, although he says that there are similarities, in temper and temperament—and I think we can all agree that the lady is one that none of us would care to anger."

At that, Dorma laughed, and Marco sighed. "I like Maria," the young physician said, plaintively. "And Benito—"

"And Benito would do anything for her," Petro interrupted. "And she is not one to abuse that sort of bond. Good, honest canal-bred."

"Precisely. And my master regards your brother's virtues as due to her influence. He, um...appears to think very highly of her now." Francisco waited to see how that was taken. He looked relieved to see both Marco and the Doge nodding. "Remember, Carlo is not nobly born either; he measures virtue by deeds, not birth. He regards Maria Verrier as the saving of Benito, and their child as glue in that bond."

"He's right about that, for both of us, I think," said Marco. "And Maria has made Benito, well, grow up, and, um, turned his path. And Alessia has been good for him. She steadied him, made him realize that he had something precious he had to protect, and to protect her, he would have to think before he acted."

"Which is why I was dispatched to this city. Carlo has long maintained a network of shall we say spies, separate from the Visconti—Montagnard faction." He coughed. "I think as a result of your mother's involvement in the latter."

"So: you were sent to watch Alessia?" asked Marco.

"And Maria Verrier, but his primary concern was the little girl. We found it odd that she had accompanied him, and left her daughter here."

Marco laughed. "Not half as odd as the truth, my friend. Which isn't what Carlo Sforza believes, but is a lot more terrifying. He chose the right side this time. Alessia's well guarded, even though that ex-Dandelo managed to kidnap her. I wish Sforza had rather sent us a message that that was planned, rather than a bodyguard. Not that we're not grateful, because we are."

Francisco interrupted him. "M'lord, I wasn't sent as a bodyguard, nor had he any idea of that plan.

He'd been excluded from Filippo Visconti's council for some time."

"If you weren't sent as a bodyguard, what were you?" asked Petro.

Francisco took a pull of his beer. "I am a soldier first, of course, but I have been Carlo's personal physician for some time. He was mostly worried about the child's health in this city." He raised an eyebrow to Marco. "He didn't know much about your medical studies and ability, Marco, but many years ago—as a young man—he came to Venice and got the bloody flux and nearly died of it. He, er, describes Venice . . . well, the filth in the canals, very unflatteringly, if you'll pardon my saying so. Of course the filth in the streets of Milan is so much better," he said, with a disarming smile. "He does fixate on certain ideas to the exclusion of others."

"I would take care not to mention that Carlo Sforza thinks La Serenissima is a noisome city to anyone else," said Petro Dorma dryly. "They'd probably make us go to war over the insult. Half of the *Case Vecchie* leave the city for high summer because of the smell, and go to their estates on the mainland, but criticism of the city is strictly reserved for her citizens. And right now I am in his debt, though I am not sure the Council of Ten would allow me to publicly acknowledge that. I owe him both for Di Lamis and your help in keeping me alive."

"Not to mention your part in rescuing Alessia. I and my family are forever in your debt," said Marco seriously.

"Carlo is still half-convinced that I helped him to survive a cunning double feint, m'lord. He says he nearly fell over backwards when he met Benito fighting his way out of the Villa Parvitto. We were sure, at that stage, that the fleet was in Corfu or possibly already laying siege to Constantinople, and that Benito was with them. It put rather a different light on our spring plans."

Petro smiled thinly, not showing his teeth, and then said: "Do convey to your master that discretion is the better part of valor when interpreting the strategies of the Republic of Venice."

"Well, he told me to tell you that his interests lay to the southwest—as long as he didn't have to deal with a direct challenge. Forgive me being so blunt. I'm not a diplomat. I'm a soldier first, and tactful later."

"You're a doctor first," said Marco firmly. "And I am going to need your help in setting up a new medical school."

"And for that reason," said Petro, "I think we will be able to persuade the Council of Ten that support for the various factions who claim legitimate inheritance of the ducal coronet of Milan should be encouraged to bicker with each other. A sudden outbreak of good relations with an old enemy would be difficult for them, or the people of Venice, to swallow. But a gradual thaw would work. Perhaps culminating in our sending a representative to Sforza's wedding. Who is it going to be, by the way? The betting is long on Eleni Visconti-Faranese. But I suspect the Medici cousin is in the running."

"Is nothing secret in Venice?" asked Francisco, looking both admiring and appalled.

"Venice has a great many secrets. It's just that people are bad at keeping them from her courtesans.

Eavesdrop in certain discreet houses and you can learn nearly everything," said Petro. "Or so I have been told."

Francisco took another pull of his beer. "Then I believe that I will be sharing my bed with the Scholar's Mistress, and not a flesh-and-blood one, while I am here."

Chapter 53

The Black Sea

The fleet set sail from Constantinople on the twelfth day of February, taking advantage of a brief spell of advantageous wind to make their way along the Bosphorus and out into the Black Sea. Benito Valdosta knew that there was no way that Jagiellon did not know they'd sailed, but hopefully most of Jagiellon's fleet-in-preparation would still be trapped in the ice on the Dnieper. If so, they would only have to deal with the fleet-at-sea, who were mostly now based at Odessa.

Benito had one serious advantage at sea: if it could find them, the roaming eye of Jagiellon could only observe the sea around them. Without referents, it had no idea where his fleet was. On the other hand, Benito knew where and how far off the enemy were. The tritons could speak at a distance across the wide ocean and knew just how far off that voice was.

Even so, the news was not encouraging.

"They're moving in squadrons down the west coast. And they outnumber your fleet by two to one," said Androcles, hovering aside the ship as Benito leaned over the prow. "Mostly galleys under oars and sail. The round ships—I think they wait for their human cargo up on the Dnieper. We do not venture into those waters."

"If they try to enter the Bosphorus, they're going to meet fireships and cannons."

"They're behaving as if they seek ships, not as if they plan invasion, Benito. I think they wait for the fleet to be free from the ice for that. In the meanwhile, you have maybe three days before the next storm."

Benito sighed. "*Next* storm? It's nearly spring!"

"There are always a few real monsters to finish off the winter," explained Androcles.

Benito made some mental calculations. "Three days of good wind and hard work will see us to Sinope," he said, as the bow-wave tossed a little foam at him. "Will we have that?"

"Hard work? Well now, that's difficult to tell. I'm no judge of how ready oarsmen are for that." The triton laughed at his own wit. "But the weather feels settled."

Benito chuckled. "You leave me to see to the hard work then."

The crews were nervous enough to need little or no urging towards it. From what Lemnossa had said, the Bey of Sinope might be less than pleased to see them. On the other hand, this was a large fleet. Big enough to make him see sense.

The weather was good enough for him to see the flags of the Ilkhan's tarkhan. The Ilkhan, ultimately, was not to be offended. All things considered, Benito doubted they'd have trouble, and he was right.

In fact, the Bey was pathetically eager to be on good terms with Venice and Genoa, and of course, the Ilkhan. Fleets of foreign northern style ships had been sighted offshore. Fishermen had not come home. Bygones ought to be bygones, rather than a return to the old days of the Brodnik pirates raiding from the rivers in the north.

Then came the storm that Androcles had warned them about. It was, indeed, a monster, and they had got into a safe port just in time.

They had to lie at anchor—and three ships dragged theirs and one was lost, before the weather abated. Then, with the galleys of Jagiellon's fleet reported barely a day's sail away, by the tritons, they set off into the open water, out and away from land.

Jagiellon had no truly maritime people in his confederation. His captains and crews were river-men, scared by the open sea. Driven out to search—as best they could. They'd been relatively successful at patrolling the western and northern littoral.

Now, according to the tritons, a large part of the fleet that was in the water was split into three, searching.

Searching, naturally, the coastal perimeter.

The round ships could do six knots with a good following breeze. Benito's big war galleys could move much faster, for short periods. The galleys and the galliots moved under sail too, when the wind was usable. Under sail, the galleys were slow and clumsy, but their rowers could rest. This was a gamble—the wind was for a brief while in the right quarter. They had a brief window in the tumultuous weather that heralded the changing of the seasons. The tritons thought it might hold for three days.

Of course, there were other problems. Mixed fleets always struggled; it was difficult to match speeds.

Benito nonetheless kept the ships together, using Di Tharra's flotilla of light galliots and the tritons to herd in the strays. They needed what help they could get, sailing both day and night.

"It's insanity!" protested one of the captains.

"It's Valdosta insanity," said another. "Which means we do it, or our crews will toss us overboard and do it anyway. They trust him, and I do, too."

The wind was feathering the clouds and coming across the water in icy squalls and flurries that seamen knew heralded a big blow, when they sighted the Genovese towers on the cliffs of Cembalo.

In the fringe of rain and sail-ripping gusts the fleet negotiated the narrow entry to the harbor to reach its sheltered water under the guns of the Genovese fortress. There they hid from the howling northerly winds and the last anger of winter for three days. They were greeted by the small Genovese trading colony there as if they were the second coming. The colony had not seen a trading vessel from home for nearly six months. They had seen the first ships and assumed this was Jagiellon's fleet. They'd had expected to be a target for it, and prepared their guns and food, until some keen eyed fellow had picked out the flags on the vessels.

"There'll be spies here, M'lord Valdosta," said Captain Di Tharra, as they conferred on the deck of Benito's flagship. It had been barely possible to send a rowboat over. Di Tharra might have to overnight here. This was going to be an ugly blow.

"I hope so," said Benito. "Jagiellon—or the thing that drives him—seems to have no idea of the frailty of ships or the strength of the sea. Or how unused to it his sailors are. He'll drive them after us—and this weather will get worse."

Di Tharra looked at the swaying topmasts even in this very sheltered harbor. "A lot worse. And those galleys of his are less seaworthy than yours. They'll have to seek shelter or sink."

Benito's smile reminded Di Tharra of the triton's. His grandfather's, of a shark.

"Never let an enemy choose his time, conditions and ground," explained Enrico. "We are three days or less sailing from Odessa. He will work that out, too, and send some of the fleet back there. But if they try to hug the coast, that adds considerable distance. It'll take the forward elements of their fleet—those that do not try to cross the open ocean in the storm—five days to reach Odessa from Sinope. And those who sail directly can barely get there—if they survive at all. Rowing both day and night—no rest, no fresh food—fighting the storm? They'll be in a poor state to face us."

"And our crews will be rested and ready," said Di Tharra.

"Ready maybe. But the town of Cembalo is not doing much for their rest," said Benito. You could hear the sound of revelry through the tower walls. Still, it was rest of a kind, if only from fear.

On the fourth, day, the Venetians and Genovese fleets put to sea in rough conditions but with a fair following wind.

Jagiellon had had his vessels all make for the Dnieper or sail for Crimea—regardless of conditions.

And now he had little idea of where they were, or how much force he had to attack the Venetian fleet with, or to defend his shipyards.

But that was by no means all. His attention was seriously divided. For now, he had problems with the Golden Horde on land.

PART VII
March, 1541 A.D.

Chapter 54

Hades

"The time has come, mortal bride, to return you to the sun and light," said Aidoneus. His voice was filled with regret, but just possibly also with a touch of relief. "It is to be hoped that Hekate will allow us to pass the gates."

"She'd better. I need to hold 'Lessi and I need Benito." Maria realized this was possibly not the most tactful thing a woman had ever said. But there was a growing certainty in her mind, and she decided to test the waters. "You're a good man, King of the Shadow Halls."

Aidoneus looked at her curiously. "I am not a man, my mortal queen. I do not think anyone has ever called me good, either."

She stalled for time, trying to read him. It was hard, even after months of being with him. "You might not be mortal, but you're a man. I should know. And you do your work well. The dead are your trust and you keep it."

He smiled. "Not many would see it that way. But,

yes. I have my responsibilities. The kingdom of the
dead is not without that. I have a duty to my dead,
and also to those who will fill my halls in the full-
ness of time."

Maria saw deeper than that by now. "You protect
the living."

"Yes. The boundary must be maintained. A few
would wish it otherwise for a while, but not for long."
He sighed.

She steeled herself. Now was the time. "You need
a queen all of the time, not just for a few months.
The way it was in the old days."

He regarded her oddly.

"And—I can't keep doing this. I thought I could, but
I can't." She said that as firmly as she could. "What
happens the next time my daughter is in danger? It
will keep happening, you know. She's a target, and not
even you and I can keep her safe." Before he could
say anything, she kept on. "And Benito... You are
a god, and you might be used to this sort of divided
living, but I'm just a mortal woman, and...and it
feels wrong. It pulls me apart."

His brows furrowed. "You intend to go back on
your bargain?"

"I intend to make a new one," Maria replied, more
sure of herself now that she saw he wasn't angry. "The
bargain was that you could have a mortal queen, just
as you had in the long ago. I intend to find you one.
No, that's not true, I intend to find you many."

"And how do you propose to do that?" he asked,
carefully.

"The Strega," she said. "They follow the old ways.
And they're poor, most of them, crushingly poor. I

think I can found a new branch of your worship among the Strega and the swamp-folk, you and Hekate, and as the reward, lift some of their poverty and give them protection."

Now he looked interested. "Would the Lion permit this?"

She almost laughed. She had him now. "The Lion doesn't care about worship. He gets his power from the land. And I know, I *know* that with all of the unmarried, poor girls in Venice, girls who dream helplessly of a great and powerful man who will lift them out of their life and carry them away, there will be a steady supply of young women who will be happy to come to you as brides."

Cynical? Maybe. Exploiting those girls? Well . . . not really. Life in the Cold Halls might be a bit depressing, but there was no doubt that it was luxurious. Many of those girls would sell themselves in a second for the life of an expensive courtesan. For a life with an admittedly handsome, distantly kind god in luxury that exceeded that?

Maria would make sure they knew exactly what they were getting into, but she was absolutely certain this was going to work. She'd thought about it long and hard.

And the one thing that *might* cause a problem with a young girl, down in the Underworld, sometimes left alone and perhaps bored for hours, days at a time, was not going to be possible. There would be no seeking of lovers elsewhere. Not with Hekate guarding all the gates.

"If you can find me a new bride by the appointed time," Aidoneus said, with more than a glint of enthusiasm, "Then I shall remake the bargain."

Now Maria looked at the god sharply. "I was not so bad a wife to you."

"Better than some have been!" the god hastened to say.

"Humph." Maria wavered between feeling insulted and relieved. She settled on relieved. Besides, it was just as well that she might have been giving less than a completely favorable picture of herself. Aidoneus would not have been willing to re-bargain, if he'd been completely pleased.

"Now, where would you go, my dear?" he asked. "I do not think Hekate will oppose your leaving. The gates are hers, the boundaries mine, but the living cannot cross the boundaries easily."

Maria bit her lip. "Alessia. I would go to Venice, my lord."

"Very well. Take my hand, my lady," he said formally.

And he led her out into the daylight streaming in through the windows of the *Casa* Montescue.

They stood there in the light, the pale lord and the earth-mother. She kissed him. Long. It would have to last him eight months. And then she was interrupted by a squeal, and a shriek, and little running feet. "Mummy!"

Aidoneus turned to leave as she scooped Alessia up in her arms. "Don't go," she said, suddenly stabbed by his expression. "I want you to meet my daughter."

Aidoneus bowed formally. Alessia responded with a giggle and a shy smile.

"Alessia knew you were there. I did that much for you," said Aidoneus humbly, looking at Alessia.

"I thought so. By the way she looked and talked, I thought so. But I couldn't hear her, or hold her, or speak to her."

Aidoneus took a deep breath. "Then, I truly understand why watching her was not enough for you. She is a charming child. I hope that we may remake our bargain, come the equinox. May I have permission to watch over you, and her? I have become attached to you, and I feel some responsibility."

"You'll have to talk to Benito about it," said Maria. "But he and I would have some privacy, Aidoneus. It's going to be difficult."

The lord of the vast halls of shadow nodded, his eyes wide.

Venice

Within days, Maria was in the thick of things again, plunging into life with the zest of someone who had only been able to view it for far too long. And the first thing she got involved with were the trials for everyone still alive that had been involved in 'Lessi's kidnapping.

Over pastries—how she had missed pastry!—and a light wine, she, Kat, and Marco sat in a window overlooking the canals. She came straight to the point. "I was watching. I saw some people you may not have. And you're doing it wrong, Marco," said Maria. "The people need to be involved. The *populi minuta*, not just the Signori di Notte. Otherwise we'll have wild rumors, things going up and down the canals, and maybe the wrong people getting hurt while the right people get less punishment than they deserve." She waved down at the canal, which under a steady spring rain was not much to look at. The few boats that went by, and their crew and contents, were shrouded in anything that might shed a little rain.

"The mob makes mistakes, Maria," said Marco.

She nodded. "They do. And so do the judges. The judges need to let people in to watch these trials. And they need to speak in a language that people can understand. I'm going out there, tomorrow, with 'Lessi. I'll get the mothers on our side. We'll make it plain that getting torn apart is a soft option, Marco."

"I suppose you are right," said Marco. "And you know, the lotos trade has suffered a bit, despite the addictive nature of it. It's . . . well let's say there were always people who believed they were different. Richer, cleverer, stronger, and so they thought they were somehow immune. The stories were exaggerated; they could take it if they wished and not if they didn't."

"Everyone would like to believe that the rules don't apply to them," Maria said sourly.

Marco nodded. "I don't think we can change that. But now . . . The trade is tainted with the Dandelos child-trade. It's something that even the ennui-filled rich don't want to be associated with."

"Except," said Kat, dryly, "that the abusers of children now know the addicts will feed their perversion in exchange for black lotos. We've shrunk the tumor, but made it nastier still."

"We will cut it out, or at least as much of it as we can find," said Marco.

That, by his tone, was the end of it. Maria nodded. At least now the people would know exactly what was going on. There would be no rumors. But there would be talk, and lots of it. The people would know the name and rank of every person pulled into the kidnapping. The judges would know that the people would take matters into their own hands—and possibly even come after the judges themselves—if they gave someone leniency because of wealth or rank.

No one was going to walk free of this. And with the women of the canals aware of what had been going on under their noses, there would be a hundred eyes on every corner, watching sharply for anything that looked like a lotos-eater.

She decided to change the subject.

"In the meanwhile, Katerina, you and I need to have a long talk about fertility," said Maria. "I probably haven't ever really spelled it out to you, but I have certain magical skills in that area. And you can both stop blushing. The Lion wants my help, you both need it."

"Um. Might not need it," said Kat, quietly.

"Wh—*what?*" Marco leapt to his feet, and hugged her. "You didn't tell me!"

Kat blushed even deeper. "I wanted to be sure."

Maria came and hugged them both. "I can find out for you for sure, too. That is in my gift."

Chapter 55

The Black Sea

Later, Benito was to learn that the greater part of
Jagiellon's ships searching for his fleet had taken shelter
where they could and not made the return voyage in
time. Even where they had found shelter the storm
had been fierce. In the Dniestr estuary, many had
gone aground, and in the swampy Danube estuary,
they had been attacked by Golden Horde tribesmen.

But that morning was a time for uncertainty. And
the Venetian-Genovese-Aragonese fleet wanted to
make sure that uncertainty was something that was on
their side, too. Benito called on Hekate, according to
the spells of the three-fold way, and brought down the
sea-mist. Within its cover, they crept toward Hacibey
and the fleet that the tritons said waited to defend the
mouth of the Dnieper.

Less than half of Jagiellon's fleet-at-sea were able to
meet them off Odessa in the early morning. The Black
Brain's naval forces still outnumbered the ones under
Benito's command, but he was confident that his hard-
ened seamen would be more than a match for the enemy.

❧   ❧   ❧

Benito tried to lean on his grandfather for advice, as the fleets neared each other, but Duke Enrico Dell'este was having none of it. "You're in command, not me."

Benito had been afraid he'd say that. When it suited him, the lord of Ferrara could be as hard as the steel he worked, and he had firm opinions on the proper way to raise youngsters. Those opinions definitely fell into the *toss-the-little-bastards-in-the-water-and-let-them-learn-to-swim-or-drown* school of thought.

After a few minutes, the Old Fox relented—just a bit. "Don't get too fancy," he gruffed. "These aren't real seamen you're facing. Just river pirates."

That modicum of advice crystallized the thoughts Benito had already been having. The oncoming horde of vessels were of the type favored by Black Sea pirates. They were single-masted oared galleys, about fifty feet long by ten feet wide, each packed with up to fifty men. They rode low in the water, with nothing much in the way of bombards. They relied almost entirely on boarding tactics, swarming their opponents with their great numbers.

For all the apparent eagerness with which they were coming toward Benito's smaller fleet, shouting war cries, he sensed the uneasiness beneath the fury. Chernobog's navy was nothing more than a pack of glorified pirates, really. Buccaneers with delusions of grandeur. On the other hand, no one in that day and age had the reputation of Venetians and Genovese when it came to naval warfare—and Chernobog's captains and sailors would know that reputation themselves.

"Let's bleed them first," he said. He turned to one of the small group of lieutenants standing nearby. "Send the galleys forward. Tell them to fire three volleys—no fewer, make sure they understand that."

The lieutenant nodded and hastened over to the signalmen standing by. Seconds later, the first of the signal flags starting rising up, passing the orders to the fleet.

Although they were the biggest and heaviest vessels in the fleet, the Venetian war galleys could move faster than any other ships at sea—at least, for the short distance that their rowers could manage before becoming exhausted. Quickly, the galleys passed between the ranks of the smaller galleasses and galliots and took up positions in the fore, facing the enemy. Once there, the rowers had simply to keep the ships steady while the cannons did their work.

The beaks of the galleys had been removed to give the heavy guns positioned in the bows a clear line of fire. There were three such guns on each ship, each capable of firing a thirty-pound shot—or, far more effective in these circumstances, an equal weight of scatter shot. There were over a hundred three-ounce balls fired by each gun, three guns across, and six galleys abreast—a total of two thousand rounds sweeping across the low decks of the oncoming fleet.

The carnage was hideous. And, as Benito had guessed would happen, terror piled onto rage on top of underlying anxiety caused Chernobog's forces to lose any semblance of discipline and order. The small galleys charged forward still more furiously, desperate to close the distance and thereby render the cannons inoperable.

Another volley. Then the third that Benito had ordered—and he'd cut that very close indeed. The galleasses and galliots barely had time to surge forward to protect the galleys before the enemy fleet arrived.

What was left of it. True, only two ships had been sunk, but the crews of most of the vessels had been badly bloodied. And they had no discipline at all left. It had been shaky to begin with, as you'd expect with such crews, and the carnage had shredded what little did exist. The pirates-in-all-but-name who finally closed with the fleet of the Venetians and their allies had no thought but to clamber aboard the enemy's vessels and butcher everyone they found.

Unfortunately for them, clambering aboard high-walled galliots—even more, galleasses—was a far more difficult enterprise than they were accustomed to. These were warships designed to fend off boarding operations, not merchant vessels. The captains and crews were trained to do the same, keeping the ships close together to make it difficult for the enemy to penetrate the line and surround any one vessel.

To make things worse, the crews had rigged over-hanging nets that they quickly brought into position, which left the boarders in much the same position as a fly trying to "board" a spider's web. These spiders had stings, too—lances that speared through the net-ting and slaughtered still more of Chernobog's sailors.

Still, it was a fierce fight, for the first half hour or so. At one point, a number of enemy ships threatened to break through the line, which would have enabled them to begin the swarming tactics that they favored. But a group of Genovese galliots led by Captain Di Tharra drove them back.

As for Benito . . .

He didn't do much of anything, truth be told, once the battle started. Despite his natural instincts—glares and scowls from his grandfather played a part, admittedly— he did not order his flagship into the fray. His job, this day, was to coordinate the tactics of his fleet, first of all.

That didn't take much, though. He hadn't even ordered the Genovese reserve forward, since Di Tharra hadn't needed to be told what to do. So...

Benito concentrated on the second principal task of an admiral in the middle of a major fleet action: Looking stern, stalwart, self-assured—in a word, admiralish. If such a word existed, which he doubted.

By mid-afternoon, it was over. Most of Chernobog's fleet was still afloat—even intact, allowing for horrendous casualties. But they'd had all the fight beaten out of them. One by one, and then in small droves, they fled from the battle zone.

At that point, in his excitement at the prospect of victory, Enrico forgot his former resolve and gave his first and only order of the day.

"Pursuit! Pursuit! Send the round ships—"

But seeing that Benito was already ordering the appropriate signals, the Old Fox fell silent and tried to look as impassive as possible.

Which was a bit difficult, given that Benito was now muttering axioms to the effect that oldsters shouldn't presume to teach grandsons how to suck eggs.

The sailing vessels wouldn't have been much use in this sort of fracas, so Benito had kept them in the rear and out of danger. But now, when the enemy ships were trying to make their escape across the open waters of the Black Sea, they'd come into their own. They could stand off and rake the fleeing vessels with cannon fire—round shot, now, to damage and hopefully destroy the ships themselves.

By the time night fell—still three hours off, this time of year—Chernobog's navy would be completely ruined. It would take the monster at least a year and probably two or three before he could hope to rebuild an effective fleet. And by then, depending on the situation with the Golden Horde, he might have great difficulty maintaining a presence on the Black Sea.

"A good day's work," pronounced the duke of Ferrara.

"Tell me something I don't know," muttered Benito, perhaps unkindly. But, if anything, his grandfather looked still more pleased.

The Genovese longboat's lieutenant scrambled up the ladder. "M'lord Valdosta. It's Captain Di Tharra." There were tears on the lieutenant's face. "He's dying, m'lord. He's asking for you. You and someone called Androcles."

Benito went across to the Genovese flagship. Di Tharra was not inside his cabin or below with the surgeon. Instead his men had carried him out to the bow of the ship. The ship was oddly silent. Yes, timber creaked. Somewhere below someone groaned. But the crew themselves were wordless, silent; united in grief and respect. Their captain had had them prop him up, so that he could see the water.

Benito took Di Tharra's hand. It was clammy and its grasp weak. "Valdosta..." he said, barely in a whisper. "I hoped to see the triton again for a last time. But I got my wish to see them."

"More than most people have done, my friend."

"I'm dying, Benito Valdosta. I have one last boon to ask. Will you take my son to the sea, and let him meet them, too? My men will see he gets my sword... and the buckler...with the tritons supporting...the uprooted tree."

"I will do more," said Benito with a calm he did

not feel. "I'll get Androcles to hand the buckler to him." He turned to the lieutenant. "Fetch the captain's buckler." The man left at a run. "And you, get me a bucket of seawater," he said to another seaman.

The bucket and buckler came almost together. Benito drew his knife, spoke the words of summoning and spilled the blood; then he threw blood and seawater into the surge at the bow. "Now help me get the captain to the rail."

Three of the sailors did so, ignoring the surgeon's protest. And there in the swirl of the wave around the bow, the sea-colored tritons moved and merged— more like shadows than solid creatures. Benito held Di Tharra's weak hand up pushing the buckler into it with the uprooted tree supported by the tritons, with the conch and fish-tongue sword. Together they tossed it into the waves.

A blue-green hand came up and caught it and pulled it down into the water, as the sailors gasped.

Di Tharra's face was pale but tranquil now. "He's a good lad. I wish I could have shown him myself... but I've seen." His eyes closed.

Then they opened again. "Benito. Get him to take the conch back," he said, his voice barely a whisper. "Tell him to give it to the tritons. It's above the fireplace."

"What?" At first the words made no sense. Then— they made altogether too much sense. *"What?"*

But Di Tharra's eyes were closed again, finally this time, still seeing the great barnacle-covered, sea-colored shoulders move in the restless waves, and the head of white-foam hair tossed back.

Chapter 56

The Dnieper river

By afternoon the galliots and galleases were pushing upriver through the cracking ice, up towards the shipyards on the Dnieper, while the round ships and the war galleys sailed to invest in a siege of Odessa.

They'd expected the city to be awash with troops and well defended.

They had not expected to have the desperate local citizenry offer them the head of their voivode on a platter. Jagiellon's soldiery had marched northwest and only the hungry populace and their voivode's household guard remained.

It was given to the sole Venetian spy to negotiate the surrender of the port.

Upstream in the Dnieper, the galleys reached the shipyards at the confluence of the Lek river. Jagiellon's shipyards, deep within his territory, did not have so much as a fortress or troops of cavalry to defend them. The galleys used the bow chasers to start the destruction. The men working in the shipyards were not soldiers, and fled immediately. Over the course of the next three hours, the galleys pounded the ribs and clad hulls to kindling and then put fire to that kindling. The heat of it was enough to melt the ice for quite some distance, but Venetians did not stay to appreciate it.

The round ships together with the galleys sailed south again, toward the lands of the Golden Horde.

Tarkhan Qishkai came on deck, looking across the breakers to the low green coast. Most of the fleet lay at anchor offshore there, and only three of the galliots made their way inwards. The water was discolored from the Danube outflow and the leadsman called from the bow as they plodded forward towards the delta. Already the blue truce pennants of the Ilkhan, and the Ilkhan's own banner flew beside the Winged Lion of Venice. Finding a safe passage in was slow work, but Venice's oarsmen had experience with the lagoon bar. The deeper water and stronger current were apparent with the lack of breakers, but mud and sand shifted.

Soon they were in between banks grown with low willows, just starting to show leaf, and chattering and clattering rush-swamp meadows. The Venetians began to relax as the familiarity to their native lagoon eased some of the memories of battle. Benito just hoped that it wasn't too soon.

The first Mongol they encountered was not on horseback but on a punt, heading upstream. He first nosed his punt into the reeds, and then peered cautiously at the flags. The tarkhan sent one of his men to bellow in Mongol at the fellow—who came out and talked volubly at the tarkhan, waving his hands about nearly as much as the average Venetian, bargaining.

"He would like a tow," the tarkhan translated. "The new Great Khan comes down to a place where the river has a big curve and a hill near where it divides into the delta. It is the meeting place for the clans from the White and Blue Horde. There is a gifting for a royal wedding there."

"It looks like you are too late to have any effect on the election of their new Great Khan, Tarkhan."

The Ilkhan emissary shrugged. "But hopefully not too late to deal with the traitor Borshar, M'lord Valdosta. Can we toss the man a rope?"

They rowed on, and after an hour they could see their goal. So, it seemed, could most of the other craft on the water. There were plenty of them, all heading that way.

The place was chosen for its beauty. A rise in the ground changed the vegetation from the low willows and sedges to oaks, in between which the short grass was scattered with vast round white tents. There were throngs of people everywhere, it seemed. And there among them, the triple red crosses of the Order of the Holy Trinity.

Benito greeted that sight with relief. Yes, Manfred and Erik had been all right, when they had sent the message. But that had been months ago. He peered across the water at two figures in the distance. No one could be that big and carrying that much steel and not be Manfred of Brittany. And by the white-blond head, Erik was next to him.

Erik was holding onto a dark-haired woman. Benito shook his head, taking in the cascade of midnight hair, the high cheekbones, the jewelry—above all, the fact that she was holding onto Erik.

An Erik that was smiling as Benito had not seen him smile since the death of Svanhild.

Benito felt his eyes brim with tears, as he looked at the Icelander. The shadow that had hung over the man after Svanhild's death was probably not gone entirely. But it was not making him desperately unhappy anymore. In fact, he looked like a man who had discovered that life was a wonderful thing.

The galliot nudged the muddy shore. Benito jumped down, not caring if he got wet and muddy, and waded in.

Erik shook his head, still smiling a great big stupid smile and put an arm around him. "Ah, Benito. Here I am in my wedding finery and you're all over mud." The other arm stayed firmly around the girl. Erik held him away. "My young friend. I want you to meet my wife, Princess Bortai."

She smiled shyly. "Your mother is a tortoise," she said in Frankish.

When they had stopped Benito choking, he equipped them all with wine to toast the happy couple. Then Benito noticed Tulkun—walking toward a ramp that was being arranged to bring the tarkhan off the galliot. "Ah. The very fellow I need," he said. "Do you know what has happened to his master?"

Erik coughed. "I killed him."

"Well, now," Benito said, his shoulders shaking. "Did anyone see you do this?"

"The clan and subclan heads of the Golden Horde," said Erik. "He needed killing, Benito. So . . . we have a problem, do we? Have I made difficulties for Manfred?"

"Oh, no," said Benito. He turned to Bortai. "Congratulations on a fine match, Princess. He's not only handsome, but he's rich too."

Erik rolled his eyes. "I am not rich. Bakkafloi is—"

Benito interrupted, grinning like a coal-scuttle. "Bakka-whatever has nothing to do with it. The Ilkhan was seriously embarrassed by the so-called tarkhan's actions. And seriously angry too. It appears that some of his friends and confederates have been making things difficult in the Ilkhan's realms. To cut a long story short, Erik, there is a price on the head of ex-Tarkhan Borshar. I believe you're the equivalent of ninety thousand ducats richer, Erik. That's more than three times what the condotteire of Venice earns in a year."

Venice

Maria poled her little boat slowly through the greening swamps. She'd talked to Julietta, the sea-woman, she'd spoken to Strega, she'd talked to swamp folk who were sometimes only half-sensible. She'd talked around and around, in circles, until sometimes she thought she would never get straight to her point—but none of these people ever came straight to a point. They had to sidle past the point, eye it carefully, walk around it, and test it for danger, not once, but many times, before they even approached it.

But she had learned a lot more of patience in the Shadowed Halls than she would have believed. And, eventually, all that talking, all the careful distribution of bundles of old clothes, baskets of food, trading for swamp-herbs and the bits of flotsam that the very poorest collected in the hope it was valuable, and all the making of connections had come down to this.

She poled her boat to the appointed place, and waited. Slowly, carefully, boats—and things that qualified as "boats" only because they floated—emerged from the reeds. All of them held women. Old. Middle aged. And—young. Many of them young. Some . . . quite pretty, under the rags, the dirt, and the starvation.

She began to talk.

"This is how it was, a long time ago . . ."

At first there was only listening. Then there were nods. Then emphatic nods. Then . . . questions. And comments. One of which nearly had her laughing, and she had to work hard to smother it.

"'Tis not a body's 'feared of dyin'," croaked one old crone. "'Tis a body's 'feared there be naught on other side. Or naught worth goin' to." She shook her head. "Don' like that Heaven priest keeps talkin' on. Don' trust them angels. Too shiny. An' no—" she moved her hips in a way that went far beyond suggestive. Then she smacked her lips. "An' never heard there was beer, either. But what you're be sayin 'bout . . . body can believe in that."

She came back, day after day. She didn't exactly think of herself as a teacher, but . . . well, there was teaching. And studying, on her part. And asking Marco a great many questions about what she read. Out in the swamp, with the help of the tritons, the neiriads, and the other sea creatures, who were only too happy to find some place to put what they were excavating out of their new sanctuary, there came to be an island. And then, a building on it.

That rose suspiciously quickly, and looked suspiciously good, far too good to have been put together out of flotsam by unskilled hands. The tritons? Marco? Aidoneus? Well, it didn't matter. There was ample room for the women, and a room for worship at the two altars—both adorned with ancient, barnacle-scarred statues the tritons had dredged up out of the swamp muck, statues with features so blurred they looked as if they had been formed naturally rather than carved by human hands. In the east, a woman with two dogs. In the west, a man, with another dog, this one with three heads.

And then, one day, she came into the temple and found a single girl there, not praying, but gazing on the statue of Aidoneus. Examining, searching, as if she was trying to make out features. One of the poor, emaciated ones, who had, when Maria had first seen her, been so encrusted with dirt that it had been hard to see the color of her hair or skin.

Now, she was clean. Regular meals had put flesh on the bones. Her hair was clean too—Strega-dark—and her eyes had sense in them, not the despair and near madness of the starving. And when Maria entered, the girl said, "You said, in the old, old days, *He* used to take a wife. You said that you've been that wife for four months of the year."

"Yes," Maria said, cautiously.

The girl turned to face her, and her eyes held determination, need, and resolve. "But you have a husband. Would *He* take someone else? For always? And not just part of the year?"

Maria did not smile. The girl would probably misconstrue that. Besides, it didn't do to seem too eager. Make the girl work for it. She would only value her bargain if she did.

"Perhaps," she said, gravely. "If you are worthy."

Epilogue

It was full moon at the Milion. As always, he came alone, quietly, with a libation of wine, and flowers this time, and gifts for her dogs. Hekate watched. He was mortal and she had her path and he had his. She had her people. And the triton had told her that she now had a grim duty to see carried out—that the shield was passed to the son. She would have to talk to Benito Valdosta about that, when he came back here.

But still she came and watched her worshipper.

And this time he did not go.

"I know you are there," he said calmly. "I can feel it, even if I can't see you."

She said nothing. He probably was aware of her. Aware that she kept her hand on the dogs to stop them going to greet him.

"The fleet has been sighted off the Bosphorus. Tomorrow they'll be here. Tomorrow, or very soon after, my master will want me to leave." He waited a moment longer, then added, "Please."

She felt a pang. She almost stepped out from the cloak of night.

"I do not want to leave without saying goodbye to you, and . . . to the dogs. I can explain to you, but all I can give them is my love. I would like to pat their heads and scratch them behind the ears, one last time." She felt it in her, the emotion . . . and it wasn't just, or even mostly, for her dogs.

He was calling them in the magical fashion that he had, and they left her and went to him, licking his face as he knelt between them and held them. She saw why.

He was crying.

"What is wrong?" she asked, in spite of herself, in spite of knowing.

He did not get up. Just held the dogs. Said nothing.

"We met at the crossroads. You have your way. I have mine," she said quietly. She had wept for others. She had not ever seen them weep for her.

He looked up at her and nodded. He even mustered a sketch of a smile.

"I watch the crossroads, the gates, the night and the hunt. You are a spy." But her words sounded uncertain, even in her own ears.

"I think . . . not anymore," he said. "I will speak to the duke. I have decided that I am finished. I have come to a crossroads myself, and I am taking another way."

"What will you do?" she asked, again in spite of herself.

"Paint, I think. I have some money set aside. The duke paid well, and I can perhaps find a small quiet place near here to live and paint." He looked up at her, then looked down at her dogs. "I could still come to your crossroads."

"Even with your skill and your magic, this city is not

safe for you. You are marked. They follow you even now." She did not say that she had intervened. Twice.

"A man makes choices," he said, and in his words was a certainty, and knowledge, that this above all was something he wanted at any cost. "Life is a series of crossroads and blocked gates. Some of them you can go around. And some you can only wait until they open. I'll take my chances."

Ripper lay down against him, and panted up at him.

Hekate knew and understood now. He'd been waiting patiently for the gate to open. He'd wait until he died, if need be. And she was the guardian of the gates.

"Get up," she said, offering him a hand. "At the crossroads, you can always take the third way. There is an island far from here, where the Shardana, the last of my people, found shelter. It is very wild and very beautiful. They call it Sardinia. I am going there. Come with me."

He took her hand and got to his feet. She did not let go of his hand, and the dogs walked one on either side of them.

The lady of crossroads chose a new path in the moonset. And this time she was not weeping and her dogs were not her only worshippers.

CAST OF CHARACTERS

Aidoneus: God of the dead; husband of Maria Verrier for four months of the year.

Alexius: Emperor of Byzantium.

Androcles: A triton.

Bartelozzi, Antimo: Agent and advisor to Enrico Dell'este.

Beg, Iskander: Illyrian chieftain, known as the Lord of the Mountains.

Borana: Admiral of Genoa.

Bortai: Princess of the Hawk clan of the Mongol White Horde, Golden Horde.

Borshar: Tarkhan (emissary) of the Ilkhan.

Bourgo, Poulo: Mercenary; creature of Chernobog.

Calmi: Venetian lord, member of the Council of Ten.

Chernobog: A demonic prince.

Dell'este, Enrico, Duke of Ferrara: The Old Fox. One of Italy's leading tacticians. Grandfather to Benito and Marco.

Di Lamis, Augustino: Milanese count; condottiere; second cousin of the duke of Milan.

Di Pantara, Marissa: Governess of Alessia Verrier.

Di Tharra, Carlos: Captain in the Genovese navy.

Dorma, Petro: Doge of Venice.

Hakkonsen, Erik: An Icelander, and bodyguard and mentor to Prince Manfred.

Hekate: Goddess of the Crossroads, Opener of Gateways, Lady of the Night, Mistress of the Hunt.

Hotai the Ineffable: Ilkhan of the Mongols.

Jagiellon, Prince: Master of the Grand Duchy of Lithuania; possessed by the demon Chernobog.

Lemnossa: Admiral of Venice.

Magheretti, Michael: Podesta of Trebizond.

Manfred, Prince, Earl of Carnac, Marquis of Rennes, Baron of Ravensburg: Nephew of the Holy Roman Emperor Charles Fredrik.

Montescue, Lodovico: Head of the formerly powerful House Montescue.

Poseidon: Earth-Shaker, old god of the sea.

Sforza, Carlo: Condottiere, "Wolf of the North."

Turner, Francisco: Doctor; soldier; friend of Marco Valdosta.

Valdosta, Benito: Grandson of the Duke of Ferrara; illegitimate son of Carlo Sforza.

Valdosta, Katerina: Wife of Marco.

Valdosta, Marco: Grandson of the Duke of Ferrara.

Verrier, Maria: Former canaler, married to Benito Valdosta eight months of the year and to Aidoneus during the winter.

Verrier, Alessia: Daughter of Maria.

Visconti, Filippo Maria: Duke of Milan.

MORE . . .
ERIC FLINT

MORE . . .
ERIC FLINT